ABOUT THE A

Timothy Schaffert grew up on a farm in Ne[...] is the author of four previous critically acclaimed novels, which have been among Barnes & Noble Discover Great New Writers selections, Indie Next picks and *New York Times* Editors' Choices. Schaffert teaches creative writing and literature at the University of Nebraska–Lincoln.

timothyschaffert.com
twitter.com/timschaffert

Praise for *The Swan Gondola*

'A highly atmospheric entertainment, full of plot twists, historical flavour and paranormal romance … Beneath the intrigue, mystery and historical window dressings of *The Swan Gondola* beats the heart of a complicated love story … Readers who enjoyed Sara Gruen's *Water for Elephants* or Erin Morgenstern's *The Night Circus* are likely to be captivated by *The Swan Gondola*.'
Washington Post

'*The Swan Gondola* will no doubt garner comparisons to *Water for Elephants* and *The Night Circus*, and fans of such historical romances will not be disappointed.'
BookPage

'Schaffert's picture of the fair is enchanting, from the buildings that shimmer with 'shattered glass that had been dusted over the whitewash' to the midway attractions, including a theatre where Cecily and Ferret briefly hang from wires and dance in midair … There are many romantic and historical delights here … It's easy to imagine this charming novel attaining *Water for Elephants*-like popularity with readers.'
Publishers Weekly

'A ventriloquist falls for a Marie Antoinette impersonator at the 1898 Omaha World's Fair. The backdrop for his pursuit – aerialist acts, midnight séances – only adds charm to this mythical slice of Americana.'   *Good Housekeeping*

'*The Swan Gondola* is a highly imaginative, vividly told tale of whimsy, hucksters, soothsayers, ghosts and, most of all, star-crossed lovers.'
Cathy Marie Buchanan, bestselling author of *The Painted Girls*

The
Swan
Gondola

❖ TIMOTHY SCHAFFERT ❖

ONEWORLD

A Oneworld Book

First published in Great Britain and Australia
by Oneworld Publications, 2014
This paperback editon published 2015

Published by arrangement with Riverhead Books, a division of Penguin
Group (USA) LLC, A Penguin Random House Company

ISBN 978-1-78074-560-2
ebook ISBN 978-1-78074-491-9

Book design by Amanda Dewey

Printed and bound in Great Britain by Clays Ltd, St Ives plc

Oneworld Publications
10 Bloomsbury Street
London WC1B 3SR
England

For Rodney

After the Fair

Autumn 1898

Emmaline and Hester, known in the county as the Old Sisters Egan, took their coffee cowboy-style, the grounds fried-up in a pan to a bitter sludge, then stirred into china teacups of hot water. They had their afternoon "shot," as they called it, at the kitchen table, sharing a slice of a wet and heavy rum cake that gave them each a dizzy spell. The sisters were sixty-eight and seventy-two.

The day had been as peaceful as any they'd ever known—so peaceful they'd only just commented on it ("So very, very quiet," had said Emmaline in her delicate, dreamy voice, drawing the words out, strumming her fingers through the air back and forth, like across the strings of a harp. "Learn to love it," said Hester, "because it's the racket of your grave"). At the uttering of the word *grave*, the house fell dark.

The sunlight at the windows seemed blown out with a sudden breath, but with a rumble and a roar and a shatter of glass. The house creaked, its joints an orchestra of great strain. Emmaline's set of china—long-since excavated from her abandoned bridal trousseau—dropped from its tall cabinet, plate by plate by plate, smashing in an even rhythm, chipping at Emmaline's heart with each staccato burst.

For all the years they'd had the farm, having moved west from the

East nearly three decades before, the Old Sisters Egan had struggled to keep the outdoors out and the indoors in, to preserve a city elegance and order in their drafty country home. They always removed their muddy boots before stepping inside. On their floors—wood planks carved from old hemlock trees—they kept Persian rugs. Their living room, every evening, glowed a shade of jaundice from the oil lamps, and they strained their eyes to read in the dim light—Hester settling in with books on animal husbandry, Emmaline with the thin dime novels that arrived by batches monthly in the mail.

Now books tumbled from their shelves, balls of yarn fell from a basket to roll and unravel, a shadow box containing the wreath of a braid of a dead niece (gone too soon) fell from its nail in the wall, the domed glass of the frame shattering. The caged birds that sang through every minute of sunlight fell silent.

The Old Sisters Egan looked at each other to share in their shock— a drama toward which Emmaline had always been inclined, but never, ever had Hester—and they took each other's hands, gripping tight. *I'm unafraid*, Emmaline thought, pleased that she had at least this last sublime split second of Hester seeking ease.

Despite all this wreckage, and some chimney bricks that dropped into the hearth and choked the parlor with smoke and soot, the Old Sisters Egan realized, from the lack of movement beneath their feet, that the house wasn't being lifted from its moorings by an unlikely late-autumn tornado; something had fallen upon them.

Hester opened the front door and took a slow step back, confused, worried that the drapery before her that cloaked the outdoors was a plot, the entire house shrouded in an act of theft or invasion. She lifted the rifle from the umbrella stand and cradled it, softly scratching her cheek with the end of the barrel.

"Oh!" Emmaline said. "Hester, it's silk!" She reached out the door and stroked the silk with the backs of her fingers.

They put on the new black coats they'd bought for travel to the Fair last month, the sleeves and shoulders overpuffed in a manner they thought fashionable. The peaks of the poofy shoulders reached their ears, and braided piping lined the seams at their sides. The coats had felt so conspicuous they had ended up not wearing them to the Fair after all, and had never once worn them even off the farm. They stepped into the silk, lifting it, swimming out, hunkering down, nearly crawling to the other side. With the barrel of her rifle, Hester pushed the drape of the silk from her path. Once they had stepped away from the house, they looked up. They might've begun to worry over the damage that had been done had they not been so overwhelmed by the sight of this deflated balloon consuming their farmhouse. They walked, arm in arm, backward, to take it all in, leaning in toward each other, their heads lifted to the roof, to the sky.

They'd witnessed so much during their lives on the farm—one summer they'd murdered a herd of cattle, shooting them to spare them a painful death from blackleg; they'd lost crops to plagues of weevils and worms; they'd built raging fires in fruitless efforts to ward off a freeze. They'd left Maine to come to Nebraska together, lured by a promise of plentitude available to two unmarried women, but there'd been no mercy. The farm had given them little and had taken much of what they'd brought with them. But this fallen, ruined balloon—it seemed a generosity of spirit dropped upon them from heaven. Finally, at least, a worthless, senseless bit of wonder. Emmaline and Hester listened to the gentle rippling of the silk, sounding like wind on wheat fields.

"Escaped the circus?" Hester wondered. When Hester squinted she could nearly imagine the silk as the skin of a runaway elephant popped with a pin. At the end of the front lane was a stone bench no one ever sat upon, and they sat on it now, to watch the balloon do nothing. Surely, any minute now, they'd be overrun by people from town, the curiosity seekers who had caught sight of the balloon falling. But rarely did people look up at the sky; their eyes were always cast down— on that stubborn earth. In Nebraska, the sky's endlessness could be too unsettling.

. . .

THE OLD SISTERS EGAN, in all the strangeness and clamor, didn't realize just then they'd seen this balloon before and that they knew well of its origins. It was a relic of the Civil War. At the Omaha World's Fair, war balloons had been tethered to the tops of a few buildings for display, balloons that had been used by both sides for spying and surveying, and this one, from the Confederacy, had been sewn from silk intended for dresses. Hester had read in a Fair guide that the balloon had been made of dress silk, and she'd pictured all the belles of the South carrying armloads of gowns to the war cause. She'd pictured the women looking as Emmaline had looked when she'd been young, before her heart got broke by a cad. She'd pictured rows of women with scissors picking at stitches, dismantling the dresses, then restitching the wrecked skirts and bodices, the monogrammed handkerchiefs and ruffled bloomers, into a vast, delicate patchwork quilt. But it had been a fanciful illusion—the balloon had simply been made of bolts of a yellow silk that would have otherwise been sewn into dresses, and when Hester lifted her eyes to the sky that day at the Fair, her hand at her forehead to shade the sun, she'd been disappointed by the balloon's lack of dainty detail.

"The pilot!" Emmaline now said with a start.

"Where?" Hester said.

"I don't know," she said, "but wouldn't there be one?"

The women leaped from the bench and walked to where the balloon's ropes led them, to the other side of the house. The brittle shards of dry grass crackled beneath their boots. They discovered the wicker basket upright on the ground, tipped just slightly, empty but for a bottle of perfume that had somehow kept from falling out: extract of sweet pea, stoppered with a cork, its neck knotted round with a rose-colored ribbon. As the Old Sisters Egan scanned the landscape, seeking survivors or victims, Emmaline took a moment to uncork the bottle and dab fingertips of scent to the inside of her wrist.

. . .

EMMALINE AND HESTER walked in opposite directions, searching. Before catching sight of the pilot, Emmaline discovered a slightly cracked mask of papier-mâché in the dirt. Crouching, she picked up the mask by the chin, with her finger and thumb. The mask hadn't much character—a simple pink face with puckered red lips and wide, curious, childlike eyes of blue. She held it up to see how things looked through the tiny pinholes, and she scanned the horizon. It was then she found the pilot.

He was alive, flat on his back on the ground not far off, his fists and his jaw clenched tight, his left leg at an awful bend. *Why doesn't he scream?* Emmaline wondered. *Why doesn't he beg us for help?* Maybe, she considered, he mistook the tall shoulders of their high-fashion coats for the dark wings of death angels. Maybe he suspected them of scavenging for souls.

Emmaline squatted next to the man as Hester pressed the barrel of her rifle to the man's left temple. Emmaline pushed Hester's gun away and she took the man's hand. She whispered a lie in his ear. "Your leg isn't broken," she said.

He snapped his fingers weakly and a card slipped out from up his sleeve: *B. "Ferret" Skerritt*, the card read, *Omaha, Neb.* And on the back: *This sleight of hand you just witnessed is only a hint of my wizardry.*

Emmaline removed her coat and lay it on the ground. The Old Sisters Egan dragged the pilot, his body between them, and put him atop the coat. They then strained to carry him in the sling of it, like on a stretcher, to the barn, where Hester kept an apothecary cabinet, veterinary implements, strips of muslin, tins of ether.

AS FERRET BLINKED AWAKE from the ether, he seemed not at all alarmed. He seemed less interested in the cast on his leg than the raggedy pajamas he wore. The Old Sisters Egan had stripped the scarecrow in the vegetable garden, brushed off the striped pajamas' straw and nettles, and had dressed Ferret for the evening. Though Hester had a closet full of men's overalls she wore when working with the livestock and the fields, they would not have fit him. For where Hester was squat, Ferret was gangly. The scarecrow's pajamas had belonged to a tall farmhand who'd absconded with a few of Hester's pistols; but the man had been no real loss. He'd been too fussy for farmwork.

Ferret, groggy, wormed his finger through a hole in the lapel.

In the barn, Emmaline had gripped tight to Ferret's foot and ankle as Hester had set the bone, jolting the leg into place. As Emmaline now sat with Ferret in the music parlor, just off the living room, she could still feel that click of reconnection as if it had happened inside her, near her fast-beating heart.

Emmaline told him her name. He only nodded.

"'B. "Ferret" Skerritt,'" Emmaline read aloud from Ferret's card. Ferret lay on a leather fainting sofa, a slit up one leg of the pajamas' pants to accommodate the lumpy cast that Hester had fashioned with swathes of plaster-powdered muslin. "'This sleight of hand you just witnessed is only a hint of my wizardry.' What more wizardry is there, Mr. B. 'Ferret' Skerritt of Omaha, Nebraska?" She slipped the business card into the cuff of her shirtwaist to practice snapping it out as Ferret had. The card fluttered to the floor with each attempt.

"None," he mumbled. He leaned his head forward to investigate the other holes and snags in his pajamas. His hair fell forward to hide his eyes—his head was a mess of tangled curls the color of straw. "I don't know any good tricks. All my magic is fake."

"Oh dear," Emmaline said. "I'm afraid the ether has wrecked your spirits." She poured him a cup of tea with a girlish elegance—her pinkies lifted, her wrists bent—as if pantomiming a party with a toy tea set. She held the cup to his lips; he took a sip then pushed the cup away. "I hope we didn't give you too much of that ether," she said. "But it was best you napped through it all, you little broken sparrow. Hester—

that's my sister—she really knocked your skeleton around. I listened very carefully and did everything she told me, but such an effort is no job for a couple of old ladies. Nothing you would've wanted to be awake for."

"Maybe that's what I'll do next," he said. "I'll become an ether addict." He wiggled his fingers in the air, gesturing for Emmaline to give him another sip of tea. He took the cup from her to hold it before his face, letting the steam warm his cheeks.

"Oh, an addict!" she said, clapping. "That's actually where Hester got the ether from. From Mrs. Peck, in town. We live just a few miles from Bonnevilla. Do you know it? Just a little bigger than a village, really. Mrs. Peck stirs the ether into her milk and sugar every evening to lessen the agony of arthritis." Emmaline thrilled at having a new audience for her gossip.

"See, you could ruin me without my even knowing it," he said. "Stir it into my milk and keep me here." He pushed his hair from his face and tucked the long curls behind his ears. He looked around the parlor. "This pretty room will be my keep."

"I'm so worried!" Emmaline said with delight.

Ferret emptied his cup, and held it out for more. "Please," he said. If it hadn't been for the tuft of beard at his chin, he would've had a child's face. In contrast, his voice was grizzled, as if from years of weariness. After Emmaline poured him more tea, he merely looked into the cup. "I was in a balloon," he said. "Did I fall out of it?"

Emmaline sat on the piano bench and pondered the question. "Well, eventually," she said. "Somehow."

"Where's the balloon now?" he said. "Is it still up there?"

"Not quite," she said. "It's up there, but not *up, up* there. It's empty. Of air, I mean. Or gas, or whatnot. It fell on the house, Mr. Skerritt, can you believe that?" She went to the window to pull back the lace curtain, to show the silk of the balloon shutting out the dusk. "We're nowhere at all. There isn't another house for another mile. I think it's wonderful. I think it's *fate*." She lowered her voice to a stage whisper, and she held the back of her hand to the side of her mouth. "But Hester is beside herself. She's furious at you. She put a gun to your head!" Emmaline returned to the piano bench and leaned forward to touch her hand on Ferret's cast. "But there's some divine reason you're here. Something tugged you from the sky."

"No, no, no," he said. "I won't believe in fate."

But there's only fate, Emmaline thought. She felt enraptured by this stranger, captivated and poised for transformation like the heroine in a novel. The letters on the pages of the novels she read each evening were always so tiny, she had to use a magnifying glass even just to skim. The words so enlarged made every sentence seem an exclamation.

"Where'd you come from, Mr. Skerritt? Where were you before?"

"Everyone calls me *Ferret*," he said. He pulled at a little thread on his pajama top where a button had been.

"Where, Ferret?"

"I'm a thief, Emmaline. I stole the balloon from the World's Fair."

"The World's Fair! We were there too. You must remember *that*," she said, gesturing proudly with her teacup toward a contraption along the wall. *That* had pedals for pumping air, and wooden hands on the ends of metal stems. She demonstrated. She pushed the cabinet up to the piano, put her feet on the pedals and pumped, and the wooden fingers, wired at the joints, played. The fingers tapped out a tune with an additional clickety-clack against the ivory. "You can change the song with a different cylinder. We ordered it from a cabinetmaker at the Fair, and a month later it arrived by train."

"I don't remember it," Ferret said. "I don't remember anything."

"I hope that's not true, Ferret," Emmaline said. She ran her fingers over the keys, striking aimless notes, in a way that seemed flirtatious to Hester, who now stood at the parlor door.

"Emmaline," Hester said, "let the man rest."

"I'll press your suit coat," Emmaline said. She left her cup atop the piano bench and collected his clothes. "I'll repair your trousers. We had to rip into them."

ONLY A FEW MINUTES LATER, at the kitchen table, Emmaline said, "I wonder what he's doing now."

Hester just shook her head and returned her gaze to a book about silk she'd bought many years before and had never read all the way through.

"Perhaps he'll never go," Emmaline said. "And then we'll have someone to keep us company when the other one dies."

"He seems cursed with some bad luck," Hester said. "I wouldn't plan on him living longer than either of us." Emmaline didn't hear Hester, though. In her mind she was already composing the will for which she had never before felt a need. She listed in her mind all the lovely things she owned that she wanted someone else to have.

FROM THE INSIDE POCKET of Ferret's suit coat, a postcard fell. Hester had gone on to bed, so Emmaline sat for a moment alone, with the correspondence in her hand. With Hester upstairs, Emmaline could allow herself to be tempted. The postcard was addressed to Mrs. Cecily Wakefield of Omaha. She touched it to her nose and smelled the extract of sweet pea.

Wakefield. She knew something of the name. There was a Wakefield who'd built the Fair. She wondered who this Cecily was, and then wondered if she wanted to know at all. Would knowing change everything?

Emmaline turned the card over, for only a glance, and she thought she spotted words as incriminating as *heart* and *love*. Ferret wrote in a small, cramped hand to fit all the words on the card. She took up her magnifying glass and read more.

October 31, 1898

To a doll-faced doll with a heart-shaped heart,

I wish this wasn't a love letter at all. I wish I was writing to tell you that I've forgotten everything about you, and that I'm never, ever thinking of you, not even for a minute. I want to tell you that it wouldn't even occur to me to sprinkle this paper with your favorite perfume because I remember nothing about that Extract of Sweet Pea, or how it smells like springtime (even in wintertime) at the nape of your neck.

I don't remember you on the bench of the swan gondola, your bare feet lifted from your slippers, a sea-green paper parasol spinning on your shoulder.

Your restless spirit shouldn't try to find me. Haunt somebody else. And when I'm a ghost too, my ghost won't go anywhere your ghost goes.

Yours,

Ferret

The reading glass shook in Emmaline's hand as she read the letter again. This distressed her, this twist. She'd got lost in the romance of the day's events, with a handsome fugitive recovering under her roof. If there was to be a love story, she'd hoped for it to be hers. *But I'm too old*, she thought as she studied the lines and freckles of her hands beneath the magnifying glass. *Or am I?*

You forget yourself, Hester always reminded her.

Emmaline decided not to despair. She would simply play a different character in this little amateur theatrical.

IN THE MORNING, Emmaline entered the music parlor, a tray in her hands. One side of the tray held a soft-boiled egg in a pewter eggcup, a few wrinkles of bacon, and a buttermilk biscuit with a dollop of sorghum. Across the rest of the tray were the implements of letter writing: an ink pot and pen, and some sheets of stationery.

"The paper's a little yellowed," Emmaline said. "So you'll need to beg Mrs. Wakefield's forgiveness. We don't write a lot of letters here, because we don't normally have much news to report."

"How do you know about Cecily?"

"The postcard in your pocket," she said, pleased to know something secret. "My eye just happened to fall on the name."

"I don't care," he said. He grimaced and rubbed his temples hard with his fingertips. "I don't care if you read it. Read it if you want."

"I can't," she said. "I've been to town already. I posted it." Ferret started at the mention of the post, but he said nothing. "You'll need to write her to let her know you survived."

"*Did* I survive?" Ferret grumbled.

Hester entered then, with a tray of her own: a cut glass decanter of whiskey, a shot glass, and three cigarettes. "In case you're not up to eating yet," she said, setting the tray on the tea cart near the sofa. Ferret took up a cigarette and began to light it.

"I beg your pardon, Ferret," Emmaline said, with a smile and a flutter of her lashes. "Shouldn't you ask the ladies in the room if they object to you smoking?"

Ferret, the cigarette between his lips, the match lit, smiled back at Emmaline, and his face snaked into that of the devil at his most pretty and corrupting. More than a hint of mischief and trouble, and a speckling of lemon-colored freckles that seemed sudden on his cheeks, gave him the look of a boy a mother never could properly scold. With a flick of his neck, he tossed his hair out of his face, and he widened his eyes. He gently took the cigarette away from his lips, lips so puffy, so thick, they seemed swollen from a tussle. Or from a long night of kissing. "May I, Miss Emmaline?" he said.

"I insist," she said. She picked up the bowl of sorghum and a spoon, and sat in the chair to eat the sweet jelly straight, like pudding.

He took the smoke in his lungs like it was a breath of bottled air, and it appeared as if he could feel the cigarette healing all the cracks of his bones, working down through him like vapor.

"You need to heal up fast," Hester grumbled. "You have to fetch your balloon off my house."

Ferret's eyes were closed. He held each puff of smoke inside as long as he could without coughing. "It's not my balloon," he said.

"You should tell us what happened," Emmaline said.

"There's too much to tell," he said, shaking his head. His face had returned to its grimace of pain.

"We've got nothing but time," Hester said.

But Ferret said no more.

BOOK ONE

Strangers

I.

EVERY TIME HER NAME crosses my mind, I whisper it. I whisper her name. Like a chant, or a prayer. *Cecily.* I like hearing it, this name of silk and satin. I like feeling the teakettle hiss of it on my tongue. And like a chant, or a prayer, it soothes my soul.

When I first wrote her name down—on the wrapper of a piece of Baker's Chocolate I happened to have in my pocket—I spelled it phonetically with an *S.* I was imagining it as *Sessily* or *Sessalee.* Or *Sissly*, even. I wrote it every way I could possibly picture it, but with no *C* in sight.

I wasn't at all unworldly at twenty-five, though it was true that I had never taken a step out of Omaha. I'd known many women of all sorts, ladies down on their luck and otherwise. A woman with a mind to bend her elbow at the bar—I would buy her a pint and let her trill away about her woes like a bird in a cage. I was quick with the nicotine when a lady had fits. And though some might accuse me of rascality, I was a gentleman always. I'd even been known to pick up the dropped hankie of an angelic who stumbled from church, her brain full of scripture.

And I wrote letters. Hundreds of them. To hundreds of women—all strangers, all around the world. But none of these letters had ever been addressed to anyone named Cecily.

2.

THE MEN WHO PAID ME to write letters of proposal and promise and regret were most often writing to women in faraway places. Some of the letters were to women the men had never met, and yet these men complimented the women endlessly on their beauty and their charms, hoping to entice them to the new city of Omaha from the old cities of Baltimore or Boston or New York, or from foreign cities overseas.

Each week, I ran an advertisement:

Literary assistance: letters of all descriptions written or edited; business letters, invitations, acceptances, letters of sympathy, love, disappointment, confession; all confidential; experienced ink-slinger for a big city paper, with a talent for drama and intrigue.

In fact, the closest I'd ever been to being a newspaper man was when I'd been a newsboy in knee breeches, hawking the rag on street corners. But if I lied in my advertisement, the letter writing, at least, was legitimate, despite all the tall tales I told to wheedle and convince these faraway women.

When I was a boy, no one had ever bothered to enroll me in any kind of school, but I nonetheless learned my way around the turns and twists of a phrase. I spent the afternoons of my childhood under the tutelage of Mr. Crowe, the city's librarian. Four different pairs of spectacles lined the broad brow of his balding head, each of a different magnification. I came to think of his round, owl-eyed specs, with their tortoiseshell nosepiece, as the ones that could see right into my heart of hearts—he put them to his eyes whenever he examined the shelves, seeking what might stir up my imagination. He first prescribed for me the stories of Hans Christian Andersen, and I read and reread them until the bindings collapsed. Mr. Crowe wasn't the first to try to save me from the fate that loomed for all boys with the worst of luck, and he wasn't the first to fail at it either. But he was the first to get me to listen close.

Sister Patience, so unsettled by the motherlessness of all us children of the orphanage, had often worried herself into nausea, complaining of her pain even to me as we'd walked to the library, her breath always sharp with the mint leaves she chewed to ease her stomach. I startled the nuns when I took to books—nothing much of anything had ever been expected of me—and soon enough I was asked to read to the other children every bedtime. During the day, the orphans acted like feral cats—one boy had even put out the eye of one girl in a tussle—but at night they sucked their thumbs and mewled, and they asked again and again for the story about the fair.

We are traveling to Paris to the Exhibition, I had read by candlelight, sometimes singeing the page when I leaned the flame too close. But it wouldn't have mattered if I burned holes through a word, or if a whole sentence went up in smoke. I knew it all by heart and still do. *Now we are there. That was a journey, a flight without magic. We flew on the wings of steam over the sea and across the land.*

Mr. Crowe collected all the books he could that depicted the Paris world's fair, and together we studied maps of gardens and galleries, and portraits of the fair's cathedrals and mosques; the harmoniums and waterfalls; the octopus, the orchids, and the canons and engines of war. From reading the official reports of the fair, we learned the particulars of making sparkling wine in a mechanical press and the weaving of French hosiery on an electrical loom.

There was to be another world's fair in Paris in 1889, and Crowe intended for us to go together—not just as spectators but as performers.

In his after hours, Mr. Crowe was a master of the art of ventriloquism, with a whole wardrobe of fancy-patterned suits that matched those of his dummy. No matter the kind of crowd or the size of it—whether in a saloon or on a stage—Mr. Crowe denied no one the exquisite beauty of his peculiar talents. He could throw his voice into the mouth of a doll with such stillness of lip, blink the doll's eyes and flap the doll's gums with such delicate twists of his wrists, you would forget the doll was nothing but wood and hinges and a ratty, yak-hair wig. You would find yourself falling in love with the soulless little thing.

He had no sons of his own (and believed his daughter to have a voice too weak for throwing), so he revealed to me everything, and I think he longed for me to become even better than he ever was. I think he pictured me someday stepping from behind the curtains of the grandest of concert halls, my voice lifting from the very back of my throat and carrying to the very tops of the balconies. "And when you retire," said Mr. Crowe, "you will write a book of betrayal. Give away all your mentor's niftiest tricks. Make a fortune telling everyone how we did it." Crowe, above all, loved books, and he longed to end up in one.

As the ventriloquist's apprentice, I grew out my mustache as much as a boy of that age could. I waxed and combed it, to best conceal my lips. And when I glanced in a looking glass, another young man looked back, a young man of fine style and dignity.

"We'll perform on top of the Eiffel Tower and enter the history books," Crowe vowed. I loved Crowe for his dream, but in my lowest moods, I couldn't imagine crossing the river, let alone the ocean. He was not my father. I was not his son. I was a thief. The only things I'd ever owned I'd stolen from someone else. I deserved nothing and expected nothing, and was certain I'd never see a world's fair.

Nonetheless, we had prepared for our journey to Paris. Crowe had a fear of heights, so we stood together on rooftops, and on ledges, holding hands. I helped him to the tops of ladders and led him along the branches of trees, all in anticipation of the Eiffel Tower, eighty stories tall. He'd been so agile and spry, so determined to overcome his anxiety, I'd not realized how old he really was. And months before the tower was complete, before it reached its uppermost point, Crowe took ill and swiftly died.

I convinced myself I'd doomed him with my doubt. I hadn't truly pictured myself in Paris. And after his death, in a nightmare, I climbed the Eiffel Tower alone, moving up along its latticework, scaling its side. I fell before I reached the zenith. When just an inch from splattering, I woke with a gasp. And in that gasp, I inherited Crowe's fear. Ever after, even just on steep, narrow steps, I could get struck with vertigo.

I never went to Paris, and I certainly never dreamed any world's fair would come to me. But ventriloquism possessed me and I became expert at the art. In the beginning, I imagined my act as something transcendent. When I got into character, like an actor, Crowe's voice spoke through me. But soon enough I became more practical-minded about it all. I strengthened my voice by saying not a word, speaking only when rehearsing, spending all my time sucking lemons and gargling tepid water, warming my throat by day with a scarf even in the summer months. At night I pressed a cold compress to my neck and tied it there with a strip of flannel. When practicing, I stood in front of a mirror to watch for any twitch of my lips. The lip-heavy *p*'s and *b*'s were impossible, so I avoided all mention of pianos and bustles. When a letter trembled my mouth too much, I did what I could to alter the word, changing its sound, reinventing the language as I went along. I spoke softer and softer, pushing each letter farther and farther back into my mouth, until every word I ever knew vanished from my lips. I cupped my hands at my ears to hear the seashell sound of a crashing ocean and to listen for the voice of my character in the distance.

And those years of practice were what led me to Cecily, in a sense.

Before the Fair

Late Spring 1898

3.

A t the Empress Opera House, where there had never actually been any opera, the talent got next to nothing—the tickets
were cheap and the hall rarely filled. Even as a vaudeville house it came
up short; you could find better at the Orpheum down the street, from
troupes that traveled in from elsewhere. But what the Empress had was
its morality plays. The ladies and gents would pay to see real live skin
and sinning and pretend it was virtuous. The plays changed every few
weeks, to allow folks to see men and women done in again and again
by infidelity, addiction, syphilis, thievery, whoredom.

Most of the performers on the nightly program were only locals
like me, but their ambitions matched those of the city itself. As our
little frontier town became more and more refined, they became certain that more and more people would be looking in our direction.
Already folks everywhere drank the beer from our breweries and ate
the sugar from our beets. They ate the slaughter of our packing houses.
The people of Omaha no longer dreamed of stepping out into the
world, because the world was coming to us. Omaha was growing beyond the city limits; its buildings were taller, its streets were paved, and
the railroad station connected us directly to Chicago and San Fran-
cisco and New York City.

I was no cynic, but I didn't share anyone's optimism. I had seen too much corruption. To my mind, Omaha had already been ruined. I saw no promise in the city's future. So while I waited for the world to come running, I lived in the attic of the Empress. The theater was an old temperamental firetrap newly wired for electricity, so in exchange for rent I slept lightly, poised to smell smoke at the first spark. Not sleeping was easy: my duck-feather mattress damn near flat. I whitewashed the iron bedstead to cover the rust, and I oiled the joints, as a squeaky bed made the ladies fidgety. I had a chair with broken springs and a little stove and a wardrobe full of worn-out costumes abandoned by their actors. I liked how I looked in them and adopted them as my own, gussying up a pocket with a square of silk or sticking a glass-ruby pin through the knot of my necktie—one day I was a Civil War soldier with a few patches of a hero's gunshot in my sleeve, the next I was some shabby king in epaulets with mangy fringe. I had top hats, plaid caps, a pith helmet. That's how people knew me, offstage and on—Ferret the ventriloquist, in the raggedy suits.

In the evenings I did my puppet show or magic or both, but all us performers had extra jobs we did in the daylight. I hadn't planned to get cozy with three of the girls in the four-girl burlesque act, but one by one they sidled up to me throughout that winter, each wanting to be my one and only. In January I took up with Ada who worked days wrapping bonbons in the back of Balduff's—the poor thing spent all of Valentine's up to her elbows in candy hearts and heart-shaped ice cream, while I forgot the holiday altogether. When I bought her a beer at Red's saloon, I thought I was being gentlemanly, but she burst into tears and refused to forgive the slight. So then I palled around with Florence, a ginger-haired cherry who hated her own freckles—I always fell into a fit of sneezing from her perfumed fading cream.

And all the month of April I dated the girl named May—when not at the Empress, May popped the corn and took the tickets at the zoological gardens, where they charged admission to see all the critters that lived in the plains just outside our city, Omaha still only a mile or two from wilderness. They kept buffalo, prairie dogs, coyotes, raccoons. One spring day we took a pleasant stroll through the zoo, arm in arm in the shade of her parasol, May looking down at the path, distracted from the eagles and owls. In front of the caged badger she finally spoke: "So go ahead and ask me to marry you, if you want," she said. And I said, "But I thought we had a good thing going," which wasn't at all what she'd hoped to hear, though I had truly meant it as a compliment. May had never before been so serious, which was why I'd liked her so much.

Marriage had seemed to me to be for men too old or too churchy for romance. I didn't know it then, but I was stunted, forever the orphaned child. As a boy, I'd feared I'd never grow up, that my rotten youth would never end. And though it did end, the fear didn't. That life I'd longed for—of being a man of worth and substance after shaking off my awful boyhood—still seemed a lifetime away. So I kept waiting and waiting.

I was waiting for Cecily, as it turned out. When I first saw her, only a few weeks before the Fair, I caught her eye, and she looked away. It was when she looked again that I straightened my back and lifted my chin. It was with that second look, as quick as it was, that I suddenly felt like I was somebody worth seeing.

I HEARD HER NAME before I saw her, that night, backstage at the Empress. Before the entertainment began, an old actor with a monocle shuffled out center stage to address a few changes to the cast. "And the part of 'violet-eyed trollop' in *Opium and Vanities* will *not* be played tonight by Odie Hansom, as listed. She will be played, instead, by Cecily . . ." and here he paused, squinting at a sheet of paper in his hand, seemingly attempting to read the actress's last name. "Cecily . . ." he said again. He finally abandoned the effort. "Cecily," he concluded, and left the stage.

As the master of ceremonies stumbled out to sing a comic song, his face painted white and his mouth a broad, bright-red gash of a smile that wouldn't stop, I shared a cigarette in the wings with the fourth girl in the burlesque revue. She was my favorite. I'd bought Phoebe St. James a consoling drink or two, ever since her traveling theater troupe went bankrupt the winter before, stranding all the actors and actresses far from home. She was content to share her troubles, and nothing more, with me. One day she'd been hamming it up as Yum-Yum in *The Mikado* at one of the city's finer performance halls, and the next she was a dime-a-dance girl at a local saloon.

"That wallpaper's truly the ghastliest," she said, gazing at the backdrop dangling overhead in the rafters. She was dressed like a fairy with a short skirt of blue feathers and silk stockings the color of her skin—little pieces of glass had somehow been stitched into the silk to make her legs shimmer in the footlights. The dancers often changed their act, but their costumes stayed mostly the same. One night they were fairies, another night pixies, another night elves, another night angels—whatever called for paper wings and short skirts.

"Maybe it's supposed to be," I said. "It's the walls of the opium den, after all."

"Why would anyone have anything to do with opium if the wallpaper is that ghastly," she said. The cigarette between her lips, she practiced her dance steps, swinging her wrists, wiggling her fanny, the wings on her back fluttering. Three little light steps forward on the balls of her feet, three little light steps back. She plucked at her stockings whenever the glass nettled her skin.

"You noticed there's no music tonight, didn't you?" I said. She stopped dancing, gave me back my cigarette, and leaned cautiously forward to peek down into the empty, shallow orchestra pit. "The musicians went on strike just before curtain," I told her.

Phoebe shrugged, then picked up a grease pencil from a makeup kit on a stool. She leaned forward into a mirror and drew a heart-shaped birthmark on a bit of exposed breast. "Unlikely anybody would notice the fiddle player anyway," she said. She batted feathery black eyelashes.

When the master of ceremonies was bored of getting booed, he ran to the opposite end of the stage spouting the foulest of words despite his painted-on grin. Phoebe took the cigarette from my lips and gave me a slap on the ass. "Time for your ol' song and dance, Geppetto," she said.

MY PUPPET, a doll I called Oscar, had rosy cheeks of chipped paint and a squat top hat atop a polished bald head. I had bought the dummy secondhand from a peddler's cart some years before, the sun having faded the doll's striped trousers and dotted vest, and yellowed the golden dragons embroidered on his tiny slippers.

In better days, he'd been a man of distinction, I figured, so he spoke with an uppity purr that was easy to do without moving my lips much, though I did still keep my mustache overgrown and unruly. My tongue lazy and slow, I created a drawl that tickled the crowds even more than his jokes about life as an elegant skinflint.

"Are you going to the Fair this summer, Oscar?" I asked him when the audience finished its feeble applause.

"Heaventh, noooo," he said. I triggered a switch that rolled his glass eyes toward the ceiling. "I unnerstan," he said, "tha' the castles are of horsehair and glue."

The crowd enjoyed the puppet's cynicism, and they laughed without mirth. *Yes*, they seemed to say, *we're all weary of the World's Fair and it ain't even begun.*

The Omaha World's Fair had seemed, to those of us in the city's lower, dirtier parts, the folly of the wealthy and their wives. The white palaces would sparkle like gemstones, they told us. Foreign flowers had been blooming all winter in greenhouses and exotic fish had been shipped in from far-off oceans to stock the lily ponds. They talked as if they could unmuddy the river and uncloud the skies. "You won't recognize yourself. How happy you'll all be to be someplace else. It's so much better than what you deserve" is what we heard them saying when they were saying all those other things.

Some of the old-timers among us had been in Omaha since its earliest days fifty years before, and they weren't folks easily dazzled. Back then, the wind kicked up the dust in summer; and in the winter it spread fires from one house of sticks to the next. Many of the settlers only settled because they had slowed to a stop on their way to the Gold Rush.

And even when I was a little boy, twenty years or so before, packs of wild hounds so terrorized the town, sinking their teeth into children and livestock, that men took to poisoning the dogs with strychnine. I'd had to step over their carcasses on my way to the library. I knew the town's worst qualities too well. No matter how many streets the mayor paved or sewers he dug, Omaha would never be Chicago. I'd never once been to the Windy City, but it was my idea of civilization. If I'd grown up in Chicago, I reasoned, I would've stumbled over the good fortune that fell in the streets. The remarkable destiny that waited for me would've been right around every corner. I would've been Dickens's Pip.

In Chicago, there was beauty and class. There was wealth and money well spent. In Omaha, the only rich men I'd ever worked among were the cattle barons in their carriages outside the auction houses. They would sit there, brooding, puffing on cigars, sending up smoke that I could swear turned into dark clouds shaped like true-to-life skulls and crossbones. They weren't ones to sully their spats by taking a step into the marketplace, so they sat in their cabs, overburdened by their fur coats, poised to hear reports of profits. As an orphan I'd begged for alms, and they would pay me to go away, not out of charity but because my raggedness reminded them too much of the dust heap they'd only themselves just recently left behind.

"There's to be a carnival too," I told Oscar on the stage, with some sense of nostalgia. "You can ride rides, and watch whirling dervishes. You can have your future told in a clairvoyant's booth."

"I already know my future," Oscar said. I played the buttons up his spine like those of a concertina, allowing me to work the movement of his hinged fingers. He opened one hand, joint by joint, and with the pointer finger of his other, he traced the line in his palm, along the grain of the wood. "The Fair ain't worth the admission fee," he predicted.

But I thought just then of Mr. Crowe, and his stereopticon, the library dimmed, the lantern lit, projecting the colorful illustrations of the Paris Expo of 1867 on the wall. He showed slides of an enormous vapor-filled balloon, a Siamese pavilion, a grotto aquarium. I could taste again, at the tip of my tongue, the sugared figs that he'd cut up and shared, and how I'd run my fingers along the ribbons of French words on the candy box that had been delivered by mail.

Any thought of Mr. Crowe could turn me sentimental. Crowe would have been tickled by the notion of a world's fair in Omaha, no matter how little the city might resemble Paris.

To close the act, Oscar did a character for the crowd—Old Poppa Popocrat of the Populist Party. With a few twists of a knob on his steel spine, I could make him sit up ramrod straight. By playing some buttons and strings in among the cog works of his guts, I could bring his hands to his chest and could slip his fingers into his vest pockets. I pumped a leather bladder near his heart to puff up his chest with a blowhard's arrogance.

I wasn't much for politics and politicking, but I found that Old Poppa could quickly turn a crowd noisy. They all loved to laugh at their troubles. The best comedy plays on your very worst fears, it seems. The money panic of five years before—the days when a farmer's crop didn't even yield enough to pay the debt on a sturdy plow—inclined folks toward clamoring for a common man's revolution. The big businesses— the railroads, the banks—overbuilt, overborrowed, overloaned; and when they failed, we all fell with them. The Populists promised change; they would give the nation back to the people.

"They light their see-gars with the sweat of our brows," Oscar said, speaking of the city's rich. "They work our fingers to the bone, then sell us leather mittens at a price twice our wages. At the slaughter-house, we work for a penny a pig, then pay the butcher double for a slice of bacon!" The audience whooped and jeered, as if at a true rally.

"And now, the World's Fair," Old Poppa Popocrat said, rocking back and forth, like in a chair on his porch. "A giant fairyland tossed up in the middle of a dead field. They say the architects are even gilding the bricks to line the walks. Yes, in Oh-me-ha, we pave our streets with gold bullion. And *you're* paying for it, one way or 'nuther, and there's *still* a fee to get in."

The crowd at the Empress was howling so, Old Poppa could barely finish sermonizing. "They drive us to drink, then sell us mugs of their beer that's half bubbles from the keg," he said, because it wasn't just the slaughter industry that had our town in a yoke—so did the breweries. So did the flour mills, the streetcar company, the newspapers that covered none of the worst scandals and true corruptions of our town. The businessmen set up shop anywhere they could sell anything of no worth to a man with little money. It was an age-old adage already: the poor could make you rich, and the rich could make you poor. "Then when we're good 'n' drunk, we buy their papers to read about ourselfs and our drunken ruckuses."

Was I any better than the city's villains, peddling pain? I took the people's grievances, twisted them around, and sold them back to them nightly. After every show, I left the stage with their angry laughter filling my soul. I would sit in the saloon and weigh and consider the success or failure of every joke and I would revise my act, sharpening its stabs.

After Oscar's rabble-rousing, we ended with a magic trick. An actor planted in the audience threw an egg up to bust on my knees, and I picked up the shell, crushed it in my fist, and stuffed it in Oscar's jacket pocket. I then tapped at his chest to unhook the door to a tiny cage within, where a talented canary rested, patient and soundless. Once released, it flew from his coat and swooped and dove just above the heads of the crowd. I loved the sigh of the ladies' delight.

When the people fell for my tricks, I felt redeemed. For a moment, I reasoned, they believed in magic. They would carry their wonder out with them into the streets.

But by the end of that summer, I would come to see things differently. I would be troubled by my entertainment, played for a fool. I would be the puppet in a rich man's grim comedy.

4.

THE BURLESQUE REVUE, bereft of an orchestra, made a music all its own, all clatter and scratch, the ladies' every step and misstep making for an uneven rhythm against the stage. Even from the wings, I could hear the huff and puff of their breaths and the smack of the kisses they blew into the audience. I could hear the popping of Phoebe's trick knee. The ladies had lightly riddled their feather skirts with down from a pillow, so when they spun and kicked, the feathers flew up and drifted in the glow, giving the illusion of their costumes falling apart little by little.

One of the feathers drifted in my direction, catching in my intake of breath. It tickled my nose, working up a sneeze. I held my hands to my face and stepped quickly back, away from the quiet of the stage. As I buried the bark of my sneeze in the sleeve of my coat, Cecily entered from the alley.

I didn't yet know that this was the actress not listed in the program, that this was that Sessaly, the "violet-eyed trollop" of *Opium and Vanities*. Her eyes were not violet, after all—they were amber. They were the color of candied ginger or a slice of cinnamon cake. Faded paper, polished leather, a brandied apricot. Orange-peel tea. I considered them, imagining the letters I would write to her. Pipe tobacco, perhaps. A honey lozenge, an autumn leaf. I would look through books of poetry, not to thieve but to avoid. *Dear Sessaly*, I thought later that night, not actually with pen to paper but lying on my back, writing the words in the air with my finger, *let me say nothing to you that's already been said.*

The light of a lantern backstage caught in her wet eyes. When Cecily gave me that first look, then the second one, she had her hands up and behind her neck. She turned her back to me. She lifted the curls of her hair that had come loose from their pins, revealing a crisscrossing of complicated buttons at the top of her dress.

"Undo me," she said.

The buttons, and their buttonholes, were absurdly small, and she tapped her foot, waiting, which somehow made my fingers more clumsy and slow. Typically I knew my way around a lady's buttons, and rarely needed more than the fingers of one hand. I squinted, wanting to be helpful but helping hardly at all. And I got distracted by the pattern in the fabric—what I had thought were flowers were actually little devils dancing and playing fiddles.

She reached back and her fingertips touched my fingertips, and without a word, she guided my hand and taught me the intricacies of the buttons and clasps. Did she even need me at all? I leaned in close to better smell the sweet pea perfume she had dabbed at her wrists. "Oh, I see," I said, and when I'd finished the task, and she'd gone on her way to the stairs, to the dressing rooms in the basement, I felt foolish for not having been more expert.

The burlesque act fell apart in pieces—without music, the girls weren't sure when to stop, so one girl slowed, another girl shuffled, another kept going. Finally, they all hopped off the stage, doffing their costumes before they'd even entered the shadows.

"The glass in this silk scratches me up good," Phoebe said, showing off the little cuts as she rolled down her stockings. The curtains closed, and the stagehands scurried, and the actresses stepped up from the basement, mostly undressed, to play the victims of the cautionary tale.

The stage glowed a bloody red for *Opium and Vanities*, the lights covered with pieces of stained glass. Only a few minutes before curtain, after all the other actresses had taken their places, Cecily climbed the stairs in her corset and underskirt, the black circles of an addict drawn thickly around and around her eyes. She studied the sight of her own mussed hair in the hand mirror she held. She used a dinner fork to tangle her hair more, twisting the tines of it through her curls.

Again she asked for my help as she turned her back to me, the laces untied. She clutched at the breast of the corset. "Tighten them up," she said. Afraid of hurting her, I tied them too loose. "No," she said. "Tighter." I failed again, and she sighed. "Pull them until I yelp."

I did as I was told. I gave the strings a sharp yank, with a zip of the laces, and yelp she did. I knotted them up with another sharp yank and another yelp. In the corner of my mouth was a pipe I had lit up. I used it in my act—it got good laughs when I would take a drag, then make Oscar cough, smoke lifting from his mouth from the popping of a capsule of powder. Cecily thanked me this time with a shy smile, her hands at her chest to cover herself. She then dropped her smile and seemed to contemplate my chin. She furrowed her brow, tilted her head in thought. I said, "Something puzzling you, sweetheart?"

Cecily swiped my pipe from my mouth. She ran on stage as the curtains parted, and she collapsed into the cushions of a red velvet sofa, puffing away without a single tickle in her throat.

She had no lines to say and yet, for me, she was the only actress worth watching. I leaned against a ladder and stared. And it was as if Cecily—and the wordless violet-eyed trollop she portrayed—knew everyone watched only her. And she ignored us all, her eyes on the clouds of smoke that rose before her.

The violet-eyed trollop figured in only two other scenes in the first act, all of them in her underthings, even the one that took place in the winter out-of-doors. *Opium and Vanities* chronicled a quick tumble down for the ladies of the bordello—one minute they were laughing it up with glasses of crushed-mint tea (simulating absinthe) and only minutes later begging at a train station, as a stagehand stood on the rigging overhead and sprinkled down bone shavings and soap flakes from a pillowcase for make-believe snow. A hose piped up steam from the boiler room below, to create a low-hanging fog. The poverty, the addiction, the bitter cold in too-little clothes—it was what turned the trollop's eyes violet, I guess.

At the end of her last scene, Cecily entered the wings, tugged at my chin, and returned the pipe to my lips. She tapped my chin again— a playful slap—then rushed down to the dressing rooms. I went over and over what I might say when she stepped back up, but I was feeling no better with words than I'd been with her buttons. I wanted to be gallant, to say something that would never occur to somebody like me.

Only minutes later she ran up the stairs in a rush, her devil-riddled dress only partly buttoned up the back. And she walked right out the stage door without a glance my way. I followed her, but she moved so swiftly through the alley and around the corner that I didn't have a chance to ask her if she might join me for a little drop of whiskey. She stepped into the street and into a phaeton with rattling wheels and a battered black hood. The driver didn't even stop for her—he only slowed the horses. A gloved hand reached out from beneath the phaeton's hood and Cecily took it, ran alongside, and she stepped up and in. And she was gone.

That was the first time I lost her. I would come to lose her again and again.

After the show, I asked Phoebe about Odie Hansom, the actress listed in the program as the violet-eyed trollop. I pretended concern, but I had never noticed Odie before. I couldn't even imagine what she looked like. I just wanted to know if there was any chance she'd return to the Empress to steal her role away from Cecily.

"Odie'll be back," Phoebe said, which seemed to me the grimmest words I'd ever heard. Phoebe and I were walking down Farnam to Ninth Street, alongside the streetcar tracks, our eyes on the sky. Those days everybody looked up at night, seeking the airship, a mysterious silver flicker that moved through the dark like a slow shooting star. It had been showing up, off and on, for months, over Omaha and country towns farther west. Whatever it was, a handful of men took credit for it in letters to the editors of the dailies. One man described it as a cigar-shaped balloon off which he'd hung his bicycle, pedaling the propellers that flung him through space; another man said he'd built a yacht powered by mysterious fuels and captained by a whole squadron of sky pirates. We didn't believe any of the stories but couldn't resist them, nonetheless.

"Odie's not sick?" I said.

"Yeah, she's sick," Phoebe said. "Sick with a drunk husband. He beats her, then cries and cries and begs her forgiveness. He buys her a couple of ounces of steak to nurse her black eye, acts like he's treating her to a fine filet at a hotel restaurant."

Phoebe had changed into a plain shirtwaist and skirt and had pinned to her hair a small straw hat. We were on our way to the saloon in the parlor of a brothel, and she hoped to look like a schoolmarm among the working girls, to avoid any confusion when she made eyes at a gentleman she liked. When you left the morality plays of the Empress, you only had to stumble a few blocks to fall into what was known as the Burnt District, where men rented women for large sums or small. The deeper you walked into the neighborhood, the more pennies you saved.

We were headed to one of the grandest houses in town, and its saloon was called the Candy Box, with walls papered in pink silk striped with thin ribbons of white velvet. Anna Wilson, the madam, was rich and charitable—the money she'd made off her well-kept ladies afforded fat donations to children's homes and hospitals. Anna Wilson claimed, with pride, that she only hired girls who'd already been ruined—a girl, say, with a fatherless baby on the way or one already in her arms. When the mothers went to work at Anna Wilson's, the babies were sent to the orphanages with the finest cradles.

I have no idea at all who my mother ever was, but I'd been told by

Sister Patience, at a very young age, "All orphans are born of whores." In the only snippet of correspondence I had from my mother—a note that had been tucked into the dapper cap of a sailor's suit I'd been wearing when, as an infant, I'd been left at the nuns' door—she'd addressed me as Mr. Bartholomew Skerritt: *Your last name was your daddy's last name (I'm right damn sure of it, don't let anybody tell you different), and your first name was the longest first name I've ever seen written down. I can't give you nothing much but I can give you a name with lots of letters in it. Sincerely, the mother you never knew.*

At the library, when I was a boy, Mr. Crowe brought out county records, and there were no Skerritts listed anywhere in them, no matter how often and how hard we looked.

"Think you'll ever bring brats into the world?" I asked Phoebe.

"Only if I marry a compassionate man," she said. Phoebe hoped to meet enlisted men in the brothel's saloon. Like everybody else, she'd got swept up in the call to arms for a war with Spain in Cuba, but in Phoebe's imagination she was a devoted lover sending off a handsome soldier. The newspapers nationwide had demanded battle weeks before and everyone was war mad. And when our navy ship, the USS *Maine*, was blasted and sunk in the Havana harbor, the phrase "Remember the *Maine*" was everywhere, in song after song and etched on teacups and pocketknives and souvenir spoons. President McKinley asked the men of the nation to prepare to fight, and the young and the old volunteered in the thousands. Those in Omaha waited to be called forward, basking in the sympathies of the town's ladies. The men haunted the saloons and bordellos, raising their glasses to their own bravery.

"What about you, Ferret?" Phoebe asked, and for a moment I feared she was asking me if I planned to enlist in that miserable war. But then she said, "Will you marry, and have little ferrets?"

"I'm going to marry the violet-eyed trollop," I said, both a premonition and a fallacy. "The one from the stage tonight, not the one at home with the steak on her eye. But children . . . no. Childhood is too awful a thing to make happen to somebody. No, nope. No, siree."

I shared with Phoebe my Baker's Chocolate, pointing at the wrapper and my many failed attempts at spelling Cecily's name with an *S*. "And you have no idea who she is?" I said. "The actress who stood in for Odie?"

Phoebe cringed from the bitterness of the chocolate. "All I know is I don't want to know her at all," she said. "She's one of the strangers who've come to town to take all the parts in all the plays." Phoebe told me about the cavalcade of performers and gondoliers who'd rowed up the rivers from Nashville. "They're here for the Fair," she said. "They move from one world's fair to the next, to work the midways, the magic shows, the illusions. The chambers of horror. All the cheap amusements."

They'd had a treacherous winter trip, in the Venetian gondolas they would use later in the Fair's lagoon. The actors and actresses sat in fur coats and quilts as they'd sailed into the weather, with umbrellas their only protection against the elements. Leading the fleet had been a novelty gondola shaped like a swan, its long curved neck pointing its beak forward into the wind and snow.

"They've been here for months, it seems like," Phoebe said, weary. *Months*, I thought, regretting all the hours already lost. But unless Odie Hansom kept irking her husband, I feared I'd never chance seeing Cecily again. I studied the wrapper, eyeballing all the wrong spellings, sensing her drifting farther away, nameless. Phoebe said, "Do you think she's pretty?"

"I do," I said, though I knew Phoebe didn't want such an answer. She'd asked with a squint, her whole face screwed up ugly. "I couldn't take my eyes away," I added.

Phoebe shrugged and sighed but did so politely. "I used to know a love spell," she said, "but you have to pluck a hair out of the girl's head and burn it. *She will not sleep or eat, and she will forget father and mother and kith and kin, and for love of me may have me only in her mind*. Or something like that."

"I used to court a lady who thought she was a witch," I said, "but she doesn't speak to me anymore." On our last evening together, she attempted to end her love for me with an alienation spell that called for driving nails through a calf's heart. She wept and wept, the bloodied, spiked calf's heart lying on the butcher's paper before her, drawing flies.

"I might very well marry you myself if you went to war and came back without a scratch," Phoebe said. She reached over to push my curls back from my face. "In a place like America, a whore's boy can be a hero if he gets in a few good licks at the enemy."

"You read that on a piece of needlepoint?" I said. I leaned my face into her hand to kiss her palm. She stroked my cheek with her thumb. "I don't fight the wars of warmongers," I said. I meant no disrespect to the men who lined up to march off, but I'd already done all the fighting I ever wanted to do. I'd spent all those years warring with bullies and thugs so that someday I could *quit* fighting altogether.

5.

FOR THE REST OF THE RUN OF *Opium and Vanities*, Odie Hansom was back as the violet-eyed trollop, her left eye black-and-blue. And no one seemed to know a thing about anyone named Cecily or how she'd come to be an understudy for that one night only. Not a soul had seen her on that stage, as if she'd been as faint as a phantom even then. The manager didn't recall hiring her and he didn't recall paying her. "The violet-eyed trollop doesn't utter a word," he said. "Why would she need an understudy?"

And Odie lied, embarrassed at being hit so hard she couldn't leave her house. "I haven't missed a day of work in my life," she said, slurring with a fat lip. All the other actresses lied right along with her as if they thought they were saving her dignity.

I had evidence. I hadn't puffed on my pipe since Cecily had snatched it; and in its bowl was the tobacco she'd burned, and at the end of its stem was a kiss of red from the rouge she used on her lips.

But the fact that she was little more than a figment only fed my curiosity. And my hopes were lifted by a few unlikely matchmakers— my fellow rats of the Omaha underground. They'd seen nothing of Cecily themselves, but they seemed to get a kick out of egging me on. These swindlers and bandits coaxed and prodded like spinster aunts certain to marry me off.

"I'm fond of the thought of you getting away," said August Sweet-briar, dandiest of dandies, who peddled tonics. We'd grown close in the year or so we'd known each other—I'd first met him at Anna Wilson's saloon, where he sold the ladies an aphrodisiac made from juniper berries and saffron. Though he was only my age, he carried himself like a man much older, often sighing with weariness or holding the back of his hand to his forehead like a fevered opera singer. He wore on his fingers handmade rings—pieces of wire twisted around little broken shards of colored glass. "Maybe you'll get in good with one of those traveling troupes that move from fair to fair to fair, and they'll adopt you into their life of endless summers." Around his wrist was always a woman's silver bracelet engraved with Old English script, a quote from Shakespeare: *I bear a charmed life.*

August interrupted me in my bath one afternoon in late May, the Fair only a few days off. I had no running water in my attic, so I bathed in a claw-foot tub in the basement of the Empress. Even with my ears full of soap I recognized August's boots on the steps—the *tip, tip, tip* of the thin high heels. He'd bought the haggard boots off a retired cowboy, and he liked to stuff the ends of his trousers into them, to show off the flowers stamped into the tall leather. August boasted that the few dents above the right ankle were from rattlesnake fangs.

"I have a solution to your mustache problem, Ferret," August said as he opened a mother-of-pearl case with a squeak of its small hinge. Inside, on a bed of blue velvet, rested a stainless steel straight razor with a handle made of scrimshaw. "You've never before been shaved with a blade this fine. I got it in a trade from a very nervous gentleman who was once very rich. He thinks he's addicted to my extract of evening primrose." August had no sense of propriety and would find me no matter where I might be in the building.

"I'm not looking to solve any kind of mustache problem," I said, wringing the bathwater out of my curls. I no longer needed to hide my lips when throwing my voice—I could keep them quite still—but my mustache reminded me romantically of my reckless youth, and of my old friend Crowe, so I was inclined to keep it always.

"Do it for the love of a lady," August said. "Think how much sweeter your first kiss will be if she can find your lips." August didn't wait for me to agree—he sat on the edge of the tub and removed his bowler, a fancy affair of gray felt. Stitched to the band of the hat was a taxidermied bluebird, with rubies where its eyes went. The short braid August wore at the back of his head was tucked under his starched collar. He began to prepare the tools to shear me: the blade, the scissors, a jar of lotion.

August had been nagging me to shave ever since we first met. "Why hide that pretty pout away?" he would whine, puffing out his lower lip. He and I worked together every now and again—we did a medicine show out in the countryside in the nearby valleys and villages, where we could make some money from the farmers' struggle. I would perform magic with my dummy as August sold envelopes of powdered corn silk and flasks of rhubarb cordial. Even at his feet just now was a carpetbag, and inside were little clear bottles of harmless cures. While some snake oil salesmen dealt in concoctions with dangerous doses of cocaine and morphine, August's fraud wouldn't stop your heart or poison your blood. Like a revivalist in a tent, he promised to end baldness with licorice-flavored tonics. He vowed to steady palsy with a spoonful of cinnamon extract, to stimulate heartsickness with love potions of water tinted brown from a pinch of burned sugar. Occasionally he would add to a concoction a few drops of alcohol—what he called *cologne spirits*—but never enough to even spin your head. "The worst that can happen is that the tonic does nothing," August said to justify his deceit. "But the best that can happen is that it does everything I say it does. I never underestimate simple belief."

"Ladies have never objected to my mustache," I said, though as I said it, I realized it was far from true. Women were often berating my mustache as grizzly and uncivilized, even when I waxed and twisted the ends.

But I'd grown that mustache as soon as I'd been able, and it hadn't left my lip since. Not only had it hidden the throwing of my voice on-stage but it had brought me a kind of respect that a hopelessly boyish face wouldn't. And in my attic garret was a cabinet stocked with grooming products and devices—special shampoos and waxes, strengtheners and weakeners, combs, curlers, snippers. I felt most like a gentleman when shopping for my mustache. And there were pretty girls behind the department store counter who attended to me.

A little sleepy from the warmth of the bath, and from the lily scent of the soap flakes, I closed my eyes and thought of Cecily haunting my bare room. I thought of my walls and how no pictures hung from the nails. I thought of how rarely I lit a lamp after dark.

And with that I leaned my head back, my neck on the lip of the tub, and closed my eyes. I nodded. August first began to trim with a pair of small scissors—the teensy *snip*, *snip*, *snip* pushed my teeth to edge; he might as well have been snipping at the ends of my nerves. He then produced from his carpetbag a shaving mug and a boar's bristle brush. He dabbed some jelly onto the remnants of my lip feathers. "The jelly's got mint," he said, opening the blade. "Breathe it in and clear your nose. It will put you at ease."

The mint didn't quite, but August's slow scritch scratch and his considering eye did manage to soothe me. He furrowed his brow, intent on his work, and I studied his face in return. I'd never before had occasion to look at him for so long. His face could use a mustache too. He looked worse than a boy: he looked like a baby, without a single sprout of hair on his chin, and brown eyes soft and wide. How had he ever convinced anyone of a cure for anything? He had the kind of gullible mug I'd looked for in a man I sought to thieve, back in my derelict days, before I took to the stage and found a little salvation in my vaudeville act.

When he finished, he went for a pewter hand mirror from a dressing room vanity, and I put my fingers to my lip. The skin somehow felt as smooth and cool as glass. For theatrical effect, he showed me only the back of the mirror, which featured stalks of cattails bending along the curve. He then turned the glass to me.

August said, "Tell me you like it as much as I like it. Please." He gnawed on his thumbnail with worry. "What do you think?"

"I think . . ." I said, pausing. "I think I look like a man with a mustache who doesn't have his mustache anymore." I held my finger across my lip, pantomiming a handlebar. "What if Cecily doesn't remember me without it?" I said.

"What's there for her to remember?" August said. "That you're the man with the terrible mustache who let her get away? It's best you pretend that that fool was somebody else altogether." He then brought out some hats from the costume closet, and tried each one atop my wet head, at a number of jaunty tilts and angles.

ANOTHER AMONG MY CUPIDS was the anarchist Rościsław. We called him Rosie the Pole, and he and his pack gathered most every evening to argufy. All the anarchists were angry, having become expert at losing awful jobs—Rosie had cut throats of cattle at the slaughterhouse and swept blood into the drains, had hacked ice from a lake and loaded the blocks into wagons, had shoveled coal into the guts of the smelting works. He was the size of two men and didn't care to be criticized, so most of his jobs ended with him slugging his boss in the jaw.

On the afternoon I lost my mustache, I posed for Rosie in his studio, attempting to look respectable for a counterfeit pass. Each of the Fair's workers was required to carry identification with a stamped photograph. With the phony credentials we rats could ease through the gates without paying a daily fee. We all had ambitions: my dummy and I would do magic tricks for tips, August would sell his fixes, and Rosie had built a rickshaw from scrap parts to taxi folks around in.

I sat in front of the camera on a stool with a gray blanket draped behind, and Rosie shoved all my wild curls up into a derby. "The razor you took to your lip you oughta take to your head," he grumbled. His studio was in a converted dovecote and greenhouse on the roof of a building on the Ware Block, with glass walls to let the sun in.

"I never realized I was quite so unsightly," I said.

"I just want your girl to fall for you, is all," he said. "I'm a sentimental bastard."

Rosie's mouth was a box of dominoes with black holes among the broken teeth, but he wasn't always seeking a scuffle. His heart was soft at times. He'd come to America for the benefit of his sister, to work hard and make money to send home to the family farm in Poland. The girl needed a dowry or she'd never snag a husband.

He now made most of his money off selling French postcards of naked Omaha women. He called the ladies his *lovelies*, and he anticipated he'd do swift business at the Fair with his pictures of Lady Godiva on horseback, Sleeping Beauty sleeping in the buff, Hamlet's Ophelia having ripped off her clothes in madness, Joan of Arc naked and tied to a stake.

With such high-minded subjects, Rosie could pass the postcards off as art to the gentlemen who might otherwise be too nervous to gaze upon the nakedness. But Rosie did truly see himself as an artist and a lover of women—he was a lumbering beast with a delicate eye for beauty.

I glanced over all the postcards stuck to his door with insect pins, to see if Cecily was among the naked ladybirds. Part of me wanted to discover her there, stripped and indifferent to any leering eyes upon her, and yet another part of me couldn't bear the thought of it.

We then sat down to a table in the studio covered with maps and pamphlets and we studied the ins and outs of the Fair. Our passes weren't illegitimate; they were just ill got. August's father owned Megeath Printing Co. and Bookshop, and had manufactured many of the Fair's official materials; August had easily swiped some.

I memorized the fairground's nooks and crannies, walking my fingertips up and over walls, down alleys, over bridges.

"'According to the 1890 census,'" August read aloud from the guidebook, "'Omaha consisted of one hundred forty thousand four hundred fifty-two souls, of which four thousand five hundred sixty-six were colored, eighty-nine were Chinese, and three were civilized Indians.'"

"Where do you fall in all that?" I said. *Sweetbriar* was a name he'd taken for himself when grown, from a book a British anthropologist had written about the natives of America. His parents had never told him his real Indian name. When his father bought Megeath's, he'd kept the name of the shop and took it as his own. And August grew up as Little Augie Megeath, his hair cut to the quick, wearing tailored three-piece suits like a little white man with dusky skin.

"Nowhere, I suspect," he said. "How does one get counted among the civilized?" He lifted his pinky as he sipped his whiskey from a chipped teacup.

"If you find out, let me know," I said.

With the Fair flat on the map before me, confined to a page, I was certain I'd find Cecily somewhere among the showmen and charlatans. Like me and August and Rosie, she'd be among the uncounted, the uncivilized, the riffraff that kept the show going for the finer folk.

In what seemed an omen, the Fair's court was shaped like a key. On the left-hand side of the map was the clover-shaped reflecting pool—the filigree of the key's bow. I ran my finger along the canal, to the end of the key's bit pointed toward the midway—the lock to be unlocked, where all the mystery was.

And it *was* an omen, a lucky one, because find her I did, on the Fair's very first day. And on that very first day, I did everything wrong.

November 1, 1898

My Cecily,

    *I've spent the evening an invalid, in a wicker-back
wheelchair. My broken leg is propped on a footstool, my foot on a
cushion. Today is All Saints' Day, and in some countries people
light candles on graves. But here where I am, wherever this is,
there's nothing but life. All the neighbors came here tonight to help
these two old sisters undo my damage. They've brought their
ladders and their strongest boys to remove the empty balloon from
the house. They'll do something useful with the silk, they figure,
even though it's all dirty with sky, stinking of glue and of the gas
that lifted it up. They've considered sewing it into new choir
gowns, which makes me think of the singers all connected by the
same dress, like a string of paper dolls.*

    *Everyone from all around is here. The farmers' wives have
brought pies baked from the apples new off the trees. A flank of
some beast cooks on a spit over a fire that the children dance
around like sprites in worship. I can hear the wolves yipping, not
howling like they should be, at the bright yellow harvest moon,
almost full.*

    *The farmers' sons have carried the dining room table from the
house and onto the lawn. It took eight of those boys. Hester, one of
the sisters whose house this is, built the table herself, cut it from
some enormous tree she felled by the river. Emmaline, the other
sister, brings out the dishes from the house, the ones that didn't
break when the balloon crashed, and a lacy tablecloth. She hooks
elephant-shaped weights to each corner of the cloth, to keep it from*

rustling away in the slight night breeze. The women cover the table with plates of biscuits and baked beets, a platter of mackerel, some jars of pickled figs, pickled peaches, watermelon pickles. It's a sight of beauty. They need all this ritual because of all the grief the land has given them. They need to connect with the earth, to tether themselves to this place they so want to leave, because they need someplace like home.

But they leave me be in my little wheeled chair, alone, writing my ghost a letter. The farmers and their wives and their children steal glances at me, and they huddle to whisper, as if I'm the apparition. And maybe I am. I'm haunted by the words that I write to you, knowing that your eyes will never fall across them.

In the dark, in the country,
Your Ferret

At the Fair

June 1898

6.

ON THE CROWDED STREETCAR I tucked my counterfeit pass into the front of my britches—over the summer, the Fair would welcome two million visitors from near and from far, and it seemed that half of them were free-market thieves. Already, on the Fair's first day in June, I spotted Mrs. Lou Decker all in black, posing as a widow in weeds. She was the famous Chicago pickpocket, well-known for the absence of her right ear.

But many of the other women on the streetcar, the respectable ones, wore white ruffled gowns. They carried white parasols, wore white hats, white ribbons, white veils. The fairgrounds were already known as the New White City, making Chicago the Old White City as far as we were concerned, and Omaha was dressing the part. The Fair's architect, a man named Kimball, went so far as to assert that Omaha's was the only *true* White City, as Chicago's buildings had actually been painted a pale brown. Our palaces were pure, whitewashed in the cleanest ivory.

I leaned out and over the side of the streetcar to see around a woman's broad-brimmed hat piled high with white peonies. Even once I saw past, to the tall walls ahead surrounding the fairgrounds like a fortress, I imagined only fakery inside, a wonderland of false fronts propped up by two-by-fours and gardens of wilting roses painted red.

But to my mind, that's what magic was. The Fair was an optical illusion as illegitimate as my sleight of hand, a summer-long dream we all dreamed together, and I adored it already. All the happy hoodwinked fairgoers would line up to be mesmerized. I would make a killing off my dummy's tricks, I decided.

I carried Oscar dangling off my back, the doll's hands latched—with a metal hook and eye screwed into its wooden wrists—at my neck. The dummy's back was against my own, his head facing out. He blinked with every bump on the tracks, making the little boys behind me giggle.

I wore an evening tuxedo from the theater's wardrobe closet, complete with tails, though it was only just past dawn. I wore white gloves, but the only pair I could find had fingertips badly yellowed from nicotine, so I kept my hands in fists, my fingers curled in. Though the tuxedo was missing a button, and the back of its collar was shiny from years of an actor's greasepaint, it would position me well in the crowd. Opening day would be packed with the highfalutin, and I knew, from all my pillaging of the Empress's costume closet, how much gentlemen owed their clothing for their positions of authority. When dressed so, I found myself enhanced with all the gestures of importance, my stride brisk, my spine broomstick straight. I quickly took up the habit of tucking my thumb into my watch pocket, and rolling back on my heels, like a man both leisurely and impatient.

When the streetcar stopped, we all stumbled out to join the others waiting at the gates. All of Omaha had turned out that morning, it seemed. An empty lot in front of the Fair's archway filled with hundreds waiting for the gates to open. The lot was like a new city of its own, as hectic as a marketplace, with people hawking goods—hot doughnuts, watermelon, roasted cashews, armloads of calla lilies. The iceman, with a face pocked like lemon peel, leaned out from the back of his wagon and stabbed at a block with a pick, sending chips into the street for the children to fetch.

The proprietor of a smoke shop jostled the crowd with his

sandwich-board advertisement for pipe tobacco and candied ginger. As the tobacconist passed, his cigar burning, a few old ladies fanned away the smoke with paper fans passed around by the undertaker promoting his parlor.

I kept my eye on the one-eared Mrs. Decker, and sure enough she went to work even as she stepped from the streetcar. She knocked into an old man, and as she apologized and helped to right him, she made off with his coin purse.

In picking *her* pocket, I impressed myself with skills I hadn't known I still had. Though I had learned how to filch any watch and wallet fifteen years before, at the nimble-fingered age of ten, from the saloon keep who'd let me sleep in a crate behind the bar, I'd not practiced the craft in some time. But I saw no violation in the picking of the pocket of a pickpocket, and I discovered that I still possessed a ten-year-old's innocent carriage, able to bump into people without even a pardon me. With just a nudge of my thumb, I had slipped in and tipped the stolen purse from Mrs. Decker's pocket right into my palm and up my sleeve.

Something about the spirit of the Fair inclined me toward feeling generous. We had all watched the buildings going up in winter, and had even skated on the frozen-over lagoon in the faint shadows of the buildings' rafters and frames. But with the first thaw, the walls of the city had been erected, hiding the kingdom away as its courts and halls took shape. Even the most cynical among us could see the myth in it. The Fair had come in the night and would draw the world near. Everyone in Omaha—angels and all—would visit the Fair. It wouldn't have shocked me to see Mr. Crowe in the crowd, his dummy in his arms. And it was at the Fair I would find Cecily, I was certain, and this time I would remember to tell her my name.

I returned the coin purse to Mrs. Decker's victim. I didn't even look to see how much money I was giving up. "You had a lady get in your pocket," I explained. "I got this back for you." The old man only eyed me with suspicion.

"Go on with you," he croaked. "I ain't giving you a reward." He then turned to his hunchbacked wife and shouted into the little brass hearing trumpet she held to her ear. "They think every act of kindness deserves a nickel."

His condescension dropped me into a sour mood. My tuxedo, it seemed, was earning me no special respect.

Though the front gates wouldn't open for another half hour, the crowd kept taking little scuffle steps forward, as more and more people arrived. But no one seemed to mind the crush. Every bump and shove just wriggled them closer to the Fair, as if they were working together to storm the walls inch by inch. They all laughed at their predicaments, at the elbows in their ribs, their hats knocked off. I'd never seen such a friendly mob in our outlaw town.

At the edge of the crowd, an organ grinder played a tinny tune, with five little monkeys with chains around their ankles collecting tips in copper cups. The grinder had put fezzes on their heads and strapped little feathered wings to their backs. The wings, not the monkeys, brought to my mind the angels of the burlesque. I missed Phoebe and the girls already.

Expecting the Fair to steal all the business, the Empress had shut down for the summer, and the performers all scattered. Phoebe had saved enough money to go back East for a few months, to join a summer troupe, and she'd been rehearsing for days—she was to play a woman blind from syphilis. One night at Red's saloon, Phoebe had lifted her skirt and pushed down her stocking to show me her bruises from bumping into furniture, her eyes having often been shut to bring her closer to her character. "Chifforobe," she said pointing to the black-and-blue mark on the back of her knee. "Leg of the bench," she said, pointing to her ankle.

Standing in this packed lot made me realize how naive I'd been. Cecily could be tucked in under any of these towering hats. Would I even know her if I saw her? Did I remember her as she really was? At least Phoebe was real, truly real, head to toe. We could have made a fine summer of it, mocking the whole pompous to-do. Phoebe would have loved those monkeys in particular. For a moment, with a pang, I longed for the summer to be over.

And with that little spark of doubt, Cecily appeared, as if I'd summoned her by giving up. And I didn't just happen to spot her in the crowd—the crowd parted for her. Or rather, the crowd broke apart, to keep from getting stomped by the slow mules of a wagon. The wagon's driver was drunk already, swaying and rocking on his perch. Or he was acting drunk—he was dressed in the tattered clothes of a scarecrow, with a hayseed's battered straw hat. He might have been nothing but a clown. "Please pardon me," he said over and over as he attempted to steer the mules away, off to the side. "Don't mind us. We won't bother you again. I beg your pardon."

Rising above the complaint of the crowd came a song, sung in a baritone so deep and loud I could feel it in my own chest. The wagon made its way to the edge, directed by a policeman with a whistle who waved the driver toward the lane that would lead them to a delivery entrance. The side of the wagon was painted with a mural depicting a bare stage with red curtains parted. Above the stage, the troupe's name swirled across a banner in purple: the Silk & Sawdust Players.

I stumbled back out of the wagon's way. Five or six actors and actresses strolled alongside, in the ruffles and frills of their underwear. The men wore undershirts and pants that sagged, and derbies and fedoras; the women wore petticoats and corset covers. And all their faces were caked with stage makeup, their kissers rosied, their cheeks comical circles of red. They seemed poised to jump right into costumes and onto a stage.

The gent who sang so forcefully had the build of a circus strong man. His hair was perfectly oiled, and he'd raked it wavy with a comb. He carried a Spanish fan that he seemed to enjoy snapping open and shut. And over his arm was the arm of Cecily.

As she passed, Cecily looked at me, then looked up and over the rooftops, knowing me not at all. But she looked my way again, and I kept looking, and her eyes, like something precious and polished, seemed too beautiful to see out of. I mean to say, when I looked at her, it seemed she might not see me at all, and I could stare without being noticed.

Cecily wore what looked to be an old wedding dress of yellowing ivory satin, but it didn't seem a costume. It just seemed to be something someone like her might wear, any day of any week. Sewn atop each shoulder was a lace butterfly with starched wings that flapped with her steps, and each butterfly's curling, twisting path was stitched in pearls all down the front of her dress.

And she carried a carpetbag. The bag was nothing special. Nothing worth notice. I paid no mind to its design of fat quail and yellow pears. Later I'd learn the bag's contents, and the contents' great value, but just then, with Cecily again walking away, the bag meant little to me. I only considered its weight. The carpetbag caused Cecily to list to one side, giving me the opportunity to be gallant.

The actors who might have volunteered to carry the bag were too preoccupied with their own whimsy. One actor walked a marionette, working its riggings, concentrating on the puppet's graceful stride as he himself tripped and stumbled over his own feet. Another actor kept stealing kisses from an actress, nuzzling his narrow nose into her double chins.

I ran up to Cecily, eager to play the gentleman, and I slipped my hand into the bamboo handle of the bag, my fingers lacing with hers. The skin of my wrist rubbed against the lace of her sleeve. When her fingers tightened against mine, I couldn't speak. It was a message, I thought. A secret. I leaned in closer, as if she might whisper something. *Not here*, she might say.

But she said nothing. And when I saw her face, and felt her tug hard at the bag, pulling it away, I realized I'd frightened her. Like a fool, I'd gone about it all backward. I'd meant to *ask* if I could assist and *then* take the handle. She had no reason to believe, despite my tuxedo, that I was anything but a thief.

Before I could explain, the burly actor with the deep voice grabbed my shoulder and gave me a good shove, sending me back to get tangled up in the strings of the marionette. While the actor and I attempted to disentangle, both of us plucking at the strings like at a spider's webbing, the troupe moved on. Once released from the puppet, I ran ahead again, hoping to apologize, but none of the actors would now let me near. They shoved and pulled and tripped. The plump actress worked her fingers into my curls and yanked me away by my hair.

"Cecily, you know me," I shouted, but she didn't glance back. "I'm Ferret the ventriloquist. I had a mustache." I trailed behind, but kept near. I intended to follow her until I couldn't follow her anymore. But when one of the actors ran ahead toward a policeman with a billy club, I stepped farther back.

The rear of the wagon had no door, only a tasseled, threadbare rug that served as a curtain. Thinking only of Cecily, I stepped up and through.

7.

WITHIN THE WAGON, in the light from a little window at the front, I saw trunks with clothes and costumes spilling from their open lids, and gowns and crinolines hanging from hooks. Strapped to the walls were dented-up instruments, some that plinked and twanged with the rocking of the wagon—a xylophone, a mandolin, an accordion.

I stumbled over a row of pretty shoes and nearly slammed myself into the wagon's wall. I worried that everyone outside would hear me inside, rolling around, so I sat atop a trunk and tried to keep still. I hugged my knees to my chest. I cozied up to the automaton seated next to me—such puppets had become popular parts of traveling shows. They did magic tricks, these bloodless characters. They were often life-size, dressed up in fancy robes and wigs, and within their guts was machinery that worked their arms and neck, animating them with a muffled clicking of gears. They were like ventriloquists' dummies, but with no ventriloquist nearby.

This automaton's skin was the texture of burlap, its wrinkles sewn deep, its nose bulbous, its wig all dirty-gray wires twisted into two braids. She slept. She wore a ruffled collar like a clown, and a silver whistle hung at the end of a chain around her neck. Her long skirt was patterned with suggestions of sorcery: frogs, snakes, a crescent moon.

As I reached up to press at her eyelid, the eyelids drifted open, as if from weights in the doll's skull. Her head turned to me, and though it moved on a slow cog, the movement made me jump. The left eye, clearly glass, was all milk white, not a single dot of color, but the other eye . . . the other eye was as real and wet as if it had been freshly spooned out of a corpse's head.

That's when the automaton opened its mouth. Her breath smelled so thickly of death, of yesterday's onions, of the blackest of pepper, I knew this old woman could only be alive. But before I could back away, the woman grabbed my wrist with the strength of a man. Despite the lack of bright light in the wagon, her one living eye continued to shimmer. One hand still on my wrist, she put the other to my throat, and she clutched until I wheezed.

"All my life," she said, her voice hoarse and broken, "little thieves have thunk they could snake past me and fill their pockets." All her weight was pressed against me, pinning me to the wall.

"I'm not a thief," I choked out.

"Them's the famous last words of all the little thieves whose necks I snap."

"I don't want anything," I said.

"There ain't a man who walked this earth that didn't want something and who didn't want that something every minute of his stupid, worthless life."

Gagging, I attempted, with both hands, to pry her grip from my throat. "Nothing," I said.

"That'd be a shame to choke to death for *nothing*," she said. "You should figure out here, in your last minutes, *something* worth dying for."

"Stop killing me," I said, my voice deflated to nothing but a slow, weak whistling.

"Oh, I ain't even started killing you yet, little thief. You'll know for sure when I'm killing ya. Now I'm just playing with ya. But maybe *that's* what you want, ay? To be the first man dead at the Fair? Then everybody would know your name for a couple of days. That'd be something worth thieving for, I'd say."

"Cecily," I said, and at the immediate mention of the actress's name, the old woman loosened her grip. But then she tightened it again. "Little thieves like you don't know nobody named Cecily," she said.

"No," I said, her grip tighter and tighter. "I don't know nobody."

"That's the smartest thing you said all day," she said. "Not knowing nothing is the smartest thing you can do for yourself, little bandit. I don't know you all that much, but you don't seem all that smart to me. But let me tell you something about that girl you say you don't know nothing about." She put her hand to my chin in a manner that might otherwise have seemed motherly. She stroked my cheek with her thumb. With her other hand, she smoothed my curls back. "You better keep knowing nothing about her. You don't have to go no further than troubling yourself with that girl to get that early death you've been wanting so bad." And with that, she grabbed me by the collar, dragged me to the door, and tossed me from the wagon.

8.

I HAD THE PRESENCE OF MIND, as I stumbled over my ankles and fell to the ground, to lead with my shoulder so as not to bust up Oscar, but I was bounced onto my back anyway, hitting my own head hard against the dummy's wooden one. Though I wasn't knocked all the way out, my wits had scattered plenty.

For a brief moment Cecily hovered over me, a glowing shadow, as I squinted into the morning sun behind her head. I was embarrassed to have her help me up, but I leaned into her as she put her arms around my waist, as she cradled me to get me to my feet. My head throbbed so, I couldn't see straight. And, in a blink, the shadow wasn't Cecily at all. The woman who held me wore a Salvation Army uniform—a cape and bonnet, and her hair was silver. "God be with you," she muttered as she righted me, and she ducked her head and slipped away.

When all the spots in my eyes left, I saw the real Cecily, but only as she disappeared yet again, as she turned a corner to follow her wagon through the service gate. As I ran ahead, a sting in my ankle from a twist, I could tell there was something wrong with Oscar too by the clack of his jaw. The thought of him back there, broken, nagged at me, but I couldn't stop to look.

The Fair's security guards were dressed as English bobbies, billy clubs and all, in domed hats and brass buttons, just for the novelty of it.

The guards were checking passes, and that's when I realized the Salvation Army angel hadn't been cradling me—she'd frisked me. She'd fingered my counterfeit pass right from the crotch of my pants where I'd hidden it, likely mistaking it for a wallet. A wizened thief myself, I always kept my money in the hollow heel of my left shoe, a heel I could push open on a secret, swiveled hinge a cobbler had tapped into place for me. At that particular moment I would have given away every dollar in my shoe to have that pass in my hands.

"I'm with them," I said, pointing toward the Silk & Sawdust Players, but the guard ignored me as he checked the pass of the driver of a flower cart. I tried walking past him but only ended up on the ground again, the guard having grabbed me by the neck and shoved.

"Get up and try to get by me again," the guard said, the tip of his boot nudging at the base of my spine. "I get paid more, the more bones I crack."

I rolled away and he left me alone. When I sat up I saw my dummy had suffered worse than I'd thought in the fall from the wagon. Oscar's jaw had gone unhinged and it hung there, speechless. I pulled a piece of string from a new tear at the seam of my sleeve and knotted it around an exposed screw and a hook, until I'd doctored him the best I could. I nonetheless worried about his innards. I relied on those switches and gears to keep him spunky. I shook him a little, and he gave off a deathly rattle.

My skeleton felt jangled from all the bullying too, and in my thinking I was a kid again—I'd got the name *Ferret* as a wily boy of a narrow, ferretlike build. I supposed I might never outgrow beatings from every sack of rusty guts who had a pound or two on me. And what would I say to Cecily now? In her eyes, *I* was the bully.

As I walked back toward the front lot, poor old Oscar under my arm, I didn't think at all about what I might say to Cecily if I saw her again but of what I should've said when I saw her before. I went over and over in my head how it all could have been different, as if there were still time to magically undo the hour if I just fussed and fretted enough. I should have tipped my hat to her, said the right thing—whatever that was—and she would have let me carry her bag and thanked me for it. And she might even have remembered me from the Empress. *Your mustache is gone*, she might have said with a wink.

But I refused to believe I'd been unlucky. Seeing her again, on the Fair's very first day, was a kind of miracle—my every misstep had tripped me right into her path. My luck was changing for the better. After all, it wasn't her that pushed me away.

Up ahead, beneath the arch over the entrance, the ticket booth had opened and the mob pulsed forth like a pack of twitchy rats toward a hole in a boat.

The summer sunlight harsh against the stark-white arch scorched us all, and those with umbrellas opened them, filling the air with the screech of steel spines and the pop of silk pulled taut. I skirted the fee by ducking in and out of the parasols of others, my accomplices barely noticing me at their sides, though we were nearly cheek to cheek, knocking elbows, as I slipped around in their shade.

I entered the courtyard tucked in beneath some lady's ruffled white parasol, my head low to avoid suspicion. The lady took my arm, mistaking me for her gentleman, and she whispered in my ear, with a lovely gasp, "Sugar." I patted her hand and somehow got away without her noticing that I wasn't hers.

Once I was out from under the umbrellas and parasols, I looked up and saw what she meant. The buildings of the Grand Court shimmered with shattered glass that had been dusted over the whitewash, to glisten like something from a confectioner's shop.

And those buildings went on and on without end. I was most stunned by the expanse of it, and all its elegance. The rotundas, the columns and pillars, the winding ivy, the rows of flags, the statues of winged horses, of chariots and bare-chested angels and warriors, everything white and shimmering as if chiseled from a salt lick—it was like looking upon an ancient city before it fell. It was not part of Omaha, but something in place of it, something else entirely. In this new place that had risen from the city's humid summer fog, the breezes seemed blown in from the sea.

Most of the fairgoers floated slowly across the pavements as if addle-headed from liquor. They seemed to want nothing other than a lazy stroll through this strange, sudden kingdom that might just ripple away in the waves of heat. This was *their* spectacle, and they were determined to be marveled by it.

I can't say *I* marveled for long, beyond those first few moments. Soon enough I felt the grit of Omaha's dirty wind between my teeth and in my eyes. The Grand Court was something I had to get past to get to the midway, to find Cecily. And the court, and all its white mansions, looked like it might go on for miles, as if you could keep walking toward the end of it and never reach the other side. I'd known this lot when it was empty—among my odd jobs over the years I'd been a wharf rat, picking up work at the riverbanks, pulling in barges and loading up wagons. Me and the other boys had climbed to the top of the tall railroad bridge, back before my fear of heights, allowing us to gaze across the fallow fields. I'd imagined the property mine. *Even just a scrap of it*, I'd dreamed. *Even just a dry corner left for dead*. A patch of land, I'd figured, would change everything. I'd get something to grow on it and live a halfway honest life.

How had they fit this court into that stretch of empty fields? I'd never guessed it'd hold so much. And there, all down the middle of the court, was the lagoon, which itself seemed as long and wide as the river.

I headed to the east end, toward the bridge with the plaster angels and cherubs with trumpets. The bridge rose up and over Sixteenth Street, over the streetcar line, then down into the bluffs that lined the river, to the midway and all its shuck and jive—despite my tuxedo, I knew the Grand Court wasn't where I'd be lingering that summer; it was on the midway I'd be able to hustle for tips once Oscar had his wits about him.

But there was no getting on the bridge because there was no getting past the elephant. The midway wouldn't open until afternoon, it seemed, and the wild animal show had been enlisted to block entry while giving the crowds a peek at the carnival's beasts. I would eventually come to know the little family that managed this zoo, just as I got to know everyone who worked the midway. A yellow-haired girl in hair ribbons, one of the daughters of the circus barker, wore a python around her shoulders like a fox stole. Another daughter, probably four years old, sat locked in the cage with the sleeping lion, one hand wrapped in the cat's mane. The barker's wife, peacock feathers rising from her headpiece, kept a panther on a leash, letting it prowl and pace. A grizzly bear wore a clown's neck ruffle. And atop the elephant, standing on the creature's back, was the barker himself, barking his guts out, in tall black boots and long red coat, boasting loudly of all the terror he'd tamed.

I stepped back into the court, realizing the midway would have to wait, and stood at the railing at the edge of the lagoon.

The gondoliers steered their boats through the still water of the canal, and swimming among them was the one shaped like a swan. Phoebe had told me about these gondolas and gondoliers sailing up the river in the winter, boats full of actors. I had pictured Cecily bundled in furs on a gondola's pillowed bench, beneath a candy-striped awning, a kettle of hot tea on a tiny gas stove, like some Russian duchess. And I'd pictured a swan gondola as elegant as the birds themselves.

That wasn't quite the case. This swan boat, though pretty with its frail, curved neck, needed paint. The yellow was nearly all chipped off its beak, and the white of its wooden feathers was faded to the color of a dirty egg. There was hardly any blue left in its eyes. The bench at the bird's tail feathers had a heart-shaped back, like on a lovers' swing, and even that looked battered, with faded velvet cushions.

And yet I saw myself with Cecily sitting on that bench, sharing a bottle of wine. The boat's ruin had a shabby romance, like it had jumped the track of some cheap midway carousel, sneaking into the court's precious waters. It was an honest wreck, and it was a welcome sight.

After looking away from the swan, all I could see was the toil of illusion. I followed the promenade toward the band shell, where speakers had already begun to speechify. I passed a patch of garden where a few women in aprons across their black skirts tended flowers, carrying what looked to be large bottles of perfume. They pinched at the bulbs of atomizers, enhancing the scents of the petals with floral extract.

Nearby, a man wrestled with a tangle of wires in a lamppost. I could almost feel the electricity, as if it buzzed unharnessed in the air, singeing and bristling the hairs on the backs of my hands. I could taste sulfur on the tip of my tongue.

This was the magic of the Fair for me. The Grand Court had been built only to be torn down and would never survive a single Nebraska winter. It all even seemed *of* the winter, like the mists that rose over the river in early December, those columns of steam and cloud that hover over the water like a ghost city. Cecily and I would fall in love at the Fair, I determined. We would lose the whole summer as we stared at each other, and then we'd let the White City collapse behind us. The place could turn to cloud and fade away like Avalon.

Already, the gondolas had passengers. As I looked down on them from a bridge, they looked up above my head. They pointed at the sky behind me. When I turned, I saw the hot-air balloon that rose from the hidden midway, its basket tethered with a rope to keep it from floating off.

The balloon was a pale yellow with a few large square patches, like patches on the knees of a boy's trousers—I thought I could even see the *x*'s of the stitching. One patch was green, another blue, and one seemed a pattern of plaid. And draped across the balloon was a giant purple banner with only one word—*Omaha*. And the balloon seemed to have no captain.

The thought of hovering up there, carried by ether, gave me the shivers like nothing else. You wouldn't get me in a tree even if the ground was squirming with rattlers. I wasn't one to hammer a shingle on a roof or to climb the ladder that would get me there. It reminded me of the dream that showed up again and again in my nights, which would start sweet, with me waltzing a pretty but faceless lady in a pavilion, under paper lanterns, only to end with us both stumbling down an open well. I would wake, my heart pounding to get out of my ribs.

9.

As I watched the balloon rise above the midway, the wind picked up. The balloon bounced at the end of its rope, tugging, the wind threatening to carry it to the clouds.

The wind would blow, then rest, then blow, then rest, and in between the gusts I'd catch snatches of the speeches from the amphitheater of the Grand Court behind me, and the oompah of tubas from the marine band. I returned Oscar to my back and wandered toward the edge of the crowd.

"These mighty sssssstructures sssstand where fifty years ago were clustered tepees of the Omaha Indianssss," the speaker said. The man shouted into a megaphone that magnified his lisp. The megaphone periscoped far out before him, its various snaky segments propped up on stilts. "The sssssilence of this place was disturbed only by the Indian war sound, by the revelry of the Indian dance, and the prairies rang with no sound but the war whoop of the aborigine. Today it is sssssurrounded by twenty thousand buildings, the homes of one hundred fifty thoussssssand people, who are the members of the rich commercial city of Omaha."

"*Whoooooop,*" came a shout from the back of the crowd, and people turned, their brows wrinkled with annoyance. I didn't have to look to know it was August. I recognized his voice and his gumption. August shouted something else, to heckle, but the wind had kicked up again and carried his voice away to get lost in the rustling of the shrubbery.

The gusts began to scatter lost things across the court. A man's derby rolled by like a runaway wheel. Handkerchiefs were plucked from pockets, sheet music spun away, stealing off with an unfinished song. Flowers were picked from women's hats. And the gondolas rocked like at sea, as the gondoliers struggled to return to the docks before their passengers fell seasick.

I waved to August, and when his eyebrow rose and he squinted one eye to sum me up, I remembered my rough-and-tumble condition. I slapped some dirt from my sleeve and from the knee of my trousers. August stood next to Rosie's makeshift rickshaw, a contraption of odds and ends. The taxi was worse off than I was, its two wheels uneven, its bench an old, short sofa of wine-colored velvet that had been tossed from a bordello saloon. Rosie had stitched shut some rips in the velvet with thick black thread. Wired to the back of the sofa was a parasol with a snapped stem repaired with string. The dainty parasol, its silk patterned with roses, cast barely an inch or two of shade.

"Did you fall into a pack of sssssavages?" August hissed. He licked his thumb and rubbed my cheek with it. He then showed me the smear of blood he'd wiped up. I pressed my fingers to my scratch.

"I'm in love," I said.

August sighed with pity and nodded. "Looks it."

The speech ended and the crowd applauded to be polite, but they were clearly eager to move on. Nonetheless, no one took the rickshaw rides Rosie offered, even when discounted to a nickel. He did, however, sell a few of his lovelies—the postcards were clothespinned all up and down the ratty silk lining of his coat. Whenever a gentleman passed, Rosie would fan himself with a picture of the three muses in sheer robes, and if the girls caught the man's eye, Rosie would lift his coat open to offer a peek at the others. Rosie liked it most when a gentleman lingered and took a great interest in the art of it. A man, perhaps feigning insight in order to ogle the nudes, might make mention of deliberate shadows and classic poses, or ask Rosie for recommendations. "I love them all," Rosie would say each and every time, and I somewhat believe he meant it. Rosie seemed to gaze upon his every lovely not so much with lust as with a longing and heartsickness, unable to decide if his love belonged more to Helen of Troy or to Salome or to Nefertiti.

After the speech, I made my first wage at the Fair. Rosie hired August and me to simply ride in the rickshaw as he pulled us along the length of the court. He wanted to demonstrate to the fairgoers that his rickety taxi wouldn't collapse, but I wasn't convinced. I worried the risk wasn't worth the fifty cents. But as I yakked on and on to August, boasting of my good luck at finding Cecily so soon, I would've been happy to have been wheeled around all morning long in that wobbling cart. And the more I talked about Cecily, the more I remembered of her, and all the rest of the day's misery began to fade to nothing.

"Just before I lost sight of her," I said, "she was lifting up her dress an inch or two, to pick her hem up from the ground to step over some mud, or something, and she was wearing ballerina slippers. At least I think so. They were pink. The ribbons were undone, trailing behind her. I don't know how she kept from tripping on them."

August blew out his cigarette smoke in a long sigh. "Heaven only knows," he said.

I sensed I was boring him, so I shut my mouth, and in the silence he whooped again. "'The war whoop of the aborigine,'" August said, quoting the lisping speaker. He rolled his eyes and shook his head. "My father is an Omaha Indian," he said, with a snap of irritation, "and he opened our bookshop before most of the cowboys of this grubby little town could read a word of English. I've been wearing a suit and tie since I was ten years old. As a matter of fact, my father took me, when I was that little boy, to Boyd's Opera House to hear Oscar Wilde speak about the pursuit of beauty." August drew out the phrase "pursuit of beauty" as if referencing a sacred text, fluttering his fingers before himself. "Here's an adorable little irony you might appreciate, Ferret:

Daddy does a particularly swift business selling dime novels all about wild Indian attacks on poor, frightened white settlers."

"Don't the Indians always end up gunned down in the end?" I said. "In those books?"

"Oh my yes," August said. "Practically every character in the book gets a shot at the redskins. Even the little girls in their gingham dresses. But, oh, the violence, the glorious violence, that leads up to it all. The scalpings. The cowboys burned at stakes."

I nodded and winked, and I finger-thumped the brim of his derby, jostling the stuffed bluebird. The lazy bit of affection seemed to cheer him up, and he took his hat off so he could put his head on my shoulder. He looped his arm through mine and told me to tell him more about Cecily. "Tell me everything," he said, "then tell me again."

A LITTLE PAST NOON, the elephant was the first to cross the bridge, and many of us fairgoers followed him, like a tribe of exiles. August and I had failed to drum up business for Rosie's rickshaw, so we were on foot now, Rosie having wisely hired a few pretty girls to ride and pose as fearless.

Some boys risked getting stomped, roller-skating around the elephant's lumbering legs, figure-eighting, ducking down and under the beast's belly.

Though August's carpetbag jingled with bottled cures, he didn't feel up to the task of hawking them. And Oscar, with his half-cracked head, was a fright. I would've been better off with a sock for a puppet, I thought. August and I wanted to simply be fairgoers like everyone else, just a couple of blokes on holiday. We deserved to be entertained.

I needed to find Cecily. She could be anywhere, playing any part, I realized. I feared it could take me all summer to find her, and even if I did find her, what if I didn't know her? She could be all decked out something awful, slathered in greasepaint, hidden by wigs.

Crossing the bridge was like crossing the ocean—the two worlds had little in common. The midway's road was hard-packed dirt, while the Grand Court's promenade was paved with bricks that shimmered in the sun a yellow gold. The buildings of the Grand Court were dedicated to Electricity, Fine Arts, Agriculture, and Government, to Horticulture and Invention, while the midway's devotion was to the devil, to hypnotists, fortune-tellers, belly dancers, swallowers of swords. On the midway were Turks racing camels, fakirs charming snakes. There was an Indian camp with wigwams, and a Filipino Village where cannibals were said to salivate every time a fairgoer passed.

To me, the midway was heaven, or at least some hell-bent spin on it. When we first set eyes on it, on that very first day, it wasn't ready to be seen. Workers scrambled to slap it all together on nothing but a lick and a promise—unlike the pristine whiteness of the court, the haphazard shacks ahead clashed in color and stripe, some tall, some short, each roof at an awkward angle to the other. Everybody seemed so roostered and frantic, you couldn't tell if everything was going up or coming down.

But many of the exhibits, even those that were only half-built, were ready to take your ticket. A dark-haired woman, her eyes painted with a Cleopatra swish, sat on a settee in front of the Streets of Cairo to puff on a hookah as a dervish whirled and whirled in front of her. A Chinese illusionist made his wife disappear with the spin of a mirrored wheel. An ostrich pulled a buggy in which was seated the Living Doll, a Cuban singer only twenty-six inches in height, and she sang a war tune called "The Belle of Havana." Overhead were strings of Chinese lanterns of pink and baby-blue paper.

There were buildings shaped like foreign shrines, with onion domes. There were thatched-roof huts of mud. There were the tall walls of Western forts and the short ones of sharecroppers' shacks. There were cupolas with candy-striped shingles and parlors with polka-dot eaves. There were railroad tracks that curved and twisted, rising high to swoop and bend, promising danger of collision and derailment, the ground far below. There were stages without theaters. On one, a clown on a unicycle juggled cats. On another, a thrower of knives aimed for his wife. On yet another, an actor stood on a fake gallows, his future widow already in weeds, sobbing her eyes out, a trick noose snug on his neck. The smell of sausage carried from a cottage shaped like a cuckoo clock. There was a beer garden and a greenhouse full of hummingbirds that buzzed so close you could almost feel their wings flutter your lashes. The bees had already fled the apiary, filling the air with threat, thumping into hats and catching in the folds of skirts.

Down the center of the midway were all kinds of sordid enterprises, the whole endeavor bringing out the city's thugs and hucksters. Riggers set up their sweat cloths, betting the kids they couldn't pick the thimble that hid the dried pea. You could lose bets on marked cards, on loaded dice, on bones and feathers. You could have your palm read by a blind beggar.

People lined up to be fleeced. The flush you felt when you lost to thieves wasn't far from the rush of love, was it? When a pretty girl flirted, you could feel that same heat in your cheeks and fast beat of blood in your veins.

That's what *I* felt anyway, that rush and pulse, when I caught sight of the automaton who'd bruised my throat. *"Her,"* I said, with a hiccup of breath. I felt a sharp sting of ache in my head.

THE WOMAN WHO'D TOSSED ME off the wagon now sat stone-still in a tall, battered cabinet in the road. The cabinet was only just big enough to fit around her, and all its walls were mostly panes of glass. Leaning against one wall was a sign: *Wake the Witch! For a nickel the automaton will answer questions you're frightened to ask!*

Though I'd hoped never to see the old woman again, I could've kissed her on her rotten, foul mouth. If she was there in front of me, then Cecily might not be far off.

"That's the woman who tried to strangle me," I told August, as I touched my fingers to the bump of my Adam's apple.

"How?" August said. "Her hands are made of wax."

"Those aren't her hands," I said. I stepped up to the booth, leaning forward to see close. "Her hands must be tucked into the sleeves."

I studied the skin of her face, which looked covered with a light cheesecloth and dusted with powder to give it the illusion of cracking plaster. My first mistaking her for an automaton was all part of the act, it seemed. She was done up to look just fake enough to seem star-tlingly real.

The witch sat hunched on a stool and wore a tall pointed hat em-broidered with a sour-faced monkey. She held a closed umbrella across her knees, and at her feet were two lightbulbs painted red. One bulb was screwed into a block of wood painted with the word *Yes!* and the other in a block of wood with the word *No!* A small plaque beneath the coin slot read: *This ancient and magical toy was discovered in the basement of an old abandoned theater in Italy! She's been taken apart and put back together and still nobody knows how she works! She's the most lifelike au-tomaton in all the world!*

I leaned over to speak into a brass horn sloppily rigged to the box, and it carried my voice inside, sending it echoing within the walls of glass. "I know your secret, old lady," I said.

August dropped a nickel into the coin slot, and the box came alive. The red bulbs at the witch's feet flashed on and off. The crank of a street organ began churning on its own, the pipes and whistles wheez-ing slowly and then picking up the notes of a tune that seemed to have no beginning or end. The woman straightened on her stool to the sound of grinding cogs, her spine ratcheting up, vertebra by vertebra, click, click, click, click. She opened her one good eye—the glass one was covered with a patch.

At the top of the booth, the word "Ask!" flickered with electricity. I again leaned into the horn, to taunt, to punish her for beating me up. I folded my hands at my chest and fluttered my lashes, lampooning a hopefully romantic pose, and I asked, "Will I find Cecily nearby?" The woman showed no reaction to the question but continued with her pantomime of mechanical, stuttering movement, her arms and wax hands lifting the umbrella to push the tip of a button on the floor. The red bulb behind the word *No!* lit with the clang of a bell. The woman then brought her umbrella back to her knees, and she drooped into her slouch, and the booth fell quiet and dark.

Her head suddenly turned as if slipping a gear on her neck. With her eye still open, she cast at me a deathly glare, her eyelid twitchy. Some drops of foam bubbled at the corner of her mouth. Then the booth lit up again, and the tuneless music rose, and a little boy with freckles and knee breeches elbowed me aside to speak into the horn.

"Is this worth a nickel?" the boy asked the witch. The witch shivered and jerked and lit the *No!* bulb.

"Don't worry, kid," I said, "that's her answer to everything." I leaned in to speak loud in the horn. *"She must be broken."*

August tapped my shoulder and pointed at a shack shaped like a dragon's head. "Cecily's with Satan," August said, and sure enough, leaning against the dragon's tooth was one of Cecily's fellow actors in devil horns, his face painted red. His back was to us as he flirted with a geisha. Written across his red cape was the Silk & Sawdust Players in the same candy-box curlicue that had been painted on the side of the theater troupe's wagon.

"God bless Satan," I said. I grabbed August's elbow and dragged him toward the dragon's maw.

To get into the chamber of horrors, you entered through the dragon's wide-open mouth, beneath giant bloodshot eyeballs that rolled up and down. You stepped up its tongue, and in.

In the lobby, where we waited for the next tour, August and I sidled up to a coffin-shaped bar where another devil served us boiled whiskey in shot glasses shaped like skulls. A squealing filled our ears—I'd later learn it was a recording of pigs at a South Omaha slaughterhouse.

A woman in black slouched forward, moving quickly through the crowd, gesturing and whispering, cupping her hand around the flame of a candle she carried. The dead black buds of roses were wired to the brim of her hat. "Come with me, come with me," she said. "There's only one way out, there's only one way out." We followed her through a creaky-hinged door.

You would walk down a dark hallway, stumble around corners, jumble up against each other. Every now and again a curtain on the wall would part, and you'd see some grim mischief lit by footlights on a stage. A family of pioneers got their gingham and bonnets all blood-ied as their papa got scalped. A bone grubber robbing graves tripped into a coffin with a corpse. On a city street a man in a wolf's mask held a dagger to the throat of a pretty young thing in a red cape. Above Little Red and the wolf, true-to-life dead blackbirds bobbed on strings like back-alley vultures waiting for the girl's guts to spill. And spill they did. I admit I admired the mechanics and particulars of the gore and shocks throughout—the wolf cut open her dress and out fell some beast's fresh offal, probably brought over by the butcher.

But I didn't see Cecily anywhere in all this mayhem. The vampire, in her underthings in a bathtub of virgin's blood, was too plump, and the woman crazed by cocaine too thin. But Little Red Riding Hood was just right. I had to look close, and the closer I looked, the less cer-tain I was. Was it her? Wasn't it?

As much as I wanted to finally see Cecily in Little Red's face, I couldn't. Cecily's nose had a pixielike lift, and her eyelids looked al-ways half-shut, like she'd just woken up. I'd already learned Cecily's every aspect by heart.

So I turned the corner, returning to the crowd. I stood at the lip of the next stage, just inches from a guillotine.

And that's when I saw her. *This* was Cecily, without a doubt. As Marie Antoinette, her head on the block, Cecily had powdered her face stark white and dabbed perfect circles of pink rouge on her cheeks. The lights fell just as the blade trembled. In the darkness you heard the soft, wet give of a cleaver through a melon and the thump of the melon into the bottom of a basket, but you saw, in your mind's eye, Cecily's flesh sliced clean through, her pretty, bewigged head beheaded. Silence fell following the sharp gasp of the spectators, then the lights blasted back on with the shriek of a fiddle, the executioner thrusting forth a wax prop, holding the head by its wig, stage blood dripping, speckling your shoes if you stood too close.

By the end of the day, and by the end of evening, I knew the actors' every step, and every drop of blood. I went through again and again, even after August left me.

Poor Oscar remained unrepaired on my back as I abandoned our plot to become famous on the midway. Instead, I memorized Cecily's queen, down to the trembling of her hands that shook the lace fan tied to her wrist and the tension of the muscles of her neck and her gentle swallows, as she offered her throat hourly to the tin guillotine.

I WAITED OUTSIDE the Chamber of Horrors as the midway closed, the lights dimmed, the entertainers and exhibitors shuttering their theaters and leading their beasts to their stables. Finally, Cecily stepped from the dragon's mouth into the light from the nearly full moon, her face still plastered with powder, her cheeks still rouged. Her hair, which that morning had been a fright of wild curls pushed up with a few combs, was now matted to her head from the wig, the curls flattened and tucked with several pins and clips. She again wore the dress with the butterflies at the shoulders.

I followed Cecily, who tagged behind a small group of actors and actresses who seemed not at all tired from a full day of performance. One tall, thin man in an untucked shirt, his face still the gray of the plague that killed him on stage, would occasionally break out in song. He swept an actress into his arms to turn and turn her in an invented waltz. They laughed like they had drunk too much, but they had unlikely drunk a drop—they were graceful, their singing melodic. But

Cecily seemed to barely notice them. She opened a sea-green paper parasol and leaned it against her shoulder. She spun it around and around as she walked. I followed its spin with my eyes, as if giving into a hypnotist's wheel.

"Oh, Cecily," the actors and actresses called back to her, in sweet singsong, after she had fallen farther and farther behind the group. They were in love with her too. "Come to us, Cecily." They delighted in their own melodrama. "Oh, Cecily, the world is so cold without you in it." They kept calling to Cecily, but they never looked back. One actress made gestures toward the moon. An actor wrapped his arms around himself. "Come back to us, Cecily; come back; come back."

"Go away, go away, go away," she called ahead to them. She held a pink peony by its long stem, touching the bloom of it to her nose. The flower was nothing special—I could see it had seen better days, its outer petals brown and tattered. To Cecily, it was prettier than it was. I wondered where she'd gotten a flower so dear to her. Had some much-loved lover left it for her?

Nonetheless I picked up my step, but just as I did, she picked up hers. I stepped up more, and so did she. We were like two cyclers on a two-seater, pedaling but not drawing closer. A few steps farther and Cecily was no longer alone. She'd caught up with the others, and they all slipped through an iron gate, going to where all the noise was. I followed them into the crowded garden lit by the frosted glow of gas lamps, where people sat at tables among trees and rosebushes raising their steins of beer. Above the chatter I heard the organ grinder's crank piano. His monkeys, in their paper wings, had been released from their chains, and they leaped from table to chair to tree. They bounced into backs and took a wig from an actor's head; they knocked over wineglasses. They stole bits of cake right from the ends of forks.

In the garden of the Storz Brewery, beer could be got for a penny a pint after hours. After a long day of keeping the Fair's illusions spinning, the workers congregated to drink and to eat the day's leftovers—the whole roasts and broiled birds—that the waitresses brought over in vast tureens from the cafés along the midway. In the first few hours after the Fair closed, everyone was here—the ticket takers, the entertainers, the custodians, and managers, the beekeepers and ostrich farmers, the Chinese acrobats and the minstrels of the Old Plantation—everyone unwinding and flirting and dropping character. As the sharpshooters of the Wild West Show enjoyed their beer in a genteel manner not befitting a cowboy (pinky up, short sips), the magician's assistant, in red satin and feathers, collapsed in on herself to demonstrate how she disappeared nightly into the bottom of a box.

Cecily walked over to Little Red and all the others from the Chamber of Horrors—actors and actresses still in their bloodied and gunshot getups. They were in the kick of some dice game. They cheered and shouted and bellowed out bawdy songs. The dice rolled, bounced, flew. Dollar bills changed hands without rhyme, without reason.

Cecily took a seat off to the side, apart from her crowd. She set the flower on the edge of a flowerpot next to her, and she began to remove the pins from her pinned-down curls, and she dropped the pins one by one into her lap.

That's when I saw August alone at a table in an opposite corner. He was in a very odd predicament—a live bird attacked the dead bird on his hat. I helped him to shoo the finch away, which returned to its nest in a potted tree in the garden.

As I licked my thumb and smoothed down the ruffled feathers of his bluebird, I said, "That's her over there." I nodded in Cecily's direction. "The one messing with her hairpins."

"Oh, she's much prettier with her head on her neck like that," August said. He sighed and whimpered and it became clear from his wobbling that he was fuddled from whiskey. "I'm in love with her too," he declared. August then lifted a shot glass, raising it to the empty seat next to him. "Ferret, I want you to meet somebody else I love," he said. When August realized that that somebody had left, he said, "Oh. Maybe if I take another drink, he'll return."

"Maybe you've had enough," I said, sitting down.

"Maybe I have," he said, sounding melancholy, falling into a slouch. He leaned closer to me, and it became clear he wanted me to put my arm around his shoulders. August rarely drank himself to drunkenness, but whenever he did, he was all affection and apology. When drunk, he became effusive, going on and on about how much our friendship meant to him, how much he loved me, and relied upon me. But what he felt for me was a different sort of thing than what I felt for him.

He put his hand to my cheek. "Thank you for saving my dead bluebird, Ferret. You're the only one who looks after me. Aren't you? Promise me you're my only one."

"I promise," I said, giving him a fatherly pat on the back. "You're a good kid, Augie." When August was sober, his attentions were flattering, and I admit, though it was selfish, I encouraged him. He saw the world in a way I didn't, and saw me as I didn't see myself. I liked being invited into his imagination, where I was some kind of handsome, hapless character, my every failing charming and comical. But whenever he fell morose and lovelorn, I felt cruel for taking any delight in the attention he gave me. More than anything, I wanted August to find happiness, though I had no idea how he ever could in a town like ours.

August gestured again to the empty seat at his other side. "We were just talking about you. Me and the gondolier. A lad named Alonzo. Alonzo with the long eyelashes." He stopped a moment, then said it again, singing it. *"Alonzo with the long eyelashes.* He can sneak you and Marie Antoinette out onto the lagoon, in the swan gondola, for a quick bit of moonlight. Any night after closing. Just bring him a bottle of wine."

"That's sweet of you to think of me, Augie," I said.

"I'm always looking out for you," he said. He looked up to me, then past me. He squinted to see better into the dark of the garden. "Your witch has taken human form," he said.

I looked to where August pointed. The automaton had changed

into a shirtwaist and long black skirt, and had twisted her silver braids to pin them properly to the top of her head. She'd washed away the makeup that had stiffened her face but still wore the eye patch of her witch's costume. The whistle still dangled from the chain around her neck, bouncing against her chest as she stepped through the garden, Cecily's carpetbag in hand. When the automaton reached Cecily, Cecily took the bag from her, and together they left the garden.

August whispered in my ear. "The flower," he said. "Take it to her."

Cecily had left the peony on the flowerpot, but August's suggestion seemed backward to me—someone else had given her that flower first. I worried I would be carrying to her the gimmicks of another man's seduction.

"Go," August said with a not-so-gentle shove at my shoulder.

I PLUCKED AWAY some of the peony's petals, wishing on each one, until the wish came true—the automaton ducked into the dim facade of the Chinese Village, and Cecily was at last alone again.

I'd left my dummy with August, and my jacket. I'd left behind much of my gentleman's disguise. I'd taken off my necktie and collar, and I'd yanked at my curls, pushing them this way and that. I'd untucked my shirt and dropped my suspenders to dangle at my sides. I had hoped for her not to recognize me from my clumsy efforts of that morning.

And yet the first thing out of my mouth was nothing but more clumsiness. "I'm the fool who tried to nab your carpetbag," I said as I stepped up to her. She flinched and quickened her pace. Her parasol was closed, down at her side, and I saw her tighten her grip on the handle like she might be apt to smack me with it. "But I *wasn't* trying to nab it, really. It looked heavy, and I wanted to help. Or, actually, I just wanted an excuse to walk with you. I'm not a thief. And I don't know why I'm telling you this. You'd think I'd never spoken to a girl so lovely before. And I haven't, I guess. Not as lovely as you. Well, except I actually *have* spoken to you before. At the Empress Opera House. You were the violet-eyed trollop, and I tied your corset strings."

Though she kept the parasol poised to batter me, she looked down at the dirt road in thought, slowing her step, sorting out all my rambling.

And then her arm *did* relax. She swung the parasol at her side, back and forth, and she looked at me briefly. She looked in my eyes, then up to my hair. She smiled at me, then returned her eyes to the ground. "*Violent*-eyed," she said. "I think it was the *violent*-eyed trollop."

"Oh?" I said, trying to seem easygoing, despite how my heart picked up to have her so near, speaking to me. "What would it mean to be violent-eyed?"

She shrugged. "Violent with anger?" she said. "Violent with immorality? Regret? I don't know. Maybe you're right. Violet-eyed makes more sense, I suppose. Even though my eyes are brown."

"Even though your eyes are amber," I corrected. I restrained myself from rattling off all the poetic allusions I'd come up with on the night I'd met her, all those lines likening her eyes to cinnamon and autumn and ginger.

"You must have watched me lose my head ten times today," she said.

"You couldn't see me in there," I said. "It was too dark. I could've been anybody."

"You were always right up close," she said. "Right in the lights."

I held out the flower. "You forgot this," I said.

"It's not mine," she said, not taking it from me.

"It is," I said.

"No," she said. "It belongs to the girl who plays the girl who gets knifed by Jack the Ripper. She got a whole bucketful of flowers from a gent. She gave me the worst of the bunch."

I sniffed at the peony. "It's not so bad," I said. Despite the raggedy nature of the thing, its sweet stink was potent enough to give me a pinch of headache.

"Did your dummy run off?" she said, nodding toward my back.

"He's scared of the old lady," I said. "Where'd she go, anyway?"

"She bets on the crickets in the fan-tan den," she said. "The Chinese magicians keep a gambling hall after hours. You can even bet on the number of seeds in an orange if you want. They train crickets to fight in rice bowls."

"I got no patience for crickets," I said. "My room's noisy with them in summer. When they keep you up at night with their clicking, you dwell on every minute that you're not asleep."

But why was I talking about the crickets in my attic? I was nervous, I guess, afraid of frightening her off. She seemed so skittish, so shy for an actress. We slowed to a stroll, and I kept my mouth shut. We began to cross the bridge that led from the midway to the New White City. Though the midway had gone dark behind us, the Grand Court still glowed. The buildings were silvery like moonlight.

"There's this one thing you do as Marie Antoinette that I love," I said.

"What thing?" Cecily said.

"You touch at the bow at your shoulder," I said. I touched her shoulder with the bloom of the peony. "You're straightening it, but you're also lingering on the ribbon, the feel of it. She's still vain, even as she walks to her death, but it's also something more tender than that, really. She's comforted by it, by the satin bow, isn't she?"

"Yes, maybe so," she said.

"A smoke?" I said, stopping, holding out my pack of cigarettes.

Cecily stopped with me and stuck the parasol beneath her other arm. She touched the pack, but she didn't take a cigarette. Instead, she took the card that kept the side of the pack stiff. I collected these cards, we all did, but I didn't have much use for them. I tacked them to the wall from time to time—pictures of boxers, acrobats, varieties of wildflowers. The characters of Dickens. This card, like the pictures in Rosie's gallery, was a color-tinted photograph of an actress; but unlike Rosie's lovelies, the actress was fully clothed in an elaborate costume.

She looked got up like a moth, with a cape of spotted ermine and a hat heavy with feathers. *Queenie Brackett* was written beneath her.

"Can I keep this?" Cecily asked, though she'd already tucked it into the waist of her skirt. "Queenie Brackett's an opera singer. She happened to be in one of the towns I was in once. I remember seeing her name on a sign."

"But you didn't hear her sing?" I said.

Cecily rocked the carpetbag at her side as she thought back and looked off at the White City. "No," she said. "I don't see much opera. But one time, in one town—I don't remember which one—I heard Viola Lorraine." She said the name like I should know it. I nodded, wanting to please her. "I heard her, but I didn't see her. I don't remember the opera. But I remember it was so sweltering hot that summer they had to keep the theater doors open wide. So me and my friend Agnes got a bottle of cider and a marshmallow cake, and we just sat right there, on the street, on a saddle blanket, and listened to all the music that tumbled out. Agnes knew the show, so she told me the story. She described it so well, I can still see it in my head, and sometimes I forget I didn't see it at all." She took the peony from me, and she held it again to her nose. "So you throw your voice good?" she said.

Cecily spoke in a voice so small, it seemed it would never carry to the back rows, let alone out into the street. Maybe no theater would ever cast her as any character who was anything less than totally silent.

I nodded, and I tossed my words into her carpetbag so convincingly, she jumped at the sound rising up from her side. "Meet me at the swan gondola tomorrow night," my voice said, echoing in her bag.

The lights of the New White City went out then, one by one, the darkness working up the court like a chill up a spine.

Cecily looked up at the clouds gray against the black sky, and she seemed startled by them, as if wakened by the dark. She began to step quickly again and crossed the bridge.

"Will you?" I said, as I followed. "The swan gondola? At this time tomorrow night? Meet me on the dock of the lagoon?" For all I knew,

Alonzo the gondolier was a figment of August's whiskey drunk, but I was determined I'd conjure him up nonetheless.

Cecily said nothing, and yet she practically ran away from me, careful to keep the carpetbag from banging into her knees. She ducked behind a row of dogwoods and out through an open gate in the wall. I followed her.

Cecily caught a cab, and the driver lashed his horse, and the rickety buggy creaked and wobbled on its wheels as it took a corner slow. She bent over the carpetbag in her lap, looking deep within it, as if rummaging around for something she'd lost.

I watched as the buggy moved beyond the streetlamp, beyond any light, Cecily only a silhouette. And when she was gone from my sight, I remained there in the lot, stitching together our conversation word for word. Though I looked in the lighted windows of the houses and tenements ahead, and caught glimpses of the lives lived there, I could see only Cecily. I saw her sitting on the street in front of an opera house, propping herself up on an elbow, eating marshmallow cake, listening to the songs the singers couldn't keep inside.

10.

I RETURNED TO THE CHAMBER OF HORRORS the next day, again and again, growing more and more poor with each ticket I bought. With Oscar all banged up from our skirmish the day before with the automaton, I left him to be repaired at a doll hospital in the back of a toy shop on the midway. I figured, with Oscar convalescing, I could abandon all plans and spend the day devoted to Cecily. I paid close attention to her every blink and nod. Having worked with any number of actresses over the years, I knew they liked to be complimented on the specifics of their characterizations. You could get a lass to spend the whole night if you offered a little praise alongside the kisses. "I could feel the woman's lack of feeling," I'd told one particularly bad actress, in between licks of her earlobe. "You made her into such a perfect nobody."

But I would never have to fib to Cecily. I would never have to invent compliments. While all the other actresses in the horror show, like Little Red, played their agony for a laugh or two, or at least seemed to give a little wink as they took the knife, Cecily was all worry and fret. She could make everything seem true, even the fallen eyelash on her powdered cheek, even the curl of her own brown hair that slipped loose from beneath the wig. Even her little trip up the step when her shoe caught in her dress. I heard a lock of her wig sizzle as it got a lick from a candle flame. She just reached up to twist away a bit of the spark, as easy as you please.

August said the cool dark of the chamber's halls eased his head, so he joined me for a few hours in the late afternoon. Though he sipped from a hangover cure of bottled dandelion milk and Saigon cinnamon, he denied having drunk too much the night before. And he denied the cause of it. "Being around all these foreigners on the midway gave me some exotic flu," he explained, his hair undone from its braid and falling forward into his face. He didn't seem at all consoled by the dark of the chamber or the playful violence. His hand trembled as he fluttered a lady's fan of owl feathers as we watched a corpse rise from the grave on the stage. "I was fevered and delirious. I can only imagine what I might have said."

I reminded him of Alonzo the gondolier, the gentleman he'd mentioned the night before, hoping it might cheer him up. *"Alonzo with the long eyelashes,"* I sang, picking up August's drunken tune. But August just rolled his eyes. "Does he exist?" I said.

It turned out he did, and August seemed to like the idea of seeking him out again, to arrange for the swan gondola ride. When we spoke to Alonzo at the lagoon, August's confidence returned, and as he negotiated with the gondolier I noticed him leaning in close. It was settled. That night I was to bring Alonzo one dollar, two bottles of red wine, and three of Rosie's lovelies. August didn't seem at all discouraged by Alonzo's interest in the postcards. As a matter of fact, he seemed charmed by the gentleman's lusts.

I was expected to pay in full, whether Cecily showed up or not. But it was well worth the risk.

AFTER DARK, Alonzo and I sat alone in the quiet lagoon, he at the swan's head, me at its wooden tail feathers. Alonzo only glanced at the naked women in the photographs before tucking them away in his coat pocket. "If I look at them as much as I want to," he said, "the beauty will wear off too soon."

August had brought me a biography of Marie Antoinette from his father's bookshop, and Alonzo kindly shared the wine with me as I read by the light from the swan's lantern that rocked from a hook overhead. Cecily's performance had little to do with history, but reading about the queen seemed to somehow bring me closer to my actress.

As it got later and later, Alonzo grew drunker and drunker and sang more and more. I was distracted by the evening ticking away, Cecily nowhere near. I would read a page of the book, and another, without concentration, none of the words even making it into my head. I studied an illustration of Marie Antoinette wearing a toy ship atop her tall wig, tendrils of her hair combed up and curled around the deck like the tentacles of an attacking squid. When I put my thumb over the queen's nose and a finger across the point of her chin, I could start to recognize a little bit of Cecily in the portrait. I put another finger across her eyes and moved my thumb to her throat.

Maybe it was best she stayed away, I considered. What did I have to offer anyway? I wore a jacket and trousers of two different plaids. The mismatched suit came from the theater's wardrobe closet, along with the tattered straw boater I wore. I had thought the costume might cast me handsomely in the part of a carefree summer lover. But now, feeling rejected, I found the suit tawdry and juvenile. I realized I had little to offer other than my infatuation. And even if she did, by some miracle, consent to spend time with me, when would I confess my whole life of missteps?

Then I suddenly remembered a pocket watch. As a boy thief years before, I'd come to fancy myself a *toy-getter*—which is what we called a thief of watches. I had one shaped like a beetle—you parted its emerald wings to see the time. One was an owl's head, and another's workings were hidden by an agate eye. One was a mandolin with pluckable strings. I had a snuffbox with a working cuckoo clock atop it. And one, I now fondly recalled, featured Marie Antoinette in the guillotine. The watch had a front and a back you flipped open; one side kept time, the other side ticktocked along with little flat mechanical figures, chopping off the queen's head one second, putting it back the next, only to chop it off a second later.

And as I considered the possibility of fate, of destiny, that watch some long-ago foreshadowing of good luck, Cecily came stepping down the staircase to the dock, her hair unpinned and combed out into its pretty, tangled mess of wild, brown curls. *Perfect*, I thought. *She's perfect. She's meant for me and only me.*

I slipped the book beneath the bench and stood to take her hand.

Her skin, so freshly scrubbed of its powder and paint, looked too pink and sore, and I longed to give her cheek a very soft, sympathetic kiss.

Cecily had brought along a young woman with hair an old woman's white. "Pearl's a dear friend of mine," Cecily said. "I think you'll like each other," and Pearl blushed with such a red fever that I worried about her. I wondered if I should ask if she was all right, or if that would only worsen her condition.

I took Cecily's hand to help her into the gondola, and Cecily whispered to me, her breath on my neck, "Isn't Pearl so very cute? Everyone adores her." Her enthusiasm was a stab of disappointment.

I helped Pearl in too, and Alonzo prepared the swan for sailing, standing next to the swan's curving neck so he could row the craft toward the center of the lagoon. I took a seat up front, and Pearl and Cecily sat on the heart-shaped bench at the swan's tail feathers.

In Cecily's lap was a thin stack of postcards tied together with twine. She unknotted the string and she and Pearl read aloud from the unsent greetings. Cecily had become friendly with the postmistress, who had told her that many of the fairgoers who dropped souvenir postcards into the postbox failed to remember to address them. Cecily had been rescuing them from the postmistress's trash bin. "I hate to see them thrown away," she said. "Someone should read them, at least."

Cecily took a pair of reading glasses from a little paper case marked with Chinese letters. The glasses, with hinges and springs, collapsed in on themselves, and she unfolded them, then set them on her nose. Somehow the old-lady glasses made her look even younger. "'My love,'" Cecily read aloud, "'I typed this on a typewriter at the fair.'" She rolled her eyes and said, "That's all it says." She looked at me, as if she knew I'd know better than to write a lover such empty words.

I leaned back to listen. Cecily could render even the lazy, tossed-off greetings of strangers into something true and necessary. After she read a few more, she took off her glasses and the three of us fell silent as we drifted on the water and watched the moon.

Finally, Cecily sat up and seemed about to speak, but stopped. "I don't even know your name," she said. "Do you know mine?"

"Yes," I said. "From when you played the violent-eyed trollop."

"So maybe I know yours," she said. "Or I did. Before I forgot it."

"My friends call me Ferret," I said.

Cecily covered her mouth with the postcard to laugh a little. "Why would your friends call you something like that?" she said. She then told Pearl, "*Ferret's* a ventriloquist. A ventriloquist without a dummy."

"He's being repaired," I said. On the midway were two cottages side by side, each with gingerbread woodwork and scalloped shingles and picket fences. One was the toy shop with a doll hospital in the back, where I'd left Oscar, the other the incubator exhibit, where live babies were displayed. Both little cottages were meant to appeal to our sympathies—from the toy shop, we'd take home our own little darlings. And next door the live babies, born too early, cooked in glass nests like new chickens. Nurses moved about like farmers' wives, peeking into the incubators, adjusting temperatures, eyeing the mercury of thermometers. For a dime, fairgoers could enter the exhibit to study the mechanics of the babies' little booths. They could cluck and coo at the unfinished infants resting in iron wombs.

"Don't you want to know how Pearl and me know each other?" Cecily asked me.

"I do," I said.

"You *do* know how we know each other?" Cecily said, with a wink.

"No," I said, "I do want to know how you know each other."

"Oh, well, Pearl's a shop girl and window dresser downtown," Cecily said. "And just before the Fair, she sewed me into a mermaid's fin for an umbrella display. I tell you, it was scandalous, practically. I had hardly a stitch on. Well, *you* tell him, Pearl."

"Oh, well, yes," Pearl said, stuttering, blushing. "A mermaid . . . in the window . . . I'm the dresser . . ."

"Have you seen Pearl's windows at the department store?" Cecily asked. "At the Brandeis? Her windows have been in magazines. She studied window dressing in Paris."

"Oh," I said.

"She's a mad genius, Pearl is," Cecily said. "She does all the electricity herself. She can wire the whole setup for all sorts of tricks. She can make a manikin vanish, then, pop, there it is again, but with a brand-new hat." She nudged at Pearl's hip with her own. "Well, *you*, you tell him, Pearl."

I interrupted, leaning forward to offer the ladies each a cigarette, which they took without any ladylike hesitation. They let me light them too. When I held the match between Cecily and me, and we both lit up, my face was so close to hers it was like we were practicing for a kiss. I looked at her eyes as she looked down at the flame. The flame rose as we drew in our breaths.

"What was the mermaid fin like?" I said.

"Oh you wouldn't believe it, it was so pretty, wasn't it, Pearl?" she said. Cecily dropped her hand with a sweeping gesture down the length of her legs, twisting her wrist back and forth, like following a flowing wave. "It stretched way past the ends of my legs, like the train of a gown. How'd you make it sparkle like crazy, Pearl? Tell him what it was made of."

"Beads," Pearl said. "Satin."

"She sewed on each individual fish scale," Cecily said, "and each individual bead."

I nodded and smiled politely at Pearl. Cecily fanned herself with one of the unsent postcards. "Pearl isn't as quiet as she seems," Cecily said. "She introduced Susan B. Anthony a few weeks ago at a ladies' luncheon. Pearl is a dress reformist. She's very much against corsets, bless her heart. She says our corsets are making us feeble. We can't breathe."

"The corset is an instrument of torture," Pearl said, her voice soft. "It doesn't fit the woman's natural figure." She shrugged her shoulders. "As long as a woman is trapped in her dress, she is disfranchised."

Cecily had dressed simply, but I noticed that the top buttons of her shirtwaist were undone, as were the buttons at her wrist, causing her sleeves to slip up and down her arms as she fanned herself. She wore boots of a damask silk, the laces up the side untied, allowing her to slip her stockingless foot in and out. Pearl meanwhile continually fussed with the pins in her hair, taking them out, putting them back in somewhere else. At one point she even had a few pins between her teeth as she twisted a curl back to tuck behind her ear. I couldn't quite imagine this mousy girl leading any political battles.

"Have you seen Cecily's Marie Antoinette act, Pearl?" I asked.

"Yeth," Pearl mumbled, the pins still at her lips.

Cecily seemed to be waiting for Pearl to say more, and when she didn't, she said, "Pearl even did a window a few months ago with a manikin dressed like Marie Antoinette. She gave her a hat that was swan-shaped like this here boat." Cecily rapped her knuckles against the side of the gondola. "The window had all these tall towering cakes with pink and blue icing. Not real cakes but paper cakes that looked real. And the floor of the window was just cluttered with women's shoes."

"It's much sadder," I said, reclining, my ankles crossed, my hands in my pockets, my cigarette hanging from my lip. "So much sadder how it all went in true life."

"How what went?" Cecily said.

"The offing of her head," I said, hoping Cecily would be impressed that I'd read up on the queen. "She'd been in prison, not the palace. All she did was iron her cap actually. They cut her hair, so it wouldn't get in the way of the blade, I guess. She had a plain nightdress of dimity. Black stockings. Prunella shoes with little heels. A poor actress gave her the dress," I added, nodding at Cecily with a wink, "or so they say. And they say she stepped on the executioner's foot. She begged his pardon. Said she didn't do it on purpose. Those were her last words. 'I didn't do it on purpose.' But in French, I guess."

"Hm," Cecily said, shrugging, flicking her cigarette into the lagoon. "What a terrible way to go." She kept her eyes on the water, and I worried I'd offended her by pointing out the inaccuracies of her horror show. But then I suspected she was just disappointed by the historical account. She preferred the queen going to the guillotine in a fancy dress and powdered wig.

Alonzo returned to the dock, a little too soon, I thought. I helped pull the gondola up and assisted the ladies from the boat. Pearl blushed again, nodding her good-byes. She stepped up the stairs as Cecily lingered with me a moment.

"She leaves work every night at five," Cecily said, making her soft voice even softer, taking three cigarettes from the pack I held open. I hadn't noticed the little purse hanging from a chain at her side, attached to her belt. She clicked open its octopus-shaped clasp, and dropped the cigarettes inside. "They have a sandwich counter right there at the store. Would it kill you to stop by there sometime and treat her to a cup of coffee, *Ferret*?" She sneered my name, but in a teasing way, a flirtation that made me blush like Pearl. "You two can talk yourselves silly about Marie Antoinette's bedroom slippers."

Cecily winked and left my side, and I sensed from the way she moved up the steps, drifting really, up toward the promenade, that she knew I kept watching. She too was playing the part of a carefree summer lover, moving slowly, humming, looking up and around, pretending to not know any eyes were on her. But I loved that she knew I couldn't look away.

November 10, 1898

Dear Cecily,

I only ever meant to write you once. It had been cold in the clouds, and I'd stayed at the bottom of the basket, huddled in on myself. I couldn't bear to stand up and look down. So all I saw was sky, even as the balloon plummeted. I'd thought that the first rattling scrape and tear of the wicker came from running aground on a cloud of ice.

I had tucked that postcard in my suit pocket, to have it next to my heart as I died.

And up in that balloon, the sense of doom made me <u>long</u> to crash. It would put an end to my fear. I romanced the idea of it, of death, waltzing it around and around in my head. But now here, in a house, broken, teetering, a couple of old-lady angels never more than a few steps away, I want to live. I want to live forever so I can always mourn losing you.

I never leave the music parlor. I sit here every day, writing you letter after letter. And Miss Emmaline posts them all for me, each one addressed to your house at the lake. It's cruel, I suppose. Everyone there loved you so. Are these letters even opened? Does someone read them? Does Wakefield? And if he does, does every word kill him a little?

Maybe Emmaline doesn't send my letters at all. Maybe she opens them, reads them, keeps them tied with a ribbon. I've been thinking of myself as a guest in this house. A hobbled charity case. But maybe I'm being held captive. Maybe I'm here against my own will. Flood, drought, freeze, bugs—all these plagues turn these farmers daft. Whole towns of people, gone mad from the sound of the wind, can hear God's voice in a turtledove. I've heard tell of a cult of farmers along the bone-dry Dismal River who took to worshipping the very insects that ravaged their crops, mimicking the chirp and posture of grasshoppers in nightly rituals, their eyes flickering yellow in the light of the bonfires.

Farmers, daft and otherwise, and the people from town—they come to sit with me. They only want to be neighborly, Miss Hester says. They bring me prayers and liquor. Sometimes they linger, like they're death watching at the side of a corpse, waiting for the undertaker. I write you letters, and they knit or stitch. A man can go batty from the needlepointing, the sound of that needle punching fabric and the soft zip of the thread. Pop, thip, ffffwiiiip, pop, thip, fffffwiiiip, *over and over, and slow.*

And though they bring me things, they also sneak things away. I didn't notice at first. If I had a loose thread at a seam of my pajamas, somebody would snap it off, and off they'd go with it. If an eyelash fell on my cheek, they picked it up with a fingertip. They scratched their fingers against my cast and carried off flecks of plaster beneath their fingernails. And they brought things of their own just for me to touch—a doll, a lock, a key, a ring, a Bible, a brush, a lily.

They don't see me as someone struck with bad luck and knocked from the sky. They see me as a man with a magical knack for staying alive. Around here, I'm the priest who fell from the heavens and lived.

Still yours,
Ferret

II.

THE MORNING AFTER the swan gondola ride, I sent Cecily a souvenir postcard. I didn't have her address, but it didn't matter. Now that I knew she rummaged nightly through the post office trash for the unsent mail, I simply dropped it into a mailbox on the Grand Court, without postage.

I'd spent much of the morning trying to decide what to say. And I was stalled right off by the greeting—I still didn't know how to spell her name. *Dear Marie Antoinette*, I ended up writing. *This is Ferret. I want us to be alone.*

Just as the card left my fingers and fell into the slot, I realized with a thump in my chest that I wanted it back. I should've written *together . . . I want us to be alone together.*

WHEN THE MIDWAY OPENED, I hurried to the doll hospital to collect Oscar. In the back room of the toy shop the shelves lining the walls were stocked with apothecary jars, some full of arms, some full of legs. One jar held bisque heads fractured and cracked; another jar was full of eyeballs. A dresser drawer spilled over with torn dresses and tiny petticoats. Miss Havelock, the young woman at the workbench, bought broken dolls from urchins, she'd explained, to harvest all the parts, and in turn she attached those parts—repaired with papier-mâché and mucilage—to the broken dolls of the daughters of the rich.

But her swiftest business in those first few days of the Fair had been the fashioning of wigs. Girls cut at their own goldilocks and brought the clippings to the hospital, in little silk purses, so Miss Havelock could sew and braid the snipped curls into wigs for the girls' favorite dolls. Miss Havelock herself had hair so fine and light—the white of the cotton of milkweed—you could see right through to the bright pink of her scalp.

"Have you ever heard him speak?" Miss Havelock said. At first I gave her comment no thought, as I was stunned by the sight of my dummy. Oscar looked better than I'd ever seen him. I'd bought him from a peddler's cart on Howard Street some time before, and though I'd polished him with oil and oiled his hinges and had restrung the rubber nerves of his fingers and joints, he'd always had the haggard look of something secondhand. But now I could swear his dead eyes looked right in mine.

"Speak?" I said.

Miss Havelock nodded like people nod when they know something you don't—quick and certain, her lips puckered primly. She turned his head to reveal a new string in his neck next to the old one. "Give it a yank," she said.

I did. "What do you wish me to do?" he said. He spoke in perfect English, sounding nothing at all like the Oscar I knew. It was a preacher's voice, high-pitched but with a spark of fire and brimstone.

Though I knew many of the little tricks and gimmicks inside his hollow chest, all the switches and levers that brought his magic to life, I'd never been inside his head. I didn't even know of any way to jimmy my way in. I didn't see a single hinge or seam on his skull.

I gave the string another yank and he said something else. "Why should I do this for you?"

I pulled the string again, at which point he started to repeat himself. "That's all he'll say," she said. "He has a phonograph in his head, but it's small."

"Why?" I said.

"I don't know," she said. "I didn't put it there."

I nearly didn't believe her. How, in all my many performances, had I never jostled a single word out of him? I paid for the repairs and shrugged a shoulder.

And I'd barely taken a step onto the midway before fairgoers were begging for a joke. It was as if Oscar's new spirit possessed *me*, as if I were the one with a new string in my neck. With a strut and a shuffle I worked the crowd and they emptied their pockets into mine. My every cheap, creaky joke was suddenly worth a fortune. And Oscar taught me all kinds of new tricks, his skeleton of wood and rubber an extension of my own bones and muscles. My hand in his back, I fiddled with buttons that hadn't worked before. He shot a flame from a fingertip, plucked a paper rose from the nose of a girl. He set a windup sparrow free from under his hat. And from his sleeve he pulled his heart, a little pillow of silk. Oscar would invite a pretty lady to press the center of it, and when she did, the heart would throb and release a puff of cherry blossom perfume.

Up his other sleeve was a marionette I'd not met before, a sad little mister no bigger than a clothespin. With the flick of a switch, the puppet dropped from a hollow in his arm and danced a jig at the end of its strings. Oscar was making the puppet tell jokes of its own when a horseless carriage came sputtering up to brake right next to us.

Montgomery Ward, the company that sold a horseless carriage in its catalogs, had been giving the fairgoers rides in one up and down the midway all afternoon, but the driver never stopped whenever he neared me. As a matter of fact, he would never even slow, and I'd had to jump out of his way a time or two, as if he seemed set on running me over.

But this wasn't the carriage from the catalog. I'd never seen this automobile before or this driver.

The man steered with one gloved hand and wore a golfer's hat of red-and-green plaid. His driving goggles turned his face insect, and the woman next to him looked just as buggy. She wore goggles too and a broad-brimmed white hat tethered to her head with a bloodred scarf she knotted beneath her chin. A piglet, with a pink ribbon around its neck, wriggled in her arms, rustling all the ruffles of her white dress.

At first they said nothing when they parked at my side, so I went on with my act. I gave them the best I had. I showed off all Oscar's new tricks, but nothing moved them. They kept their goggles on, and they eyed me like scientists, like I was a specimen on a slide. They wouldn't laugh, they wouldn't smile. I felt unnerved by their scrutiny and concluded they didn't want jokes or magic. So I would offer them the wizard's voice. I leaned forward, easing Oscar closer to the man in the auto. I pulled the string to his phonograph.

"What do you wish me to do?" Oscar said. "Why should I do this for you?"

With that, the man turned slowly to face the woman at his side. Though their eyes were still hidden by the goggles, I could see this glance was somehow meaningful. The woman lowered her face, looking down and off as if remorseful, and the man lowered his face too. I pulled the string again twice.

"What do you wish me to do? Why should I do this for you?"

The man stuck his gloved hand into his coat and pulled from it a wallet that bulged and bent. He took from it some bills, then offered forth, with his ungloved hand, a shocking sum.

More shocking than the sum was the hand itself. The bills were held between two fingers of metal, the whole hand a skeleton of steel bones, each finger joint on a minuscule hinge. Whoever had crafted the hand had added a few prettified flourishes of art here and there. A fleur-de-lis had been cut into the center of the metal palm, and a vine of roses scrolled, engraved, in a wreath all around his silvery wrist.

I practically curtsied at the sight of the cash. "I thank you ever so much, sir," I said, faking the gestures of a grateful beggar. All my deep disdain for the rich eased for a minute, and I allowed myself my greed. I was happy to bow and scrape and shuffle if it meant spending it all on Cecily, on a month's worth of moonlit rides in the swan gondola and on bottle after bottle of the finest wines and box after box of chocolates.

But as I reached for the money, the man's steel fingers snapped back like the spring of a mousetrap. "I'm not tipping you," he said. "I'm *buying* your doll."

"Oh," I said. I pulled my hand back and brought it to my mouth to gnaw on my thumbnail. I considered the offer for only a moment. With the money the man held out, I could've easily bought a new dummy, a new suit for myself, and a new hat, and still wooed Cecily, but what kind of act would I have had without Oscar? Mr. Crowe had insisted no dummy was expendable. "As far as the audience goes, the dummy's the brains of the act," he had told me many times. "The audience would be happier if you weren't there at all." And besides, I was deeply fond of the doll. He had a character all his own. "Well, I'm sorry, it's not for sale," I said. "This is my act. I can't sell Oscar."

The woman then pushed her goggles off her eyes and onto her forehead. Her piglet squealed like he'd been pinched. The man brought his metal hand back to his wallet, and when he held it out to me again, there was even more money—a whole summer on the swan gondola, with a string quartet on the dock, serenading us every night.

"I'm sorry, sir," I said. I studied that hand and ran my eyes along his coat sleeve, estimating where the fake arm ended and the real one began.

After a moment he nodded, and he returned the money to his wallet. He then held out a calling card. "If you change your mind," he said, "let me know."

Wm. Wakefield was all that was written on the card. I'd seen his name all around the Fair, and his signature with all its sharp points.

"I think I might've heard of you," I said.

"You might've," he said, as he fussed with the automobile's devices before jerking forward and scooting on along. The woman with Wakefield looked back as they drove away, and she tossed some dollar bills into the air behind her. I skipped forward, and I swatted at those bills, grabbing each one before it fell to the dirt.

AS THE SUN WAS SETTING, August approached me with not a single bottle of tonic in his bag. He put the cigarette he was smoking to my lips for a puff. "That cigarette's the only potion I have left," he said. "I've made a killing on my cures." The cigarette tasted like strong tea sipped from a gas pipe. As I coughed, squinting, handing it back to him, he explained it was for the treatment of asthma. "It's quite medicinal," he said, smoking it himself and inhaling deep like it was a gulp of spring breeze. "Crushed plantain leaves and belladonna," he said. "Some saltpeter."

The Chamber of Horrors wouldn't close for another half hour or so, so I let August lead me to the Chinese Village. August was feeling successful and full of luck. With a wiggle of his fingers, he flaunted his ring: a piece of wire he had twisted around a tiny, naked, porcelain baby. "The little doll was my prize in a piece of king's cake at the New Orleans café, up the way there," he said. "I chipped my back tooth on it, but I rarely win the prize in anything. So now I wear it for luck. And my luck is your luck, my dear."

We stepped past the joss house and through the rock garden to a silk curtain embroidered with cranes in flight. A young man stood at the curtain dressed like a barkeep, in a slick satin vest that burned with the pattern of bright-red dragons in a tussle. He plucked August's cigarette from his fingers with a sneer. "Smoke makes the fighters sick," he said, as he lifted the curtain to allow us entry.

The den was crowded and noisy, everyone huddled around a low table. From the sound of the cheering and the groaning, some sort of match had been won and lost. But I couldn't see what any of them were looking at. When I'd been only as tall as a man's pants pocket, I could have a good evening of theft by working the cockfights and dogfights, weaving in and out among men's legs, lifting their wallets and watches and coin purses as they stood mesmerized by the brutality, knocking me aside with their knees, yelling their lungs sore at the battling, bloody creatures. I had never been able to stomach it, so it had been particularly sweet spending the money that otherwise would have kept the fights going all night.

Now at the back of the crowd I stood on my tiptoes to see the last of a fight between insects. So these were the cricket fights frequented by the automaton. It wasn't unlike a dogfight in practice—creature against creature—but on a much smaller, less violent scale. In a small wicker basket atop a table, one cricket kicked at another as it curled in on itself. When the fight was declared over, a tall Chinese woman dressed in a shirtwaist and long black skirt stepped forward to collect her bug. She imprisoned it in a tiny bamboo cage.

No sooner had the one wrestling match ended than another began. That's when I saw the automaton at the center of the crowd, sitting on her knees right at the table, having changed from her costume, her hair braided and pinned, her makeup rubbed away. She dropped some coins into a basket that a man dangled from the end of a long stick as he worked his way through the pack of gamblers.

A cricket was then passed around in a teacup through the crowd, for appraisal by all. The automaton held one lens of a pince-nez up to her good eye, and she examined the insect before passing the cup to the next gambler.

When the teacup reached us, August held his ear to it. "The ones that chirp the loudest," he told me, "are the ones that wrestle the hardest."

I couldn't take my eyes off the automaton. When I had seen her before, the very sight of her sent a shiver through me; I felt embarrassed, like a boy tripped by a bully. But seeing her here, with her head lowered, as if in prayer, crushed by the crowd but alone, I felt just a pinch of affection for her. Truth be told, I was glad Cecily had someone to look after her so fiercely.

Once the crickets had been examined by the crowd, they were weighed on an apothecary's scale, then tossed into the basket on the low table. The men and women leaned forward to watch and shout. The crickets' wranglers coaxed the insects forth by tapping them with straws, but all the bugs would do was pace the periphery of their boxing ring. They engaged in one little scuffle before leaping away from each other. "They should've put a lady cricket in with them last night," August said. "It makes the boys bloodthirsty." I became so engaged with the ruckus, I was startled when the fight ended before it had even really begun. And it was only then I discovered the automaton had slipped from the room unseen.

I RAN INTO THE MIDWAY, my feet knocking around in the ill-fitting shoes I had borrowed from the theater's costume closet because I'd liked the handsome point of the toes. I had apparently missed the automaton's exit by only a heartbeat or two, as there she was, moving briskly past the foreign villages all closing for the night. I followed her at a safe distance, stepping forward on the balls of my feet to keep my heels from clomping against the hard dirt of the road. I kept my hand behind me, my finger between the teeth of my dummy to stop his jaw from clattering with my every step. I froze in my path when she paused a moment. I worried she had heard me. But no, upon listening closer I realized she had been arrested by the seesaw melody of a bush full of crickets near the picket fence of the toy shop with the doll hospital. She reached among its leaves to capture one in the palm of her hand. She watched it, held it to her ear, then delicately placed it upon a branch.

The automaton then went to the next fence and followed the lane to the cottage, the one that housed the incubator exhibit. I grabbed hold of a few pickets and leaped over, nearly losing a loose shoe.

I walked to a side window and looked into a room still partly lit by a few burning lamps. Inside stood one lone nurse in a starched cap and long white dress, a deep-blue cape across her shoulders. All along the walls of the room were the metal cabinets equipped with gauges and tubes that seemed to heat or cool, each box equipped with a coiled pump that lifted and fell with the rhythm of breath. The doors to the cabinets had foggy glass windows, babies sleeping fitfully within each one.

Painted on the wall above the machines: *Live Babies! Infant Incubator—A wonderful invention! Visited by 207,000 people at Queen Victoria's Diamond Jubilee Exhibition, London 1897.*

The automaton walked through the room slouched, but the bend of her back gave her a buzzardlike authority. She went directly to a closet, and on an upper shelf was Cecily's carpetbag.

And while the automaton prepared the carpetbag, opening it atop a center table, tucking a blanket inside, the nurse stood at one of the cabinets, fumbling with the keys on the iron ring of her belt. She stood on her toes so she could reach the cabinet's lock without having to remove the key from the ring. And upon the opening of the cabinet door, I saw a baby swaddled tight in a pink blanket and fast asleep, a thermometer above her little nest. The nurse lifted the baby from the cabinet and walked to the very window at which I stood. I took a step to the side, again fearing I'd been caught, but the nurse saw only her own reflection in the glass. The nurse rocked back and forth on the balls and heels of her feet, smiling, quite taken with the sight of herself with a child in her arms. Had the glass not been between us, I could have reached across to touch the pale down of the infant's head.

The window was open a crack, and I heard the automaton grumbling above the wheezing of the machinery. "Your maternal nature'll only lead to awful despair," she said. "Bring the child to me."

"Despair?" the nurse said to the baby, smiling, with a slow shake of her head, as if such a thing was unthinkable. *"Despair?"* She then carried the baby to the table, waltzing a few circles, singing a one-word song, "Despair despair despair." The old woman held the bag open, and the young nurse again stood on her tiptoes to cradle the infant's head as she placed the baby inside.

THE AUTOMATON HURRIED from the cottage and down the lane, the rush of her legs in her black skirt sounding like the flapping of a bat. She somehow didn't see me, though I hadn't the presence of mind to duck behind a shrub. She had hold of only one handle of the carpetbag, and the carpetbag gapped open, unclasped, at her side. The baby wasn't in any danger of tumbling out—as a matter of fact, she was probably better off getting a breath or two of the summer air. I took my shoes off so I could follow close without clomping.

The midway was empty but for a few workers closing up shop and leading their beasts to their stables. A man in a long white robe with an ostrich on a leash looked up at the sky and stopped. He called out something in some foreign tongue to a group of belly dancers in a nearby pavilion, and the dancers stepped out and they too looked up.

"The airship!" someone shouted. There was a flickering of silver light crossing the sky. It looked as if a sliver of the moon had broken free and drifted away. Others stepped from the buildings and gardens. They pointed at the airship. They squealed and laughed and chattered.

All last spring and winter, whenever the airship had shown up at night, we could only ever see a little spot of light, and it inched forward so slowly, you thought you could hear its chug-chug-chug if you listened close, cupping your ear.

Within minutes the midway was full of the Fair's workers knocking into one another, bumping into the automaton, everyone distracted by the tiny light of the airship. But still the old woman wouldn't slow her furious pace. She just wove through the growing, clumsy crowd. Two barefoot boys ran by me with sparklers sizzling in their hands, and they waved the fire in the air, as if trying to signal the pilot above. This inspired more fireworks, including some that spun around on the dirt, spitting sparks this way and that. One of the boys lit a rocket's wick with the end of his sparkler, and the rocket shot off with a terrible shriek, then burst with a blast of red, white, and blue just above the palmist's fortune-telling booth. Up ahead the folks who drank after hours in the beer garden all stumbled out into the road with their mugs and steins, and they celebrated the airship, raising their glasses to the sky. Some of them drunkenly fell into dancing with each other to the miserable tune cranked from the organ grinder's hand piano. Even his winged monkeys climbed a wall to point and shriek. But the automaton kept on, oblivious to any danger posed to the baby she carried in the open bag.

Finally, the automaton slowed, stopped, and looked up. She pushed herself taller on the balls of her feet, as if to see the airship better, and she held one lens of her pince-nez to her eye.

I crept forward on my stocking feet. I peeked into the open carpetbag. The baby's eyes glistened, wide and wet, catching the specks of light from the fireworks. Amber eyes, just like those of the violet-eyed trollop. Brown like a wren's feather. A minnow. A tuft of rabbit's fur. I'd already considered all the shades when trying to write Cecily a love poem.

The little girl seemed not at all bothered by the noise. She'd already shoved herself out of the tight swaddling of her pink blanket, and she entertained herself with her fists at her mouth. She happily gummed at her knuckles. Her cheeks sparkled too, wet with slobber.

And for the first time, my dummy spoke unprovoked. "What do you wish me to do?" he said, somehow louder than before, his voice crackling with scratches. "Why should I do this for you?"

The automaton snapped her head my way, her one good eye wide and bloodshot, more of those bubbles frothing at the corners of her mouth. If there hadn't been a baby in that bag, she'd have likely beat me with it. Instead she looked down at the child, and I saw the old lady soften. She reached in to touch the girl, tucking the blanket. She slouched even more, growing older and older before me. For a moment I thought I might even have to take her arm, to help her keep upright. I wanted to tell her not to worry.

She then shot me yet another noxious look. "You're seeing things," she said, and she tossed in my face a handful of ash. It was pepper mixed with snuff, enough to blind me. As I blinked away the sting, she rushed ahead. This was no black magic—it was an old tactic of theft. I'd known at least one woman who'd worked as a sneeze-lurker, who would slip from around a corner, toss a handful of spice and dust into a man's face, and make off with his wallet.

I stumbled forward, blinking and sneezing. When I could see again, I saw Cecily up ahead, a long summer shawl wrapped around her shoulders. She had again wandered away from the other actors, and while everyone else looked up to the airship, she looked down, watching her feet, her ankles, her legs, as she practiced the steps of a dance.

The old woman walked up to Cecily without even nodding a hello, and Cecily took the bag from her, saying nothing. She looked into the bag, tilted her head with affection. She puckered her lips, kissing the air. The automaton gestured for Cecily to rush, and though Cecily did follow the old woman, she continued with her made-up waltz, circling and weaving, like a tuft of cotton caught in a slight breeze. I stood and watched the two of them work up the road toward the bridge, the old woman constantly trying to hurry Cecily along, Cecily constantly falling behind, until they turned a corner and away, beyond my sight.

I'd had only the quickest of glimpses, but in that baby's face I'd seen not only Cecily's eyes but also Cecily's nose, her chin, the dimples in her cheeks, and the curl of her lashes. She couldn't possibly resemble anyone else. It was as if the child had never had any father at all. Was Cecily widowed? Abandoned? Was her baby feeble? And if she was feeble, would she just get sick when stolen from her glass egg? She had been small enough to fit in the carpetbag with some comfort, but not nearly as small as some of the smallest of the premature infants in the incubators.

I'd only known this baby a matter of minutes, and I was already feeling fatherly.

IN THE BEER GARDEN, I took a seat at Rosie's table as he and a few of his fellow anarchists fussed over the war that raged in Cuba. The whole Fair was a monument to imperialist pigs, they complained. "America is a plague," whispered Zigzag the hobo clown, his face still painted with a black grin and red freckles. "It's a killer pox." Like a jumpy pyromaniac, Zigzag lit everything that would light. He touched the flame of his match to a fallen leaf, to a paper rose, to the lace of a lady's dropped hankie, to his own cuff.

Rosie had already abandoned his rickshaw business. No one would ride for fear of looking lazy. He still sold plenty of his lovelies, but he had to give postcards to every guard who threatened to throw him off the fairgrounds. "It's exploitation," he groaned, but Rosie was the type of man who could find injustice even in the cheap steak he sawed at. "This is some ugly slaughter," he said, pointing at the steak with his knife, chewing with his broken teeth.

He introduced me to Mandelbaum the lion tamer, a slight-built man with hair wispy and gray. He wore a red suit—the gold buttons buttoned unevenly, the epaulets off-kilter. He held out his hand to me, and his undone sleeve slipped up his forearm, revealing a crisscrossing of terrible scars. "Mandelbaum has been mauled twenty-seven times, twice just today," Rosie said.

And next to Mandelbaum was Josephine, an entertainer in the minstrel show of the Old Plantation. For the show, they put her in the sackcloth dress of a slave and tied strips of muslin in her curls, and she played the piano as others danced. But, Rosie explained, Josephine composed her own ragtime tunes. "'The Draggletail Rag,'" he said, boasting and looking upon her with his lovesick eyes. "'The Weasel Rag.' 'The Breaky-Leg Rag.' 'The Belly-Full Rag.' Her songs are sold in New York City, for pity's sake. This girl's too good for this Fair. It's undignified. They've got her playing the music for cakewalks and buck dances. A couple of old white men run the whole show and fill their pockets. It's an insult to her and to her entire race!" Rosie sawed more at his grisly hank of steak, his indignation at a high pitch. Josephine and Rosie shared the steak and drank from the same glass of red wine. She started to speak for herself but stopped when Rosie leaned forward to give her a quick peck on the lips. "Exploitation," he said again.

Rosie and the ragtime player, the clown, the nervous lion tamer all looked to me to hear my tale of frustration. For once in my life, I wasn't troubled by a thing.

"Exploitation," I said, nodding. "The uncooked babies, for example. In the incubator exhibit." I brought it up only so they might tell me more about it.

"God almighty I hate that live-baby exhibit," Zigzag said. "That's the *first* thing we should set on fire when we burn this fair down."

Josephine said, "The whole thing is out-and-out humbug."

"How do you mean?" I said.

"You pay a quarter at the door to see orphans and circus children in the pink of health acting half dead," she said. "You stand there and wring your hands, your heart in your throat, worrying about them in their glass coffins. And you leave saying, 'It cost me a quarter, but I would've spent fifty cents to see such humanity.'"

"How do you know?" I said, hoping it was true. It was a relief to think that Cecily's little girl was just an actress like her mother.

"It's the midway," she said. She peeled off a piece of fat from Rosie's steak and popped it in her mouth. "Everything's for show."

"Even war," Zigzag said. He complained of all the relics of battle on display at the Fair. He wanted to set fire to the cyclorama that re-created the Battle of the *Monitor* and the *Merrimack*. He wanted to puncture the Civil War balloon. Zigzag, too jittery to sit still, moved the anarchists on to a rapid debate of the efficiency of assassination. If President McKinley were to come to the Fair, should they shoot him? Poison him? Lynch him? I found it amusing to see Rosie contemplate such violence—though it wasn't unusual for him to leap ham-fisted into a fight, I couldn't picture him ever dealing anyone a fatal blow. I suspected he just wanted to impress Josephine with the staggering depths of his dissatisfaction.

August arrived with a cricket in a bamboo cage. "Admiral Dewey lost his every match in the fan-tan den," August said. "They were fixing to squish him, so I bought him out of slavery." August tapped the cage, and the cricket jumped around in a fit. "See? The humiliation has already stirred up his killer instincts. Where'd you stumble off to, anyway?"

I shrugged, thinking I should keep my discovery to myself. But then I leaned in to whisper in his ear: "Want to know why I got beat up for trying to take Cecily's carpetbag?" I didn't want to start rumors— a husbandless mother didn't have an easy way around in the world we lived in—but I was anxious to tell somebody something. Anything. I wanted to talk about Cecily all night. I wanted August to promise me that Cecily *didn't* have a husband at all, that I'd be a good father, that the incubator exhibit was a fraud full of well-fed babies.

"Oh do tell me there's something gothic inside," August said. He held tight to my arm and leaned against me. He spoke close, his breath hot on my cheek and smelling of cloves. "A mummified mermaid? A secondhand prosthetic leg?"

I turned my head, my lips at his earlobe. "A baby," I whispered. August gasped, genuine. I said, "She keeps her in the incubator during the day."

"Such skullduggery," he purred. "From a carpetbag into an incubator? Then from the incubator to the carpetbag? I hope you're dreadfully suspicious. The baby could be a victim of a kidnapping. Or of scientific experiments in a country laboratory. Or maybe Cecily doesn't even come and go with the same infant—maybe she's some kind of hand-maiden of death. Did you think of that? Maybe she and the automaton practice a nightly bloodletting in a terrible den of monsters. Like vampires in a penny dreadful. It could all be worse than anything you could ever imagine."

"Yes," I said, though I hardly listened. "It could be. She might be married."

"Oh" was all August said.

But it wasn't the notion of a husband that worried me most. I already had so little I could give Cecily, what could I possibly give to a baby? Suddenly, I understood Cecily's hesitance.

As the anarchists playfully discussed how they might drown President McKinley in the lagoon, I put my hand to my chest, to the rich man's calling card in my pocket. I touched the corners of the card through the fabric. I had no true intention of selling Oscar, but I did consider his worth. How much might a man like William Wakefield pay?

12.

When the Chamber of Horrors started on fire the next day, smoke rolling through the pitch-dark corridors to choke us, I first suspected, not lightning but Zigzag the clown anarchist. But it had been raining all morning, heavy, fixing to flood the whole Fair and wash it downriver. Oscar, soaked to his wooden bones, weighed double on my back.

Not only did I hear the sharp crack of thunder but I could feel it like cold steel in my spine and joints. It startled Cecily out of character, and the executioner too, and they both grabbed at each other, clutching arms, their eyes meeting for a blink of sympathy. But in a moment, they returned their attention to the guillotine.

Cecily's neck went on the block, and they played out the beheading.

After the curtains closed and the others slogged on, the water squishing in their socks, I peeked through to the stage. "Cecily," I called softly. "Cecily." Cecily stepped forward with a candle in her fist. I handed her an envelope.

"What's this?" she said.

"I explain in the letter," I said.

"What's the letter say?" she said.

I hesitated. I scratched my wet head. "I'd rather not say," I said.

"Why not?" she said. "What's in it that's so terrible? Why should I read something that you don't want to say?"

"There's nothing terrible," I said. "Nothing terrible at all. It's just that I agonized over the letter. I put just the right words in just the right order. You need to read it all in a letter. It's a confession, of sorts."

"A *confession*," she said. "What are you confessing?"

"Why can't you just open it and read it?"

"Ferret," she said, sighing, "to read, I have to have my specs. Like an old lady."

Finally, after taking a deep breath, I spoke. I kept my voice low. "I don't know if the automaton told you. Last night. I know about the baby. I saw the girl in the carpetbag." Cecily lowered the candle, dropping the light from her face. "Please don't be upset," I said. "I said it much better in the letter." As if hoping to impress her, I added, "I write letters for a living."

"Why are you telling me this?" she said.

I shook my hands with exasperation. "Because you *told* me to tell you."

"I didn't tell you to tell me anything," she said.

"You told me to tell you what was in the letter," I said.

"But why did you write it in a letter? Why would you talk about such things?"

"Because you have to know that I know," I said. "I want to spend time with you, Cecily." I reached up to touch her hand, to raise it, to return the candlelight to her face.

"Oh, Ferret," she said. "Please, please, please, you'd be so much happier with Pearl. I promise." All her breathy *p*'s made the candle flame sputter.

Before I could object, there came a clanging down the hall, and fast footsteps, and chaos, as someone ran through the winding corridor with a bell in hand, shouting, "Fire, fire, fire, fire!"

I helped Cecily from the stage—or more rightly, I caught her as she tumbled down, her legs tangled up in her endless petticoats and layers of satin skirts. As we rushed ahead, squeezing all the flounce of her gown around narrow corners, I put one arm around her waist to keep her from tripping. She leaned in toward me, complaining of the awful pinch of her tiny velvet shoes.

All the creatures and fiends from the Chamber of Horrors ran from the hallway, and we were shoved along, out through the mouth of the dragon, into the storm. A devil looked up, and the deluge washed away the red paint on his face. The rain matted the wolf's whiskers and cleansed the blood from the Ripper's hands. A dark angel, a skeleton bride, a man with a noose hanging from his neck, a ghost in sheets and shackles, they all rushed for cover as they scattered along the midway, sliding in the mud. A cloud of black smoke rose overhead like a snort from the dragon's snout.

Just steps from the Chamber of Horrors, my umbrella's ribs got twisted and its silk ripped. Cecily's wig and costume wilted in the rain as I held the spindly umbrella over her head, all her overskirts and underskirts growing waterlogged and heavy, dragging her down. There was no keeping the bottom of her dress out of the mud, though I tried. With one hand I held the umbrella over her head, with the other I carried her train like a courtier. Within seconds she was a muddy mess, her dress a wreck. "In here," she yelled above the storm and its locomotive roar. She gestured toward the Mirror Maze.

The building was closed for repairs, some drunk having tripped his way through, cracking every mirror he slammed against. I pushed aside the sawhorse blocking the entry and Cecily moved into the maze.

"You stay here, and I'll go look in on the baby," I said, following her. A glass case seemed the worst place for an infant in a storm.

"She's not at the incubator exhibit," Cecily said, panting and snuffling, as if she'd swum up from underwater. Cecily pushed the tall wig from her head and it fell onto her dress, rolled down the satin, and onto the floor. She began undoing the knots and ties at her waist.

"Then where is she?" I said. "Your baby."

Cecily said nothing. She shook her hips, shaking off layers of the sopping costume. I was pleased to watch her undress even as I wondered if it would be more gentlemanly to look away. But she beckoned me forward to help her with yet more knots and clasps. "I want to see the broken mirrors," she said. "Let's go get lost." As we stepped forward into the maze, layers of her costume loosened and dropped, giving way to bodices, hip pillows, bustles, ruffles, pleats. She shrunk away, piece by piece, the wreckage of her gown falling off. She stripped to a long skirt of pink satin and a chemise as lacy as a muslin nightdress. She stepped lightly, her feet still in the too-tiny shoes so as not to step on shards of glass. I watched her every reflection, and the reflections of reflections, in the mirrors. A few shivers worked up her spine from the damp.

Cecily bumped along slowly in the dim maze, knocking her shoulders gently against the walls, feeling her way through. Eventually we did seem a little lost, every turn another twist, until we didn't know forward from back. If the skinny tip of a cyclone had hit us, we would have been sliced to ribbons as we spun around. But that didn't keep me from wanting to follow Cecily deeper and deeper into the maze.

We found the broken mirrors, shards and shatter still hanging off the frames, breaking our reflections into pieces. We walked past. We would dead-end here and there, caught in corners and wrong turns, and as we corrected and doubled back, we'd brush shoulders and touch hands, and it became something like a waltz, graceful and smooth. And every time we turned again, our touches lingered longer. I felt her breath, still shaky with her shivering, against my neck, and her fingers stepped along my open palm, tapping, tapping, tapping. I looked in her eyes every chance I got, and I got more and more chances as our little waltz began to slow down to nothing.

Cecily leaned back against a cracked mirror, the crack reflected, repeated, in all the other mirrors, casting the illusion that every mirror of the maze was broken.

She plucked the handkerchief from my pocket and turned to her reflection to scrub away the smeared powder from her face. "My baby's not sick," she said. "So don't feel sorry for us."

"I don't," I said.

"The live-baby exhibit needed more live babies, and I needed somebody to watch her while I got my head chopped off every day. That's all. There's nothing more to it."

I looked at her face in the mirror as she wiped at her cheeks. "Can I ask you something?" I said.

"No," she said. "I don't like it when people ask me if they can ask me something. It always turns out to be something nobody wants to be asked."

"I'm going to ask you anyway," I said. "Do you have a husband, Cecily?"

"If I told you I did, would you leave me alone?"

"No," I said. "I would just decide not to believe you."

"Then why'd you ask?" she said.

I shrugged and winked at her. "Seemed the gentlemanly thing to do." I took her elbow and began to turn her toward me. She leaned back against the cracked mirror again, and as she looked down at her sleeve, she traced her finger along the petal of a rose in the lace.

"Her name's Dorothy," Cecily said. "My little girl. But we all call her Doxie, for some reason." Cecily lifted the watch from my pocket. She messed with the watch's stem, watching the hands spin on the dial. She returned the watch, but it now told the wrong time. "She's with Mrs. Margaret, the witch in the booth on the midway. When it looked like it might storm, we kept Doxie home. Mrs. Margaret is *very* protective."

"I noticed," I said.

"She's been like a mother to us." She gave me a squint, and furrowed her brow. "Can I ask *you* something?"

"Well, that happens to be my *favorite* question," I said, laying it on thick, intending to be comical. "Ask me anything at all."

"Did you used to have a mustache?"

I buttoned a button of her chemise, a little one at her wrist. "Yes," I said.

Cecily squinted again, and she reached up to run her finger under my lip, tracing the ghost of a fancy, twisting mustache unlike any I'd ever had.

Before I could lean in to kiss her, a spark of sunlight distracted us. The glimmer bounced from mirror to mirror, glinting in my eye. It was only then I noticed I couldn't hear the wind anymore. "The sun's out," Cecily said, and she took my hand. Hand in hand, we wove back through the maze, winding our way out easily, following the slant of sun. At the wreckage of her costume, Cecily picked up some silk and wrapped it around her shoulders like a shawl but left most of the dress behind for someone else to gather later.

Out on the midway, the sun seemed even brighter than before. People stepped from the buildings and from under the eaves, peeking out from beneath their umbrellas and blinking at the sky. Rainwater rolled down gullies in the muddy road. The barkers went right back to work, shouting and beckoning, begging people into their booths. "Chiquita's spirit can't be dampened by a summer storm! Come watch her dance on her little two legs!" A camel roamed without a rider, stopping to nibble on the thatched roof of a hut in the Filipino Village.

But the ruins of the Chamber of Horrors were the real attraction. The fire was out, but smoke billowed. A fire wagon emptied its tank on the building, and the arc of water made a faded rainbow above the dragon's head. The pale colors sparkled in the sun.

The show was over. Word traveled among the chamber's performers as they gathered in the wet road, and a few of the actors wept, even the Big Bad Wolf who disemboweled Little Red every day and night. "I don't have another job," he said, returning his mask to his face to hide his tears. Even if the building could be repaired, it wouldn't be for days.

Cecily didn't seem to mind. As a matter of fact, she seemed happier than I'd ever seen her. "Good-bye, Ferret," she said. She whispered, "I'm going to go get ol' Dox and spend the rest of the day with her." But before she'd skipped away entirely, she returned to me. "Hey, just take Pearl out for an hour or so, please, please, please," she said. "You really will like her quite a lot. Just an hour. Or two." I nodded, though not at all politely. She could sense I was irked, so she smiled at me, then stuck out her lower lip to mock my pout. Then she kissed me on that pouty lower lip of mine—just a quick peck. She ran away, stepping lightly through the mud, and I could see from her limp how those little shoes pinched and pained her. I couldn't bear the sight of it.

I kicked off my own shoes, took off my socks, and I ran after her. I called her name, and when she stopped I knelt at her side to take her ankle in my hand. She steadied herself with her hand on the top of my head as I removed her peacock-blue shoe and replaced it with mine. "Ferret," she protested, but I wouldn't listen. "Chivalry is *dead*, already." Her foot on my knee, I tied the laces as tight as they'd go.

"Don't let them trip you," I said, standing. "They're too big for you, but they're better than those pretty little traps." I'd left her blue shoes footless in the mud. I kicked them away. "Mine won't leave you hobbled, at least."

Cecily cast me a skeptical glance, an eyebrow lifted. "So you're going to go around in bare feet like a heathen?" she said.

"I was born barefoot," I said, winking. "I grew up barefoot. I've always hated shoes. I could walk in a ditch of needles and not feel a thing."

Cecily lifted her petticoat higher up, above her ankle, and studied the shoes. She playfully tapped her foot against my naked toes. She bit her lip, like with melancholy, and she looked up. "Ferret," she said, then paused. "Ferret, you're a very nice man—"

I interrupted, as I knew this compliment wouldn't be going anywhere I wanted it to. "Bring Doxie to the swan gondola tonight," I said. "Just the two of you. After the Fair closes." I tapped my toe against the toe of her shoe. "Please?"

She looked vexed by the invitation, but then said, "Do you promise to go see Pearl? At least walk her home from work? This evening? I have a good eye for these kinds of things, you know? I think you two could fall in love without even trying much."

This time I wasn't insulted by the suggestion. It was beautifully halfhearted, at best. I smiled and nodded, and this got me another quick kiss on the lips before she turned and headed toward home.

13.

THOUGH THE MUD hardly kept anyone off the midway that afternoon, my business was sluggish, everyone's spirits were sapped. Not only did no one stop for my jokes, nobody even slowed. Oscar and I resorted to following fairgoers, mocking a lady's hat perhaps, or insulting the mustache of the man at her side, until they paid us to shut up and go away. And Oscar had been soaked by the rain, so most of his tricks fizzled and flopped. His sparks sputtered, his joints squeaked.

My heart wasn't in it either. I was fretful. If Cecily and Doxie didn't join me in the swan gondola, I reasoned, they probably never would. Why, after all, would Cecily trust me? I closed my eyes, trying to again feel Cecily's kiss on my pouting lower lip. I gave my lip a pinch. The kiss had been so soft and quick, it had been almost nothing at all. But the taste of her lips had lingered—she'd been wearing some kind of balm the flavor of cucumber and rose.

When I opened my eyes, an old man in a black swallowtail coat stood before me. He wore the white gloves of a footman. He had hardly any hair but what hair he had needed cutting. The pale gray hair hovered over his skull like a halo of smoke. He said nothing. He only nodded, expecting me to perform, so I began my routine. He was generous with his laughter, but the laughter was silent. It shook his whole body, sent his head back, shut his eyes, but never reached the volume of a wheeze.

After several minutes of this, the man finally held up a hand and shook his head, as if he could take no more hilarity. He smiled and sighed, exhausted. He reached into the front pocket of his coat as he stepped forward. In his hand was not a tip but an envelope of a fine linen paper, its red wax seal stamped with the letter *W.* Across the front of it, in an elegant hand, was written: *The Ventriloquist.*

The footman tromped away, holding up the legs of his trousers to keep the cuffs from the mud. And I read the invitation.

> A Masquerade Ball,
> to "Remember the *Maine*,"
> on July 1,
> on the roof of the Fine Arts Building
> in the Grand Court
> of the New White City,
> after dark.
>
> William Wakefield, President of the Board of the Omaha World's Fair, King of the Knights of Ak-Sar-Ben, invites you to the Sinking of the (miniaturized) Battleship *Maine.* The USS *Maine* exploded and sank in the Havana harbor, on February 15, as the city celebrated Carnival. The lagoon will stand in for the harbor as we watch from the roof as the toy ship sinks. Our spectacle is a tribute to the Americans who've lost their lives in the Spanish-American War thus far, and those lives still to be lost in the name of Freedom.
>
> Please come masked, and in costume.

Beneath the type, Wakefield had scrawled me a message in pencil.

> P.S. Bring along any friends. And bring along the dummy.
> P.P.S. I'm the man in the car, with the silver skeleton.

. . .

I'D HEARD OF the Knights of Ak-Sar-Ben, but they were rich, and I was poor, so what did I care? It was a kingly court of the wealthy looking to improve the city. They took the name of the state of Nebraska and turned it in on itself, spelling out, symbolically, how backward things had got, everything topsy-turvy in the city of Omaha, with its saloons and whores and gambling dens. The knights hosted coronation balls and parades. They built the Fair. When they gathered for court, they wore crowns and ermine capes, and jester's tights and pantaloons. The men painted their faces like harlequins and drank wine from golden goblets. I could just picture them all eating grapes fed to them by skinny boys dressed as sprites. Appalling. At Ak-Sar-Ben Hall, for ten cents, the common folk could stand at the railings of the upper reaches to look down upon the dance floor, during the knights' famous masquerade balls. Yes, the rich bastards let us watch them waltz, and charged us a dime for the privilege.

I had never attended and I never would. They spent thousands of dollars on their revelry so they could raise hundreds for orphans and poorhouses. *William Wakefield*. Of course he'd be the king. Wakefield was the king of all.

And he still is, as far as I know. And always will be.

I should've killed him when I could've.

November 18, 1898

Dear Cecily,

    Forgive the rusty thumbprint at the corner of the page—my every fingertip is red. Emmaline brought me a plate of gingersnaps and broiled marrowbones. She dusted the snaps with cayenne pepper, which helps the night seem not so cold.

    I've been letting Emmaline read the letters I write to you. I'm letting her read this one, even as I write it. She sits with her cheek near mine, criticizing my handwriting, complaining that she can hardly read a word.

    There's been no talk of how long I might or might not stay. The Old Sisters Egan and me grow sleepy at the same hour, grow chilled at the same temperature of an evening.

    And I've told Emmaline about you, about the Fair, about Doxie. I tell her I'm only telling a ghost story, but Emmaline tells me I'm wrong. Ghost stories have ghosts in them, she says.

    But you, Cecily, haven't so much as said boo to me.

    Emmaline's starting to think that I'm the ghost. And who can blame her?

    Emmaline wants you to know that her favorite character in my ghostless ghost story is the baby in the carpetbag. But that shouldn't surprise you. That's Doxie's way—she just has to purr a little and we're all in love. Write more about Doxie, Emmaline begs, sitting here at my shoulder, tugging at my sleeve like an impatient child. Cecily would want to know more. Mothers never tire of hearing all about their babies.

    So if there's no ghost story to tell, I'll tell you a fairy tale.

When I went up in the balloon, on the last day of the Fair, I took Doxie with me, and I wasn't afraid at all. I didn't cower in the basket. When you have someone to protect, someone to look after, bravery runs through you, sharp, like the fear used to.

And we didn't crash, and my leg didn't break. We floated to the farm just in time to wrestle it back to life. Doxie was crowned queen and heir of all the acres of nothingness. She rests in a basket and does nothing but magic. The creek bed is wet again and the corn has grown tall. When we wake up every sunny morning, it's summer, with a chance of rain, no matter what.

Your spinner of tales and teller of lies,

Ferret, again

BOOK TWO

Lovers

14.

Aᴜɢᴜsᴛ's ᴄᴀʀᴘᴇᴛʙᴀɢ ᴡᴀs no longer sufficient for his business, so he'd taken to wheeling around a trunk full of his potions and tonics. He painted on the side of the trunk *August Sweetbriar, Omaha Indian*, and he parked in front of Buffalo Bill's Wild West Show. On the day of the storm and the fire, I found him sitting on the trunk, smoking another of his asthma cigarettes, lines of red and yellow paint across his cheeks. Stuck into the brim of his hat, next to his bluebird, was a tall gray feather.

"War paint," he told me, winking, touching his finger to his colors. He found that the closer he could match the white folks' idea of a witch doctor, the more he sold. And with the rain having weighed everyone down and quickly given them sniffles and chills, he was making a fortune off sweat-inducing extracts of dwarf elder and marigold alone.

I sat next to him on the trunk and showed him the invitation from Wakefield. "Oh my," August said. "Are you taking me to the masquerade ball, my love?"

"Not a chance," I said. "What's Wakefield's story, anyway? I see his name on ice trucks."

"*Billy Wakefield*," August said, bewildered by my bewilderment. "You've lived in Omaha all your life, and you're asking me about Billy Wakefield?"

"I am," I said.

"Yes, darling, Billy Wakefield is an iceman. In the summer, his lake is a resort, and in the winter they cut the ice off it. He's ice and fire and everything in between. He has money in the smelting works, a meatpacking company. He deals in linseed, sugar beets. He's everything, and everybody knows him."

"I don't," I said, "and I don't want to."

"We have to go to his party."

"No," I said.

"It's almost a month away," he said. "That gives me plenty of time to change your mind."

I took my dummy's hand in mine and pressed my thumb to the center of it. His fingers curled around to grip my knuckle. What was it about my shabby doll that would make a man like Wakefield so interested?

"Oh, and such tragedy. There was even a song," August said, glancing over the smoke of his cigarette, contemplating.

"A song?" I said.

August nodded and thought some more. "'The Ballad of Billy Wakefield's Little Boy,'" he said. "It was *very* popular. It broke all our hearts."

And so August told me the story behind it. Like a lot of men's misery, it started with all the bad business of the nineties, the corruption, the failures, the debt. The railroads, running out of money, began staging locomotive collisions for spectacle, driving two trains at top speed right toward each other on the same track, just so people could watch the catastrophe. Billy Wakefield, a lover of toys and sport and grand productions, took his son to a locomotive collision in the deserts of western Nebraska. In his zeal, he arranged to have a gazebo built as close to the track as he could get, so he and his boy could sit in the shade. A little *too* close, it turned out, because when the trains crashed and the boilers exploded, debris flew. The little boy was killed and Wakefield was maimed, his arm lost. "I can't really remember the song," August said, "except that it rhymed *rails* with *coffin nails*. Oh, and there was a whole other ballad too. When the mother died. She dwindled. She fell ill. Her ballad rhymed *the boy's life so brief* with *she died from grief*."

And I pitied Wakefield just then, no matter how rich he was. Whatever role he played in his own demise, he'd been punished more than any one man deserved.

15.

STILL BAREFOOT, I took the streetcar to the Empress in the late afternoon to slip my filthy feet into a pair of shoes. I was grateful for the task of taking Pearl for a stroll—I'd had nothing else to do but worry. I'd arranged for Alonzo the gondolier to be waiting with the swan gondola after dark, but I still fretted that I'd be sailing the lagoon alone.

Brandeis & Sons, the department store where Pearl worked as a salesgirl and window dresser, was only up the block from me. Though the store had everything anyone could want, I'd only once or twice gone inside.

A handful of ladies carrying signs marched in front of the store, and I first suspected nothing but gimmickry. The Brandeis men, the store's proprietors, were kings of hullabaloo. They often appeared in front of the store themselves, holding balloons by their strings, and at the ends of the strings were tickets you could exchange for a man's suit, a lady's hat, or a jeweled stickpin. The men, like a couple of boys, would release the balloons to rise and roam above the city before drifting back to earth to get caught in trees and on the roofs of houses. Even I, as unlucky as I am, once found a Brandeis balloon tangled in the wheels of a parked carriage. The prize was a silk-lined box of crystallized dwarf oranges so fancy that I chose to save them, but I saved them too long, and they turned on me before I had even a taste of one.

As I neared the store I was amused to discover that this wasn't a sales gimmick but a protest. The women carried picket signs—*Harlots in underwear! Activities unbefitting ladies!* Their chanting served only to draw people in. I had to elbow my way to the window to even get a glimpse at the offense.

It was quite something, that window display. With everything behind plate glass, you couldn't hear all the whirring and rumbling of motors and engines, so it looked like it all moved on air or by magic, or clicked along on the tiny gears of a windup music box. Overhead hung a banner—*America by Road*—and three manikins rode bicycles as a rolled-up canvas unrolled behind them in a continual loop, unspooling painted landscapes of fields and rivers. The cyclists were women, and they wore bloomers, not skirts, and they were decked out in red, white, and blue. They wore scarves patterned with stars and stripes that blew in a wind stirred up by an electric fan offstage. Their motorized legs pedaled fast, spinning the bicycles' wheels.

Pearl, too, was a magician.

"If you put your daughters on a bicycle," a protester shouted in my ear, "you've given them the freedom of a whore! You've soiled your little doves! Do you even know where your girls are?"

"Yeah," a heckler called back, a cigar plugged into one corner of his mouth. "She's in the store spending my money on a pair of them natty pants." The others who'd gathered there chuckled, which just encouraged him to heckle her more.

I went to the front doors, and even after stepping just one foot in, I felt like somebody might kick me right back out. Even when I straightened up to give the illusion of dignity, I could feel a stitch or two in the seams of my suit pop and unravel. Fortunately, I was as invisible as I ever was.

Shoppers and clerks hustled quick and graceful, as if they too were electrified manikins linked by a single wire. Cash registers clunked and rang and their drawers sprang open and slammed shut, while a violinist stood at the center of the grand staircase, fiddling softly. The whole place was selling patriotism by the yard, the flag's stars and stripes even fashioned into petticoats in honor of the Spanish-American War. The manikins wore cavalry caps and army-blue dresses with gold braid and brass medals, the ladies' arms bent into a salute. You could get belt buckles with eagles painted on them and suspenders patterned with the mug of the mustachioed George Dewey, admiral of the navy.

You knew these shoppers were rich because they shopped for winter already—the place was stocked with fox fur collars and chinchilla overcoats. Imagine a life so leisurely you considered, in the heat of summer, what you might wear when it got cold.

I did find something I could afford, however. In a glass counter of scarves and neckties, gloves and collars, were handkerchiefs stitched with initials. I bought one for Cecily—its corners were embroidered with yellow roses, and along one edge was a pink cursive *S*.

Before the shopgirl could tie the box closed with a ribbon, I heard Pearl call my name. In the millinery corner, at a counter, Pearl stood surrounded by hats on severed heads.

"Well, there you are," I said, walking to her.

Pearl produced from behind the counter a comb, and she leaned across to fix me up. It embarrassed me a bit. Had I even looked in the mirror before I'd left my room? She touched the fingers of one hand to my chin, and with her other she ran the comb through my hair. I watched her face as she watched the wayward sweep and swoop of my curls. She squinted and grumbled, then finally gave up. She held out a mirror.

"Ah," I said, looking at myself. "You parted it in the opposite direction. It would never have occurred to me."

"You must have got caught in the storm," she said.

"Do I really look so all in fits?" I said. Back in my attic, I hadn't thought to change. I'd been rushing through the day, anxious to return to the swan gondola at nightfall. I smiled and winked. "Seems I can't go anywhere anymore without someone doing my hair or shaving my lip." As her face lit up apple red, I remembered: *Ah yes, Pearl blushes.* "It was raining pitchforks," I said, hoping to change the subject so her cheeks could cool off. I told her about the lightning and fire in the Chamber of Horrors. I stepped back and tugged at the knees of my trousers, showing off the mud caked on the hems.

"Is Cecily all right?" she said with a gasp.

"She is," I said. "She is." I decided to show Pearl the hankie I'd bought Cecily, because I didn't want anyone wrongheaded about anything at all. "Is this the right sort of thing," I said, holding open the box, "to buy a lady?"

Pearl seemed to fall into a little bit of a swoon. But when she looked at the hankie, and ran her finger along the curve of the letter *S*, she blushed herself into a sweat. "Oh," she said, bringing her fingers to her lips as she looked into the box again. "I'm afraid the shopgirl gave you the wrong handkerchief."

I looked at the embroidered letter. My hand began to shake. I was making matters worse and worse. *She thinks it should be a* P, I thought. *She thinks it's for her.*

"Oh, Pearl," I said, "I'm so sorry if you thought . . . I didn't mean to . . . You're a very lovely girl, and sweet to boot, and there's no reason at all that I shouldn't want to . . . that *any* gentleman shouldn't want, wouldn't be honored to . . . well, to buy you things and take you around . . . but this handkerchief is for . . . well, it's for Cecily. Who I'm very fond of."

"Oh no, no, please, I know, I know, don't say another thing."

"And it's not that I *couldn't* be fond of you, or *wouldn't* be fond of you, if . . ."

"Ferret," she said, sternly. "Please." She took the box from me. "The girl gave you the wrong handkerchief. You need the letter *C*, of course." When she saw I was too dim-witted to catch on, she said, "For Cecily." She paused again. "*C* . . . for Cecily." I think she even gave the

C an extra *S*-like *sssss*. She stepped from around the counter as I mulled it all over. "I'll just go swap it out for you and I'll be right back," she said.

Now I was the one blushing. As I waited, I ran my finger through some light dust on a shelf, drawing the letter *C*, which looked to me like half a heart. I then touched at the glass eye of a wax head that wore a hat upon which toy ships with flames of red silk sank in a sea of blue crepe—a naval battle in the Havana harbor. When Pearl stepped up to my side, the box nicely tied shut, I said, "Who would wear such a hat?"

Pearl held the box to her chest. She twisted her finger through the box's ribbon. "Well, we haven't sold one yet, so I wouldn't know," she said. "But people do like to feel like they're supporting the American troops at war."

"By wearing a hat?" I said.

Pearl shrugged, and I worried I was being difficult. I was still burning a little from my embarrassment, I guess. I took the box from her. "I can read and write, in case you're wondering," I said. "As a matter of fact, I don't know if you've ever seen my advertisement in the *Omaha Bee*. I offer literary assistance. I write letters and whatever else needs written. I've written a hundred letters, probably, to women with all sorts of names."

My boasting didn't seem to impress her. Instead, she seemed distracted, melancholy. She held a finger to her lips in thought. "Maybe you wrote *me* a letter once."

"Oh?" I said. She put her arm in mine and led me deeper into the store. Despite all her blushing, Pearl seemed nothing at all like the nervous girl I'd met at the swan gondola.

"Yes, yes," she said. "Do you remember something about . . . about . . ." She looked up and off in thought. "Pearl the girl of the ocean blue?"

"Hm," I said. "No. No I don't think I quite remember . . ."

"A letter of proposal?" she said. Though I couldn't possibly remember every letter I ever wrote, it seemed I'd remember something like

Pearl the girl of the ocean blue. It seemed a little too plucky for my style. "He was far too dull to write the letter he wrote," she said. "I always suspected he'd copied it from a book. But if there are people like you—who *sell* love letters—then . . . well, perhaps *that's* why he didn't sound himself." There'd been a pinch of disapproval with her mention of "people like you."

"And you didn't accept?" I said.

Pearl sighed. "He was very kind," she said. "But he should have written me a letter himself, don't you think? I actually liked the bit about the ocean. It made me sound like a girl in a song. But that was one of the reasons I wouldn't accept, you know? To have such a poetic proposal of marriage from someone who wasn't poetic at all? I came to my senses right then, and I knew I couldn't marry him."

"You mean to say you didn't marry him *because* of the letter? It couldn't have been from me then," I said. "I've never written a proposal of marriage that wasn't accepted."

"And it's even worse than all that," she said. "I even used the words of the letter against him. 'What ocean?' I said to him. 'I'm Pearl the girl of *what* ocean? *I've never even seen the ocean,*' I said to him. At that time, I'd never been to Paris. I'd never been to New York. I had never been anywhere. How could I even be the girl in those lovely lines? 'How dare you ask a stranger to marry you,' I said. I was really very awful to him."

I honestly did take great care to assure that the letters I wrote had the character of the sender. I figured into the fee of the letter the price of a pint of beer or a cup of tea, and I would sit with the sender for much longer than necessary, listening to every word. I found that my work as an entertainer gave me a good ear for voices. I picked up on any habits of speech or odd snippets of vocabulary, and I worked it all in, in a literary manner. It was my best bit of flimflam. Whenever they tried to write the letters themselves, they only sounded like somebody else. They needed a mimic in order to ring true.

"Whatever happened to the poor sap?" I said, but before she could answer, we'd reached the men's department, and she'd embarked on her scheme to get me in a new suit. The linen suits were on clearance—two dollars and fifty cents—and though I'd spent my last nickel on the embroidered hankie for Cecily with a *C*, Pearl opened an account for me, so I could buy the suit on time. I was no stranger to credit—I was living on jawbone all around town—but I'd never had credit in a place like Brandeis & Sons. And I'd never before been treated with such respect. Pearl left me to a manager named Mr. Foswig, who brought me a thin cigar and a snifter of whiskey so smooth it didn't burn its way down my gullet in the manner of most whiskeys I'd known. With each suit I tried on, Mr. Foswig appraised me in the way he'd appraise a man of only a finer feather, as if I'd be wearing this suit someplace of consequence. And when we'd made our selection, and the tailor had pinned and chalked the coat and pants and carried the suit away, Mr. Foswig brought me the catastrophe I'd been wearing when I'd walked in. But it had been attended to miraculously—the mud had been sponged away and some gaping seams stitched shut. My hopeless shoes had been polished and the cobbler's shoddy work redone. As Mr. Foswig helped me on with my coat, he told me my new suit would be ready in the morning. Pearl returned with her umbrella and hat. "Walk me home?" she said.

"I think I'll buy a two-dollar-fifty-cent suit every week," I said as I studied my cigar out in the sunlight. I was quite unaccustomed to wearing suits that had never been worn before. "I feel like a million bucks just having tried it on." The protesters had left for bigger and better scandals apparently, and the cyclists in the window still happily traveled as their bicycles spun in place. "Do you cycle?" I said.

"I do," Pearl said. "I sold my piano to buy a bicycle, but we're all doing that. Sales in the sheet music department have dropped. It seems we're spending all our money on tires and patches. I wonder if they'll stop writing songs entirely."

"If they were smart," I said, "they would write songs about bicycles, I guess."

Pearl put on a pair of eyeglasses, their lenses tinted red. When I raised an eyebrow at the sight of them she explained they'd been prescribed by a homeopath. "Iridology," she said. "There are doctors who can read your health in the colors and shadows of the irises. All your pain and disease sits waiting in your body, and they can see it all in the eyes. I've had dizzy spells to the point where I see things in the room that aren't there."

"What things do you see?"

"Well, it's hard to describe." Her voice, already so low and soft, grew softer and lower. "I see myself, but I'm somewhere else in the room. Like a ghost of myself, haunting only me." Pearl turned bright red, of course. "There's a spot of indigo in my left iris, and the doctor says it tells of an imperiled ovary." She whispered that—"imperiled ovary." And she kept whispering. "He worries my ovaries are afloat inside me. They're *untethered*, was what he said. So he feels that if he can see the damage in my iris that he should be able to correct the iris and therefore correct the damage. The glasses are meant to chase away the little spot of deep blue in the ovary part of my eye."

"Maybe it's the glasses giving you the dizzy spells," I said. This iridology didn't seem all that far from August's cure-alls.

Pearl laughed again. "My doctor thinks it's because I don't wear a corset," she said. "He disapproves of dress reform." And suddenly, Pearl wished me good night, one foot up on the front steps of a boarding-house for women—its name, the Juliet, was etched in stone above the doors.

"Can't I buy you your supper?" I said. "A glass of wine and a plate of hash?" I still had hours to worry before that late-night gondola ride.

"But you spent your money on the hankie," she said.

"Brandeis isn't the only place I have a line of credit, you know," I said. "A man of my means has debt all around town."

"You're very sweet to offer, Ferret," Pearl said, "but Cecily would be furious with me."

"No, she wouldn't," I said. "Didn't you hear her on the swan gondola? She wants us to like each other."

"Don't you know anything? What she really hopes is for us to not like each other at all. I'm sure it would be much easier for everyone if you fell in love with me and I fell in love with you, but that's not going to happen, is it?"

"No?" I said.

"No," she said. "Tomorrow you'll go to the store and you'll put on your new suit, and you'll go find Cecily, and you'll tell her that Pearl is a perfectly decent girl, but she's just not the girl for you. *There's only one girl for me and that girl is you.* That's what you'll tell her. *I* should be the one writing letters of literary assistance. At least I know how to spell Cecily's name."

"How do you spell it anyway?" I asked, and she told me. I asked again, to make sure I had it right. And then I spelled it out loud myself. As Pearl headed up the front steps to the door of her building, I said, "I'm sorry about the proposal."

"What?" she said.

"The proposal of marriage. *Pearl the ocean girl*, or whatever it was. I'm sorry it didn't work out. I hope I wasn't the one who wrote it."

"But I hope you *were*," she said. "What a charming coincidence that would be, wouldn't it? If it had been you who'd written that proposal of marriage? And I had rejected it? And then here we were?"

"And if we fell in love after all?" I said. "And got married? It'd be a story we could tell people."

"The story you'll tell people will be the story of how you met Cecily," she said. "I'll be that awful extra girl who tagged along on that first gondola ride. *What was her name again, love? Pearl, was it?*" She took off her red glasses, showing off her ocean-blue eyes, as she opened the door. "But I don't mind. I'm much more interesting as the girl who is forgotten." And with that she slipped inside and away, turning to smoke behind the door's frosted-glass window.

16.

M Y STOMACH SO IN KNOTS, I had to nurse one of August's tonics late into the night. Some sort of extract of some sort of weed. "You're only to take a dessertspoonful," he explained. "Any more than that and it could turn devil on you." So I only touched my tongue to the wet underside of the cork of the little blue bottle—just for a lick or two, enough to give me a pinch of ease every now and again.

I waited and waited alone on the heart-shaped bench of the swan gondola. Alonzo the gondolier had jilted me too. The lights of the Fair had been doused for hours, it seemed. And the later it got, the more I lost my mind. When I checked my watch, I could've sworn the hands were working their way counterclockwise. A few minutes later I realized the watch had quit altogether, and wouldn't wind up, so I plunked it overboard.

I blamed my nerves on the nerve tonic and pitched the bottle too. I shouldn't be frustrated with Cecily, I thought. I should *want* Cecily to be cautious, after all. A mother, alone, with a little one, had no choice but to step lightly.

But when I did hear her steps, at long last, they weren't light at all. They weren't even hers, they were mine; she clumped along in the shoes I'd put on her feet. I recognized the tap of the cobbler's nail against the brick. I'd often cussed those shoes and their noise, but just now it seemed I'd never heard a prettier tune.

I leaped from the bench. I ran up the stairs from the dock to the promenade. "Can I help you this time?" I said, walking up to Cecily, who gently rocked the carpetbag at her side.

"Please," she said.

I took the bag and looked in on Doxie. As she slept, she smacked her lips. Her little lashes fluttered with a dream.

"What do you suppose she's dreaming about?" I said.

"Me," she said. "I'm all the poor little urchin's got." She folded her hands in prayer and fluttered her own lashes, mocking sincerity. She then elbowed me in the ribs. I didn't tell her yet about my own orphanhood. But I couldn't help but wonder what my life would have been like had my mother cared enough to keep me near. Snuck around in a carpetbag seemed a fate that would have suited me well. I'd been born as scrawny as a wet rat, and not much heavier—I would've made an excellent incubator baby.

"I can't fault her," I said. "I might be dreaming about you right now myself. Are you really here, looking as beautiful as that?"

Cecily smiled and tugged up at the fabric of her skirt, lifting the bottom of it above the tops of her shoes. My shoes. She'd cleaned off the mud, and wore a pair of wool socks to keep her feet from swimming in them. She did a little jig. "I'm stealing the shoes for good," she said. "Walking right off with them. I like how they look." They were nothing but calfskin, but they suited Cecily. She most often dressed like no one else. Her skirt, shiny and striped in purple and pink, seemed the same fabric as the cushions in an ice cream parlor. And around her waist was a belt of her own invention—the buckle was a gilt-framed miniature of a blue wasp that had once hung on a wall.

I told Cecily there'd be no gondolier to row us through the lagoon, but she said she was just as happy to simply sit. I helped her into the swan gondola, and when we all went to the bench at the back, the front of the boat seemed to lift, like the swan was waking and about to stretch its bent neck.

Cecily took Doxie from the bottom of the bag, and the baby squealed a little, her voice skipping across the still water. Doxie drifted back to sleep, my finger in her grip. I ran my thumb over the soft skin of her knuckles. Cecily said, "I wouldn't have blamed you if you'd got tired of waiting for us tonight." Then she said, "I think I was half hoping I'd be too late."

I leaned in close. "Why would you half hope for something like that?" I said.

"Because I want nothing to do with you," she said, her voice a whisper.

"You're breaking my heart," I whispered back. I pushed a lock of her hair aside so that I could kiss her ear. She let me. I then unbuttoned a button of her lace collar, and I kissed her throat. She put her hand to my chest, to feel my fast heart, and she smiled at its telltale rattling around. "I'm worried," she said.

I put my hand over her hand on my chest. "About what?"

"That your heart's going to give out."

"Let it," I said.

Cecily ran her thumb over a drop of perspiration on Doxie's forehead, wiping it away as it rolled toward her eye. Doxie's pale hair was dark with sweat, the curls matted to her skin.

"Oh," I said, remembering the handkerchief. I took the box from beneath the bench, and I undid the ribbon for her, and opened the lid. "I saw Pearl today," I said. "Like I promised. She set me right on the spelling of your name. I almost bought you a hankie with an *S* on it."

"You just can't stop talking about Pearl, can you?" she said, her voice light. She only glanced at the embroidered initial before plucking the hankie away from the tissue paper to dab Doxie's sweaty head.

"Sure I can," I said. "Watch me."

She touched the hankie to her own forehead. Then she held it to her throat. She said, "Does this town *always* suffocate everybody to death?"

"Every summer," I said. "No survivors."

"I wouldn't have come out to meet you at all," she said, "but it was too hot in our room. She wouldn't sleep." She moved Doxie into my arms, and I sat bolt upright, afraid of even letting the baby's head loll an inch. It seemed that the slightest bit of jostling and her baby bird bones would crack. I'd not held many babies in my life, but I became expert in an instant. Doxie whimpered a little, then quieted as I situated her head softly in the crook of my arm. I tugged her collar down from her chin so she could breathe easy. "Walk me home?" she said.

"Already?" I said.

"It's not a short walk," she said.

The fairgrounds were never empty, not even in the hours past midnight. Workers patched cracks and hammered and pasted and untangled wires. They touched up the paint on columns and statues, and watered the flowers. Maybe it took a whole army of workers working late to keep the walls and angels' wings from falling in.

For all I knew, putting Doxie in my arms was part of a plot to stop me from asking Cecily questions. I lagged, afraid of tripping over my own feet. I tried to keep my stride smooth so as not to bounce the baby awake. And we fell far behind Cecily, who seemed to have become oblivious to us, as she walked ahead at a wicked pace, swinging the carpetbag at her side.

The Fair's architects, perhaps with an eye toward mystery and intrigue and midnight gondola rides stolen across the lagoon, had riddled the tall walls with secret doors and gates—or maybe they just wanted the workers sneaking in and out, so the Fair could seem maintained by magic. We rats of the underground had already found many of the secret entrances. Cecily pushed at the door concealed behind a trellis of grapevine. We then walked across the lot, and into the dark streets.

Cecily got so far ahead, into the shadows, I worried I'd lose her.

But I didn't want to call out and risk waking Doxie. It wasn't that the girl needed sleep—she slept all the time, for hours and hours in the incubator. I kept quiet because I simply liked the idea of her so peaceful in my arms. And I was hypnotized watching her as I cradled and rocked her. Doxie was an artist of sleep. A master at it. A sleeping beauty. A somnambulist. With such plump, pink cheeks, how could anyone but a great actress convince the fairgoers she was a premature infant, at risk of breathing her last? They all gathered around her glass bassinet to watch her live another minute, then another minute more.

CECILY WAS LIVING in a fine-looking boardinghouse of two floors, with a long porch and a whitewashed fence, in a neighborhood that slept through the night, unlike my own, which rattled with thieves and drunkards in its alleys at any hour. But the Silk & Sawdust Players had infested the place, building nests of costumes and props. Hanging from the branches of the tree in the yard were cages of trained birds. The empty back and front of a two-man horse costume was deflated on the lawn, as if the horse had sloughed off its skin and left it behind. The skeleton of an old-fashioned hoopskirt sat near the rosebushes.

Cecily waited for me at the front gate. "We call it the *pensione*," Cecily said, trilling the word in a foreign way, even fluttering her lashes. "It means 'hotel' in Italian, I think."

There were actors and actresses, some sleeping, some sleepless, on the porch, on the porch roof, on the grass, some smoking, some drinking, some tossing lit firecrackers, some getting firecrackers tossed at them.

"Ol' Dox has to work tomorrow in the live-baby exhibit," Cecily said, taking the girl from my arms. "It's easy money, so I hate to have her miss another day. But I'm guessing *I* have the day off now. The Chamber of Horrors is still smoldering." I kissed the baby's forehead, and Cecily's cheek, and we made plans to meet in front of the incubator exhibit at eleven in the morning. Cecily and I would spend the day together.

"Now run away quick," Cecily said. "Mrs. Margaret might still be awake." She reached up to pull at a curl at my forehead and to let it spring back. "And she *sure* don't like the looks of you." Cecily then turned and left me, and I could have spent hours watching her with her baby, and listening to the lullaby she hummed. She carried Doxie with one arm, as if the child weighed no more than a bag of sugar.

I LEFT OSCAR at the Empress the next morning. On my way to the Fair by streetcar, in my freshly tailored lilac suit from Brandeis, I rolled up the trouser cuffs an inch or two more to show off the snakeskin slippers I'd got on credit to go with the suit. I wore a necktie of green silk and a straw boater with a yellow hatband. The streetcar passed so close to a garden wall, I was able to reach out and pluck a pink-lipped snapdragon from a pot, and I stuck its stem behind my ear.

When I got to the incubator exhibit, Doxie was tucked into her booth, but Cecily was nowhere. I looked inside and breathed on the glass. I wrote *Hello* backward, with my finger, through the fog. I longed to spring her from her prison, but she looked so content. Too content? Maybe she wasn't acting after all. Were all those pipes and tubes pumping in some kind of gas? And as I looked to the top of the cabinet, to watch the lift and fall of a coil, I saw a little swan folded from paper.

I took the swan into the palm of my hand. I hated the idea of undoing all the paper's twists and folds, but I could tell that something was written within—letters slipped from the folds and out onto the wings. When I first began to dismantle the bird, I thought I might be able to carefully follow its construction and perhaps return it to its form later. But with just a tug at the bird's beak and an untwisting of its neck, I lost all sense of the swan's design.

Ferret,

Don't you already miss my little paper swan? I can put it back together for you, if you'd like. An actress who plays a geisha in the Japanese tea garden taught me how to fold it.

I can't spend the day with you after all, but you have no choice but to forgive me. The girl in the Flying Waltz fell when her wires snapped, and she broke both legs and an elbow, so I have a new job. Unlucky her, lucky me, I guess. They say the wires are perfectly fine. It was a freakish accident unlikely to repeat. So I'll be spending all day learning the ropes (hee-hee). Don't tell anyone that I told you it's all a trick—we're to look like we simply took wing. The wires are attached to the straps and springs of a corset under my gown. Come watch me practice—it's the little blue theater at the end of the midway, the one with the dome.

Cecily-with-a-C

I'd never before noticed the blue theater, but the midway grew every day, inching past its fences, threatening to spill into the river. It was becoming stranger and stranger all summer long, with new shows up in a matter of minutes and old ones falling just as fast. While the Grand Court could fool you into thinking it was all marble and stone, the midway was marzipan melting in a candy shop window.

A banner that stretched across the dome of the blue theater promised *The Flying Waltz & the Waltzing Dwarves*, and sure enough, the hall was full of folks shorter than my hipbone. Women in their underthings sorted through trunks full of child-size ball gowns, and men polished their shoes or practiced their steps. Others rushed around as if the curtain were scheduled to rise any minute.

"When's the first show?" I asked a woman who sat on a trunk lid to unashamedly roll a purple stocking up her bare leg, her underskirt hiked up to her hips. She pointed her toes, lifting her foot high, and she rolled the stocking so slowly, it was as if her little leg was a mile long.

Despite her languid movements, she opened her eyes wide at my question. "Oh don't remind me!" she said. "It's only two days away! Only two days."

"Only two days" carried through the hall, all the others repeating the phrase, passing it from person to person, sending it across the room like an echo. They hurried their steps a beat.

The theater had only a stage and a piano and was otherwise bare. Even its floors were dirt. Either the seats had not arrived or they weren't arriving at all, the audience expected to stand.

"How long's it going to take you to look up?" came Cecily's voice, dropping from overhead. I looked into the arch of the dome and Cecily hovered above, smiling down at me, wiggling her legs. The dome was lined with mirrors and dotted with lamps, giving her pale dress a shimmer and sparkle.

"I'm getting dizzy just watching you," I said.

"Go up on the stage," she said. "Silas and the boys will help you get strapped in. Then you can come dance with me."

"Oh, no, no. I can't," I said. "I'm afraid of heights."

"No, you're not," she said. She spun herself around, circling and circling. "No one's afraid of heights. That's just something people say."

"No, no, I am," I said. "As a matter of fact, I wish you'd come down. And not go back up."

"The fear's all in your head, Ferret."

"Well, yes, it is," I said. "Where else does fear go?"

Some of the dancing dwarves were suddenly upon me, tugging at my trousers and the sleeves of my suit coat, pushing and pulling. "It's nothing to be afraid of," one of them said.

"No, nothing at all," said someone else. "It's not even real. She's not really flying. It's all a trick."

I said, "I know, it's not that, I just . . . ," but somehow I allowed them to rustle me to the stage to truss me up in a harness and belts. Silas, it seemed, was a little man in a felt cap, and he stood on a ladder to remove my jacket and to buckle leather straps to my shoulders, attaching me to thin wires that led to a track in the ceiling.

I didn't want to look cowardly. "It's all in my head, it's all in my head," I chanted to myself, concentrating only on the sounds of the words. But the chanting didn't help. I felt a shot of panic, my face dripping with sweat. Just as I said, once again, "I can't," I did. I was. Up in the air. A group of stagehands as little as all the others turned the crank that tightened the wires that lifted me near the arches of the dome.

My stomach felt like it was lifting even higher than I was and twisting inside me. If I'd been able to catch a single breath and find a single word, I'd have begged for help.

Cecily swam toward me, kicking her legs, fanning her arms. She took my hands and pulled me to the center of the track that ran straight across the room. The dome arched above us. "See?" she said. "I've cured you of your fears."

"No," I said. "I'm still scared."

Cecily rolled her eyes at me. "What, exactly, are you afraid of?" she said.

"Falling," I said.

"We all could fall," she said, spinning around and around and away from me. Overhead, her wires were attached to a contraption of propeller blades and wheels that worked along the track. I tried to swim toward her, swinging my arms and legs, but only moved backward and only an inch or two. She danced over to me and around me, pulling me into her arms, taking the lead, waltzing me in circles.

"So where's your dance partner?" I said.

"Sleeping off a drunk," she said. "When his partner fell yesterday, it rattled him."

"I imagine so," I said. I looked down, and my stomach jumped again. I closed my eyes tight.

"Don't worry," she said. "It was a simple fix, they tell me."

"You look beautiful," I said, when I could open my eyes again. She lifted my arm to spin around and beneath it, as if there were no wires to tangle.

"You always say that," she said. "But this time it is true." She backed away to show off the dress. It was one she'd made, when she'd danced onstage once before. The sheer fabric, she said, was something called white illusion. And looking through the gown you saw another gown beneath, one of "chameleon silk," she said. When she spun for me again, the lights that bounced around and off the mirrors caught up in that silk, shifting the colors from pink to blush to blue, then back again.

Someone sat down at the piano below and began to play for us. The piano player was then joined by a woman with a fiddle and a man with a cello, and Cecily took me in her arms. At each shoulder was a muslin rose that sparkled with the crushed glass she'd dusted on the petals.

"I didn't even know you could dance," I said. I was starting to understand my way around the wires, and the harness, and I was able to follow Cecily's lead as we waltzed along the track, our feet kicking around each other, but gracefully in rhythm.

"How *would* you know?" she said. "We're strangers. You don't know anything about me."

"So then tell me something," I said.

"There's nothing to tell," she said.

I loved listening for the rustling of her body, her elbows, her legs, hidden and moving beneath the silk and skirts.

"How'd you learn to dance?" I asked.

"From the other candy factory girls," she said. In New York City, she told me, where she'd lived before taking to the fair circuit, she dipped orange peel in chocolate in a chilled room. "Even in the summertime I went to work in a fur cap. And some nights, when the other girls weren't worn out from the long day, we went to the Hans'1 and

Gret'l, a dance hall uptown. See, what you did was"—and she slipped away from me to dance alone—"you started dancing with one of the other girls, then a couple of gents would break in, and you'd dance with the man you got, if he was halfway handsome." And here she returned to me, and we held each other close and turned on our wheels. "And if you were lucky, he took you to the saloon after and bought you a bowl of turtle soup or something."

The tinny music below swelled into something dramatic, as if a whole orchestra had joined in, and Cecily and I matched it with our steps. I pulled her in so close and so sudden, she shuddered. She then followed my movements, my hips pushing hers this way, then that, my legs scissoring around her skirts. We rushed from one end of the track to the other, the flounce of her gown flowing around us. I held her right hand in my left one and I felt her grip tighten, squeezing, and we rushed the waltz more, fearless, testing the wires and the wheels of the track.

"And where'd *you* learn how to dance?" she whispered in my ear.

"The girl shop," I whispered back. "The whorehouse." She put her head to my neck and buried her laughter in my collar. "It was legitimate," I said, and I laughed too. "It was a job, even. I got paid. I was fifteen. Anna Wilson, the madam, taught me all the steps so that the girls could practice on me, and they could invite their gentlemen to dance and seem ladylike. Anna fancied herself running a finishing school."

"I hate to know how you got paid," she said.

"The girls would only *dance* with me," I said. "That was all. They thought I was a kid."

"You *were* a kid," she said.

"I was never a kid," I said.

"Did you even steal a kiss, ever?" she said.

"Sure," I said, "kisses I got."

Our dancing had slowed as the music had trickled away to nothing. She leaned her head back to squint at my face, summing me up.

She put a thumb to my lower lip. "They're kind of irresistible," she said. "Those lips."

"So don't resist them," I said. And so she didn't. She put her lips to mine, and we kissed. Up to then I'd felt foolish to be so in love with someone I'd known so little. But the kiss, as kisses do, changed everything.

But the kiss stopped before it was meant to end, as I was dragged away from her, the wires pulling me back so fast I thought I was falling after all. I rocked forward and faced the ground. I felt that twisting in my gut again. My arms grabbed at the air. My heart sped. But I was still attached to my wires, and was only rushing back along the track. When I was above the stage, I was lowered, and I was unable to land on my feet. My legs buckled and I fell to my knees. I gasped, and though my hands and knees were on the boards, and I'd survived, I still thought myself doomed.

A man my height grabbed me by the harness and lifted me like a puppeteer, setting me upright, and he began undoing my belts and straps. His hands seemed to wander when he got to the clasps near my crotch. "I beg your pardon," I said, lowering my voice to a gruff scratch as I pushed his hands away.

"I beg *your* pardon," he said, glaring at me, lowering his voice too. "You're in my harness. Get out of it."

Once I was freed of the rigging, I just wanted to be back in it. I felt severed.

I looked up to Cecily as I walked toward the door. She gave me a smile and a shrug, and the shrug somehow worked something loose, dropping her an inch with a jerk. My heart stopped again, and I stepped forward, my arms out, as if I might be able to catch her. But she stayed in the air. "A wire must've caught," she said, shrugging again. "Meet me out front at five," she said. "We'll walk the midway."

I nodded, but I worried I should stay. I wanted to demand she get down. "Go," she said, sensing my hesitance. "You're making me nervous."

. . .

CECILY SOMEHOW SURVIVED her day of waltzing, and I would say we made a dashing couple as we strolled the Grand Court that evening, her in her gown of white illusion and me in my lilac suit. But she wouldn't let me buy her a fine dinner or even a glass of wine. "We'll eat our supper like hummingbirds," she said, and we moved from booth to booth within the Manufactures Building, sampling evaporated apricots and strawberries drenched in clover honey. We had some canned lobster on crackers, and some Chinook salmon, and a few spoonfuls of cured figs. We had ox tongue and tulip tea. We had a few tastes of orange wine and of something they called sparkling Scotch ale that rumbled our stomachs.

Back on the midway, we visited the tent with the whale—a five-hundred-year-old beast the size of a ship. We walked its entire fifty-foot length. With Cecily distracted by the stench of chemicals and decay, I suggested hiring Doxie myself. "What does she get for a day in the incubator?" I said. "What if I paid her the same rate to help me with my act?"

Cecily held her hankie to her nose like a railroad marauder. She lowered it to say with some irritation, "What could she possibly do?"

"Well," I said, "I could set her up in the pram and put a little bonnet on her head. I could throw my voice and make her say funny things. She could cuss or something. Something babies don't do. Folks would love it." The idea of it all seemed to be wrinkling Cecily's brow with worry, but instead of shutting my mouth, I felt compelled to say more and more, the suggestion sounding worse and worse with every word. I'd only meant for the idea to show my affection and my concern.

"But why?"

"It would get her out of that glass box," I said.

"She doesn't mind the incubator," Cecily said. "She doesn't mind it at all. And she can't be out in the hot sun all day."

"I would keep her in the shade," I said, but when she shook her head and furrowed her brow more, I said nothing else.

Outside Cecily wouldn't speak. She only nodded politely and smiled a tight smile at anything I said. I begged her to sit for a silhouette, and this seemed to cheer her up. But in the artist's studio, atop a stool, a blast of light casting the shadow of her profile large against the wall, she had time to weigh the slight. Looking at her shadow, I saw her chin quivering. She lowered her head.

"I need to leave," she said.

The silhouette maker said, "I'm nearly done." He snipped his scissors through the black paper, even cutting around the roses at her shoulder.

"What's wrong, Cecily?" I said. She didn't answer.

As soon as the light was turned away and her shadow vanished, Cecily stood from the stool and headed for the door. I took the silhouette from the silhouette maker's hand before he could paste it on white paper and place it in a frame.

I caught up with Cecily on the midway. "You think I'm a terrible mother," she said.

"No, no, no, no, no, no, no, no, no, no," I said. "No, no." I took her elbow and turned her to me. I held the silhouette in my palm. Cecily looked at it, but I don't think she saw it. She wasn't thinking of it at all. "I think you're a wonderful mother," I said. "That's why I want to help."

"Help?" she said, snapping at me. "Oh, there are plenty of people who want to help *me*. I'm helpless." She then stepped close, her voice dropping to a fierce whisper. "I'm a woman with *circumstances*. There's all kinds of help for the likes of me. If I want to auction Doxie off, there's people all over Omaha who'll pay more than you."

"Cecily, I'm sorry," I said. "I wasn't . . . I didn't mean . . ."

Cecily put her hankie to her mouth again. She breathed deep. She calmed down. She lowered the handkerchief and spoke softly. "Do you know of a Reverend A. Foltz?" she said. She began to walk away slowly, and I walked alongside. I told her I didn't know any minister by any name. Not a one. "You'd think he was sweet on me. He shows up at the boardinghouse every Monday morning, in a rat-gray carriage coat, no matter how hot it is. Mrs. Margaret and me, we don't even know how he found out about Doxie. He brings me little pamphlets with little sermons in them. He manages something called the Child Rescue Institute. He rescues babies from their own mothers. He's paving his way to heaven with all the little souls he saves. I bet the bastard reaches in and yanks them out of the womb."

I now remembered hearing of this reverend and his rescue. It was easy to get him confused with all the other Pied Pipers of Omaha, snatching babies from their cribs. A man like Reverend Foltz needed children to fill his little schools for the unfortunate, so he could add on towers and turrets, new wings and hallways. He longed to fill gymnasiums and natatoriums with all his saved babies. The bigger the academy, the bigger the bronze statue they'd someday insist on casting in his image. He probably lunched every day with all the fallow-wombed old ladies with more money than sense. The very idea of him at Cecily's door, lurking like a hungry undertaker, quickened my pulse. "Maybe I should stop by the boardinghouse myself on Monday morning," I said. "I could give Reverend Foltz a sermon of my own."

The suggestion, and my voice quivering with rage, seemed to please her. She smiled but shook her head. "There you go again," she said. "Trying to save me."

I looked at the silhouette in my hand and studied the uncanny resemblance. It looked exactly like her. And I thought of my own mother, of course, and my own sad little self and how I'd once decided, for a few months at the age of eight, that I was the secret son of Sister Patience, the orphanage nun. I'd studied her face for my nose, my eyes. And I'd managed to convince myself she spoke to me in a code I could crack. I memorized every word she said to me throughout each day, and at night I wrote it all down. I puzzled over it, substituting one letter for another, scrambling the words around, seeking a confession. That fantasy faded, but later I sought my identity in the spoils of my thievery. Whenever I lifted a purse I sat in the alley and weighed the value of even its most worthless objects, learning about the lady's character from the perfume she wore or the pills she took. A piece of hard candy in a strawberry shape. A wedding ring tucked away for an afternoon. My every fiction told the story of my mother somehow.

"Why doesn't your old automaton get after the minister?" I said. "She's not shy about strangling a gentleman."

"The only thing in the world that scares Mrs. Margaret is religion," she said. "She's had a long hard life, poor thing. She's been damned to hell so many times, she hates to tempt fate."

And later that night, in the beer garden, I found myself almost grateful for Mrs. Margaret, and her devotion, as I sat and watched Cecily waiting. Cecily wasn't ready yet to tell the old woman about me, so while she drank wine with the Waltzing Dwarves, I stayed at the opposite end of the garden with August and Rosie and the anarchists. But I couldn't take my eyes off her, and she couldn't take her eyes off me.

When Mrs. Margaret swooped in like an old crow, in a black bolero jacket complete with a lapel of half-molted black feathers, carrying that carpetbag, I hated not following them when they left. Mrs. Margaret could learn to like me, I was sure of it. We weren't so very different. Things had never been easy for me either.

August told me to open my hand, and he shook into my palm a paper mermaid. "I bought it at the fortune-teller's booth," he said. "It's sensitive to your temperament." The paper's coating allowed it to respond to the palm's sweat and salt.

"That seems ominous," I said when the mermaid curled itself into a tight little tube.

August read the chart on the back of the envelope to properly diagnose. "Passionate," he said, with a dramatic sigh. *Proof*, I thought. Even a cheap novelty knows. Had the mermaid curled on the sides, or flipped over, it would have read as "fickle" or "false."

17.

CECILY LAY BACK on a chamomile lawn. It was late morning, the sun hot, and August had brought a tea party right to us, into the gardens behind the Horticulture Building. We sat in the shade of topiary trimmed into the shapes of sea monsters attacking sailing ships. The gardens expanded north into the miles of empty fields behind the New White City, making this spot nearly silent but for the squawking of hawks circling overhead. The Fair sounded as if it might be miles away. Above the muffled noise of its calliopes and marching bands were the click-clack of a croquet mallet and the bubble and slosh of a stone fountain. We could even hear the squeaky turn of lawn mower blades as an old man cut the grass.

"This is how I would look," she said, "if it had been me." She closed her eyes and twisted her body, bending her legs in an awkward pose. The theater of the Flying Waltz had closed before it opened, and she was jobless once again. This time it was the gentleman's wires that had snapped. He had somehow managed to not break a bone when he'd hit the dirt, but he nonetheless sought a lawsuit.

I stood to help arrange Cecily's collapse. I stepped over and around her, composing. I turned a wrist and an elbow. I pushed her fingers into a fist. I removed a shoe, but just from her heel, leaving it clinging to her toes. I unbuttoned a button of her dress and pulled at a curl so it rested on her forehead. I rustled her dress—she'd decked herself out head to toe in cherries. There were red cherries and green stems in the pattern of her pink dress. Her red straw hat, tossed aside on the grass, was garlanded with wooden cherries and silk blossoms. She'd tied a red scarf around her waist.

August stood to critique my work. "I can't bear to look," he said, looking closely. "The terror is absolutely lifelike."

I positioned Oscar in the grass too, as if he'd been bent and broken from a fall, and I dropped to lie next to Cecily and to pose my own crippling. I kicked one leg over her legs and linked one arm with hers. The chamomile was soft and smelled like baked apples.

August attended to his tea party. He'd even packed a small samovar shaped like a keg, which he set up on his medicine trunk.

"What am I going to do now, Ferret?" she said. She looked past me, to the carriage I'd bought Doxie. Doxie reclined inside, under the shade of an umbrella of lace and ribbon. I'd come into a little money, with several literary assignments in recent days. Many people had employed me to write letters of complaint to the editors of the dailies. Everyone was afraid of the strangers invading our town to visit the Fair. *The Fair was intended to save us*, wrote Mrs. Mattie Ish, the chiropodist of Twenty-fourth Street, *but they'll kill us with all the illness they bring in from the outer reaches.* My clients complained about the overcrowding of the hotels and streetcars, of late-night noise and early-morning drunkards. *The city has doubled its number of thieves*, wrote Mrs. Pfeiffer, the phaeton-maker's wife of Leavenworth Street.

"You're an actress," I told Cecily, "so you'll act." I took her hand in mine and slipped into her palm a clipping. I'd bought an issue of the *Omaha World-Herald* that morning, to see if they'd run any of my letters of complaint, and had come across the advertisement for auditions. A play called *Heart of the White City*, a melodrama full of stunts and effects set in Chicago, was to premiere in the fall on the stage of the amphitheater on the Grand Court. Yes, the White City of the title was

Chicago's, not ours. Omaha's biggest spectacle was the story of some other town. *My dummy*, I thought, *would have a heyday with that.*

Needed: *A cast of hundreds*, the advertisement said.

August, listening in, leaned forward. "Speaking of actresses," he said, "Ferret told me you collect cigarette cards." He handed her two photographs—one of Sarah Bernhardt and another of the opera singer Adelina Patti. Patti wore a bridal gown and Cecily studied the picture. She turned the card to read the back. "She's Lucia di Lammermoor," August said. "She has a mad scene. There she is just before her dress gets bloody. I've heard that Patti licks the blade of her knife after she guts her groom."

August returned to his copper samovar and spooned crushed pine-cones into the base to fuel its flame. When he poured some hot water from the spigot into a china cup, the samovar hissed and squeaked. He dropped in a candied violet.

"Too hot for tea," I said.

"But that's why we drink it, isn't it?" he said. "And why we drink whiskey? And why we smoke like fiends? To work up a sweat to cool us off?"

"Nah, we just go crazy from the heat," I said. "We're just trying to cook ourselves from the inside out."

"I'd love some, please," Cecily said.

"A little honey, sugar?" he said. "A little sugar, honey?"

Cecily and August, pleased with themselves, both shot me cold glares of playful derision, casting me from their tea party. I lay back again, charmed by their conspiring against me.

As August sipped his tea, he said, "I actually *saw* Sarah Bernhardt as Camille, here in Omaha. Well, rather, I saw her *dressing* for *Camille*. I didn't have tickets to the show. I was fifteen and I stood across the street from Boyd's Opera House, with my opera glasses, just hoping for any glimpse of her. And there she was." He put the cup down, and seemed to lose himself in the dream of it all. "There she was, in the window of an upstairs dressing room. In the heat of the early evening, by the open window. Naked. Naked as sin. I hadn't expected to be lucky enough to see her at all, let alone without a stitch on. It felt like some miracle from heaven. It was a message from God that I was a man with the gift of luck. And magic. I was a man who could aim my opera glasses, and Sarah Bernhardt would appear naked in front of them."

"How'd she look?" Cecily asked.

"Well," he said, nodding toward the card in her lap, "just like *that* but without clothes."

I picked up the card, and I gave it a sniff. "Pretty," I said. "It smells like roses."

August sighed. "It would, to *you*," he said. He looked to Cecily and rolled his eyes. He leaned in toward her to conspire some more. "It's essence of Rhine violets, of course."

"Of course," Cecily said.

Afterward, August wrapped up his tea things in silk scarves and put them in a box, and the box in his trunk. He put the leftover scraps of scones in his pockets, to drop them into the lagoon later, to feed the river fish. "The fish in the lagoon are starving," he said. "Meanwhile the foreign fish in the ponds here probably dine on anchovies and caviar."

"The river fish oughta picket," I said.

He wheeled his trunk away, to leave the garden, to go sell his medicine at the Wild West Show. "He loves you," Cecily said, as I helped her up from the grass.

"And I love him," I said. "He's the dearest friend I've ever had." I picked up Oscar and brushed off his coat, then returned him to my back.

"But he loves you differently than you love him," she said. I handed her her red straw hat, and she situated it atop her hair, which she'd kept coiled up into a Psyche knot. Even her hatpin had a cherry at the head of it.

"Do you mean to say," I said, taking the handle of Doxie's buggy, "that he loves me the way I love you?" I'd said it hoping to sound debonair but immediately felt devious for using August's affection in this way. But once I said it, I could only wait. My heart seemed to thump harder, louder, every second she stayed silent.

She paused at my declaration. She slowed her step. She clicked her tongue as if about to speak, but then didn't speak at all. Finally she said, "You don't love me," but she said it teasingly, girlish. And once again she insisted, "You don't know me."

"You don't have to know a girl to love her," I said. "That's the funny thing about love."

She put her arm in mine as I pushed the buggy toward the lane lined by rosebushes. I said, "This could be us every day."

"This isn't even us to begin with," she said.

There was a trick I'd always longed to do, to impress a lady in a garden. I'd come prepared. In my pocket were aniline crystals in a corked vial, and as Cecily looked across to the caged alligator near the garden's fountain, I dusted the crystals across the petals of a white rose, then brushed them away with the cuff of my sleeve.

"This is a magic rosebush," I told her. "Lend me your perfume."

Cecily took from her chatelaine purse a scent bottle shaped like a pistol that fit in her palm. It was yet another dainty thing inspired by the war. The thin barrel of the gun was filigree and silver, and she unscrewed it from the crystal handle that contained the extract of sweet pea. I splashed the perfume against the rose, and the drops splattered and seeped, turning the rose red.

"How's the trick work?"

"No trick," I said. I broke the stem from the bush and I bowed as I handed her the flower. "Magic."

She held the bloom to her nose but drew her head back quick, her nose scrunched up. "It smells like rotten fish," she said, smelling the aniline. And with that I shot up a spark from the magic ring of flint I wore. The spark fell on the rose, and the petals went up in a fast flame. Cecily dropped the burning rose on the cobblestone path.

She lifted her skirt an inch or two and tapped out the flame with the toe of her shoe. I explained the particulars of the trick as we continued with our walk, but I don't think she listened. She read the back of one of the cigarette cards August gave her. "Do you know what chemicals might color my hair?" she said. The opera singer, she explained, had bolts of red in her tresses.

GETTING LITTLE Doxie to her job at the live-baby exhibit that day was a complicated business. In an alley between buildings, Cecily switched Doxie from the pram to the carpetbag, then went off to meet Mrs. Margaret, who would alone escort Doxie to her shift in the incubator. Though Cecily checked in on Doxie often every day, she never spoke to the nurses or gave any indication she was anyone but a disinterested party. Mrs. Margaret did all the dealings. "They don't ask Mrs. Margaret any questions," Cecily said when she returned to me, childless. "She's too terrifying." I'd been enjoying sitting on a bench waiting, the pram parked in front of me. When people peeked into the buggy and only saw Oscar where a baby should be, they cast me a disdainful glare, like they'd fallen victim to a prank. I would just wink at them, tip my hat, and give them a polite *Good day to you.* "But if anyone suspected Doxie belonged to an unmarried woman," Cecily continued, "they might get that itch people get when they're itching to save something. Mrs. Margaret says Reverend Foltz of the Child Rescue Institute stops in every day to satisfy his lust for the destitute."

Cecily nervously chattered away, wringing her hands, as I escorted her to the auditions for *Heart of the White City* in the auditorium at the west end of the Grand Court. She so much wanted the audition to go well and to return to the stage. "Sometimes I think I'm only truly happy when I'm in the skin of someone else," she said.

We left the baby carriage parked just inside the theater door and I returned Oscar to my back. We stepped through a lobby so full of mirrors you couldn't avoid your own glance. A secretary at a desk—an old woman in a hat piled with real roses and thorny stems—eyeballed Cecily, scrutinizing her character.

"You're pretty," she said, but she wasn't extending a compliment. She was just summing her up. "Can you sing?"

"Oh, oh my, well, yes, I . . . I'd well . . . yes . . ." and she cleared her throat and began to trill the first few bars of a song that began "When the war is o'er."

"Not *now*," the old woman said, interrupting with a snap of disgust. "You audition in *there*." She nodded toward the doors to the theater. "I'm just asking you. Can you sing?"

"You just heard me sing," Cecily said.

"This is a very, very, very important production," she said, rifling through papers. "It'll be the most extravagant Omaha has ever seen." The theater had been built to house only this one play and it would be torn down when the play closed. The stage and its mechanisms were vastly elaborate. Real fires were to be put out by real water from tanks pulled by real horses. There would be a hot-air balloon and a locomotive on a track.

The woman handed Cecily a page of script—a snippet of a monologue delivered by Heart, the melodrama's damsel in distress. *When I was a little girl growing up plucking chickens in the fields of Illinois*, Heart says, *I never dreamed of a place like this. At the very top of the Ferris wheel, I could look out on those fields, so colorful, like a patchwork quilt.*

As I sat in the theater itself, as Cecily stepped toward the lip of the stage to read her few lines, I got all caught up in the thought of her as the star of the show. The theater had pillowed seats of velvet, and the walls were covered in deep-blue silk that was flocked and rucked to resemble a restless night sky, the stars stitched with silver thread. The gilded chandelier overhead was strung with pink crystals. The stage was flanked by columns with pink veins crackling through the granite. The theater looked like the inside of a jeweled egg. Everything was in place but the machinery of the show itself—the melodrama would require multiple stages that revolved on wheels; it would be rigged with tanks for pyrotechnics, and hydraulics for the spin of the Ferris wheel. Even the roof was rumored to crank open, as if the producers had employed the moon to run through a month of phases in only an hour or two.

But for now there was nothing on stage but construction and framework, and Cecily strained to lift her voice above the hammers and saws. She stood up on the balls of her feet, stretched her neck forth, opened her mouth wide. But her words fell short of even the third row where the director sat, the man leaning forward, trying his best to listen. I sat up straight myself, stretching my own neck, as if I could somehow help her voice carry farther.

When she finished, a command thundered up from several rows back, from the far reaches of the theater. "Again!" a man shouted, and when I looked to see who spoke, I saw Wakefield. He stood, raising his silver claw, gesturing broadly with it, summoning her voice forth. Strapped to his head were binoculars that scoped out from his eyes. He appeared to be wearing a silk smoking jacket with velvet lapels, and he held a pipe with an *S*-shaped stem. "Heart is . . ." he said, and then he paused, thinking. "Heart *is* a frail thing, it's true. She *would* speak so as not to be heard. Hers is a *gentle* nature. And the actress *must* communicate Heart's frailty. But she must do so as loud as she can. Heart's weak voice must bounce off the rafters. So, please . . . let Heart be heard." He then barked, "Try again!" while stabbing the air with his pipe.

Cecily nodded, she smiled, inspired, and she stepped forward, so close to the front of the stage I worried she'd tumble into the orchestra pit. Her feet were only half on the boards. She cleared her throat. She breathed in deep. And she read again.

Her voice was even softer than before. It sounded like she was speaking into a pillowcase. When she finished, she didn't even wait for Wakefield or the director or anyone to say anything. I don't think she even finished the sentence she was in the middle of. She stopped and walked to the stairs at the side of the stage, folding and folding the page of her script, making it smaller and smaller. Cecily kept twisting the page this way and that as she passed me. I grabbed her hat and ran to her side, and we walked up the aisle, past Wakefield, who only nodded politely. I had half a mind to sell him Oscar right then, right off my back, if it meant he'd give her a part, any part, in the play.

But I didn't have to sell anything. In the lobby, the secretary held out a sheet of paper with a list of the characters Cecily had been assigned in the mere minutes between her audition and our walk up the aisle. "You're lucky," the secretary said. "No lines to learn."

Cecily would not be playing Heart, but she had four different parts instead:

Factory Girl

Dance Hall Girl

Ferris Wheel Girl

Fire Victim

"You get fit for costumes next week," the secretary said, "and the week after that rehearsals start. And just because you're nothing but a face in the crowd, don't go thinking we won't notice if you don't show up." She eyed her up and down. "You'll be getting paid good enough for what little you do."

As we left the theater, I gave Cecily her hat. She strutted some as she walked alongside me, as I pushed the pram. "They just couldn't put the show on without me," she said, quite pleased.

"Of course they couldn't," I said.

I suggested we go fetch Doxie and spend the afternoon in celebration. "They won't unlock her cabinet for us," Cecily said. "They don't know I'm Doxie's mother, remember?"

"We'll steal her," I said, and she clapped her hands. She loved the idea of kidnapping her own infant.

At the cottage that housed the incubator exhibit, I pushed the carriage, with Oscar tucked inside, down the cobblestone lane. Fortunately there was only one nurse on duty, so Cecily engaged her in conversation, her sea-green paper parasol open, spinning around on her shoulder, doing her best to hide me as I picked the incubator's lock without any special picklock—I used to sell French pocketknives equipped with a variety of tools, and I still carried one with me always: it held within it a cigar cutter, a glove buttoner, a tin opener. The ear-cleaning spoon proved the perfect key, and I managed to turn all the lock's tumblers.

"I'm a disciple of the Reverend Foltz," Cecily told the nurse, her quiet voice serving her well in this particular performance. "And my heart goes out to these little lambs. Wherever will these children go when the Fair ends? What if I wanted to adopt the whole litter?" The nurse was made so fidgety by her questions, she stuttered and stalled and lowered her eyes, busying herself with the folding of diapers. I easily lifted Doxie from her coop and slipped her beneath the blanket to cozy up with Oscar.

IT WAS A LOST, lazy afternoon and evening. We stood in line for a ride in the swan gondola, but the thought of sharing our private yacht with other fairgoers, in the bright light of day, made the whole endeavor a little less appealing, so we stepped away. Instead, we nestled in the swan bench on the merry-go-round of the midway, in among the carousel horses with their blue manes and bared teeth. The ride proved to be Doxie's favorite, and for once she didn't nap. Her eyes wide, she watched all the color spin around her, and she seemed to grab for the sunlight that sparked on the carousel's mirrors.

As I held Doxie, Cecily held Oscar across her knees, his head dangling off the side of her lap.

On one of the last of our many spins around the carousel, I swore I glimpsed Wakefield watching. Not only did I think I saw him standing in the road, a cigar between his silver fingers, but I thought I saw the woman with the piglet too. The woman—who I'd assumed to be his wife or his mistress—wasn't easy to miss; she wore a red dress, and the netting of a red veil across her face. But when our swan swam back around, they were gone.

November 20, 1898

Dear Cecily,

When I think back, I think I see Wakefield everywhere we ever were. In my memory, he can't keep his eyes off us. Wasn't he in the Indian camp as we watched a girl braid together a corn shuck doll for Doxie? Didn't he eavesdrop on our fortunes as we got our palms read? I can just see him aiming a telescope at us from a rooftop as we lay back in the grass to gaze at stars.

Tonight, on the farm, it seems colder than it is. I stand at the hearth as I write this letter, with the mantel as my writing desk. I don't leave my room often, but Hester made a cane for me. It's a polished branch of old gnarled wood. I worry that my leg, when the cast is broken off, will look just as rotten and twisted as this cane. My leg hurts as much as it ever did. The cast is crippling me, bending my knee the wrong way, chipping away at any bones left unbroken. I haven't seen a doctor. Hester doesn't trust them. So I don't trust them either. I only trust the Old Sisters Egan. I want my world to shrink more and more, so that all that's left is this farm.

I don't want to die, but I don't want to walk among the living.

I can see your absence everywhere, in everything. I could look at a rose, but instead of seeing the rose, I would see you not holding it. I look at the moonlight, and there you are, not in it.

Ferret

18.

THE SILK & SAWDUST PLAYERS slept even in the hallways of the boardinghouse and sometimes three to a bed. Cecily, with Doxie on the way when they had all left Nashville, had become sick from the winter trip up the river, so they'd given her her own room at the boardinghouse to thaw out. She kept the room, even after Doxie was born, and sweetened it up with touches of her own. The room had faded yellow wallpaper patterned with hornets on gray roses, so she tacked up covers of fashion magazines, illustrated with women in winter coats, and she hung a bright-blue ukulele on the wall above the bed. She tucked the cigarette cards into the edges of the mirror of a vanity. She made a chair from an overturned washtub, with embroidered pillows for a cushion. Behind a silk screen painted with pink apples was Doxie's crib, rented from the landlady.

Before rehearsals were to begin for *Heart of the White City*, Cecily decided to get her hair dyed red. The sword swallower's wife in the Turkish Village of the midway sold me a tin of henna and dried indigo leaf, and she wrote out instructions in broken English. After everyone else in the boardinghouse fell asleep, we snuck downstairs to the bathroom. Cecily left the door to her room open so we could hear Doxie when she cried. The little girl had her days and nights mixed up; she slept all of every day and fussed often after dark. In the hall, we heard the thundering of Mrs. Margaret's snores. "Mrs. Margaret's still so furious with me," Cecily said, "she has to take a sleeping tonic at night."

Doxie had been fired from her job as a living baby due to our mischief. I was relieved—I knew next to nothing about babies, but it seemed to me she was getting too old for that box. And the whole incident had led Cecily to confess our love affair to Mrs. Margaret. I still avoided the woman in the days after, sneaking in and out of Cecily's room, in and out of windows, over eaves and down rain pipes, after dark and before dawn. And though I wasn't pleased by Mrs. Margaret's violent determination to keep Cecily all to herself, I understood it. She wanted Cecily to trust only her. Mrs. Margaret, after all, had helped with Doxie's birth, staying right there at Cecily's side, holding her hand, every minute of all the many hours it took for an elderly midwife to coax Doxie out into that little room at the boardinghouse. It seemed that Mrs. Margaret had often been at Cecily's side when Cecily would have otherwise been all alone. And for that, Cecily would forgive the old woman anything.

In the bathroom, Cecily and I stripped naked, then stepped into the tub, hoping for the water to cool us off. Cecily sat with her back to me. I poured half a bottle of prune brandy into her hair to clean it of its fats and oils. Up in her room, I'd made a paste of the henna powder, mixing in a glass of red wine, some spoonfuls of paprika, and the juice of three lemons.

After I worked the henna into Cecily's hair, I touched her shoulder, where there was a tattoo of a heart. I had seen it before but had never asked about it. I now ran my fingers along the heart's curves and leaned forward to whisper in her ear. "How'd you get this?" I said.

"Doxie's father was a tattooist in Nashville," she said. "He worked the midway of the world's fair there, and sold tattoos for fifty cents in a striped tent. His name was Mercury."

"Did something happen to him?" I said.

Cecily sighed. "I hope so," she said. "But probably not. He tried to talk me into getting tattooed all over, and I was so in love I almost did.

It would have taken two months, me and him alone in his parlor, his eyes only on me. And when I was covered neck to boot in tattoos we would go on the road on our own."

I hated hearing she'd been in love once before me. But I only said, "I'd pay a buck to see that," and I kissed her shoulder.

"We had quite an awful act in mind," she said. "See, I'd pretend to be blind, and I would go on stage and tell the audience that I'd been nabbed by savages, and held captive, and tattooed, and then I would describe the tattoos, and how beautiful they were. Angels and doves and all that. But the audience would be horrified, because what was really on my skin would be fiercely ugly. Cross-eyed devils. A serpent with the mean eyes of a drunk. All the very worst things Mercury and me could think of. And after I left the stage, Mercury would get up there and beg the audience not to reveal the truth to me. 'Let her at least have this illusion, folks,' he'd say. And they'd be so full of pity, they'd give us all the change they could spare. And they would tell their friends about it, and they'd all line up to see how tragic I was."

"That's no kind of life," I said.

Cecily leaned back in my arms, her hair sticky with paste. We stayed that way until daylight, very softly singing every song we knew with the word *red* in the lyrics.

Once the morning's birds started up with their whistles, we followed the last instruction—a blast of sunlight to turn the hair hot. We grabbed our clothes and stepped lightly on the stairs to keep them from creaking. We crawled out the window of Cecily's room to sit on the roof of the back porch, me in only my underdrawers, and Cecily in a kimono patterned with sea horses. As Cecily ate a freckled pear, I read to her from one of the pamphlets the Reverend A. Foltz had left behind: *From Hell to Heaven, and How I Got There*, about how he had become a lush at the age of eight.

"'In early childhood,'" I read, mocking an evangelist's vain humility, my fingers a deep bloodred that wouldn't fade for days, "'I struck off to swim in a dark sea of sorrow whose sad waves ever beat over me.'"

July 1898

19.

WITH CECILY IN MY LIFE, and my mind on fatherhood, I often thought about how little I had otherwise. I combed my hair and shaved my chin by looking in a little shard of broken mirror propped up on a windowsill. *I don't want to still be telling jokes at the Empress at thirty*, I told my twenty-five-year-old self. And I could just see myself at thirty saying, *I don't want to still be at the Empress at forty.* And if I was still at the Empress at forty, I'd say, *Why didn't you kill yourself at twenty-five?*

I had long had ambitions for a larger theater, a bigger audience, perhaps traveling in a vaudeville circuit. *But what if I left the stage?* I wondered. What if I went to work in the offices of the *Omaha World-Herald*, to write obituaries and theater reviews? My letters to the editor were sometimes the liveliest pieces in the dailies. I'd recently read an article about the professional life of the literary hack—instead of writing correspondence, I could write articles for magazines, or poems and stories. I had it in my head that it would impress Cecily if I became dignified. If I became respectable, she would see how serious I was about her and Doxie.

"A hack can get twenty dollars for a thousand words," I told Cecily. We were at the Fair after one of her afternoon rehearsals, sitting in the replica of a restaurant of a White Star luxury liner, the cardboard waves of a fake sea bobbing up and down on a motor outside the porthole. A string quartet strummed some slow sonata in the corner. We sat on a settee at a marble-top table, Doxie in my lap in a dress I'd bought her with a gingham apron. She toothlessly gnawed on my thumb. "It don't even matter what the words are. Every word pays the same. I could easily write a thousand words about anything, even the proper knotting of neckties, which I don't know much of anything about at all."

We'd been served oysters soaked in a puddle of champagne in a seashell. Cecily swallowed an oyster and looked perplexed. "You're going to help people knot their neckties?"

"Is that what I said?" I said.

"No," she said, smiling. She dabbed at her mouth with a linen napkin. She nodded at my dummy, who sat propped up in a chair. "Look how sad you've made him."

And he had indeed looked sadder somehow, ever since I'd started thinking about selling him to Wakefield. I'd kept the invitation to Wakefield's masquerade ball all month long, having stuck it in the pocket of my winter coat hanging from a hook in my room. It was perhaps unseemly to be so attached to a doll. "He'll be fine on his own," I said. "He's the one with all the talent."

A waiter in a white jacket brought us the bottle of red wine we requested, and poured us each a glass. I asked him to bring more oysters. I was feeling flush already, with the thought of Wakefield's money and the possibility of legitimate work. A professional hack could make upwards of six thousand a year, according to the article I'd read.

Cecily leaned back in the settee with her glass of wine, slouching in the silk pillows. She looked perplexed again, squinting, like she was figuring math in her head. "It just seeeeeeems to meeeeee," she said, "well, how should I put this? It seems to me that if you quit ventriloquism to write about how to knot a necktie, you'll soon enough be writing about how to knot your own noose." She nodded her head sharply, pleased with what she'd come up with.

"I like that," I said. "That's clever. I'll buy it from you. I pay a penny a word."

"I'm quite serious," she said.

"I won't write about neckties then," I said. I put my hand on her neck and gently strangled. "I was just using neckties as an example."

"I was too," she said, putting her hand over mine.

"Why would I hang myself," I said, "if I was happier than I've ever been? I'd be taking good care of you and Doxie."

"And, see, that's what troubles me and ol' Dox," she said. "We don't like the sound of that at all. If *I* left the stage for *you*, I'd hate you with all my heart eventually."

"How could I ever hate the two of you," I said. I moved my hand up to brush a few strands of hair from her cheek. "And how could you ever hate me?"

"Let's not try to find out," she said sternly.

So I promised Cecily I'd not sell Oscar at the masquerade ball, and it was a promise that was easy to keep. I didn't want to part with him. But Cecily insisted we all go to the ball nonetheless. She had felt some affection toward Wakefield ever since the auditions, when he'd stood to give her advice. Though he hadn't given her the lead, he had seemed to believe, for those few moments at least, she might be perfect for the part. And she'd been flattered to end up with any role at all.

August fled to the Indian camp to buy feathers and ribbons for masks he would make us of satin and paper. And when the midway closed for the night, we rifled through the trunks in the wagon of the Silk & Sawdust Players parked behind the Chamber of Horrors. The building still seemed to smoke, casting a gray haze against the night, though the fire had been out for days and days. In the light of an oil lamp, we tried on costumes—all of us but Rosie, who would only go so far as to tie a bandana over his mouth, bandit-style.

"You're dancing on the graves of dead soldiers," he grumbled, not amused by Wakefield's plans to sink a toy battleship in the lagoon. Typically I'd join Rosie in his indignation, but I'd begun to think of myself as a man who'd come into some luck. And as a man of some luck, I'd come to think that luck might suit me after all.

Josephine, Rosie's ragtime girlfriend, wore Cecily's Marie Antoinette costume, the wig still collapsed and snarly from the storm of early June, the skirts still dirty and snagged. August tied a thin red ribbon around Josephine's throat.

"All the women of France wore red ribbons around their necks," he said, "after Marie Antoinette lost her head."

Pearl wore Chinese pajamas she bought off a man in the fan-tan den—roomy trousers and a long jacket patterned with golden tigers.

And Cecily, of course, was the most smashing of all, dressed as the enemy. She put on a red gown with pleats of yellow stripes, so when she walked she seemed to be waving the Spanish flag. She carried a spindly fan that looked a little war-battered itself, some of the torn black lace hanging loose from the fan's ivory ribs. August stuck a tall comb into the top of her hair and draped from it a black veil that fell over her shoulders and down her back. She wore no mask but pinned the veil up to cover her face so only her eyes were showing.

We could hear the party long before we reached it, and we picked up our step to get there quicker. From atop the roof, a man with a high-pitched voice started the evening off by singing the tune "After the Ball" into a speaking horn, and his warbling echoed across the lagoon. We sang along and danced on the bricks on our way across the Grand Court. August tossed himself into my arms for a spin, in a costume that he called Oscar Wilde as Warrior. It consisted of a linen suit coat and vest on top, and a buckskin kilt and knee-high moccasins below. Through the buttonhole of his lapel he'd stuck the thick stem of a sunflower. He'd bought the kilt and moccasins, and his mask shaped like the snout of a mountain lion, from an Apache staying in the Indian camp.

"Don't tell anybody who you're supposed to be," I whispered in his ear.

"People dress up like Wilde for fancy-dress parties all the time," he whispered back.

"Not since he went to jail," I said, my voice still kept low. "What'd they call it?"

"*Gross indecency,*" August said, not whispering anymore, practically shouting it, as he danced away from me and toward Rosie. Rosie comically swayed and dodged but nonetheless flirted back, bumping his hip against August's.

"Are you drunk?" Rosie said.

"No," he said, as he ran a peacock feather along his own cheek. "Only happy. We should *all* be more like Oscar Wilde. Did you know that in prison he campaigned for the release of some children who'd been jailed simply for poaching rabbits?"

"Do you even listen to yourself?" I scolded. "*Prison*. He's in prison." But August only raced ahead toward the stairs that spiraled up the side of the Fine Arts Building. He was no innocent, but he worried me. His longing for love, and his gentle heart, would lead him into enough trouble and pain. But if he was ever locked away in a cage, he'd die in a day.

No one ever asked to see my letter of invitation, though I had it at the ready the very second I stepped onto the roof and into the crowd. All day long I'd practiced my best devil-may-care, in hopes of impressing the rich man with my indifference. But once I got into the thick of the circus, I couldn't pretend that I wasn't intimidated. I held the invitation in my fist, prepared for someone to call me a fraud and rustle me out and away.

There was a maharajah who'd likely blackened his face with burned cork, his turban strung with rubies and sapphires. A Cleopatra had greased-up catlike eyes and a live snake coiled up her arm, its head pinched between her fingers and its forked tongue darting. There was a chimney sweep, a Humpty Dumpty in an enormous papier-mâché egg, a fisher maid with strings of wooden fish dangling from her shoulders. There were men as women, and women as men, and men and women as children.

"The statues are alive," Cecily whispered in my ear, and it was so; these weren't plaster of Paris nudes, but actors and actresses in little more than loincloths, unflinching on pedestals, their every inch of skin powdered white. Every now and again they'd change their pose, slow and smooth and graceful, but otherwise remained as still as marble.

August had made me a mask of raven's feathers, and I dressed like Oscar, in a pair of striped pants and a dotted vest. Oscar hung off my back, a mask across his eyes too—a mask of tiny feathers August had collected from the bottom of the canaries' cage in the aviary in the Agriculture Building.

As we moved through the crowd, Cecily's hand in mine, I looked for Wakefield. A harlequin on stilts bumped into me, and his marionette knocked off my derby with a brickbat, as he high-stepped through the crowd. Meanwhile, I rapped my ankle against the tiny Chiquita, the "Living Doll" who stood no taller than a goose.

"Knock into me again," she shouted up, "and I blow out your kneecap." She flashed me the pearl-handled pistol tucked into the cleavage of her low-cut ball gown of velvet. I had no reason to think it an idle threat. The ball seemed to have no rules. The roof was frantic with freaks and drunks, opium eaters and cocaine inebriates, men and women swapping pipes and spoons, and snorting from snuff bottles.

A troop of men were dressed in the khakis and neckerchiefs of Teddy Roosevelt's Rough Riders, those cowboys who had galloped into Cuba to chase out the Spanish. They offered us Havana cigars, cut the tips, and lit a match. Cecily took one too, but after the first few puffs she felt a little queasy.

"Remember the *Maine*!" a sailor shouted over and over as he maneuvered through the crowd with a torch. We then all moved to the front of the roof to see the toy battleship chug through the lagoon.

"There was no attack of the battleship *Maine*," Rosie said, returning to his disgust. He tossed an empty whiskey bottle over the side of the roof to break on the bricks below. "It blew up on its own." Those around us shushed him and glared, but his protest only grew louder. "There's all kinds of proof. The furnace was too close to the explosives. *The Spanish did not torpedo our boat in the Havana harbor!*" And with that, he got the fight he wanted. A man dressed as Gretel, in a blond wig and dirndl with low neckline, with candied cherries over his nipples, swung at Rosie and missed. Rosie swung back, and he missed too. A few ladies shrieked, men bellowed, and then the toy battleship exploded, smoke rose, debris flew, and the boat sank into the lagoon in flames.

WE ALL LINGERED until long after the party wound down, the roof mostly emptied of its revelers, the floor littered with feathers and confetti. As we headed toward the stairs, with intentions of going to a saloon in full costume, Wakefield called after me.

"Did you enjoy the Carnival, Ferret?" he said.

Cecily and I let the others leave without us, and we walked to where Wakefield stood, at the edge of the roof, where he looked out on the debris in the lagoon. He wore a tuxedo, but his attire was white where it should be black, and black where it should be white. He carried a cane of onyx—its brass handle the head of a gryphon—but he didn't lean on the cane at all. Instead he simply tap, tap, tapped at the floor, clicking out a little rhythm.

"I did," I said, "Mr. Wakefield."

"Call me Billy," he said. His voice was muffled by his mask, a papier-mâché skull that covered every inch of his face. He held a cigar between the silver bones of his fingers, and he put the cigar to a hole in the skull's toothy grin to smoke.

"And you're *Mrs.* Wakefield?" I asked the woman with the piglet, who'd stepped up to him. Her eye mask of purple feathers was pushed up off her face and into her girlish ringlets of black hair.

"*Mrs. . . . ?*" she said, exaggerating her shock, with a laugh that echoed across the rooftop. "*Mrs.* Wakefield? I'm his *sister*. Can't you see we're twins?" But Wakefield stayed behind his skull.

"Very pleasant to make your acquaintance," I said. "And this is Cecily."

Billy Wakefield held his metal hand out, and Cecily hesitated, unsure what to do. She then put her hand in his, and he held it there for a moment.

"Cecily's in *Heart of the White City*," I said. "She plays a factory girl . . . and a fire victim . . . and, um . . ."

"Dance hall girl," Cecily added. "And a Ferris wheel girl."

"Oh?" he said, as if he didn't recall.

At the same time, the woman who wasn't Mrs. Wakefield leaned in toward me, squinting to see through my raven feather mask. "Your *eyes*," she said. "I've never seen such a blue in an eye. Billy, his eyes are the blue of that stone scarab I bought in Cairo. At that bazaar."

"Lapis lazuli," Billy Wakefield mumbled.

His sister grinned wide as she pet the squirming piglet in her arms. "I shall *dig* out your eyes, and *wear* them as earbobs!"

Cecily and I chuckled but only politely. We weren't quite sure if she meant to be funny.

"I'd like to see your act," Billy Wakefield said. "You'll take the stage, won't you? Tell us a few jokes?"

"Oh," I said. "I don't . . . I'm not . . . I couldn't . . ."

Billy Wakefield reached into his coat and took from it a golden dragon's head—the jaw was on a hinge, and its diamond-studded teeth clenched down on a fat mouthful of folded bills. He peeled off from that wad of cash more money than I'd expected to make all summer on the midway. I again refused, just to be coaxed and convinced, and he only peeled off more. I then took the money. I'd actually had no intention at all of leaving without that pretty payday.

"It would be a great honor," Wakefield said. "I understand you were an apprentice to Crowe, the master ventriloquist."

"And how'd you come to know that, sir?" I asked.

Wakefield shrugged one shoulder, as if to say, *I know all, of course.*

Wakefield's sister complimented Cecily on her dress, but then peered at the front of it, puzzled. "Do you even have a corset on, in under there?"

"I don't always wear one," Cecily said.

"You're a revolutionary!" she exclaimed, taking Cecily by the arm and leading her toward the rooftop's stage, where some servants unfolded folding chairs for one another. "Not so long ago, if you went without a corset, we all thought you were a whore."

"Better they think me a whore," Cecily said, "than an actress," and Wakefield's sister let off another echoing laugh.

"Can we be best friends, my love?" the sister said.

Billy Wakefield then took my arm, and we followed the two of them. "I used to see Crowe, when I was a boy, on the stage of the Eden Musee," he said. The Eden Musee had been a dime museum downtown that had featured oddities and cheap acts before burning to the ground one winter. Wakefield's voice was so soft, so tucked away in the skeleton mask, I had to tilt my head toward him to listen close. "His puppet seemed so alive, you so much wanted it to truly live. I so wished for the puppet to just one day jump off his knee and stroll around on its own. It broke my heart that he didn't exist. I could even somehow convince myself that he did indeed live, that he was real, that it would be entirely illogical for him to be only a puppet. Crowe's lips didn't move, and the puppet's voice wasn't Crowe's voice at all! And the puppet could speak while Crowe gargled brandy! And Crowe and the puppet could sing the same song at the same time! It got so that I was having nightmares—I would sometimes dream I awoke locked in the box where the puppet was kept."

No one had spoken to me of my dear old Crowe for so long, I felt a little catch in my gullet. "Crowe had magic," I said. "I only know tricks." I could only dream of my dummy giving a boy such nightmares.

We walked up to the stage where the band had played. I took a seat on the piano bench for an audience that grew only slightly—one of the statues, a burly Hercules who now wore a robe over his powdered skin, stretched out in a chair in the front row. A few of the waiters joined us, as did the harlequin now without stilts, and an ancient old cuss with a buggy whip.

I froze. Not a funny word came to mind. All the jokes I'd told on the midway, or on the stage of the Empress, seemed worth even less than the pennies I'd made from them. I sat there, everyone staring, Oscar silent on my knee. If I dared to open the dummy's mouth, Wakefield would know, right away, he'd paid me too much.

I'd never had a minute of stage fright in my life—all fear of performance had been scared out of me as a waif when I'd had to steal to keep from getting beaten. I'd always had to be friendly, to gain the confidence of whoever I wanted to sidle up to and thieve. I had begged, I'd danced, I'd sung all the most popular songs. I'd been every bit as real and magic as Crowe's dummy.

And that's what Oscar started telling my rooftop audience. I opened his mouth and he spilled my guts. "He had a little groundhog pelt for a pet," Oscar said, mocking my poverty, looking up at me askance. I didn't even try to keep my lips still. "He kept it in a rusty birdcage and pretended to feed it grasshopper legs." I paused for the audience's nervous twittering. "He used a fish skeleton as a hair comb, and he greased down his cowlick with the mush of a rotten peach, and by the time he got to the whorehouse to beg for alms, his head was swarming with bluebottles."

At first, I seemed to only be making everyone unhappy. Though his skull mask still hid his face away, Wakefield nonetheless looked mirthless, sitting stone-still, his silver hand folded around the head of his cane in front of him. His sister, so full of laughter only minutes before, only smiled a tight smile as she petted her piglet.

"He's so poor," Oscar said of me, "he's thinking of selling his eyeballs for earbobs." At that, the sister sneered, clucked her tongue with

offense, and whispered loudly to Billy Wakefield, "That was my joke."
Billy Wakefield nodded with impatience.

Just when it seemed I might be dragged out and lynched, Cecily
saved my neck. She started giggling. A little tee-hee-hee at first. A
little *pffft* between her puckered lips. A little squeal, a little "oh!" And
the giggling grew. And grew. A bubbling up of gentle laughs that
shook her shoulders and gave her hiccups. And she couldn't stop. She
doubled over. She threw her head back. Even when she wheezed and
snorted, I'd never heard anything more like music from heaven. And
there was nothing fake about it. The poor thing was a genuine mess. I
had her in stitches.

"Ferret bought old empty ether tins from an addict, then sold them
back to him full of piss at double the price!" Oscar said.

Cecily held both her hands tight to her mouth, but that only worsened her convulsions. She wept and sniffled. And it was infectious, of
course. It was a delight to see someone so pretty so off her head. And
once the others started laughing at her, they got to laughing at me too,
even the old codger with the buggy whip. Suddenly, Oscar couldn't
utter an unfunny thing.

AFTER I FINISHED with the act, I suspected Billy Wakefield would
want us gentlemen to engage in some buying and selling of my little
dummy's soul, but it turned out he didn't want to talk business. He and
his sister weighed Cecily and me down with the party's picked-over
remains: a half-empty box of candied plums, a few half-drunk bottles
of champagne, a half-eaten fairy cake. Billy Wakefield tucked a half-
smoked cigar in my inside suit pocket. "It's half gone," he said, "but
half a Havana is better than none. Smoke it with this," and he shoved
into my arms a bottle of cognac that had only a few gulps left swirling
around at the bottom of it.

Billy told the man with the buggy whip to take Cecily and me anywhere we wanted to go in the private coach, even if it was just to circle the block for hours.

And that's practically what we did. Cecily and I got in the coach and closed the curtains after instructing the driver to drive nowhere in particular. I finished off the cognac and studied the French words on the label. I couldn't help but think I'd earned Wakefield's respect at the expense of my dignity. Though my boyhood had not been quite as miserable as I'd portrayed, I'd been every bit as poor. I'd bared my soul for the rich man's amusement.

"Was I really all that funny?" I asked Cecily, as I unwrapped the tissue from a plum to tear it up and feed it to her.

"Yes, but it breaks my heart," she said, putting her hand to her chest, "to think of you as that little boy." She took my hand to lick the plum's honey from my fingertips.

"I'm glad Doxie has you," I said. I leaned forward to kiss her, tasting the sugar on her lips.

After we kissed for a while, she started in with that giggling again. "Pissing in the ether bottle . . . a pet gopher pelt . . ." She wept and wheezed with the comedy of it all. "It's not funny . . . it's the worst kind of . . . tragic . . ."

I lifted her dress to duck in beneath, and I lightly bit at the inside of her thigh, getting a shriek from her, in among the giggling. "Do you have a corset in here?" I squealed, in imitation of Wakefield's sister, mixed in with a pig's oink. "Are you even wearing any drawers?" Cecily laughed more and shooed me out from beneath her dress. I held the bottle of champagne to her lips, and we kissed awhile, and then we kissed some more, all night long. We fell asleep, and in the morning a stick of sunlight slanted in bright from where the curtain didn't close all the way. The coach wasn't moving. We had stopped at the very edge of the river. Had we gone out the wrong door, we would have fallen into the water. On the other side of the coach, in a thicket of grasses, the driver slept on a saddle blanket. We apologized and apologized, and begged and begged his forgiveness.

"For goodness sake, why didn't you wake us?" Cecily asked.

"I hated to bother you," he said.

We helped him up. Cecily had had her dress off in the night, and it was now only partly back on. I suspected her immodesty in allowing the front of it to slip about her naked breasts, revealing a nipple or two once or twice, may have been for the benefit of the driver we'd so cruelly left to sleep on the ground.

The driver drove Cecily to the boardinghouse, and me to the Empress. As I reached up to offer the driver a tip—which the driver refused—he handed down another invitation, with Wakefield's same wax seal, as if the message had somehow reached us as we'd traveled by coach.

Will you and Cecily please join me at my house above the lake
for the fireworks on Independence Day? Please arrive in time
for quince brandy and cake. Bring Oscar.

20.

WAKEFIELD LAKE was at the very end of a long, long streetcar ride. The tracks even passed the far ends of the Fair and kept going north. There was little out that way but a cemetery and a carriage factory and a few churches without steeples.

But many of the people on the streetcar were dressed for the lake— or undressed rather, in bloomers and knee-length swimming costumes. There was no other reason to take the Blue Line this far north. It was as if Wakefield had arranged for the city to pay for the laying of tracks right to the front door of his country resort.

Oscar sat on the bench next to me, and Doxie lay in my lap, her head on my knees. It never occurred to us anymore to tuck Doxie away. For all appearances, we were a family. We were a father and a mother and a baby girl. And I no longer worried at all about dropping Doxie or holding her wrong. I didn't fret over carrying her or holding her, any more than I'd fret over carrying my own heart or my own kidney inside my bones.

Cecily and I had decided we'd go to the lake in the late afternoon, and we would have our supper on the beach before heading up to the house to knock on Billy Wakefield's door. After stepping off the streetcar, we followed the cobblestone lane past the luxury hotel painted pink and pale blue, past the day-trippers on the beach in their brightly striped swimming suits. The beach was crowded, and waltzing had already begun on the dance floor on the wharf, paper lanterns bobbing in the breeze. Fireworks were already crackling against the sun's glare.

The streetcar ride had taken longer than we'd thought it would, so we skipped the beach and began our walk up the winding path toward the Wakefield house situated atop a hill that overlooked the city. The house was also farther up and away than it seemed, far from anything at all, and it was sunset by the time we reached the locked gate. At the center of the gate was the gilded letter *W* in loopy cursive above a key-hole the size of my head. The lane behind the gate wound through a peach orchard.

Had Billy Wakefield forgotten us? Cecily playfully shook the gate, rattling it, squeaking its hinges. "Let us in, let us in," Cecily said, "or we'll huff and we'll puff and we'll blow your house down."

The sky was dark enough now for us to see the fireworks blast red, white, and blue and spider down and out, the lake waters mirroring all the shimmer.

Mrs. Margaret had prepared us a picnic basket, despite the fact that she still disapproved of me. We spread a thin blanket over the hard dirt of the road to sit and wait and eat. Mrs. Margaret had packed a tin of walnuts, some candied dates, a jar of pears in syrup, some bread and honey. Wrapped in butcher's paper and tied over with twine was a boiled chicken.

Night fell, and I held Cecily in my arms, and Cecily held Doxie in hers, as I leaned back against the stone wall of the estate. We dropped off to sleep, despite the endless crackling of the fireworks. But we didn't sleep long, only just long enough for me to dream that Cecily and I sat there in that very same spot, on that very same picnic, while we ate deviled swan's eggs, and a fire in the peach orchard raged out of control behind us.

We woke to the sound of the gate screeching open on its hinges. "Oh, for goodness sake, there you are," Wakefield's sister said, exasperated. "Gather your things now, we'll go on up. Hurry, hurry, hurry, now." She kept her piglet on a leash tied to her wrist, and it galloped toward our picnic, trampling on our apple cores and empty tins, getting its hooves caught up in the rib cage of our chicken bones. Wakefield's sister yanked on the leash and scolded the pig. She stood smiling impatiently, bouncing on her feet, as we wrapped the food that remained and folded the blanket.

"Please, please," she said, "hurry, hurry, rush, rush." We moved too slowly for her, and she began to help us, grabbing at our cups and dishes, and Doxie's bottle, and stuffing them in our basket. She picked up Oscar and slung him over her shoulder. "Not the time to dawdle," she said. Once everything was gathered, she rushed up the path, her heels on the dirt clip-clopping in rhythm with the pig's feet.

"Shouldn't we close the gate?" I called to her. I carried Doxie, and Cecily carried the basket.

"No, no, no," she said, barely glancing back, waving us on. "Leave it, leave it. Leave the gate." Her hasty state made Cecily and me feel the need to dash. We didn't know the winding path, so we listened to the woman's heels, and the piglet's hooves, though they stepped along so quickly up the steep hill, and around the madman turns of the road, we couldn't keep close. Wakefield's sister began to whistle a bunch of notes with no tune, and the whistling grew fainter and fainter as we slipped farther and farther behind. It was as if I were still in the dream, but instead of wildfire, we fought a river's current.

"Why are we running ourselves ragged?" Cecily asked me, but she likely knew I had no answer.

Finally, panting, our sides splitting with ache, we reached that strange house with no corners. Wakefield House seemed to be all turrets and silos and wrought-iron spires, with pointed roofs like witches' hats. It looked as if it might have no corners at all but for the three square chimneys that rose to different heights. A porch wrapped all around the front of the house, curving around its turns.

The lamplight from the parlor spilled out onto the empty lawn, but our shadows were somehow cast ahead of us. Our shadows slipped through the front door before we reached the porch steps.

The sister propped Oscar up in a chair in the hallway, scooped the piglet into her arms, and beckoned us forward, her own various shadows dancing and sparring with one another, each cast by one of the many lamps and candles lit throughout the house. The house was noisy with light, if such a thing could be said. Even if the rounds of the house had had corners, there wouldn't have been a dark one to hide in.

I nearly made my wildfire dream come true when I bumped into a hall table and toppled a candelabra. Cecily rushed to gather the candles that rolled across the carpets. We then walked slowly down the hallway, holding hands, following all those chaotic shadows that the sister and the piglet cast behind them. Now that we weren't running, and the blood wasn't pumping so loudly through our ears, or our feet stamping against the wood floor, we could hear the house roaring. And the farther we went down the hall, the louder the roaring grew, and we could feel the floorboards rattling under our feet. We could see the tapping of the picture frames against the wall. A blue china panther, crouched to prowl, jiggled along a tabletop and right over the edge. We heard it shatter in our path.

The sister's shadows had vanished, so we followed the noise now, and we found our way into a conservatory of sorts, a parlor of glass walls, a glass roof slanting overhead. French doors open wide swung slightly on their hinges, as sheets of music from the grand piano were blown about, among leaves and flower petals that had been shaken from the branches and stems of the many plants that grew there in pots and vases.

We weren't sure what we were seeing when we looked out the French doors and through the glass walls, but whatever it was began to thump my heart to a different beat. I kept back, to keep Doxie from the thick of it, but Cecily crept forward.

OUTSIDE THE FRENCH DOORS was a lawn, and at the center of the lawn, a cyclone rose. It was only as tall as the house, and only as thick as a coffee can, the very top of it opening wide into a funnel that dissolved into the gray night above, unattached to any cloud. Except for all the violent spin at the heart of it, it didn't move—the tip of it remained inside a box attached to pipes. At first I'd foolishly assumed that the wild thing had been caught, the box and pipes part of the rich man's fancy tornado trap—in Nebraska, in summer, tornados seemed to touch the earth like demons dropping down from heaven, mindful, spirited.

But then I saw that the pipes led to more machinery, to what looked like a giant fireplace bellows pumped up and down by the efforts of the old servant I'd met weeks before—he'd been the one to bring me the invitation to the masquerade ball. The man pushed down on the handle with all his might, leaning all his meager weight into it, then he pulled the handle up, nearly knocking himself over every time. Up and down, up and down he went, and the cyclone spun and corkscrewed, knotting and unknotting itself.

"Get as close as you dare!" Billy Wakefield shouted above the rumbling. He leaned back from the wind. His hair had come loose from its part, and the wind blew it across his cheeks. "But don't get too close! It's liable to rip the tongue right out of your head."

And I believed it. I could feel the power of it enter my mouth and thunder around inside me, like it was loosening my guts from my bones. I held Doxie tighter and stepped backward.

But Cecily stepped closer, even as she leaned away, pushing her feet into the earth, digging her heels in good. The wind puffed up her shirtwaist, billowing her sleeves like balloons, her skirt flapping. It sucked the pins from her hair, and her curls flowed loose in front of her. She held out her arms, her fingers spread out like a conjurer's, and I swore I could see little bolts of silver lightning snapping from her fingertips.

And she allowed that wind to pull her forward one fraction of an inch too far.

All that came next came quicker than half a blink, but it was just enough time for my mind's eye to see the end of everything. When Cecily lost her footing, it was as if she turned to air, so fast was she snatched away by the cyclone.

What I saw next didn't happen at all. My fear played out before me so vividly, that I sometimes still see her as she never was. I see her carried up through the funnel and shot out the top. I see her waltzing through the night, like the dancer on wires she was. I see her flung to the earth to be broken to pieces.

But all the time he'd toyed with the wind, Billy Wakefield had kept a watchful eye. The tip of his boot was at a switch, and with a quick flick of his toe, nature was defeated. The twister stopped twisting, and when a twister don't twist, there's nothing left of it. Cecily was caught up in the cyclone barely at all, only enough to give her a few quick turns, lift her off the ground a few feet, and send her stumbling across the lawn to collapse in a patch of rosebushes.

I ran forward, holding Doxie near, cradling her head in my hand. I stepped over and across the metal cage that had held the cyclone. Inside the cage were the slowing blades of an electric fan that had helped to keep the wind spinning.

We all rushed to Cecily, even the old servant, and we carefully unpinned her from the thorns that had snagged at her clothes and scratched her skin.

"Say something," I said, looking into her eyes, putting my thumb to a scratch on her cheek.

"Stir up the storm again," she said.

ATOP A TABLE IN A ROOM that Billy Wakefield called his library were science books open to pages of formulas and diagrams. Wakefield unrolled a scroll of blueprints and weighted the corners with brass owls. He attempted to explain to me the mechanics and chemical reactions that made his cyclone tick—something to do with dry ice and vortexes. The tornado was to play a starring role in *Heart of the White City*, if he could manage to contain its rage.

I tried to follow it all, but I was feeling like my head was filled with bees. The fast pumping of my blood—from the running uphill and from the fear—and a touch of intoxication from the reek of whatever magic smoke fueled the tornado made me blissful and mindless.

All I really wanted to do was remind myself, over and over, that Cecily was alive.

"What would have happened if you hadn't shut the machine off?" I asked. I realized this was the first I'd seen of Wakefield's whole face, when it wasn't half hidden by masks or goggles. I looked for scars but saw none. I was caught by his eyes, which were somehow quite warm and gentle despite their color of fog.

I swished the quince brandy around in the bottom of my snifter like I'd seen men do. Cecily reclined on the leather sofa, Doxie on the cushion next to her jabbering and grabbing at her own toes. Wakefield's sister sat perched on a footstool, dabbing some kind of ointment on Cecily's cuts, something she had muddled together with a mortar and pestle.

"But I *did* shut the machine off," he said.

"But what if you didn't?"

"But I did, is what I'm saying."

"And what I'm saying is what if you didn't?" I said.

Wakefield's sister sighed and spoke up without looking away from Cecily's minor wounds. "Boys, boys, it's very simple," she said. "It would either have twisted her poor little neck or rocked her brain around in her skull until it snapped it from its stem."

"*Or*," Wakefield continued, "she would have floated to the top of the cyclone like a champagne bubble." The old man who had pumped the bellows of the cyclone machine refilled Wakefield's snifter. "And," Wakefield added, "she would have dropped into my arms, giggling."

When the sister finished spooning the pulp onto Cecily's skin, she set the bowl on a bookshelf and picked up her snifter. Doxie had begun to fuss, so Cecily took her into her arms. As she kissed Doxie's head, Cecily said to the woman, "You never did tell us your name, I don't think." She held the back of her hand to her mouth to lick at the medicine, then let Doxie lick some too.

"Oh I didn't? Oh, it's just the same as his." The sister nodded toward Billy. I dropped into the sofa next to Cecily and I took her hand in mine. I held it to my lips to taste the medicine myself. It tasted of apricot and vinegar, with some kind of mint vapor, and even just having it at the tip of my tongue sent a chill through my snout and down my throat in a sharp swallow.

"The same?" Cecily said.

"He's Billy Wakefield with a *y*," the sister said, "and I'm Billie Wakefield with an *ie*. He's William. I'm Wilhelmina."

"You two don't look so much alike," I said.

"Oh, we don't?" said Billie with an *ie*. "Are you sure? Well, that's strange. I always thought we did." She pulled down her sleeve to cover her hand and held out a silver spoon and clawed at the air with it. "Now do I look like Billy?" she said.

"Not in front of the children, Pickle," Billy said. "They aren't accustomed to your ugly wit." Cecily and I paused, but then we laughed a little, because they weren't truly being cruel to each other. We both slouched deeper into the sofa cushions, and I daresay we could've stayed there for days. Wakefield was a man I could look up to. He was likely in his forties, and I admired him and his inventions, his novelty tornados, his giant miniature battleships. For him, entertainment was an expensive hobby, not a means of living. He could devote himself to his imagination.

And I admired the clutter of his crooked library—though the walls were curved like all the other walls of the strange house, the bookcases weren't. The bookcases, all different widths and heights, the tops of them stacked with even more books, overlapped in places, as if they'd been shaken away from the wall by an earthquake. And I could tell the books were read, not just collected, by the way they were shoved onto the shelves when not another book could possibly fit. Bookmarks and strings poked out the tops of them. Their pages were torn and stuffed back in, their covers were warped from having been left out in the rain. And the room had that rich, dusty, sweet smell of old pages constantly fluttered open, that cloud of vanilla and tobacco that watered your eyes.

"You know what you oughta do?" I said, feeling a little drunk. The old man had refilled my snifter too, and I'd shot the brandy back in one swift gulp. "You oughta put your cyclone in its own booth on the midway. Cecily could learn her way around it. She could be the star. The Girl Caught in the Tornado. She would get swept up in it and dance her way right back out of it." Of course I never wanted Cecily within two steps of that tornado ever again, but I was happy I'd suggested it, as it seemed to please Cecily to picture herself in such a show. With Doxie nestled in the crook of her arm, Cecily looked up and off, the snifter of brandy at her lips.

"You're a natural-born humbug artist," Billy Wakefield said. He sat in a wing chair by the fireplace. "Speaking of that," he said, "let's talk about Oscar."

"And with that I retire to my cold, lonely quarters," Billie said, standing. She held her snifter out to the old man for another pour before leaving. "I mean no disrespect, Ferret, but there's nothing I despise more than a ventriloquist. There's just something quite unsettling about those dolls, wouldn't you say? It almost seems they can see out of those glass eyes. If you sell my brother your dummy, I will throttle you with my bare hands. Good night, children," and with that little threat, she left.

I DIDN'T WANT TO TALK about Oscar either. I could see him in my head, sitting there alone in the hallway, slumped forward in the chair, waiting for my breath of life. There were indeed objects I'd grown attached to in my lifetime but only a very few: the letter my mother had tucked into my baby blanket when she'd abandoned me, the pipe that Cecily smoked onstage on the very first night I ever spoke to her. And Oscar.

The impulse to sell him suddenly seemed like a dark one. It was human nature to grow attached to a possession. In fact, it was *in*human to have no affection of any kind for the pieces of your life you carried around with you. I felt a kind of loyalty to Oscar. To sell him meant I put no value on my own personal history, my own memories. I wanted Oscar right there, always on my knee, until I looked as old and raggedy as he did.

"Oh look, the war," I said, to steer the conversation off. The *Omaha Evening Bee* had been tossed onto the Persian rug. The news of our victory in Cuba had stirred the day's patriotism into a fever pitch. By not spending our day at the Fair, we'd avoided endless parades stomping over our feet. I read aloud the headline: "'All warships but one blown up and are burning on the beach—pride of Spain's navy meets the same sad fate as the lamented *Maine*.'"

And even as I read it, I wished I'd kept quiet. I thought about Wakefield's toy ship on the lagoon, and I suddenly felt embarrassed for even having taken part in his Carnival. "This is independence?" I said. "Getting into fights just so we can win something? That's freedom?"

"War is necessary to the national temperament," Billy Wakefield said.

"Then why aren't we all too sad to do anything today?" I said. "Why doesn't it wreck our temperament every time a soldier gets himself riddled with bullets?"

"Because the military man dies for his love of country," Wakefield said. "He dies as an American soldier, not as a civilian like you and me. We celebrate him as a hero. And we show our respect for the family by letting the widows, the children, weep alone. *Respect.* We allow them to be prideful in their private grief. When a widow, shrouded in black, crosses your path, you feel the full weight of her sacrifice. You and me,

Ferret, we couldn't begin to understand it all. We're not soldiers. We're not even soldiers' wives. It's a different heart, a different love. We can't fathom it."

"Oh, *I* understand it, every bit of it," Cecily said, stretching her arm to hold out her empty glass for the old man. Doxie held her arm out too, reaching for the glass herself. But Cecily was already slurring her words, and Wakefield shook his head discreetly at the servant, and the servant stayed still. "War is all about *men* acting like *kings*," Cecily said, bringing her empty glass back to try to get one last drop from it. "And we women get to worship, is all. When a man loses a wife, he marries again in a few months." I looked to Wakefield to see if he might be offended by Cecily's mention of a dead wife. But he didn't flinch. He didn't move at all. I knew that Cecily knew about Wakefield's tragedies—we'd only just spoken of them on the long streetcar ride. I pinched her leg, hoping to remind her. "For a few weeks," Cecily said, "he wears a black hatband. But a woman loses somebody, she's hat to boot in a black weeping veil for two years. And you can't just mourn a husband; you gotta mourn every old uncle and cousin too. And your cousins' cousins. My mother was from a sickly family, and she started wearing black when my daddy died too young, and she'll go to her grave in black. Not me, boy. If I married a dead soldier, you'd see me out in that parade, proud of my man."

I still had some brandy in my glass, so I poured a few swallows of it into Cecily's. I kissed her cheek. "I'm sorry about your daddy," I said.

"Miss Cecily," Wakefield said, "it is because women have such strength that they must mourn for us. If a man is allowed to indulge in the pain of loss, he's ruined for all else. When a man loses his wife, he *must* marry again, or he'll be lost forever. Blessedly, my sister has been my strength. Man is weak. When we see a widow in black, we know that love is constant. And it's that privilege of love we fight battles for. For Americans, war is not waged by the bloodthirsty. War is a sentimental endeavor. For all our bluster and brutality, we are fighting for what's in our hearts." He began to drum his silver fingers on the arm of his chair, and he said, "You children make a very spirited debate. I guess this is why we send the young men to fight, while the old men ponder the inevitabilities and make the sensible decisions."

"I don't mean to argufy, Mr. Wakefield," I said, and I did wish I hadn't brought it all up. What did I know from war and peace? I'd spent much of my life taking things and having things taken from me. If there was anything I should know inside and out, it was that some men had some peculiar notions of decency, and you had to fight to keep things in line. "But there's just something about *this* war," I said. "We're fighting it because we like the *idea* of fighting it, don't you think? The blood's not even spilling in our own fields. Nobody's going to really remember the *Maine*."

But before I'd even finished my sentence, Wakefield threw his snifter at the fireplace, and it shattered against the andirons. "Enough!" he barked, and it so alarmed me, I lost my breath. Cecily jumped and I feared Doxie might cry. The old servant stepped forward, having produced from nowhere a dustpan and brush, but Wakefield shooed him away, waving his hand. "Leave it, Morearty," he snapped. "For God's sake, just leave it be for now."

Morearty sniffled and nodded, and stepped back. The old servant shuddered with weeping he tried to hide. "Oh, Morearty," Wakefield said, "I'm not angry at you. I'm simply . . . embarrassed. Now sit down, my dear friend, and pull yourself together. Pour yourself a snifter of that brandy." And the old man did just that, though none of it seemed to ease his weeping. He sipped the brandy as he dabbed a tea towel at the corners of his eyes.

I stood. "I apologize, Mr. Wakefield," I said. "I'm not a very polite guest. We'll be going."

"No," Wakefield said, "no, please. Please. *I* should apologize. I should apologize especially to you, Miss Cecily. It's undignified for men to talk war and politics in front of a lady."

Cecily shrugged, easing the tension with her pretty smile. "Ah, well," she said, "as far as ladies go, I'm not much of one." When she kissed Doxie's forehead, I then realized Wakefield hadn't made a single gesture in the baby's direction all evening, despite all the mewling and gabbing she did. He hadn't cooed at her. He hadn't tickled her chin. He hadn't even asked her name. I respected his tragedy, the loss of his young son, but how could anyone not be charmed by Doxie's beauty?

When Cecily squeezed my elbow, I knew she meant for me to hurry her away.

"Thank you for the brandy, Mr. Wakefield," I said.

"No, please," he said. "We haven't finished our business, have we?"

"We don't have any business," I said.

"You let me buy your dummy, and I'll buy you a new one for your act," he said, in a rush of words. "I know a buyer at Brandeis; I'll put him to the task of finding you the finest one ever made. I'll even pay for him to go to London—or Bora-Bora—or wherever the hell the best dummies are."

"No," I said. I wanted to ask him why, if he could pay anything for a dummy, he was so smitten with mine. But before I could speak, he stood with a happy stamp of his boot, practically bouncing up from his chair.

"Ferret," he said, smiling. "Miss Cecily. Come with me." He picked up the brandy bottle in his silver hand, patted the still-weeping Morearty on the back, and stepped into the hall.

"Let's leave," Cecily whispered in my ear. "I have an awful headache." She took my hand and brought it to Doxie's warm forehead. "I always get a headache whenever Doxie gets a fever. I always know it when she's sick. I feel it in my own blood. I want to go home."

As we followed Wakefield, I gave our regrets again. "We really do need to be getting back," I said.

"And how are you doing that?" Wakefield said, without turning to look at us, without slowing a step. "Getting back, I mean."

"The same way we got here," I said. "All the streetcars keep late hours this summer, for the Fair."

"If you spend a minute or two more with me," he said, "I'll send you back with my own driver, and you'll still get home much sooner than if you take the streetcar, with all its stopping and going, going and stopping."

"Sir," I said, "Cecily has a little bit of a headache."

This stopped Wakefield midstep. He turned slowly on his heel, and he gave us both a good looking over. "Oh?" he said.

"I think you poured too much booze in me," Cecily said, and I noticed her cheeks were as red as Pearl's often were.

"I'll have Bugsy bring the coach around," he said, and he slipped around a corner. We heard the cranking and bells of a telephone, and the hollow echo of his voice as he summoned the driver. We heard his footsteps go farther down the hall, and the squeak of a door. When he returned, he handed Cecily a bottle. The glass was dark blue and the label bore a doctor's name in elegant print. "Take a few swigs now," he said. "Then a few more when you get home. But no more than that. Your ache will leave your head."

He reached into his trousers pocket for his hinged dragon, and he spoke to me without looking in my eyes. He looked at his bills, ran his thumb along the edges. Each bill was a big one. I had never seen so much money in one place. "And I'd like to finish up business with you, Ferret, before you leave." He hesitated, then held out the cash, dragon and all. "The dragon is twenty-two carat," he said. "It's yellow gold from China. The eyes are diamonds. The nostrils are rubies. It's meant to be clipped to a lady's dress."

I might not have taken it from him had he not let go, letting the dragon fall. I caught it. I ran my own thumb along the edge of the bundle. I looked at Cecily. She looked at me. I thumbed through it again, keeping track of the sum, but kept losing count of the bills. I was distracted by the wealth I held in my hand.

And I put the dragon, and the money, in my own pocket. I traded Oscar for Doxie.

I couldn't help but think about all the things I could buy that little girl. She could sleep in a bassinet with a new mattress. She could go to a doctor when she needed to—her head did feel a touch too warm. I could buy her new dresses, and new dolls with dresses that matched hers, with wigs woven from her own hair clippings. In a booth in the Manufactures Building of the Grand Court, there'd been a girl's wardrobe on display—a fur coat and muff of Russian squirrel, a nainsook slip trimmed with lace. The more I pictured her, the richer she got.

Wakefield had no more to say to us then. He thanked us for the evening, gestured toward the doorway, and told us the coach waited at the front steps. And he headed back up the stairs to his library.

It was only then that Cecily said, "You *can't* sell Oscar."

"But I did," I said, as we passed where Oscar had sat. He was no longer there—he'd already been snatched away, by a servant, I assumed. But that empty chair was an awful sight.

In the coach, Bugsy drove us fast along the winding road, down through the orchard. "Take her," Cecily said, handing Doxie over. "Thinking about Oscar is just splitting my head open more." She then uncorked the remedy Wakefield had given her and guzzled back much more than a few sips.

"Stop," I said, putting my hand to her wrist. "Don't take any more until I ask August about it."

"No need," she said. "It's working already." She rested her head on my shoulder, and though the coach wheels seemed to be knocking against every rut in the road, she dropped right off to sleep. Her fingers loosened, and I took the bottle from her fist. The druggist was someone named Goodfellow, in someplace called Hot Springs, South Dakota. On the back of the bottle was another label, with a number and a dosage and a name: *Mrs. William Wakefield*.

WITH WAKEFIELD'S MONEY, I paid Cecily's rent at the boardinghouse. I bought Doxie a new crib, and Cecily a new pillow. In the days after our visit to Wakefield's, Cecily had got in the habit of having headaches. "How do you live with this heat?" she asked me a time or two, looking at me with suspicion. I bought an electric fan that kicked up cool breezes from a block of ice in a porcelain bowl.

I bought a typewriter, used but newer than the one I'd had, and I would drag it out the window with me, onto the porch roof, where I wrote letters, wearing only my trousers, my feet bare, my shirt off, the sun on my naked back. I wrote a letter to the editor of the *Bee* on behalf of yet another engineer who took credit for the airship we saw in the night skies. The engineer promised to eventually unveil all mysteries. *All will be revealed*, I wrote, *at the Fair.*

And I wrote love letters for other men's lovers and poems for lonesome wives. But every love letter was inspired by Cecily. Sometimes, in seeking the right sentiment, I got lost in a past afternoon, trying to put it all into words. I drank tea with a chip of ice in the teacup, and daydreamed.

August had brought us his samovar when he'd heard of Cecily's headaches, along with little silk pockets of crushed leaves and dried nettles. He recommended skullcap and lavender. Cecily had quickly emptied the bottle Wakefield had sent home with us, and her headaches would ease for a while, but then come back double.

"This is nothing but swamp root," August complained, sniffing the fumes from her medicine bottle, when he visited our room one afternoon. He found us in the dark, lying in our bed. Cecily often skipped the rehearsals for *Heart of the White City*, but she never got fired. The sun somehow felt a thousand times hotter in the Grand Court, she said, in the dazzle of the daylight against the ivory. But we had grown happy to go nowhere. Our new wealth had spoiled us. We were butterflies caught in a net.

August threw the curtains open and I covered Cecily's eyes. "She's having a really bad one today," I whispered.

"I suspect she is," he said. He ran his finger through the dust of the wardrobe and kicked at some dirty clothes strewn on the floor.

He picked up an empty bottle, and another one. Wakefield's butler, Morearty, had kept her stocked in tonics of various kinds. "Remember," Morearty would say, "just a swig or two every now and again." And on the days Cecily did go to the theater, and Wakefield happened to be there, he would give her even more new potions to try. I would have hidden the bottles, or thrown them away, but Cecily complained that she was in pain if she didn't take a sip of syrup every now and then.

"What does Mrs. Margaret say about all this?" August said.

Cecily got up from the bed and walked to the open window. She picked up a pack of cigarettes, lit up, and blew her smoke outside, leaning her elbows on the windowsill. She wore only her corset cover and an underskirt. "Mrs. Margaret is ignoring us," she said. "She won't even speak to me in the hall. She hates Ferret."

"Have you been to a doctor, Cecily?" August said. He lay back in the bed, where Cecily had been. He curled up next to me and Doxie, and put his hand on my shoulder. I hadn't dressed for the day either, and was in nothing but my underdrawers.

"The headaches aren't *crippling*," she said. "They're just a nuisance."

August kissed Doxie's forehead. "I brought you more tea," August said, dropping the silk pocket on the bed between us.

"Aren't you just selling the same remedies?" I said.

"Ferret, what I sell is water and nectar mostly," he said, sighing with frustration as he stood. "Some herbs, some extracts. Maybe a few drops of beet juice for color. It's harmless. I tell people to be careful with it, just for the charm of the act. *That's* what people are paying me for, Ferret. Just the humbug of it. But this stuff . . ." He picked up a brown bottle, uncorked it, and sniffed. "This, for example, is Jamaican ginger. Druggists aren't even allowed to sell it to Indians. It's intoxicating. But you white people are allowed to guzzle it by the gallon."

When August left, Cecily blamed his distaste on his jealousy—he was simply peevish because we rarely went to the Fair anymore. I suspected she might be right. I knew I could trust August, but wouldn't

Wakefield know something about doctors, and pain? He'd had his own arm ripped off. His wife had been sick, and she'd died. He could afford the best treatment in the biggest cities. He would have insights that would otherwise be deprived us.

But she did seem to ease up on her medicines, and we sought other advice. Even the midwife who delivered Doxie came to the room one afternoon. "Your womb hasn't recovered from the violence done to it in childbirth," the old crone told us, as she held her hand against Cecily's stomach and eyed Doxie with accusation.

I recalled Pearl's tinted spectacles, and how they'd been prescribed by a doctor to still her ovaries. When Pearl stopped by the boarding-house with some bottles of lemonade, she blushed at the mention of her red glasses. "I threw those horrid things away," she said. She'd been to a lecture, she explained, and had become enlightened. "It's all hog-wash. The doctors will blame the womb for every lady's every malady," she said. "They want us to believe that being a woman is an illness in and of itself."

But Cecily's headaches had become so constant, I was willing to believe not only in every cure but also every ailment. If her aches could be ended by steadying her womb, then I hoped for her womb to be hectic. I hoped for her to be sick with something that could be cured so easily.

A FEW DAYS LATER August and Pearl returned, and this time they brought Rosie. Rosie wasn't the type to go visiting, and the massive bulk of him shrunk the room. The crystals of the lampshade jingled as he walked across the floor. He bumped his head on the paper lantern that hung from the ceiling. As he sat on the overturned washtub, we weren't so much intimidated as confused by the sight of him making a social gesture. August made us all tea, and the cup, tiny in Rosie's fingers, seemed it might shatter with his every slurping sip.

August called the tea *scandal water*, as tea parties were typically circles of gossip. "Rosie has a few snatches of gossip himself," August said.

"You're fueling the war with those patent medicines," Rosie said.

Cecily wore a kimono, her hair fastened up with a whalebone comb decorated with a constellation of little gold stars. She sat on the edge of the bed drinking her tea, facing the wall, her back to all of us. "I quit taking the medicine . . . for the most part," she said, with some irritation. "I just endure the pain."

"That's good," Rosie said. "If it's a pain you can live with, then you don't need to kill it, do you?" Cecily only shrugged. "The government put a special tax on those medicines that advertise in the paper, you know," he said, the teacup held near his chest, one pinky out. "The nostrum tax. For the war. They tax all the cheap medicines that you get from any druggist. The poor don't have any doctors, so we buy the celery tonic that's half water and half liquor, or something worse, to keep us wanting it. It costs fifteen cents to make and we buy it for a dollar. And since the government needs the money, they'll approve any drug. And the newspapers get rich off the advertising. And we all get poorer, because we're paying for the battleships that'll blow up in the harbors."

Cecily set her cup in her saucer and leaned over to place the saucer on the desk, next to my typewriter. She stood up. As she spoke, she looked down to smooth out the wrinkles of her kimono, pretending to be perfectly calm. "So my headaches are sinking our ships, is what you're telling me," she said.

"And maiming our soldiers," Rosie said. "Then they come home. They can't work. They can't afford doctors. And they start taking the tonics too. Even the whiskey's medicinal these days."

I stood, and I took Rosie's teacup from him, and August's. "Maybe you should go," I said, though it felt cruel to be dismissive. Rosie only wanted to see Cecily feel better. He loved us. And I could see the line of logic Rosie followed. I just didn't think there was any hope of it helping. "Cecily's headaches aren't political," I said. I cast a glance at

Pearl then too, so she knew we wouldn't need medical advice from her women's societies either.

"But they are political," Rosie said. He put on his hat and walked toward the door. "The more headache medicine you take, the more headaches you get. And then you take more medicine."

"Oh, Rosie," Cecily said, suddenly smiling, chipper. She rolled her eyes to mock his seriousness and stood on her toes to kiss Rosie on the cheek. "Don't worry about me. I'll be sure to write President McKinley and insist he stop banging around in my head."

Her good-byes were cheerful then, with kisses all around. But after they all left, Cecily's smile dropped, and she leaned back against the door. She rubbed her temples with her fingertips. I walked up to her and kissed her. "Ignore Rosie," I said. "He's been angry for years. The Board of Health chased him out of his own tar-paper hut down by the river bottoms. They were afraid all the squatters living there would bring back the cholera. And they were probably right. So what does he know?"

And though Cecily left the boardinghouse for rehearsals every day that week, I became doubtful she ever took the stage. She wore a perfume I'd never smelled before, not the same sweet pea scent I'd grown to love but something spiced, musky, and when I asked her about it, she said she'd simply stopped at the druggist on her way to the theater and treated herself. I became suspicious of the slightest things—a sprig of wool violets stuck into the knot of her hair, a blush of pink rouge on her cheeks. And she would claim to buy herself more than just new perfume—she had charms on a bracelet, such as a little golden Buddha with a tiny glass diamond set in his belly.

She said she'd stopped at Brandeis for the reindeer-skin driving gloves she brought home one evening.

"But you have nothing to drive," I said.

"You don't have to drive anything to have driving gloves," she said.

At the end of the week, we left Doxie with the landlady and I bought Cecily dinner at Bridenbecker's, a restaurant on Farnam Street.

The proprietors listed their menu on a chalkboard (pig's head, pig's tongue, pig's tail, pig's feet, fried halibut, coffee jelly in cream, Charlotte russe) and a fiddler played in the corner, mostly hidden by beer casks. I reached across the table and took her hand in mine. On her bracelet was a frog set with glass emeralds. I flipped the frog over with my thumb, and on the frog's golden underbelly, I saw the initials *W.W.* The letters were minuscule, practically invisible, but they were somehow as shocking, as bold, as if Wakefield had carved his bloody initials into her flesh.

My hand began to shake. It wasn't jealousy firing up through me. It was fear. It was the same worry I'd had over Cecily's headaches—his initials on her wrist might as well have been a black spot of cancer. I felt her slipping away from me, like a breath I couldn't catch.

Cecily gave my hand a squeeze, gripping my hand tighter. "Billy gave that to me," she said, without even a flinch of shame.

"It must be real emeralds then," I said, my stomach churning.

"Oh not at all," she said. She pulled her hand away, and she touched at the frog. "I wouldn't have accepted it if it was anything of worth. He just gave it to me as a joke. I told him how I'd taken ballet lessons as a girl, and how I'd been in a troupe that was terribly untalented. 'It was a real frog salad,' I said. And he thought it was funny, my calling it that. And the next day he brought me this."

"I didn't know you were in a ballet," I said. "Do you speak to Wakefield often?"

Cecily sighed. "No," she said. "Not at all."

"But you just said you talked to him one day, and he gave you a gift the next. That's not 'not at all.'" She glared at me, rolled her eyes, and took a sip of wine. "Do you talk to him every day? In passing? Do you sit down together?"

Cecily leaned over, breathing through her nose. She grit her teeth and spoke slowly. "*We . . . exchange . . . pleasantries*," she seethed. Then she said, "Your jealousy is insulting."

"I'm just curious," I said. "Why do you talk to him? About ballet? About frogs? Or anything? And if you just exchange pleasantries, why would he give you a gift? With his initials on it?"

"I don't know, Ferret," she said. "He probably gives gifts engraved with his initials to everybody he sees. You know how the rich are. They think they're royalty. We're all supposed to be tickled by the attention." She smiled, and took my hand again. She looked me in the eyes. "I have a confession," she said. "He's been giving me something new. A headache powder. I've been taking it, and it's been working. I didn't want to tell you because I didn't want to worry you. But I'm *so* relieved. It's made all the difference. And it's not like the patent medicines Rosie and August were talking about. You can't even buy it at the druggist. And doctors around here don't know anything about it. It comes from a very esteemed doctor in New York City." She took her hand away and took another drink of her wine. "So that's why I accepted a bauble from Billy Wakefield. To be polite."

"How much of the powder do you take?" I said. "How often do you take it?"

My questions, or the brusque way I asked them, made Cecily angry again, and she refused to answer. Then she said, "Billy struggled a great deal with his wife's illness. He has insights."

"What do you know about his wife?" I said. "And what makes you think this is an illness? Do you think you're ill?"

"For God's sake, Ferret," she said. "Don't do this to me. Don't tell me I'm well when I'm not. Don't patronize me. I have to take these things seriously. You don't know what it's like. I have a child to look after."

"No, I don't know what it's like," I mumbled.

Cecily sighed, tilted her head. She realized she'd upset me, but she continued. "How *would* you know?" she said, pitying.

"Let's leave," I said.

"Our food's coming," she said.

"No, I mean, let's leave Omaha," I said. "Let's go."

"To where, Ferret?" she said, with a hiss of spite. "Where are we going?"

I took her hand again. "It doesn't matter," I said.

"Of course, because nothing matters to you," she said. "We could live our whole lives in that boardinghouse, never taking a step outside, and you'd be perfectly happy."

"Yes," I said. "I can't think of anything that would make me happier."

"And what happens when you stop loving me? Then what will we have?"

"I could never stop loving you," I said.

"Your romance is sweet," she said. "But you talk like a—a child." She clucked her tongue. She shrugged her shoulders. "You're a child." She looked down at our hands, and she stroked my palm with her thumb. "Billy says you don't want me to get well. He says you want to keep me sick."

I snapped my hand back. I dropped my fist against the table, rattling the silverware. I yelled. "Nobody cares what Billy says," I said. I then grabbed Cecily's wrist, pinched the frog between my fingers, and wrenched the charm free from the bracelet. I threw it across the restaurant, above the heads of the other diners.

I regretted my rage even before I looked to see Cecily so startled. She held her hand to her mouth, and her face was deep red. She trembled. She wept. I began to apologize, to beg her forgiveness, but she stood from the table to leave. I threw some money on the tabletop just as our dinner arrived.

I followed her to the boardinghouse, staying a few steps back. We didn't speak. We returned to the room together, and I paid the landlady who'd sat next to Doxie's crib reading a novel by lamplight. When the woman left, I shut the door, and Cecily and I undressed in a silence that pressed against me, that stilled the air in the room. I worried that every second that passed gave her more time to consider my wretchedness, my worthlessness. But I feared that anything I said—even *I'm sorry*, even *I love you*—would just be more evidence of my ignorance. Or worse, would lead to some truth she was too afraid to tell me, some twist ending she was waiting to reveal.

We put out the lights and got into bed. She turned onto her side, her back to me. That awful silence kept me from sleeping. Then I heard a whimper, and I looked over to see her sobs gently shaking her. I stroked her arm, her shoulder. I got up on one elbow to speak into her ear. "I love you so much," I said. "I never want to lose you."

She turned to me and put her arm around my shoulder. "You can't ever leave me," she said. "You can't. I can't be alone again."

IN THE MORNING, we didn't speak of the night before.

I WOKE CECILY BEFORE SUNUP, kissing her cheek, her neck, her naked shoulder. She ran her fingers through my hair. I undid the tiny buttons at the front of her nightgown and kissed her chest. I licked her nipple, and I ran my tongue along the sweat beneath her breast. I unbuttoned her gown further and kissed her stomach and kissed her hip. Her fingers caught in a tangle of my hair, giving my curls a yank. I flinched and looked up to see her smiling at my pain. She gave my hair another light pull, and another shot of pain, and this time I growled low and pushed myself up to bury my face between her neck and her shoulder, lunging, my teeth lightly gnawing on her skin. She shrieked and laughed, and she wrapped her arms around my shoulders, her legs around my hips. As we kissed, I held my hand at the back of her head, and pushed her head forth as I pressed my lips harder against hers, my tongue against hers. I lay on top of her, and she wrapped her arms tighter, pulling me closer, pushing herself beneath me, her wanting more and more of my weight to hold her there.

We made love, and by dawn we were tired again, and we napped an hour more, not having untangled our arms and legs. We woke drenched in sweat and the smell of each other, but we didn't even run a washcloth over our skin. We threw on whatever clothes were nearest on the floor, took Doxie from her crib behind the screen, changed and powdered her, and left the room. And we still hadn't said hardly a word to each other. The silence, the not speaking, comforted now. The silence was as light as mist. But the room, where we'd been so happy to be trapped, seemed to be losing every breath of air with every ray of sun that slipped in. Our movement stirred the dust that caught in the morning light.

For a while we just walked, talking little, mostly just leaning into each other and moving slow as Cecily pushed the pram and I held Doxie, feeding her her bottleful of milk. Despite Pearl's politics, Cecily now wore tinted glasses prescribed by an iridologist—Cecily's lenses were blue to treat the equilibrium part of the eye, an effort to end her headaches. She wore a shirtwaist patterned with bars and notes, and a few lyrics, like a sheet of music. I wore only an undershirt and trousers, and a derby, my suspenders dangling at my sides. And I was barefoot again.

We'd walked so far away from the Fair, we decided to keep going, to the Howard Street flea market, where the rag-and-bone peddlers parked their carts full of junk and shoddy. The goods, if you could call them that, were collected from all the world over—anything from a dented tin cup from a cowboy's satchel to a chipped teapot of blue-and-white china from a London parlor. It was here that I had first found Oscar hanging on the side of a wagon alongside a whole colony of broken dolls, all of them strung together on a clothesline, a chain gang of misfits missing limbs or stripped naked.

I carried Doxie in the crook of my arm and held my derby up between her and the sun to give her some shade. Cecily pushed the baby carriage along the street, all the while weighing it down with snatches of fabric and secondhand dresses. She was expert at bargaining, casting some kind of hex on the peddlers whenever she lifted the tinted lenses up from in front of her eyes.

"Nobody's going to buy that ratty old dirndl," she might say, and the seller would somehow agree, and he would sigh, and he would take whatever pitiable sum she offered.

Back in the room, we ripped the dresses apart at the seams. The landlady rented us her sewing machine, and her sons carried its cabinet up the stairs and crammed it into the only corner it fit. Cecily had to sit on the edge of the bed to work it, her granny-like glasses perched at her nose, and she began to patch together street skirts and shirtwaists of her own invention, turning things inside out and upside down—the velvet from a hat for the belt of a skirt, the sateen lining of an old coat for the sleeves of a gown.

CECILY SKIPPED that afternoon's rehearsal, but the next day she insisted I go with her. I told her there was no need, I'd been foolish, I'd been jealous. I told her I trusted her, I trusted her more than I'd ever trusted anyone, but she said the walk, the sunlight, would do Doxie good, and that I might enjoy seeing all the actors and actresses muddle through the awful script, missing cues, dropping props, stumbling over the half-finished sets. It was unsightly, she said. And it must be seen to be believed. So I went with her to the theater at the Fair.

Wakefield was indeed in the lobby. He was the first person I saw inside, and I bristled at the sight of him. How could a man so important have such leisure? Had he nothing better to do than lurk and linger? He was the boss of every factory in town, and producer of every entertainment. He paid us our wages at the end of the day, then took it away when we went out for the night.

But I was pleased to see how little notice he took of Cecily. Or, at least, he took no more notice of her than he did the other actresses. And the actresses did gather. All the girls likely knew who he was, so they reacted to his lazy stabs at flirting, his cold nods and awkward winks, as if he were the most charming gent alive. As it turned out, he gave them charms for their bracelets too. He had a pocket full of them.

"Did you see the frog I gave Cecily?" Wakefield asked as I wheeled the pram into the lobby. He leaned forward, his hands behind his back, to look in at Doxie beneath the umbrella. He didn't even offer the baby the slightest flicker of a smile.

"I did," I said. "She lost it."

"A shame," he said with a shrug.

Despite his seeming indifference, he invited Cecily and me to dinner in a rooftop café on the Grand Court that night, then again a few nights later. Whenever we dined with him, we could have been anyone—he asked us nothing, and responded to nothing we said. But he boasted, and we genuinely enjoyed his tales of influence. And he seemed to enjoy our enjoyment. We loved it, particularly, whenever he started anything with, "Now don't tell anyone . . ." The phrase was always followed with some privileged bit of knowledge. We were not to tell anyone many things: that President McKinley would visit the Fair as soon as the details and negotiations for peace with Spain were settled; that the New White City was already turning pale gray from the smoke of the smelting works and would need a thorough whitewash before fall; that a Salvation Army lieutenant had been arrested for taking a hatchet to the genitals of a statue of a naked cherub she'd found offensive.

And he told us just a little about Oscar, and his reasons for buying him. "Sentimental attachment," he said. "Nothing more than that. My son had a very similar toy." And to think, I deeply pitied him just then. He sniffled and plucked a handkerchief from his pocket, but he explained away his sudden red eyes and runny nose as symptoms of allergy. The lagoon, he said, and the humidity, were turning the structures mossy and soft with mold. The framework of the New White City was warping around us, cracking the plaster walls, threatening the domes over our heads. *Don't tell anyone . . .*

IN THE DARK OF OUR ROOM, Cecily lifted money from Wakefield's dragon to hire me. "Write me love letters," she said. "Nobody ever sent me one before."

I ate a cold grape from the bunch we'd thrown in with the ice. When writing love letters to be sent to other women by other men, I'd grown lazy. I peppered them with lines lifted from the published love letters of others—from John Keats to Fanny Brawne, or those letters written by that Portuguese nun.

But the very second she requested a letter I started composing one in my head, with words all my own. "Find me some paper," I said. "Quick."

Cecily carefully ripped a blank page from the front of a book. As I wrote, I read aloud. "'If I was a poet, I could tell you how beautiful you are. You have plump red lips like wax cherries. You have long eyelashes that catch the snowflakes when they fall. Isn't that something a poet might write on a valentine, my love?'"

"You've never even seen my eyelashes in the snow," she said.

I rolled forward to kiss her ankle. "But I will," I said. "The winters here are fierce."

"The Fair's over before winter," she said.

"You won't leave with the Fair," I said. I kissed her leg.

"What if I do?" she said.

"I'll die," I said.

"Why would you do something like that to me?"

"You wouldn't know about it," I said. I kissed her knee. "You're gone by then. You leave me when winter comes. And then I die. And you never know." I ran my lips along the inside of her naked thigh.

Cecily put her fingers to my chin and tilted my head up to look in my eyes. "But you'll write me love letters, and you'll tell me you're dying, and then the letters will stop, and I'll know then."

"I can't send you letters," I said. I brought my face up to kiss her lips, and I touched my tongue to hers. "I don't know where you are. You and little Doxie don't have a home. You move from boardinghouse to boardinghouse. That's no way to live."

After we kissed for a while, I got off the bed and went to my hat, upturned on the floor. Inside the hat was a ring box, and inside the box a ring with a heart, and at the heart of the heart, a cluster of little diamonds. I'd paid cash for it at Brandeis, and Pearl had helped me pick it out. Pearl had put it on to model it, and I'd held her fingers with mine, tilting her hand from side to side, wondering if the little diamonds had enough sparkle.

I got on my knees beside the bed, put my elbows on the mattress, and took the ring from the box. "Won't you marry me?" I said.

Cecily's eyes turned wet, and she sniffled, and she took a deep shaky breath as she let me put the ring on her finger. She held her hand against my cheek, and she looked at the ring. "Write it to me in a letter?" she said. "Your proposal of marriage? I want to have something to show Doxie when she gets older. She'll want to see it."

"Then will you say yes?" I said. "Because you haven't said yes yet."

She nodded. I turned my head to kiss her wrist, to kiss her palm.

Dear Cecily, I wrote, but I could think of nothing else to say. I was too happy, my heart too full. I didn't want to think in words.

CECILY'S HEADACHES had grown mild, lessening to a feeble pulse at her temples that she could almost convince herself was pleasant. "I just think of you kissing me here," she said, tapping at her forehead, and I kissed her right there, right then, as we entered the Fair as fine new citizens, not workers, of the New White City. Cecily had somehow convinced me she felt invincible. With her headaches cured, she would cure me of my fear of heights. And I felt inclined to believe her, somehow.

The manager of the Civil War exhibit offered to let us ascend in the basket of the tethered balloon, to the end of its rope, to watch the sun set.

I felt my vertigo spinning my head before we'd even lifted an inch, but I said nothing. I wanted, more than anything, to be fearless for Cecily. If ever my life had been touched with magic, it was in those days when Cecily wore my ring. I had no doubts, no troubles. And my contentment became contagious—even Mrs. Margaret finally forgave. She'd come to Cecily's room that morning to make amends, in her way. "Marry the devil himself why don't you," she told Cecily, as I sat on the edge of the bed putting on my socks. "Why should I trouble myself about it?" she said. And with that, Cecily threw her arms around Mrs. Margaret, and kissed and kissed and kissed the old woman's jowls. Cecily let Mrs. Margaret take Doxie for the day, to a park down the street, but Mrs. Margaret refused to use the pram. Instead, she returned Doxie to the carpetbag. "Doxie likes to be rocked in it," Mrs. Margaret explained. "She likes to be right at my side."

I held on to the edge of the balloon's basket, digging my feet into the floor of it, holding fast like I had on the night of Wakefield's cyclone. This was worse than the Flying Waltz—at least then, dancing with Cecily, the wires had given the illusion of safety. Cecily now held tightly to my arm. "Squeeze my hand as hard as you need to," she whispered, and I wrapped my fingers so tight around her hand that the heart of her ring left a deep red imprint in my skin that didn't fade for hours.

As we rose, Cecily leaned out over the side of the basket to take in the sight of the city and the river and the countryside beyond. I watched with horror, too easily picturing her tumbling out and dragging me over. I begged her not to lean over the edge. As we bobbed in the air, she pointed to the horizon. "I think I can see the boardinghouse!" she said, excited, as if the house was her home.

She turned to face me and she now held both my hands, helping me feel anchored. "Let's steal the balloon," she said. "Steal me away,

Ferret. Kidnap me. We'll just live wherever the balloon comes down. Just you and me. We'll take new names. New lives. We'll hide."

She looked at me, on the verge of tears, and it felt too dangerous to say anything at all. If we stole the balloon and lived where it landed, we'd be leaving Doxie behind. I couldn't speak. I didn't want her to think that I would ever want such a thing. But neither did I want to scold her for spinning a yarn, for slipping into a minute of fantasy that didn't hurt a soul. To me, she could say anything she wanted to say. Anything at all. But I had to leave her alone in this. Doxie—she was my little girl.

When Cecily took her hands back and started to twist my ring off her finger, I was struck with worry. In some sense I'd been waiting for her to take it off ever since she'd first put it on. But then she said, "Propose to me again. But like it's the first time. This is the story I want to tell Doxie. That you proposed to me in the balloon."

And so I did. I asked her, again, to marry me. And again she wouldn't say yes. She wouldn't say the word. She let me put the ring on her finger, and she kissed me. She wrapped her arms around me, and she put her cheek against my chest, listening to the fast beat of my heart. "You really *are* afraid, aren't you?" she said.

Thanksgiving (the night of) 1898

Dear Cecily,

I often wonder what would have happened had I cut the rope somehow, when we were up in the balloon together. What if I'd dropped the sandbags and let us drift off? I sometimes picture us living near an abandoned little town, even deeper in the country than here where I am, way out where everything dried up or flooded, where all the harvests reaped only worm-eaten crops. We would've gone to the city to steal Doxie back, but otherwise we would never leave our broken-down farm, spending our nights starving to death in each other's arms in secret, watching the fireflies blink.

Today, for Thanksgiving dinner, the sisters opened their doors to all their neighbors from miles around. The ones who came were the ones most grief-struck by the holidays, by the empty chairs around their tables and the quiet rooms down their halls. Emmaline and Hester cooked all of yesterday and today, and they covered the dining room table with turkeys and pheasants and sausages, with mincemeat pies, and plates of salted alligator pears, and a chowder of scalded oyster liquor and cream. You wouldn't know from the feast that the Old Sisters Egan's farm had been strangled and choked years ago.

And though the house was packed to the belfry, no one made a noise. They whispered and crept, respecting me, their oracle.

And I called out to them, asking them into the parlor, whenever they peeked in. One by one they sat down next to me, and I offered them little.

Ever since falling from the sky, I've resisted playing the part they so need me to play. I'm not a priest or a pastor. I don't know anything about what they've lost, or where their lost ones have gone. But it seems, with so little effort, I can offer them a moment of calm. At first it felt like deception. It felt like a theft to promise them anything. But the comfort I could lend lifted my spirits too. It warmed my heart to see them feel a snippet of hope.

When the first woman sat down with me today, I didn't know what to tell her. And she seemed to need me to say <u>something</u>. The only words I could summon were the questions on Oscar's phonograph. Oscar's questions seemed like something a wizard would ask. <u>What do you wish me to do? Why should I do this for you?</u> And with that, I had to ask nothing more. And more and more of them came into my parlor to hear those same questions.

They brought me old tintypes of their fathers, their grandfathers, their brothers, their sons. They brought me locks of a daughter's hair and a page torn from a wife's diary.

I still gave them next to nothing. But they were thrilled with even a sentence, no matter how cryptic. I spoke my nonsense, and they nodded, making sense of it. And where's the harm?

What if all they need is a whisper of faith? It's not mischief I'm up to. These good people just need to know, after years of struggle, that the prayers they've been praying, Sunday after Sunday, have finally scared up an angel.

And my talents as a thief finally serve a holy purpose. Back as a boy, as a wharf rat for the river men, I learned to see the rage before I saw the fist. I became a prophet of abuse, seeing every slug coming from a mile away. And in the street, fleecing strangers, I learned the habits of a man's elbow in a stiff suit coat, and the meager give of a lady's corset whenever she went to turn. As a thief, you anticipate surprise. When a man's hand goes here—as it always does and always will—your hand goes there, and you take what's his. You look for the fall and flutter of his shadow and you let it serve you in your crime. You dance your own shadow like a puppet, or you allow it to dodge the sun and slip away, and all in all, you know that his gaze will go from here to here to here so you go from there to there to there. You calculate gullibility in just the way a gentleman stands. You detect a lady's character in the spin of her parasol.

Here on the farm, I put the back of my hand to the foreheads of men and women and children to calculate the damage of their fevers. I feel for their pulses in their wrists, and attach meaning to the rhythm of the beats. I press my fingers to their throats. I sniff at a baby's sour breath.

And I only ever tell them what they could have figured out for themselves.

F.

21.

W HEN WAKEFIELD sent along yet another invitation, I accepted on the spot. Morearty stopped by the boardinghouse, having driven himself down in a one-horse buggy. *Ferret & Cecily* was written across the front of the envelope he handed me, our names made nearly illegible by all the swirl and flourish of the pen. I barely glanced at the card before starting to fan my sweaty neck with it. I told the old butler, as I leaned back on the picket fence, "Tell Wakefield I said 'Why the hell not?'"

It makes me sick to cast back with my mind's eye to my arrogance. My vanity. I could've simply declined. Why hadn't my instincts led me to hide Cecily away, to keep her to myself, out of sight of everyone?

The truth was, I was proud. As proud as Wakefield, in my way. I wanted him to see how Cecily loved only me. I wanted the richest man in Omaha to want everything that was mine.

The cyclone machine is now divinely unstoppable, the invitation read. *I've thrown together an afternoon of devastation. When we arrive in Pink Heron, Nebraska, it will still be a place on the map, but when we leave, all the maps will be wrong. Don't eat lunch, for we'll have a lavish early afternoon dinner in the Peacock Room of the condemned Pink Heron Hotel, so that we may watch the town destroyed by my tornado while there's still good sun to be had.*

And beneath the engraving, Wakefield had scribbled, *F&C, Dress in your finest, as you'll be hobnobbing with snobs. W.W.*

We met the other guests at the train station early Sunday morning, to be ferried by private car to the depot of a town called Blue Creek, the stop that got us the closest to Pink Heron. But, of course, had Pink Heron been easily reachable by rail, it might not have perished. The countryside was riddled with new houses and new schools abandoned, whole towns pristine and empty. People had flocked to Nebraska for the land, only to discover they'd bought acres of desert. A few summers of insects, heat, drought, and flood, and the people fled their new houses without even taking down the curtains.

Wakefield hadn't told us we would leave the luxury of the private car to sit in the back of a long hay wagon pulled by a team of local steeds. There were three such wagons for all the party's guests, and most everyone was amused by the novelty of it. Wakefield had had chairs and tables set up in the carts for parlor games and rounds of cards. A few pretty maids in linen and aprons had been tasked with standing next to the tables with enormous parasols, dropping some shade on us all. But most of the women had their own shade, sitting beneath their elaborate hats decorated for their trip into the country-side, with wildflowers and thistle and milkweed woven into the hatbands.

Each cart was equipped with a fiddler in an evening coat who played what sounded to me like lullabies. Two old men at my table bickered about whether the tune was Schumann or Schubert, and then they bickered about which of the two was the greater composer.

Cecily and I were likely the party's clowns, dressed as we were. Cecily had lifted bills from the dragon's head to return to the Howard Street market. For me, she had plucked from a peddler's cart a swallowtail coat, and she'd made me a vest out of that dismantled dirndl she'd bought before. My stovepipe hat was a little bit crushed, but she pinned onto it a moth she'd knotted from a silk hankie. "Wakefield always digs up the best characters," old Schumann said, and I nodded and half bowed in my seat, taking it as a compliment.

"Like all those spiritualists," Schumann's wife said, and the others at the table clucked their tongues, rolled their eyes. They chuckled, but disdainfully. ("Yes, yes, yes," they all said. "Yes, those spiritualists.") "All those séances we've sat through. All those ghosts we've summoned."

I'd been to a few séances myself. Some of them were held in public halls, as theater. A clairvoyant could get good work in those days— with the century about to turn, everyone, rich and poor, seemed mindful of other worlds and the afterlife.

I closed my eyes, dropped my jaw, and placed my fingertips atop the table, all to their amusement. I hummed demonically, as if falling into a dark trance. Everyone laughed some more. "Is that you, Aunt Nannie?" Schubert said. "Who pushed you down the stairs, Aunt Nannie?"

We made introductions. Schubert owned a brewery, while Schumann had the vinegar works. "Ah yes," I said, "I do all my best pickling with your vinegar." This made the old men, and their old wives, laugh some more. "Ferret Skerritt," I said, flicking my card out from up my sleeve. "Ventriloquism and magic tricks."

For herself, Cecily had fashioned a gown from a tablecloth patterned with grapes and grasshoppers.

"It's just Russian crash," she told Schumann's wife when the woman asked about the gown's fabric.

"I wouldn't say so," Schubert's wife said. "It looks Parisian."

Schumann's wife held a pearl-handled lorgnette to her eyes and leaned in to examine the dress. "I tore all the rucked-velvet roses off a dreadful hat and stitched them on wherever there was a threadbare spot," Cecily said, lifting at a rose at the low-cut neckline. The women seemed amused by her ingenuity. All the front and back of her dress was scattered with those patches of roses. I couldn't take my eyes off Cecily, or the sweet freckles across the skin of her chest.

To punish me, most likely, for my war talk on the Fourth of July, Wakefield had seated me at a table with a game called War in Cuba—you pulled back the spring of a little cannon to shoot wooden balls at a row of tin soldiers on hinged pegs on a board. When it was Cecily's turn to massacre Spanish troops, I kissed her ear and ran my fingers over the back of her neck. She lifted her chin like a cat getting scratched, so I kissed her throat too. She fumbled with the cannon, sending the ball skittering.

Schumann, or Schubert—I'd already lost track of who was who—made much of having caught the ball easy with one hand, keeping it from rolling off the cart altogether. Everyone applauded his dexterity, as if he'd saved the day from ruin.

AT DINNER, ON EACH PLATE, there was a scrawny bird we didn't know. Cecily and I, too shy to ask the uppity among us, concluded it was partridge or squab, though we tickled ourselves by speculating otherwise. "Canary?" I whispered to Cecily. "Rook?" Cecily whispered back. This went on for a while. *Swallow? Sparrow? Finch? Hummingbird? Butterfly? Mosquito? Gnat?*

The dinner was served on the hotel's china which had been found left in a hutch. A maid ladled lobster bisque from a tureen into our tiny bowls, and old Morearty poured us a wine that was a deep bloodred. The old butler's hand shook, and drops of wine stained the sleeves of nearly all the fine men around the long table.

Once we'd all picked the meat off the little bird bones, Wakefield stood. "Let's raise our glasses to a man named Dudley," he said, lifting his snifter. Morearty now dribbled our sleeves with that quince brandy Wakefield favored, and the maid handed out Cuban cigars. We all looked around for this Dudley, but Wakefield said, "Oh he's not here.

He ran off long ago. He built this hotel on a hill, thinking a town would rise up around it." He raised his glass higher. "God bless his blind ambition, and thank God none of us were born so stupid."

The rich men laughed, and so did their wives, but their laughter didn't sound at all jolly. It sounded like a noise they'd all invented for occasions when laughter was called for.

"Flood the town and make it a lake," one of the youngest of the bunch said, as he leaned back in his chair, rocking and balancing on the chair's back two legs. He wore a vest striped with purple and gold. I would later learn his name was Baker, of Baker Bros. Engraving Co. Everyone there, other than us, had their names on Omaha buildings. "Turn this hotel into a resort. You'd probably make a fortune without even trying. Some men have the golden touch, and others don't. It's that simple. You do, Dudley didn't."

Wakefield's sister, who'd been seated far at the other end of the table opposite her twin, leaned her own cigar into the flame of the butler's match. It was a skinny cigar wrapped in ivory paper. "Finally, I'm interested," she said, drawing out that word *finally* with a long, long sigh. "Destiny. Is that what you're speaking of, Mr. Baker?"

My old friend Schubert spoke up before Baker had a chance to answer. "There's no such thing," he said, gruff, dropping his fist on the table. "I was destined for nothing. Less than nothing. My father was in debtors' jail when I was a newborn, so I came into the world owing people. Everything I have I got on my own."

"By the sweat of your brow, and all that?" Billie said, smirking. "And *luck* had nothing to do with it? Nothing at all?"

At Billie's mention of luck, the table fell gloomy. No one among us said anything. Wakefield, after all, had all the best luck in the world but had paid too dearly for it. His shoulders slouching, he lowered himself into his chair. He drank up the dregs from the bottom of his snifter.

"You have not misunderstood me, Billie," Schubert said. "I do not believe in destiny, and I do not believe in luck."

I leaned over to whisper, my lips to Cecily's ears, and was only just about to ask her *Do* you *believe in luck?* when the same question was put to me.

"Well, do you, Ferret?" Billie said, raising her voice to call down the table. I felt my stomach lift and fall, like I was back in that balloon. "Ladies and gentlemen, we have with us today an honest-to-God waif," she said. "Raised in the street by thieves. Does someone like you, Ferret, trust in luck?"

I looked at the others all looking back at me. *Raised by thieves?* What did she know about me, and how did she know it?

I took Cecily's hand in mine, the hand with the ring, and I brought her fingers up to my lips for a kiss. "I'm the luckiest man alive," I said.

Everyone at the table was so grateful for my gesture, for the easing of the tension, they applauded, and they clucked their tongues at the very sweetness of it all. A few of them tapped their spoons against their glasses in celebration. "Hear, hear," old Schubert said, raising his snifter though there was nothing left in it. "Well done."

"Do you know who believed in luck, Pickle?" Wakefield called to Billie from far down the table, cupping his hand around his mouth like a megaphone. Pleased to have another reprieve from the somber mood, everyone perked up, raising their eyebrows.

Who who who, they all asked, filling the room with owls.

"Dudley, the founder of Pink Heron, Nebraska. There'd been a crippling drought when he arrived in these parts, but only a week later it rained. It rained so hard, it left a little pond, where he spotted a pink heron one sunny afternoon. It was a sign, he thought. Fortuitous. A symbol of luck and prosperity."

"Oh that's too too utterly marvelous," one of the wives said.

"Now," Wakefield said, "let's go tear his dream to pieces."

And with that, the guests pushed themselves from the table. The room filled with the scratching of chair legs against the wood floor. The men and women chattered and bellowed, and they made those laughlike noises again.

Though Wakefield intended to capture the wreckage with his motion picture camera outside, he insisted that all the rest of us keep to the rooms of the pink hotel, where we were to watch from the windows. Even the men who fancied themselves adventurers, who wanted to be out in all the whirl and wind of it, respected Wakefield's wishes. He was a living rebuke to the dangers of daredevilry.

Cecily got up from the table too fast. She grabbed hold of my arm to steady herself from the spinning of her dizzy spell, and I helped ease her back into her chair. There was no water left in her glass, and she'd emptied the pitcher too—she'd been guzzling it all through dinner, blaming the cook's heavy hand with the saltshaker. "I just need one more little sip," Cecily said, touching her fingertips to her temples. She looked up at me and said, in a tone that sounded like accusation, "Headache again."

I picked up her glass and left the dining hall to seek out the kitchen. When I found the doorway and stepped inside, an old woman wringing her hands in her apron looked at me wide-eyed, as shocked as if I'd stumbled upon her in her underskirts. I hadn't been among the rich long enough to know that the servants got embarrassed if you caught sight of the dishes in the sink and the pots on the stove.

"I just need a splash of water," I said. *I'm not one of them*, I wanted to add.

"Let *me*, Mr. Skerritt," Morearty said, suddenly at my side, taking the glass. "I'll bring it to you." He smiled broadly but gently, politely indicating I needed to leave the kitchen. He kept still, the glass just staying empty in his hand.

When I returned to the dining hall, there was no one left, not even Cecily. I followed the voices of the crowd to the lobby, and once there, I glanced through an entryway into another hall, to see Cecily and Wakefield off alone, sitting on the bottom steps of a grand staircase. Cecily held a snifter of brandy.

It certainly didn't surprise me that Wakefield had swooped in. The drapes were drawn and the hall was dark—Wakefield lured her forth, I assumed, promising that the shadows would chase the ache from her head.

When I walked up to them, they were both intently studying the fabric square that he'd pulled from the pocket of his dinner jacket. He held the fabric open in the palm of his metal hand.

"Oh, Ferret, look at this," Cecily said, setting down the snifter and plucking up the fabric. She stood from the steps and walked toward a window. She elbowed the drapery open an inch or two to let in just enough sun to glisten the jewels woven with gold thread into the mesh of the square. The jewels were all circles, some round, some oblong.

"But they aren't jewels at all," she said. "They're the backs of beetles. Billy bought this from a market in Egypt."

"We match," Wakefield said, walking over to us. He pointed toward the grasshoppers in the pattern of Cecily's dress. "We're both covered in insects." When she held the fabric out to him, he said, "I want you to keep it."

"I can't," she said. She then said to me, "It's very rare. It's only made for the women in harems."

"Dead bugs?" I said. "Morbid. Where'd your dizzy spell go?"

Wakefield said, "I gave her the tiniest pink pill," he said, "and her headache left in an instant."

"In the three seconds I was down the hall, you got a pill down her throat?" I said.

"Ferret . . . ," Cecily said, scolding.

"Would you like one?" Wakefield asked me, taking a vial from his trousers pocket. "It might cure you of that disposition," he said, not so kindly.

"No need to be rude about it," I said, moving my jaw around like I was gnawing on a toothpick.

"Really, Ferret," he said, "your determination to keep your lady in pain is quite ungentlemanly." We were then interrupted by another of his servants, who handed him a pith helmet and a pair of goggles. He then left us for the lobby where his guests gathered, and he assured everyone he'd be safely tucked away in a duck blind. Some ladies attempted to discourage him, but they did so too politely, for he left without a hitch in his step.

"He's leaned too close to such spectacle before," one woman said.

Baker, the young man of the engraving company, said, "Well, he still has another arm and two legs to lose." He sat at an upright in the parlor and played a melody that got him scolded by the old ladies who flapped fluttery lace fans with the quick wrists of disgust.

"I don't know what's so insulting about the tune," I whispered to Cecily.

"It's 'The Ballad of Billy Wakefield's Little Boy,'" she whispered, still enraptured by the beetle-backed hankie that she hadn't given back after all. "About the train crash that cost him his life."

"How do you know it?" I said.

"Me and Pearl had the girl play it for us at the store the other day," she said. There was a piano in the sheet music department of Brandeis, and when you picked a song that you might want to give a listen before paying the nickel, you took it to one of the shopgirls who would plunk it out. "We had her play it for us a few times, then a few times more. It's so sad. We just couldn't stop listening to it."

The butlers and maids had situated chairs at every window, upstairs and down, and on the pillow of every chair was a pair of opera glasses. Cecily and I roamed the halls, looking for the room with the best view of the valley below, of the few empty houses and barns, and the blacksmith's shop, and a red schoolhouse with a silver bell on its roof.

Suddenly, Billie was there in the hallway with us, her piglet in her arms. "Please ignore my bad manners at dinner, won't you?" she said.

"It's shrinking," I said of the runt.

"Piglets don't stay piglets," she said. "This is Mr. Swift. The piglet you met previously was Mr. Cudahy, who has moved on to capture other hearts." Cudahy and Swift were the names of a few of the packing houses of South Omaha.

Billie told us we were to watch the cyclone with her, in her suite on the top floor. She had been there a few days already, she told us, "living in the light of an oil lamp, like a pioneer girl in a soddy." The hotel had been abandoned but not emptied. Rooms were full of beds and vanities, draped with sheets, as if only shut up for a season. But there were also the dried husks of crickets and locusts in the corners, and cobwebs spun in among the chandeliers. Weather had cracked the walls and warped the wood of the floors. But in its day, if it had ever had a day, the pink hotel had been handsome. The wallpaper was flocked and the beds were brass.

The three of us sat on a davenport that old Morearty had pushed up to a bay window, Billie scooting in between Cecily and me. Her red gown was so full of frill and crinoline, its satin and lace spilled over into our laps. Billie took her own binoculars from an alligator-skin case, an elaborate set of spectacles with a strap she buckled at the back of her head. The glasses rested on the bridge of her nose, and the barrels, made of whale tooth, telescoped with a turn of a tortoiseshell wheel between her eyes. Once she had it set, her hands were free to cradle the fidgeting Mr. Swift.

I was still stinging from her scrutiny at dinner. Yes, I'd spent some time with thieves in my youth, but also the nuns, and it'd been years since I'd done much of anything dishonest. "I think you think you know things about me," I said, looking through my own opera glasses, holding them by a silver handle, to watch Wakefield walk down the hill. The only other men down below were two burly farm boys on either side of the cyclone machine, which had doubled since I'd seen it last, with two bellows now and a more complicated system of pipes. It sat on a wheeled cart, and the farm boys pumped the bellows with all their muscle and might.

"I know a thing or two," she said. "I probably know more about you than Cecily does."

The tornado began to bend the air, the wind of it starting to bat at some thistle.

"Cecily, did you know," Billie continued, "that Ferret got his name from his police record? Ferret is called Ferret because a ferret is something like a weasel, and do you know that old expression? When something is an impossible task, it's like catching a weasel asleep? The police found it impossible to pin a crime on the young weaselly Ferret Skerritt."

It was an insulting insinuation, this notion that I had something to hide. "Why would you go to all the trouble?" I said. "I hardly seem worth it." As the tornado worked itself into a good fierce conniption fit, the farm boys ran into the barn and out the door of the other side. They were tugging hard on a rope now, dragging the cyclone machine along on its wheels. As the tornado neared the barn, shingles flew off the roof and twirled in the air, a few of them smacking against Wakefield's duck blind as he turned the crank of his camera. The barn's weather vane pointed its iron arrow in every direction, faster and faster, spinning and spinning until it too spun off, stabbing the end of itself into the dry, cracked ground. The others in the hotel shrieked and yelped at the violence and threat, and all their noise echoed up through the hallways and floorboards.

"I don't want to see any more harm come to my brother," Billie said with a weary sigh, adjusting the wheel of her glasses to telescope the lenses an inch or so more. "I'm the only one in the world he can trust. You can't possibly imagine what it's like being Billy Wakefield. People will crawl out from anywhere to take advantage of his good nature." The tornado then began to lose its steam, turning into a puff of nothing, having only scattered some hay and torn a barn door off its hinges. "I think he paid much too much for that dummy of yours."

"I'll gladly buy it back from him," I said with a shrug, and before the words even left my tongue, I knew I could never manage it. Too much of the money was already gone.

"Oh, Ferret," Billie said, slapping my knee, "don't be so sour. There's no need to get owly with me. I'm your dear friend and I wouldn't dream of offending you. And it seems you've been a very, very good boy for the last several years. There's hardly anything on you at all. And I'm sure Cecily's record is as clean as a whistle, though I can't find a damn thing on the girl." Billie pushed her glasses up onto her forehead. "It's as if she never existed," she said, as if Cecily wasn't right at her side. Billie stood from the sofa, releasing her pig, letting it scurry away. "I'm spontaneously bored," she said. "I'm going to go see what I can pilfer from the rooms."

As she was about to step into the hallway, Billie clucked her tongue and snapped her fingers, remembering something. She went to a grip next to the vanity, and she took from it a book that she then dropped on the sofa between Cecily and me. I flipped open the book's cover with my pinky. *The Female Offender*, it said on the title page. *The Criminology Series.*

"I marked a particularly compelling paragraph on page one twenty," Billie said, and she left us.

Glancing over her shoulder toward the door, Cecily whispered, "That one smiles real pretty but she's mean as a rattler."

"And I have a feeling we're about to find out she's even meaner than we think," I said. I read aloud from the marked paragraph, from a chapter on the tattoos of prostitutes and other women of the clink.

"'Five women bore the half-length likeness of a young man; four showed two clasped hands; nine a heart, that well-worn symbol of love'"—that bit about the "well-worn symbol of love" was circled in pencil—"'three a kind of ribbon; two a branch with leaves, and two a leaf only. Eight had a bracelet, or a funereal cross, or a rosary, a ring, a star, a ship with sails, or a flag with cannon. Two women were tattooed in nine places, one in eleven, and another in fifteen. All these marks were on the upper part of the body; rarely on the legs or chest; and eight were on the joints of the fingers.'"

Cecily twisted her neck around, her pretty face a scowl, as she attempted to see her own back. She ran her fingers over her skin, as if she might locate the heart by touch. "Can you even see it?" she said.

"You can," I said, pushing down the petals of a velvet rose at her back, "when the dress droops a little, when you slouch. But even then you can only see a little."

"I've *never* been in jail," she said. "Except for once, and that was just to visit."

I kissed again the tattoo on her naked shoulder, then glanced back to the book to read more. "This is underlined too. 'Among prostitutes, those who are tattooed are the most depraved.'"

"That bitch is itchin' to get her eyes clawed out of her head," she said.

"An eye for an eye," I said, kissing her eyelid. "Tooth for a tooth," kissing her cheek.

The farm boys had kicked the tornado back into a fury, and as the machine neared the school, the bell rang like one in a firehouse as a city burned. The rest of the hotel whooped at the sight of the cyclone huffing and puffing at the school's feeble walls. I tugged down at the front of Cecily's dress, and I pressed my lips against her breast. She ran her fingers through my hair and kissed the top of my head. I reached over to the curtain to pull it closed, as if the ghosts of the town below were looking up, aiming their opera glasses at our window.

AT THE END OF THE DAY, Pink Heron, Nebraska, still stood. Wakefield's cyclone felled only the school. The farmers who'd abandoned the town had built their houses and barns to survive the winds of the prairie, and Wakefield seemed to find such fortitude exasperating. He admitted defeat and ended the party.

But first he put us to work. "The sun's about to go out!" he shouted in the hotel's parlor, gathering us all up and rushing us out the door. He wanted to film us scrambling from the hotel and running for our lives. "The tornado is coming!" he directed. "You've watched its destruction from the window of your hotel! You're the finest ladies and gentlemen of all the land. You've mastered nature. You've built industries up from nothing. But you can't keep a cyclone from flipping you inside out!"

It's no small task to get a rich man to run, but Wakefield did a fizzing job of it. It was quite the comedy act—he slapped at the ass of a railroad magnate as if herding cattle. He chased and stomped and waved his arms to get everyone into a rooster's state of frenzy, and then he ran out to crank his camera to capture the chaos. Mrs. Brandeis, of the department store Brandeises, stumbled and fell and rolled through a patch of clover. Klopp the printer stumbled too, but was able to right himself by knocking over Krug the brewer. Sunderland of the Omaha Coal, Coke, and Lime Co. lost a shoe, and Mrs. Kimball, the architect's wife, lost her towering hat of osprey quills. None turned back.

We were all well past winded when we reached the hay carts that had brought us to Pink Heron. "Just think," Wakefield said, running down to send us off, "you may see yourselves life-size on the screen of Edison's Vitascope Theater!"

Cecily, still panting from the run, shrugged a shoulder and rolled her eyes. She and I had been to the theater on the midway and had left for want of story. There'd been only a handful of snippets of nothing much: an actress dancing with an umbrella, and a comical mismatch between a short fat pugilist and a tall skinny one. And the irony was not lost on either one of us when we realized we'd paid a dime to see an elephant march across the screen and raise his trunk when we could've spent half that to see an elephant living and breathing in the circus ring next door.

"It'll be *better* than the Vitascope show at the Fair," Wakefield said, as if he'd caught sight of Cecily's shrugged shoulder and eye roll. "Because this will be a *drama*. A cyclone tears a town apart, sending the fine folks of the hotel running away in horror!"

Morearty placed a wooden crate next to the horse cart, as a step. After most everyone else had boarded and taken their seats at their game tables, Cecily put her right hand in my hand for balance, and took the hand of young Baker who had leaped first thing into the cart to help the ladies up. Cecily tripped a little on the crate, her foot caught in her dress, and her sweaty palm slipped from Baker's. I caught her easily, and she righted herself. But when she tried again to step up, she fell, and the full weight of her in my arms caused me to stumble too.

"I'm losing you, Cecily," I said, nervous. "Cecily," I said, sharper, needing her to help herself. I didn't realize she'd gone rag doll, her arms and legs entirely limp. We both fell to the ground, my arms around her waist. Her eyes were closed. I put my hand on her chest to feel for the beat of her heart, and I thought I might burst into tears. I was terrified.

Baker looked down and chuckled. "She just needs to sleep it off," he said. "She's had a gulp or two too many of the oh be joyful up at the hotel."

"She's not drunk," I snapped. I knelt beside her. "Could someone bring her some water?"

"She needs to loosen her corset, of course," a woman said with a cold absence of alarm.

Billie Wakefield, who'd suddenly appeared with her piglet, said, "She doesn't wear a corset."

"Oh, well, that's unfortunate," the woman said.

To some relief, but only a little, Cecily began to blink herself halfway awake, and her hand clutched mine tight. "Ferret," she said, woozy, "hang on to me. I'm going to fall over."

"You already fell over, sweetheart," I said. "You're okay. Somebody's getting you some water." I glanced up to shout at all who hovered over us. *Is someone getting her some water, for Christ's sake?*

Though even a sip of water was yet to come, Wakefield brought over one of his guests, a woman barely taller than a child. "Cecily," he said, "this is Dr. Lankton. She's a homeopath. Tell her what's the matter." The lenses of the doctor's spectacles were smaller than her eyes.

"Actually, no, don't speak," Dr. Lankton said as she lowered herself to her knees with no worry about dirtying her dress. "Just hush."

"I just need to sit down for a minute," Cecily said, still flat on her back.

"Hush," Dr. Lankton said again. The doctor's every movement was unspeakably slow. It was all I could do to keep from begging her to hurry. She undid the buttons at her own wrist and pulled off her linen glove. She pressed her fingers to Cecily's throat. She took off her other glove, and she felt just beneath Cecily's jaw. She looked me right in the eye as she did so. I thought she might have a question for me, so I said "Yes?" but the doctor wasn't seeing me at all—she was merely looking off in contemplation, considering whatever swelling or softness might be there beneath Cecily's skin. She put the back of her hand to Cecily's forehead, and then poked around on Cecily's gut.

"The girl's lucky," one of the wives said to one of the other wives. "Freda knows her way around the most miserable creatures. She serves those shame-struck pitifuls over at the Open Door."

The one to finally bring some water was that cocky young Baker, who handed Dr. Lankton his silver flask. She gave him a stern glare of skepticism that didn't quite fit on her girlish face. "I emptied out the liquor," Baker said. "It's just water from the pump over there."

"Can you sit up, Cecily?" she said, and Cecily did, with my help. The doctor held the flask to Cecily's lips. "It could just be a summer cold," Dr. Lankton said, "but it could be something else."

"She took a pill," I said, and I shot Wakefield a look.

"Just one of these," he said. He handed Freda Lankton the bottle and she merely glanced at it. The label didn't seem to suggest any danger to her, but she kept the vial, putting it in her pocket.

"I'd like to check you into the hospital for the night," she said, "and have an eye kept on you." The hospital. Though I hated the idea of it, I couldn't wait to get her there. I couldn't wait for her to be seen, to get better, to be sent home.

"You're just hungry," I said, full of hate for those little cooked birds on our plates.

"I ain't going to the goddamn Open Door," Cecily said.

"Ungrateful!" came a scandalized voice from overhead, along with all kinds of other buzzing. *What did she say? Did she just say what I thought she said?*

The Open Door was a clinic and shelter for unmarried women, a charity frequented by prostitutes. "No, you're not going to the Open Door," I said, as much for Cecily as for all the others listening in.

Dr. Lankton, her feathers forever unruffled, only smiled. "I'll grant you it's not the Paxton Hotel," she said, glancing up to wink at Paxton the hotelier. "But we do very well for our girls."

"Don't be offended," I said to Dr. Lankton. *You have no right to take offense* was what I meant. "She's not well," I said.

"We'll take her to the nuns at St. Joseph's," Wakefield said. "I shove enough money up their habits, I oughta be able to get her a private room."

"Ho-ho-ho" those old men laughed in that pompous, knowing, witless way of theirs.

I'd never felt more alone. I was alone with Cecily, floating in a rowboat in the middle of the ocean.

"Is there a hospital closer?" I said.

Wakefield said yes, but added, "I'm sure Cecily would rather we didn't trust her care to rural medicine. If you're worried about expense . . ."

"No," I said.

Dr. Lankton stood, brushing dirt from her dress before returning her gloves to her hands. She said, "Can we do whatever possible to make the dear thing comfortable for the ride to the train station? Gather some pillows so she can lie down?"

Cecily leaned over to whisper in my ear. "I just want to go back to the *pensione*," she said. "I just want to hold my baby girl. She's not feeling well, I'm sure of it. Whenever she has a cold coming on, I feel it in my own bones first."

I looked up at Wakefield, who hadn't heard Cecily's objection—no one had, because she'd spoken in such weak voice. And they'd all already grown impatient with our troubles. They'd seated themselves at the tables in the hay carts, and they'd resumed their games, but mirthless, irritated.

Wakefield gave orders to some servants, who then rushed off to carry them out. I realized, with a chill up my spine, that we needed Wakefield's help. I said, "We will very, very much appreciate anything you can do for us, Mr. Wakefield."

"Of course you will," Wakefield said.

I held Cecily in my arms. The two farm boys who'd been managing the cyclone machine carried down from the hotel a fainting sofa of a cool-blue damask satin and installed it at the rear of one of the hay carts. Though Cecily at first tut-tutted the efforts of Baker and me to carry her onto the cart, she found herself too rickety on her pins to even take a few steps.

The setting sun was still scorching hot as the horses and drivers carted us away from the bedraggled town of Pink Heron. One of the servant girls had been assigned to shade Cecily with her broad parasol, and she did a shoddy job of it. She seemed too infatuated with the handsome-faced Mr. Baker to keep her mind on her task, and the little slip of shadow would off and on drift away in inches. For the first several minutes of the ride down the road, I called the girl's attention to her clumsy work; finally I reached over to snatch the parasol away. I sat with Cecily's legs in my lap and tilted the shade toward her. I loosened the laces of her boots, and I stroked her bare ankles with my fingertips.

Soon enough the sun dropped, and the temperature fell just enough to not be suffocating. And then it turned a little cool with the dark. The coolness was helped along by the squeaky-hinge song of frogs always nearby, as if the cart followed the line of a river.

Cecily stopped squirming, stopped flinching with discomfort, and even slept a little, and I felt relieved too. I could have stared at the night sky, at the stars, for hours and hours, as Cecily rested. The servants held linseed-oil lamps above each table so the guests could see the spots of their cards.

"Two queens," Baker said, tossing his cards to the center of the table, certain of having won. Then he said, "Might Cecily be passing a stone?" Baker had made any number of diagnoses along the way, hoping to cast himself as the hero in the day's turn of events.

Dr. Lankton laughed at him, which pleased me. I had enough time on the ride back to worry over Baker's concern. Cecily, despite having not a penny to her name, was pretty as a daffodil. And if a young man of means set his eyes on my girl, what sort of odds did I have? Didn't men like Baker, and Wakefield, get whatever they wanted, even if they didn't want it all that much or for all that long? The whole sordid melodrama played out in my brain, the story ending with Baker taking my girl away, and though I didn't realize it at the time, the sad tale was a comfort. It kept me from dwelling on what had Cecily so weak.

"A wicked stone will definitely double a girl over," Dr. Lankton said. "An astute analysis, Dr. Baker." She tilted her hand, and I saw the two kings in her mitt. She tossed the cards atop Baker's queens. "Two butchers beats two bitches every time," she said.

Cecily woke, then fell back to sleep. She slept with her neck against the cushioned roll of the fainting sofa. On the silk of the parasol had been painted a garden scene in watery blues and cloudy pinks, and she dreamed herself there, or so she would tell me later in a letter.

Your fingers were cupped in my hands, she would write. *I overheard some word of stones, and at that, your fingers were the cool wet rocks from a brook. And I felt my aches, my fever, leaving me, one deep breath at a time.*

22.

A s I waited for any word of Cecily's condition, a young nun—a novitiate in a white habit—brought me coffee with chips of ice in it. Whenever I asked to see Cecily, the nuns would tell me, with squints of concern, in the gentlest of voices, that she simply couldn't be seen.

"I'm sure you understand," they would say, always, every time, and I would say, "Yes, I understand," but I never did. And the novitiate would bring me more coffee, her eyes a startling, wide-awake blue. She always seemed about to say something, but she would never utter a word.

Two or three times a day, during those four or five days at St. Joseph's, I would be allowed to look in on Cecily. Most often I could *only* look, and only as she slept. "She only ever sleeps," the nuns told me.

"Should she be sleeping so much?" I would ask.

"Oh, yes, yes, she should," they would say. "She's awake all night, so she needs to sleep all day."

"Then maybe I can see her at night," I said, "when she's not sleeping."

"No one can see anyone at night," they said.

St. Joseph's was a hospital that tended to charity cases, but the building was new, and the novitiates scrubbed the place until their blisters bled. The smell of the bleach sometimes burned your nose and pinched your lungs.

Cecily had a sunny room, with a window that looked out onto a courtyard garden with grapevines winding around a gazebo and the pickets of a fence. Ravens gathered and then fled with grapes in their beaks.

"She might like to see this," I said once. "Can't we get her up to look out the window?"

At the suggestion of it, Cecily woke, and I went to her bedside.

"It's me . . . Ferret," I told Cecily as I stroked her cheek.

"Where have you been?" she said.

"Here," I said. "Always. They won't let me see you except when you're sleeping. And they won't let me wake you."

"But I never sleep," she said. "I can't sleep at all." And her eyes drifted shut. At her side, atop the bed covers, was always a book, and each time I peeked into the room, the bookmark, a yellow feather, had been moved deeper down. I liked to imagine my silent, blue-eyed novitiate reading to her.

When not at the hospital, I tried to see Doxie at the boardinghouse, but Mrs. Margaret refused me. And the actors of the Silk & Sawdust Players assisted in the refusal, bullying me away just as expertly as they had on that first day of the Fair. They all had so little to do, they could afford to stand sentry at every entrance. And I didn't even know where, in the house, the baby was. I appealed to the landlady, reminding her that I was the one who'd paid the rent. "You are an accomplice," I told her, "in the child's abduction." But she was unmoved by my demands. Mrs. Margaret had her convinced that *I* was the reason Cecily had been hospitalized and that Doxie would be doomed in my care.

Who could help me? I wasn't Doxie's father. Cecily wasn't my wife. What laws were there to protect someone like me? I felt so desperate, I considered seeking out Wakefield. But I'd not seen him in the hospital halls even once. I assumed he was back at his theater in the Grand Court, seeking affection from his cast of hundreds.

So I waited. I spent all my hours in the chapel, waiting, waiting, waiting. "I'm just downstairs waiting," I told Cecily, when I could. I drew some comfort from the deep sympathy in the novitiate's eyes, and she seemed to be everywhere, casting me glances like an angel.

When Cecily was better, everything would be remedied, I assured myself. We would fall into our new life. We would get Doxie baptized, in a long silk gown. We'd get a house together, maybe even a little farm just beyond the fairgrounds. We could conspire on a show and take it to the stage. We could start our own theatrical troupe.

One afternoon, August, Rosie, and Pearl brought Cecily a kimono wrapped in tissue in a box, and Cecily woke just long enough to tug at the box's ribbon. Together, we watched Cecily sleep, her little soft snores puffing at her lips like she was blowing us kisses. Pearl took a manicure set to Cecily's fingers, scratching away at the ends of her nails with a tiny file.

"They ain't doing nothing at all for the girl," Rosie said. "Let's leave with her."

"You won't succeed at kidnapping," August said. "There's nothing more fierce than an Omaha nun. They've got shotguns tucked away in those habits. In a frontier town, you can't fend off evil with a crucifix." He came to the side of the bed and scooted me over in my chair, to share the seat with me. He took a chamois cloth from Pearl's manicure kit and began scrubbing the nails of Cecily's other hand.

THE NEXT MORNING I sat in the chapel as always. I'd gnawed my thumb bloody, chewing and peeling at a hangnail. I hadn't slept, and I was on the verge of madness. I took out my pocketknife. I pressed the tip of it into my wound as if I could dig out all the damage I'd already done to it. But at the first sharp stab of pain I was startled from my delirium. I then leaned forward, pressing my forehead against the pew in front of me. I stuck the tip of the knife into the soft wood, and began to carve Cecily's name. Part of me wanted to get caught, to get punished, but it mostly felt a holy act. It felt like worship, scratching the letters in deep.

I froze at the sound of footsteps, having only carved in the *C-e-c-i*. I pulled back the knife, tucked away the blade. I hid my vandalism by holding my bloody thumb over the letters on the pew.

Then came the ting of a tin bucket on the tiles of the floor, and an echoing bang as the handle dropped against the bucket's side. I heard the sloshing of the water and smelled the bleach. I heard someone slip into the pew behind me to sit. I recognized the scratch and crunch of the starched folds of a habit.

I turned when I heard her speak to me.

In the split second before I saw the novitiate's blue eyes, I'd hoped to see Cecily there, in nun's costume, in the middle of a plot to escape. *Ferret.* I'd heard the song of Cecily's soft voice in the way the nun whispered.

At first I wondered how she knew my name, but then I realized this was that little dove in white who was everywhere, always. She was omnipresent, like her Lord. She mopped, she scrubbed. She changed the beds and fluffed the pillows. No matter how noisy the bristles of her brush, the patients paid her no mind. It was as if she'd made a sacred vow to fade away.

"She's gone," she whispered.

I asked my questions as I rushed to leave. I wanted to be every place at once.

My clumsy stumbling was like something from a nursery rhyme.

"Where'd she go?" I said as I stood from the pew and knocked over the novitiate's bucket.

"They took her away," she said as the water spilled.

"To where?" I said as I slid on the soap and the bleach.

"Who knows," she said as she knelt to the floor to sop up the mess.

"Who knows?" I said.

"Go," she said.

I squatted down next to her, nearly weeping from frustration. "But *where*?" I whispered.

"The child," she whispered back. "They'll fetch the child first, I suspect."

The child. I stepped from the chapel, but had no idea where to find a door. The few times I'd left the building, I'd had to be taken by the hand. I'd never learned my way around the hospital's sprawl, every corridor alike, every window looking out on the same lawn of burnt grass. Whenever I'd been led up the winding of the halls and the spiraling of the stairs to Cecily's room, she had seemed housed in a tower, locked away by witches.

I returned to the novitiate's side, to whisper, "Which way to the door?"

"Heaven help us all," she said. She stood up and took my arm, and left behind the wet floor, the bucket overturned, the brush in the aisle. She led me from the chapel, down a hall, around a corner.

"Who is *they*?" I said.

"Who is *they*?" she said.

"You said *they*. *They* took her."

She held out her other arm, curled her fingers, clawed at the air, pantomiming Wakefield's silver fist. "Him," she said. "And his butler and his driver."

"That can't be," I said. "He's not been here at all." But even as I said it, I felt my stomach sink.

EVEN THE NUNS were villains in this ballad of mine. My novitiate explained it all to me on our long walk down an endless hall.

As I'd fretted in the chapel every day, hour after hour, with my hands folded in my lap, my head bowed, in all the postures of prayer, Cecily hadn't slept at all. Somewhere down a hall, around a corner, and up some stairs, and down more halls, and around more corners, and up more stairs, Cecily was seen by medical doctors, midwives, homeopaths, and healers of all stripes. Every waking minute, every minute I didn't see her, she'd been fiddled with, her temperature taken, her blood drawn, her skin needled, her reflexes tip-tapped. She guzzled beef tea to feed her iron-poor blood and they collected her urine to puzzle over its shade of yellow. Pills were tucked beneath her tongue. Electrostatic shock was shot through her joints. They sought illness in every inch of her with their spyglasses and stethoscopes. They went water witching in her ear canals and became students of her pupils.

And all the while, there sat Wakefield. He read to her and held her hand, and he promised her he could make her well. Whenever she asked about me, she was told I had trusted her fully to their care. And here is how she betrayed me: she believed Wakefield. And she believed the nuns. When she asked to see me, they told her I couldn't be found anywhere.

"It's unforgivable," Wakefield told her. "And it's the same mistake I made when my Myrtle took ill. I hid. I ran away. I couldn't bear to see her in pain. And I couldn't bear to let her see me cry. So I couldn't be found when she needed me most. For all their bluster and fight, men are weak, weak creatures."

WHEN MY NOVITIATE led me to the front door, she still held on tight. "Lean on me," she whispered. "Act like you're on your last legs."

I *was* on my last legs. Or at the moment it seemed so. Pretending to be weak came easy, and I was grateful to have her there next to me.

In the lane out front, a carriage and driver sat parked. He seemed to be there to serve the hospital's patients. My novitiate helped me into the carriage and instructed the driver to take me wherever I needed to go.

. . .

WHEN I REACHED the boardinghouse to collect Doxie, I expected a battle. But there was no one on the stairs to stop me. No one in the hall. I went to Cecily's room, and the door was unlocked. And there stood the wicked Mrs. Margaret in costume, in that skirt patterned with frogs and crescent moons, her black boots with white spats. She was in the middle of twisting the wiry hair of her own pig-snouted, pumpkin head into a skinny braid.

"I'm the only one here," she said. Mrs. Margaret nodded toward the empty crib as she tied a girlish pink ribbon to the end of her braid.

"Where'd they go?" I said. I can't say I didn't wish for that stubborn hag to drop dead right then and there, but I didn't pick up the scissors to stab her. The scissors were on the sewing machine just at my side, and I only took them in my fist to threaten. I just wanted to worry her. I wasn't leaving that rattrap without word of Doxie, and it was beginning to seem like the only way to eke out an ounce of civility from the old witch was to hold a blade to her throat.

No sooner had the light from the window glinted on the metal of the scissors than Mrs. Margaret had her full weight against me, pushing me to the wall, her knee in my groin, her arm cutting off the wind in my pipe. She gripped the hand that held the scissors and forced them so close to my ear, I could feel their pointed tip going too far in.

"When you gonna learn that I'm just trying to keep you out of trouble, Ferret?" she said. "It's pity I feel for you, deep, deep down in the cold black guts of my heart."

I couldn't see anything for all the watering of my eyes. I couldn't breathe, and when I did sneak a gulp of air, I choked even more from the stench of whatever had died in her mouth.

"Now the nuns'll lie to ya, Ferret, but Mama Margaret, she'll tell it to you like you gotta hear it. But you gotta be smart enough to even *want* the truth. Are you? You gotta tell me. Or nod your head. Are you smart?" But I couldn't speak. And I couldn't nod. "Can you hear a word

I'm saying?" she said. "Or do I need to dig out all the earwigs clotting up the sound?" She pushed the point of the scissors in deeper, and when I started to flinch from the pain, she backed up and let me drop to the floor. I coughed and clung to the bed.

"Now the person you wanna go after with scissors is Billy Wakefield," and she ran the point of the scissors up along my cheek. "He stol'd your girl right from under your nose." She stuck the tip of the scissors up one of my nostrils. I slapped her hand away. "He got Cecily good and scared. And he made sure the nuns kept you napping in that chapel, praying for help like a good little ninny. And now he's taking her away in his own private train."

This isn't a city where the sick can get anything but sicker and sicker, Wakefield had told Cecily. The whole profane town stood on the sacred boneyards of Indians. Omaha was blacking our every lung with its filth and soot. The hospitals were hot with poxes and fevers. *I know where to take you,* he'd promised. *I know all kinds of secrets about the wind and water. Your health is out there somewhere. We only have to find it.*

"No," I said. "She loves *me.*"

"She loves you *not,*" Mrs. Margaret said. "You were nowhere when she needed you most." She put on a mocking frown and tapped at her own chest with the points of the scissors. "It's a story that stabs you in the heart."

"I was there," I said, pushing myself up from the floor. "They told me she needed rest. She wouldn't get better without rest. I wanted more than anything to be with her."

"You don't have to convince *me,*" she said. "You should've *fought* to be at her side. People like you and me, we gotta fight tooth and nail, cradle to grave." She called out to me as I ran from the room. "From the hole between your mama's legs to the hole they shovel for you, you gotta be kicking and screaming every goddamn minute of it." She raised her voice more as I ran down the stairs. "Your problem, boy, is you got uppity. You thought your luck improved. But it didn't, and it won't. You're no better than the worst of us."

I slammed the door behind me, hoping to shut out her screeching, but before I had even crossed the front yard to the street she was at an upstairs window. "Oh, Ferret, love, I forgot something," she sang out, singsongy. "I'm to give you this letter she wrote you. She snuck the envelope into my fist when I handed her Doxie. She knew not to trust anyone else with it."

"I'll come up for it," I shouted back.

"I'll drop it down to you," she said.

"No, I'll come up for it," I said again.

"No, I'll drop it down to you," she said again, and she held the envelope out the window and lit it on fire with a match she struck with the broken, banged-purple nail of her thumb.

By the time the letter had fallen, burning, to the lawn, most of the words had been lost. After dropping to my knees to pat out the flame, I then collected the ashy snippets that had flaked away, whole words, and parts of words, and fragments of sentences, that had drifted into bushes and flowerpots, landing on leaves and petals—*it's not so, when, the rain, a mother, you don't*. At the end of the block, I was lucky enough to nab a cabbie unafraid to snap the reins. It was only half past noon and he was cross-eyed with liquor already. "You can't get me to the train station fast enough," I told him, and he laughed at me with teeth half-black from chaw.

"This broken-down nag's got a wild streak or two left in her," he said.

With one hand, I clutched the side of the carriage as we bucked away, and I pressed the other to my chest, holding the last of Cecily's letter close, its charred and fragile pieces of linen stationery tucked into the inside pocket of my coat. I could still feel the heat of it and smell its smoke.

I didn't know what to believe.

Mrs. Margaret's flame had burned through the center of the letter, and I'd yet to read much of what little writing was left. But the ride was so rough as we galloped, I didn't dare risk lifting the paper from my pocket and having the wind carry it away. I even held both hands tight against my coat, and the people we passed might have thought we were in such a rush because I'd been shot through the chest.

"You're either escaping a lady or going after one," the driver called back to me as he slowed in front of the station's towering columns.

"Yes," I said.

"Lady troubles are the best troubles to have," he said, with a smile and a sigh, as if touched by the romance of it. I noticed then something quite dapper about the black-toothed lad, with his felt daisy in his buttonhole and a polka-dot necktie dressing up his tattered tweed suit. I paid him double, and was nearly trampled by the speckled horse of a passing carriage as I stepped into the busy street.

The stately Burlington Station—blocks of marble and a roof of red—had only just opened that summer, in time for the Fair, and it swarmed with travelers. At the top of the facade was a clock cradled in the arms of a white angel, and I checked the hour hoping to see that time had stopped.

I ran through the lobby and onto the staircase that spiraled down through the floor, my feet slipping out from under me on a freshly polished step. I grabbed hold of the brass banister before nearly braining myself on the marble, but not without accidentally kicking an old lady in the shin and nearly sending her for a spill—an old man at her side kept her from falling by grabbing her sleeve.

"I'm so sorry," I sputtered to them both, as I ran off.

The lower level led out to the canopied platform, where Wakefield's private car pulled away, at the very tail end of a long train. Unlike the sleek, dark cars of other rich men, Wakefield's had all the marks of his showmanship, painted a canary yellow, its roof in peppermint stripes. In the railing of the observation deck were the curls and twists of a wrought-iron *W*.

The train was leaving the station at a snail's clip and I could have easily leaped onto that deck and slipped in through the back door, but for Wakefield himself. He stood out there, alone, with a teacup in his flesh hand and a cigar in the silver one.

He didn't seem at all surprised to see me.

I walked alongside the car's deck, quickening my pace as the train began to pick up speed.

"Where are you taking her?" I said.

He only shook his head. He plugged his cigar into the corner of his mouth and looked down into his tea.

I said, "What's stopping me from pulling you off there and pushing you under the wheels?"

"Because you want what's best for Cecily," he said through the side of his mouth, with exasperation. He tossed the tea from the cup out onto the rails, then spat his cigar from his mouth. "You're not good for her, and you know it."

"I could charge you with kidnapping," I said. "She's my wife to be."

"You were killing her by inches," he said, his voice building. "Keeping her and that baby in that dark dusty room. You don't even know the difference, do you? And why should she trust you? You were willing to sell off your whole livelihood when you sold me that dummy. You don't have a care in the world. If only we could all be like you, Ferret."

He had to shout his insult above the clangor of the trains. My instinct was to pull him from his perch, not to beat him but to make him stand in front of me as he spoke.

I ran ahead, and off the platform, as the train switched tracks. I skipped over the rails and followed alongside the car, running past Wakefield. I leaped up to knock my knuckles against the windows. I called Cecily's name. I ran along, knocking, calling. And then I saw her. Cecily came to the window and pressed her palm against the glass.

I reached into my coat pocket and so very carefully took from it the burned letter. I cradled it in my hands and held it up, hoping she could see it, even as I knew I was losing yet more of it, more of its ashen message blowing away word by word. She furrowed her brow. "She burned it," I shouted, though I suspected Cecily couldn't hear me at all. "I couldn't read it." I clutched the charred letter to my chest as the train left the rail yard, chugging quickly away, Wakefield no longer on the deck.

Before she left my sight, I watched her lower her eyes, lower her chin, and turn her face away from the window. The wind picked up, and I lost a few more pieces of the letter. I clutched quickly at the paper and ashes. But then I opened my hands. I let the wind carry the last of the letter away.

November 26, 1898

Dear Cecily,

*I haven't told Emmaline yet what becomes of you, and she's fit
to be tied. She always reads the ends of books first, she says. She
reads books for their sentiment, for their characters. If she's flustered
by suspense, she worries too much. So she reads the end before she
begins. At that point, there at the end, the dead are dead, and the
living have lived.*

*Hester, meanwhile, says we should live all of life back to front.
We should be born old and age younger. Our baptism should be a
ritual of our funeral. We should die as infants, content in our
mothers' arms, having lost all our learning and all sense of
disappointment. If only we could die, she says, not knowing we'd
ever grieved.*

*Emmaline has begun writing her own book, but no one can
read it. It's not that she hasn't shown it to us—we just don't know
what it says. She wakes from dreams with symbols and shapes in
her head. A new alphabet comes out of the end of her pen. Even she
doesn't know what it means. The dreams began on the night I
arrived. She suspects I provoked them. I'm heaven-sent, she says.*

*On some mornings she can interpret some of her dream
writing, but only vaguely. All we know is this: they're instructions.
We're to build something. And we're to build it beneath the roof of
the barn. We're anxious to begin, but we don't know how. We
don't even know the materials to use.*

*I probably have no business diagnosing sanity in a letter that
I'm writing to a ghost. But I don't detect any madness in her*

hieroglyphics. Every time I look at the pages, I feel on the verge of literacy. If we can puzzle out one little word, one if, and, or but, then we'll find our way to all the others.

She has drawn a blueprint, of sorts, based on what little she understands. The drawing consists of circles circling, spiraling in and out of one another. But her circles don't really mean circles, she says.

Emmaline calls it the Emerald Cathedral, because a man whispered the name in a dream. The man is someone she used to know, she says, but she doesn't like to talk about him. Before this man left her for someone else, when she was young, he gave her a ring. "An emerald for Emmaline," he told her. She hasn't dreamed about him in many, many years.

We're <u>grateful</u> for all the suspense. We wouldn't ask her to dream any faster than she does. The mystery of it is where the magic is. What if the Emerald Cathedral can never be built? If that's the ending, we don't want to know it.

Ferret

September 1898

23.

In the looking glass looking back at me was the mug of a man wanted dead or alive. In those weeks after Cecily left, my curls grew long and unruly. I took no scissors to the thicket of beard that crept onto my chin. My vest gapped open where the buttons were gone. My collar had warped. And in my eyes I saw no hope left.

I had no work, and I had no money. For a time, Wakefield's golden dragon head had seemed to cough up cash on its own, but the bundle had grown thin, the dragon swallowing it up. My literary correspondence had dwindled. I sat at the typewriter, back in my attic at the Empress Opera House, struck inarticulate. *There's nothing worth saying*, I found myself typing in the few letters I wrote for others.

A bottle of rum in the evening with August and Rosie would lift me a little, but the first glint of morning sun, and soberness, would drop me even lower than before.

I did take some comfort from the postcards Cecily sent, though she didn't send them to me. She sent them to Pearl who, in her mercy, would share them with me. I would meet Pearl, in my wrecked state, at the lunch counter at Brandeis for coffee and cold lamb's-tongue sandwiches.

On a card from New Helena, Nebraska, Cecily wrote only: *Feeling quite well. Took the waters. Leaving today.*

On the back of a picture of bathers in a warm-water plunge in South Dakota, she wrote: *Doing better. Took the waters. Leaving today.*

A new note arrived every three days or so. No sooner would she leave one mineral spring sanatorium than she would leave yet another.

She took the waters in Colorado, Wyoming, Idaho, and Oregon. And she only ever wrote as she left a place. If she'd written on arrival, I might've caught the next train to wherever she was.

The words on the postcards were hollow—like she was shouting down a well only for the echo of it. But I was grateful for them, and they would lift me even higher than the rum could. She sounded lonely and lost without me.

ON MY BIRTHDAY, Pearl baked me a harlequin cake—one layer was chocolate, one white, one pink. "The pink has the last of the summer's rose leaves," she said. She had plucked them from the garden behind the Juliet, the women's hotel where she lived. "I snipped them to pieces and powdered them with sugar."

We had our sad little party on the unlit stage of the Empress, which had been set for a new play. The theater was to open again in a few weeks for its fall season, but Phoebe, and all the others from last spring, had not been invited back. The theater had a new manager, a gentleman in white linen and checkered hat, determined to go legit. The play didn't even have a moral or much of a plot. I'd watched a rehearsal one afternoon. Two actresses I didn't know played two sisters I didn't like. The sisters paced a kitchen, dredged up old slights, and puzzled over their dead father's ledgerbook.

The play would have no opening or closing acts, no vaudeville or burlesque. So even if I'd still had Oscar, I wouldn't have had a stage.

Much of the kitchen was only painted sloppily on a backdrop. Pearl and I sat at a table that wobbled, sloshing the tea in our cups. She served the cake alongside a few dried apricots from the fruit market. I picked up a sliver of apricot and inspected it for dust. "The filth of the streets gets on the fruit," I said, taking a bite nonetheless. "And the filth gives you typhoid fever." I'd been studying a magazine sold in August's father's bookshop—a periodical for doctors called the *Omaha Clinic*. With my new medical knowledge I often reflected back on the summer, diagnosing Cecily from afar.

"This week it's the apricots?" Pearl said, gently ribbing me. "Last week it was the oysters from polluted ponds." Yes. The sewage oysters Cecily and I had eaten at the Fair, feeling elegant.

Pearl then gave me my gift. "A novel with a villain," she said. "Do you know the story of *Trilby*?" On the cover was an angel-winged heart caught in a spider's web.

"I do, a little," I said, though I hadn't read the book. You didn't have to read it to know it. It sold millions. It was all the go. People slapped the name Trilby on anything they wanted to sell. You could wear a Trilby hat and eat Trilby chocolate. You could dance a Trilby waltz and play a Trilby rag. There were Trilby freckle creams and card games and china dolls. And there were endless sermons against the book's naked ladies and gothic evil. But none of it mattered to me. What did I care anymore about other people's amusements?

"It's a horrible novel," Pearl said. "Well, not horrible in that it's a poor story but in that the incidents in it are horrible. Trilby is a beautiful young woman who falls victim to Svengali, an older man. He's a mesmerist. He puts Trilby in a hypnotic trance, and she becomes his lover. She's beautiful and he's hideous. Nothing ends well." She leaned forward to whisper, wobbling the table some more. "His first trick is to cure her of her headaches."

I tried to read the book when I was alone in the attic, but it was mostly about artists in Paris. I learned very little of the villain's methods. Instead I returned to the *Omaha Clinic*. I read about the medicinal properties of orchids. *Travelers in the deserts of Persia sustained themselves on tonics mixed from the flower's bulbs. Even just being in the presence of such strange blossoms was curative. Orchids needed no soil, so the Japanese would simply hang the plants from their ceilings.* My mind drifted, imagining myself stringing orchids up by their stems, in a hothouse where Cecily could sit and sip orchid-bulb tea. She would return to me, and I would cure her.

ON THE OPENING NIGHT OF *Heart of the White City*, I returned to the Fair for the first time in weeks. I knew I would not see Cecily on the stage, but I would, at least, see her characters. I would see her factory girl, her dance hall girl, her Ferris wheel girl, her fire victim. And there was a part of me that wanted the constant ache of seeing Cecily everywhere, in everything, her shadow crossing my shoes, the scent of her extract of sweet pea caught in the garden. I wanted to sail alone on the swan gondola, with Cecily at my side.

I tamed my hair with a messy pomade August had concocted in his kitchen, a perfumed slop mixed from wax, mutton lard, and orange flowers. It slicked all my curls straight and made my hair darker and wet like from a rainstorm. I ran a string of dental silk between my teeth and brushed with August's powder of French chalk and myrrh. I splashed my bloodshot eyes with a tonic from the oculist, a tepid water peppered with sea salt.

When I reached the theater at the Fair, the girl behind the gilded bars of the box office laughed at me. "There hasn't been a ticket for weeks," she said.

I refused to be disappointed. I leaned in close to the window, and I hooked a finger around one of the thin bars. "Do you know of any scalpers?" I said.

The ticket girl winked and tapped at my finger. "Go look on the midway," she said. "It's full of degenerates after dark."

She was right. I found no ticket scalper, but rogues of every other stripe loitered and skulked. The midway had become more sordid than ever; it was the Fair's back alley. The puppeteer's Punch-and-Judy show was bloodier and filthier than before. In front of the big top of the Wild Animal Show, a man-size birdcage featured a woman inside swinging, in a costume trimmed with red feathers, nothing on beneath her skirt. She performed acrobatics that made her feathers flutter up so fast you risked missing something obscene. Young men stuck green carnations in their buttonholes, limped their wrists, fluttered their yellow hankies, and sold their kisses to Oscar Wilde types. Grass skirts wiggled off hips in the Hawaiian Theater. Women undid their corsets for the X-ray machine. Hard liquor flowed from the lemonade stands. From an apple cart a peddler sold opium pipes.

And the lovelies Rosie had been selling under cover of his coat had now crept out, every bare inch of them in the full glare of the midway's lights. He'd parked his rickshaw in front of a souvenir shop. The photographs were pinned to the umbrella and propped up in the seat. They were stuck into the spokes of the wheels. He'd even strung up a clothesline, the pictures dangling from wooden pins, as shocking and delicate a sight as a lady's frilliest underdrawers. Rosie had pictures pinned to his suspenders, and even one playfully tucked into the fly of his pants.

On the brim of Rosie's hat was pinned a lovely I recognized—one of the young, motherly nurses of the incubator exhibit. I knew she had likely been an actress only playing the part of a nurse, but I still worried about her, posed as she was, naked but for a nun's wimple atop her head. "I'll buy it," I said. She'd been one of the ones who'd been sweet to Doxie, so I paid to take the picture off the market or, at least, this copy of it. "Some of these girls have fathers, you know." I harrumphed, holding out my dollar bill.

Rosie had grown used to my foul mood. He rolled his eyes and held out a half-dollar piece. "Men of the clergy get a half-price discount," he said, with a sneer.

I didn't take the coin. Instead, I folded up the card, smaller and smaller, and gazed into the window of the souvenir shop.

We were about as far from an ocean as we could possibly be, so landlocked were we there in the West, but the shop was stocked full of souvenirs made of seashells—little mother-of-pearl prairie schooners with dried sea horses in place of oxen, and figurines of mermaids holding ears of corn. I stepped inside. Nestled in among the knick-knacks was an oval bottle not much bigger than a robin's egg, and made of abalone shell. When it caught the light, the cloud-colored shell shimmered faintly with pink and pale blue. The gilded tin stopper was shaped like a tiny crown, and it was attached to a little stick of pinewood. The idea, the clerk explained, was for a lady to attach the bottle's chain to her charm bracelet, and she could turn the stopper when she wanted a bit of scent, the little stick grinding the perfumed seeds inside.

It cost only a half-dollar, so I stepped back out to take the coin Rosie had offered, and I returned to the clerk. Before I'd even left the shop with the bottle, it throbbed cool in the palm of my hand like a talisman. I rubbed my thumb over the smooth shell.

I twisted the stopper, to grind the seeds, and something about the scent—a mix of licorice and lilac—was tranquilizing. It already reminded me of Cecily.

I FOUND AUGUST SWEETBRIAR in the Indian camp, where he'd built himself a tent among the wigwams and tepees. He had hammered to-gether a rectangular frame of scrap wood and hung up rags for walls—curtains, tablecloths, tattered ball gowns torn apart at their seams. Fairgoers lined up at the front of the tent, and he would lift the flap with his wrist and wave people in, one by one, with a witchy wiggling of his fingers.

August no longer practiced only medicine. He told fortunes too. The tent, though spacious, had no chairs, so he would sit with his subject on a rug spread out across the dirt. He would either diagnose and prescribe a tonic, or he'd have the man or lady shake a large kid glove that was filled with chicken bones left over from his previous day's supper. August would spill the bones onto the rug and study how they fell.

When he saw me standing in the line outside the tent, he closed up shop, sent everyone else away, and pulled me in. I could smell the spot of perfume at his throat as he hugged me close.

His hair had grown past his shoulders. I ran my fingers through the snaggled ends of it. When I stepped back, I saw he wore only a woman's petticoat that sagged on his skinny hips. Around his neck was a long necklace that nearly reached his knees. Knotted up in the necklace were misshapen pearls, seashells, and turtle bones. His cheeks and chest were crossed with white and yellow lines of paint.

"I've gone native," he said, cocking a hip. "We all have around here."

I ran my fingertip along the two-headed snake scribbled up his arm. "What's all this mean?" I said.

"Oh, darling, I have no idea," he said, "but I hope it means something awfully savage. Would you like some tea? I have the samovar." Before I could answer, it seemed the whole tent would be trampled. A stampede passed so close, it shook the wooden frame and blew the walls like sheets on a line. The riders wailed and hollered, and the horses' hooves kicked up a thick cloud. I bent over with a coughing fit from all the dirt.

"You do get used to it," August said, when we could hear ourselves speak again. He went to a tent pole to secure it, pushing it deeper into the ground. "It was fairly quiet around here when it was all just an exhibit of everyone being peaceable and pretty." He dusted the samovar with a peacock feather.

I had indeed noticed that things had changed in the Indian camp. The camp had been designed as a high-minded tribute to "the lost man," according to the Fair's diplomats. It was an important anthropological exercise, they'd explained. Before, the white folks had stepped polite and curious among the rituals, even a little stooped at the back, like they were examining medical oddities under glass in a dime museum. They wore thick goggles to keep their eyes from stinging from all the dirt kicked up by the strutting of warriors. They hesitantly accepted offers to bang a drum or blow through a flute.

Meanwhile, farther down the midway, Buffalo Bill's Wild West Show made a fortune by staging mock scalpings and stagecoach massacres. Those Indians—most of them white men in face paint and loincloths—warbled and shrieked all day long, then spent their nights in the suites of the fine Paxton Hotel.

When the old warrior Geronimo arrived at the Fair as a one-night-only one-man show, selling the buttons off his coat and letting young ladies pose on his knee for a fee, he inspired the men and the women of the camp.

Now, for a nickel, you could be right in the thick of it. You could suck alfalfa smoke from a pipe—a penny a puff—while sitting along-side a man claiming to be an Indian chief. Everything cost you, even just a plug of that buffalo pemmican you could barely chew without ripping out a tooth. You could place bets on which man would catch the maiden in a love chase on horseback and get tickets to glimpse a baby that had been born in a tepee a few days before—Little Spotted Bear swaddled in a pelt. But the biggest spectacles were the sham bat-tles staged in the open fields, stealing some business away from the Wild West Show. Rumors floated through the Fair that virgins had been abducted and businessmen scalped, right there, within the Fair's fences, only steps away from the New White City. These rumors were designed by the tribesmen themselves. All the threat and naked skin drew folks closer and closer.

In August's tent, I lay back on the rug next to the center pole that kept the roof up. The roof was nothing but a threadbare bedsheet pat-terned with stars, thin enough to let some light in. August stood nearby looking into a gilt-framed mirror he'd hung on one of the tent posts, twisting his hair up into a little bun and locking it into place with a thin-handled spoon. On his ankle was a stringy bracelet, and I touched its charms—a silver dove and a heart.

"It's a mourning bracelet," August said, lifting the hem of his pet-ticoat an inch or two higher, moving his ankle around to show it off. "That's what I tell people, anyway. 'They're strands of my dead lover's hair,' I tell people. 'The bracelet helps me see what's not there to be seen.' But it's just hair out of my own head." He lowered himself to the rug to sit cross-legged. "Do you want me to tell *your* fortune?" he said.

"I don't have a fortune," I said. I sat up too, cross-legged, facing him. Our knees touched. "All I have is *mis*fortune."

"Well, yes," he said, taking my hands in his, palm to palm, "misfortune *is* your fortune." He closed his eyes tight and furrowed his brow, as if studying the ether. "It's all I see for you."

"Try to see something else," I said. "I don't want any more bad news." I looked down at our hands and I laced my fingers in among his. He rubbed softly my thumbs with his thumbs.

"You're such a broken little sparrow, aren't you?" he said. He nearly whispered it. "How'd you ever survive the kind of life you lived?" He leaned forward to kiss my forehead. He then moved his head to press his cheek against my cheek. I put my head on his shoulder.

"If you look in my future," I said, "see me there with Cecily, please. And with Doxie."

August shrugged my head away, and he leaned back. "I've learned that *I've* lived other lives," he said. His hair had fallen loose already from its knot, and a lock of it dangled in his face. I reached up to push it back, tucking the strands behind his ear.

"How do you know?" I said.

"There's a woman here in the camp, and she told me," he said. "We sat under the moon and drank some sort of wicked brew. When we got drunk enough, we ate a locust, and that's when we saw this flurry of images. I've been stitching it all together in the days since."

"Who were you before?" I said.

"One hundred years ago, I was one of the wives of a warrior," he said. "I was a wife, but I was also exactly who I am now. I was a man, and I was a wife. Like a double life, like you might have in a dream. And a French fur trader fell in love with me, and he stole me away from the warrior. We lived in a plantation house in New Orleans, and he bought me beautiful dresses and beautiful wigs. He taught me French, and I wrote a journal of my captivity. In my vision, I could see myself as I was then, and I could see over my shoulder, see what I was writing. But I couldn't read it, because I don't know French now."

"You only believe in all that voodoo because you want to believe in it," I said. "You're too romantic."

"I am," he said in a whisper, looking in my eyes. "It's a curse I've been carrying around for centuries."

"Then you know the pain," I said. I touched my fingers to his wrist, to feel the feather-soft beating of his pulse. His pulse quickened. "Did she ever even love me, do you think?" I said. "Does she love me still? Is she thinking about me?" In that moment, I would trust his every word. I just needed him to say it, to tell me that Cecily loved me, so I could believe him. It was childish, I suppose, but something about being there with him, snug in his sympathy, made me pitiful. I wanted to rest my head on his chest and listen to his heart.

But August stood, turned away, and walked to the wall of the tent. He took deep and broken breaths, his hands on his hips, looking down at the ground.

"August?" I said. "What's wrong?" August said nothing. He didn't move except to breathe. "Augie?" I said.

August ran his fingers over his cheek, smearing his paint. He then took a lace handkerchief from where he'd tucked it into the waist of his petticoat. He dabbed at his nose. "You will see her again," he said, with a sniffle.

I stood and walked to August's side. "What is it?" I said.

"It was only a glimpse, and a blur at that," he said. "It was mostly nothing more than a shiver up my spine. But I'm certain. You'll be with her. I see her hovering against a wall, up above your head. Like a picture in a magic lantern." I looked back and up, following the line of his sight. "Will you go now?" he said. "I need to collect myself."

If it hadn't gotten so late, the play about to open, I would've begged for more. I wasn't typically inclined to believe in any kind of soothsaying, but I could have spent hours analyzing his visions of Cecily, his voice gentle in my ear like a hummed lullaby.

THE MYSTERIOUS AIRSHIP flew again above the Fair, and many of the hundreds turning out for *Heart of the White City* stood in the street to watch the flicker of light in the night sky. A man in a top hat took his opera glasses from their leather case and focused them on the passing ship. Others followed suit until the promenade was crowded with gentlemen in full dress and ladies in gowns standing still, staring up, their binoculars to their eyes. I slipped in and out among them, as graceful as a vapor, not knocking a knee or brushing a sleeve, twisting myself this way and that. By the time I'd reached the front door, I'd lifted the ticket I needed.

I took my seat, which was smack-dab in the theater's middle, my view partially obstructed by the woman in front of me, her hat decked out as the Chicago World's Fair—white buildings with balsa walls and a tin Ferris wheel that turned with a click-click-click with every nod of her head. And she nodded often, an agreeable sort flanked on each side by a gentleman taken with her flair for vaudeville.

I was afraid I'd be caught in my counterfeit seat, but when the lights dimmed and the pit orchestra's music thundered from far below, I quit worrying.

As the curtains opened, Heart arrived in Chicago in the back of a hay cart pulled across the stage by a team of actual horses neighing and snuffling. All in the audience applauded the audacity of it, and the stunts and sets only got trickier and fancier with each plot twist. When snow fell on poor Heart peddling matchsticks in a winter scene, big electrical fans blew shaved ice into the audience, speckling our cheeks and sending up chills. A scene in a pillow factory featured a cast of hundreds on a tiered platform, actresses plucking real ducks, stuffing real pillows, stitching them shut. Plucking, stuffing, stitching, plucking, stuffing, stitching. That alone would've been a sight to behold, but then out came Wakefield's cyclone at low spin. The cyclone machine was far gentler than before, sending only white feathers fluttering across the theater to hover and sway. Many in the audience reached above their heads to try to pluck the down from the air.

When summer arrived, live butterflies were unleashed from the wings and they flew out to light on our sleeves and flutter against our ears. And as my eyes followed the stumbling flight of one, its wings seemingly too heavy to keep it afloat, I cast a glance along the wall, and there she was. August's vision, in a sense. *Cecily*, up above.

CECILY AND WAKEFIELD were arriving late, stepping up to the balcony to the private box nearest the stage.

She came home, I thought. All my fear, all my anger and dread from missing her for days, fell away at the sight of her, as if I had only to meet her in the lobby after the show, take her arm in mine, and escort her, with magic and grace, back to the rooms of our past. I didn't even feel any ache of ire toward Wakefield. He'd brought her back to Omaha healed. He was only a device of our reunion.

The relief worked on me like a swallow of morphine.

I then noticed that I wasn't the only one looking. Many in the audience had let the aim of their opera glasses drift away from center stage and up to where Wakefield sat with Cecily on a blue settee. A waiter brought them champagne, and the popped cork shot from the bottle to fall and bounce off the lip of the stage. The men and the women stared and whispered.

Wakefield had had their private box built so near the front curtains, he and Cecily were practically among the performers. The box even seemed to lean forward, threatening to tip them into the footlights. The railing of their balcony was garlanded with smilax and lilies that drooped and spilled forth, so much so an actor might pluck one without even stretching his reach.

"May I?" I asked the woman next to me, holding my hand out for her opera glasses. Though a tad taken aback at the request, she nonetheless shared.

The glasses, shockingly powerful, bolted me so close so quickly, I felt the fear and dread return with a thud in my head and gut. Any of my newfound forgiveness was gone in a blink. I studied Wakefield and Cecily. He somehow seemed indifferent, as if he sat alone. Cecily had no help with the tricky clasp of her cape.

"Rushing the season with that fur," I heard someone mutter to someone else.

"Owl," said someone else altogether. Cecily's cape was a gray fox riddled with feathers, as if the pelt had been let into the henhouse. "I saw that cape in a private showing, upstairs at Brandeis. Owl feathers. And an owl's head at her shoulder."

The owl's eyes flickered in the light from the pyrotechnics on the stage. I heard a gentleman say, "The furrier plucks out the eyes and swaps them for agates. And the beak is made of gunmetal, with some gold at the tip."

"Disturbing," a woman said.

When Cecily shrugged off the fur, I thought I could hear a gasp rise up from them all.

"Wearing *red*?" someone said, appalled.

"When out with a widowed man?"

"My glasses, please?" the woman next to me said, holding out her hand. I returned them to her, then returned my gaze to Cecily.

Look for me, I chanted to myself, *look for me, look for me, look for me*, watching Cecily stare into the champagne she didn't drink.

Cecily then picked up her own opera glasses, and she scanned the audience before her. And the audience, feeling caught in their scrutiny, shifted the aim of their glasses back to the stage with a snap of their necks.

I, however, kept my gaze steady.

I stood up.

The men and women behind me hissed at me, insisting I be seated.

And Cecily's glasses stopped. She saw me. And she didn't look away.

"Excuse me, excuse me, excuse me," I whispered, high-stepping over the legs and feet of the men and women as I headed for the aisle, jostling against their knees, tripping on the dust ruffles of gowns. I steadied myself by grabbing ladies' shoulders and the tops of men's heads. The men and women grumbled with disgust at my maneuvering. "Pardon me, pardon me, pardon me," I said. They slapped me and shoved, only tumbling me more. Finally I fell, stumbling into the aisle. I got to my feet and rushed to the lobby and up the grand staircase.

But when I arrived at their box, there was no one inside. They'd fled. Were they fleeing *me*? I heard fast footsteps, heels clanging against metal stairs, and I walked toward the noise. I reached the top of a spiral staircase and spun down along its bends. A backstage door, when I reached it, was locked.

I walked back to the private box, stepped inside, and took a seat on the settee. Cecily had left her glass on the railing, half full of champagne. I picked it up and pressed my lips to the lipstick on the rim, and drank from it. I raised my glass in a toast to all those who stared up at me, and with that gesture, they snapped their opera glasses away, back toward the stage, as Heart arrived at the Chicago World's Fair. A scrim fell away to reveal an ornate and sturdy facade made of genuine marble and granite, the ornate stonework standing in for the paste and plaster of the actual White City of 1893.

And at my feet was Cecily's handkerchief. I picked it up and ran my thumb along the letter *C* stitched in the corner. It was a message to me, I was certain.

I finished Cecily's champagne, then poured myself more. I was in no hurry. I felt my whole body slow, my blood, my heart. Cecily and Wakefield had run from me. The thought of it, of myself as a threat to their happiness, was bliss.

24.

THOUGH I DOUBTED Rosie's capacity for murder, I did worry when I first saw all the stolen documents—President McKinley's schedule, his seating plans, maps of his paths, copies of his speeches, photographs, even swatches of fabric of the suit he'd be wearing—and the manner in which the anarchists studied them in a dark corner of the beer garden, the way they scrawled notes and arrows and circles throughout the blueprint of the Grand Court. The anarchists had been discussing assassination all summer with what had seemed idle and harmless complaint. But if a man had had a mind to truly shoot the president, it became quite clear that the Peace Jubilee would be the day to do it.

Our soldiers were still dying in Cuba—keeling over from yellow fever—but we were told the war was won and done with. The fever was an epidemic, not an enemy act, the senators said. The battling, at least, was over, and it became unpatriotic to consider the war anything but the most dramatic of victories. President McKinley, the ink still inky on his peace treaties, would get a hero's welcome at the Fair, and thousands and thousands were expected to turn out for the Peace Jubilee of speeches and parades in late September.

With autumn chilling the air, a man could vanish into that crowd, could tuck any kind of weaponry into his coat, could hide within a scarf, and not be at all conspicuous. And McKinley fancied himself a man of the people. He wanted to shake hands with the common folk and lean in to hear their every question and concern. "He keeps his ear so close to the ground," one newspaper said, "he gets grasshoppers in it."

I doubted the anarchists' toil would amount to much, so it was the list of dinner guests among their papers that disturbed me the most. *Mr. and Mrs. Wakefield.* The sight of it—that *Mrs.*—had sickened me. Had they married alongside some burbling hot spring, a wreath of pansies in her hair, a daisy in his buttonhole? I refused to believe it, no matter how likely it seemed.

She had run from me at the theater, and had been hiding ever since. I had even stood at the front gate of the Wakefield estate one day, in a downpour no less, waiting for someone to come in or go out. A pack of dogs had kept me from climbing up and crawling over. They growled and barked and threw themselves against the gate, driven to break through and lunge at my neck, to swallow my throat, to keep me from telling the truth.

So when I saw that the Mrs. would be dining with her Mr. at the president's table, my plan had been a simple one. I would leave her a note. *Meet me on the roof,* I would write. And I would place the note beneath her plate.

Or perhaps I would say even less. I could drop the handkerchief she had dropped for me, the embroidered letter upturned, and when she saw it, and looked around, I'd be there nearby. I'd leave through a door, and she would know to follow.

Rosie and I spent a week scheming, mapping out my quiet ambush, and the plot grew more and more complicated. To infiltrate a president's event, even just to drop a hankie, would take a cast of thousands, it seemed. We enlisted the aid of an entire network of anarchists strung throughout the Fair, the Fair far thicker with anarchy than I'd realized— waiters, managers, florists, janitors, cooks, and maids all having settled themselves deep within the Peace Jubilee's inner workings.

It began to feel patriotic, my stolen moment with Cecily. With the anarchists so fixed on all the mechanics of it, my love affair seemed destined to save the president's life.

MY ROLE THAT NIGHt was that of a waiter. One of the cooks in the kitchen tied back my long hair with a piece of twine used for the trussing of game birds. Another waxed my beard with a few fingers of lard, twisting the end of it into a dandy curl.

I stood entirely still at my station, holding a carafe of wine, a tea towel over my forearm. "You're to do *nothing*," a woman manager told me, with a scold's snap of her tongue. I lurked behind a palm leaf, watching the room become more and more frenzied in preparation for the guests, the staff giving the forks one last polish, the maids fussing with the flowers so the petals sat just so.

My hand was in my pocket, and in my pocket was the scent bottle—the little souvenir I'd bought Cecily. I was risking rubbing the sheen off the shell, so much did I run my thumb over it for luck.

I'd convinced myself that all success with Cecily hinged on that bottle. I'd even rehearsed in my room the many ways it might go. Would I simply press the bottle into her palm without a word? Would I ask her to hold out her hand, and would I place it there? I could give her the bottle first, or I could give it to her last, before turning and walking away. She would be pleased with the little cheap gift. It would take back to our lazy summer, to the way we drifted along in the swan gondola, and the carousel, to our long afternoons collapsed on the chamomile lawn. And she would remember that she couldn't live without me.

The tables had been arranged in a hollow rectangle, and the dinner guests began taking their places just minutes before six. There were a hundred of them in all, one hundred of the city's most notable. Somehow it hadn't occurred to me that the men and women from Wakefield's cyclone party would be in attendance, so when I spotted Mr. and

Mrs. Brandeis, and the Kimballs, and the Rosewaters, I attempted to sink into my suit and hide myself away.

In my fidgety determination to become invisible, I dropped the carafe, and all eyes turned on me. The carafe shattered at my feet with a sharp crash, soaking the bottoms of my trousers with red wine, and splattering the skirts and pants of anyone nearby.

One of the women, in ivory, squealed with horror at the sight of her dress freckled with wine. Her escort, as it turned out, was the dreadful Baker, the pompous young man who'd seemed so proud of himself at the Pink Heron Hotel.

"Look alive, chap," he snapped, glaring right into my eyes. I froze, a swallow of spit caught in my throat. I was convinced I'd been caught. I was caught, and in seconds I'd be hustled out by my collar. Baker probably knew that Wakefield had stolen Cecily from me, and he would see right through my efforts to lurk unseen. I'd be lucky if I wasn't arrested and charged with some kind of treason. There were likely all sorts of laws against former thieves sneaking into presidential dinners. "At least make an attempt to save your own dignity, man," he said. "Maybe gather a damp cloth for the poor dear?"

A waiter appeared right then with the cloth in hand, and Baker made much of kneeling before his lady to blot the spots on her dress. Another waiter attended to the spill with a mop.

Baker hadn't recognized me. Of course he hadn't. Even if I'd walked right up to him and shaken his hand and told him my name, I still wouldn't exist, because he would never remember anyone who didn't matter. I was only a waiter, and a clumsy one at that.

My absence made me feel bold.

The woman who'd told me to do nothing suddenly appeared in front of me. She snatched my arm tight and led me away while giving my elbow an ungentle twist. "Pretend to fold napkins," she said, pushing me up to a table. "And do a better job of doing nothing this time."

When I picked up a napkin, I noticed all the other napkins that had already been folded and laid out across the table—they'd all been tucked and twisted together into the shape of swans. *Swans.* It felt like a symbol, a promise. A row of maids lined up at the table in a rush, the skirts and puffed sleeves of their aprons fluttering, and each one gently lifted one linen bird into her two cupped hands. They cradled the swans one by one to the tables as the guests were led to their seats.

EVERY LADY IN THE ROOM wore a hat, and every hat looked big enough to snap a lady's neck. Their faint shadows were tremorous with all the gossip. I watched as a puzzled bee buzzed from one patch of velvet flowers to the next. There was a hat with a whole bird's worth of plucked feathers, and another with an enormous silk bow with the wingspan of a hawk. There were wax apples with leaves of lace and strawberries of blown glass. One hat with bells tinkled and chimed with the lady's every nod.

And then there was Cecily, utterly hatless. She looked even more beautiful than she had at the theater, but I would've needed opera glasses to study her. The president's table was clear across the hall from me.

How was it that I couldn't simply walk the vast distance and sit at her side? How had she become someone I wasn't allowed to know?

All those hats in the room set to bobbing at the sight of Cecily. Wives leaned past their husbands to speak to the other wives. The faint shadows in the room shivered with all the gossiping.

I was proud of how she so scandalized the room without saying a word. She simply sat there, indifferent to them all, her eyes on the swan on her plate, thinking only of me.

AT EACH PLACE SETTING, clipped in the hinged beak of a little silver dove, was a card with a guest's name in a scrolling and looping script. Where *Mrs. Wakefield* was to be seated, I had left a plea on the back of the little menu atop her plate. At the bottommost of it I'd etched, in a faint scratch of pencil: *When you see this, meet me on the roof. Please. Ferret.*

And I'd carefully placed the handkerchief, near the leg of her chair, embroidery up. It served no purpose in the plot. It was only a sentimental gesture.

I'd been so afraid of Wakefield seeing the note somehow that I'd barely pressed the pencil's tip against the menu. I'd inched the message as close to invisible as I could get it. At a glance you would see only a smudge, much of the mark fading into the grain of the linen paper. The plan: After the dinner plates had been cleared, as the staff served the dessert in a flurry of bowls and spoons, the ice cream melting beneath everyone's very noses, a waiter would lean over to place a spoon at Cecily's side and whisper in her ear. He would prompt her to read the back of the menu. She would do so, then send a glance around the room. Her eyes would find their way to mine, to linger, then look away. She would wait for Wakefield to fall into a conversation with President McKinley to his left, and she would slip from the table. Her ice cream, molded into the shape of the battleship *Maine*, would sink into a puddle as she and I hid on the roof.

But that's not how it went. Not quite, anyway. Cecily did sit in the right place. Wakefield did indeed ignore her for much of the dinner as he busied himself with impressing the president. The waiter did whisper in her ear, and Cecily did flip her menu over to look at the back of it. But somehow in the plotting of it all I'd forgotten something key—Cecily wouldn't be able to read a word of my note without her glasses.

It wasn't that I'd forgotten about the glasses themselves—she'd often asked me to carry in my pocket the little paper case decorated with Chinese letters. But they were so part of her character, I'd forgotten their purpose.

So when I saw her twist her pretty face into a terrible squint in her effort to read the writing before her, I feared all was lost, or even worse.

She might turn to Wakefield and ask him to read it to her. For all she knew, the words on the menu could be as dire as an anarchist's warning. When you're in a room with a president, I realized, it was as if you were all made of china. Your every move seemed under scrutiny by everyone else, because even the weakest tip-tap could shatter the whole royal works.

I felt myself flush with sweat. I brought my thumb to my mouth to gnaw nervously on the edge of my nail. And then, without a thought, I stepped forward.

Every waiter I passed, every maid, shot me a look of shock, as if they knew all about me. They knew I was a man broken by love and jealousy—there was no telling what I might do if I stepped from my corner. They could only help a fool so much.

The presidential table was set atop a long platform, so everyone in the room could see McKinley slurp his turtle soup. The floor creaked beneath my feet as I walked up, but no one could hear anything above the chatter of the crowd and the rattling of spoons. And I was nothing. I was a waiter. I was confident in my invisibility. If I'd been an anarchist intent on murder, I'd have had a bullet in the president's brain in a matter of seconds.

I crossed the dais, walking behind them all as they ate their ice cream. I ducked down to pick up the handkerchief she hadn't even noticed, and I placed it atop the table, the letter *C* showing, and whispered into Cecily's ear. "Meet me on the roof," and I nearly wrecked the whole operation in my impulse to stay. She wore, again, the extract of sweet pea. The smell of her perfume worked into my senses and surprised me with its familiarity—it carried with it our entire lost summer, and every minute of it worked up into my thoughts. I needed to kiss her ear, her neck.

Nonetheless, I moved on. As I passed behind the president, I saw a thin thread loose from a seam, and without pausing to think, I quickly twisted the thread around my finger as I passed behind his back. I snapped the thread off without even slowing my step.

I twisted and untwisted the thread around and around my finger as I left the platform and walked through the hall. *I'll give it to Doxie someday*, I thought, with a pang of regret. *I'll tell her it came from the president's suit.* Ever since I'd first thought of making Cecily my wife, I'd been thinking of all the things I'd save for our little girl, all the fragments of our first summer together.

25.

DESPITE ALL OUR careful plotting and planning, I hadn't realized there were *two* rooftop gardens. I sat for several minutes, sunk with exhaustion, my head in my hands, on a stone bench in the one garden where Cecily wasn't.

I twisted the president's thread around my finger some more. I closed my eyes and calculated. I pictured Cecily standing, walking, leaving the dining room. I counted the steps down the hall, tapping them out with the toe of my boot. I counted the stairs, imagining the time it would take her to climb them so weighted down by the trappings of her dress.

Cecily once told me that rich ladies kept their skirts stiff by wearing crinolines spun from glass.

"No wonder the rich girls look more sour than the poor ones," I'd said, whispering in her ear, slipping my hand beneath her kimono, running my fingers over the skin of her thigh. "They're bleeding from all those snips and cuts." She had then taken my hand in hers to move it up her thigh, to between her legs. She writhed against my fingers. I watched her, as she closed her eyes, as she opened her mouth. I put my hand to her neck to feel it arch, her head falling back. I loved hearing her every broken breath. I held my mouth to her mouth, to let her breathe into me, my lips only barely touching hers.

But when I finally stepped from the wrong garden and saw her waiting in the right one, her back to me, she looked as light as a cloud. There was no taffeta, no crinoline to hide the bones of her hips. The silk of her sky-blue gown clung to her, as if she wore nothing underneath.

I had wished this other garden into existence. I'd conjured it up. *She lost her way*, I'd promised myself. *She's here.* I'd stepped back into the corridor, to look up and down, and had it not been for a slight gust of wind that had pushed at the garden door, and the squeak of the door's hinges, and a shift of pale shadow, I would have risked never seeing her at all. The door to Cecily's garden was tucked around a corner, behind a twist in the hall, hidden by a slope. How had she ever found her way in?

Out on her private corner of rooftop, she stood between two tall urns spilling over with ivy and she gazed across the Grand Court. The evening sky beyond her was a spatterwork of heaven-like colors—some lavender, some robin's-egg blue. "Cecily," I said, softly, as if I might frighten her away if I spoke too loud. She didn't hear me, and when I said her name again, I ended up startling her anyway.

"Oh," she said, "there you are," with an edge of annoyance. She turned to me, sending sparkles glinting up and down her dress as the setting sun caught metallic threads of silver. The threads had been woven into the silk, into the blooms of fireworks bursting.

Her arms were bare, and she rubbed them for warmth. Her hair was done up again in a Psyche knot, some of the curls coming loose and dangling down, like she'd just woken from a nap beneath a tree.

"I was waiting in the wrong place," I said. I smiled at her, but she didn't smile back.

"I figured you just couldn't kick the habit of abandoning me," she said.

"I've never abandoned you," I said. I spoke as softly as before. I didn't want her to think I was trying to stir up an argument. But I was desperate to explain. "I've never left you. Never. Please believe me."

"I don't want to talk about it," she said. She looked down at her hands. She ran a finger along the lines of her palm, like a fortune-teller tracing a fate. "That's the only reason I came up here, Ferret. To tell you that I won't talk to you. I have nothing else to say about it." But she didn't leave the garden.

"Cecily, I was *there*," I said. As I stepped closer, I saw how pale she'd become, all her summer color having faded away. "I was there in the hospital. That's what I've been wanting to tell you for weeks, Cecily. It kills me that you think I wasn't there. I was *there*. The nuns only ever let me see you when you were half asleep. They lied to you when they said they couldn't find me."

"The *nuns* lied," she said, scoffing, rolling her eyes, and despite her paleness and her finery, there she was again. There was Cecily. "The *nuns*."

"Yes," I said. "And Wakefield. Ask him. Tell him to tell you the truth."

When I stepped forth to take her hands in mine, she pulled away. She shook her head. She shrugged, and the shoulder knot of her dress dropped down her arm. "I won't listen to this," she said, her weak protest rising just above a whisper. "None of it matters."

I reached over to push the shoulder knot back up. "The truth doesn't matter?" I said, but I said it gently, running my fingertips over the goose-pimpled skin of her ice-cold arm.

"No," she said. She shook her head, then she looked me right in the eye, almost defiant. "*No*, frankly. No. The truth *doesn't* matter, to be honest. Whether it's true or not, I believed it. And isn't there something wrong with that? Isn't that troubling? It was so easy to believe that you would leave me. I'd been expecting all along for you to just run away. And I can't live like that. I can't live every minute wondering when I'm going to be alone again."

"You're not being fair," I said. "I never did anything to make you think I'd ever leave you."

"Except for the time *you left me*," she said. "When I was *sick*."

"I was *there*," I said again, raising my voice, and I suddenly remembered the little dove with the mop and bucket. "The novitiate," I said, and I began to stumble over my words, rattling them out, excited to remember. "The novitiate. You remember her? Always cleaning? Always everyplace? She knew I was waiting for you. She knew I was in the chapel. She can tell you."

Now Cecily's eyes seemed to fall on me with pity. She started to say something, but stopped. She returned to the railing, to look away. "I don't remember the novitiate," she said, weary. She then spoke calmly, patiently. "Maybe I'm *not* being fair. *But it doesn't matter*. We don't *have* to puzzle it all out, Ferret. We don't have to worry over it all. This isn't *Heart of the White City*. This isn't a show. We don't have to have a scene with the novitiate." She said "the novitiate" with a pompous air, mocking the drama of it. "We can simply let it all go, without a fight. I'm with Billy now." She looked back to me, and she shrugged again, again knocking that shoulder knot off. "I *married* him. I'm married now. I have a daughter to look after."

"I love Doxie," I said. *Daughter* . . . I found it insulting the way she said it. Yes, your *daughter*, I know her. I know your daughter. I know your daughter's name. Remember?

"I know you love her," she said, looking down again at her hands, and my feeling of insult faded as quickly as it had sparked up.

"*He* doesn't love her," I said.

"He does," she said, matter-of-fact, certain. "He does. He loves her very much."

"He doesn't," I said.

"How would you *know*, Ferret? We've been away for weeks. You don't know anything about us anymore. We've been away even longer than you and I were together. Did you even realize that, Ferret? Do you have any sense of time at all?" When I said nothing, she said, "No, not you," but she wasn't angry. She spoke gently. "The days just trip along, one into the next. We should all be so lucky to care so little."

I'd hoped she wouldn't see how misted my eyes had got, as I'd been concentrating on keeping my tears back. If I so much as blinked, the tears would drop, and I didn't want to cry alone over all of this. If I cried in front of her, I was just the helpless little boy she worried that I was.

So the first tear felt like defeat. But somehow it seemed even more cowardly to wipe it away. I blinked my eyes, and more tears fell. I sniffled, then cleared my throat, lowering my voice. "I'll be whoever you want me to be," I said.

In a spat between lovers, you can shore yourself up when the other one buckles. You become the strong one in front of the weak one, just like that. She stepped forward, and with a kindness that killed me, she wiped my tears with her thumb. "You don't need to play a character, Ferret," she said. "You need to be who you are."

She rubbed at her bare arms. "I'm getting cold," she said. "I'm going in." She dropped her eyes from mine. "Good night, Ferret."

As Cecily walked past me, I took her arm. I held it. I wouldn't let her go, but she didn't try, anyway. I pulled her to me, her back to my chest. I held her there, against me, wrapping my arms around her. I put my lips to her ear and whispered, "I *never* left you." I said, "I never once left you."

At first, Cecily seemed to be simply indulging me, kindly letting me hold her, petting my hand with hers, sighing with that pity again. But then her sighs grew heavier. She began to shiver, and I held her closer. And her shivering turned into shaking, and she wept. She fell slack in my arms.

Finally, she elbowed me in the ribs, and she shook herself away. She turned to face me, but stepped back, her eyes wide with rage. "Then why'd you burn my letter?" she said. She yelled at me, but with my mind so muddled I couldn't think of what letter I'd burned. "I poured my soul out to you in my letter," she said, "and you *burned* it." I'd never seen Cecily like this. She shouted above her sobbing, half bent at the back like a madwoman, clutching at the skirt of her dress. "I told you that I loved you in that letter, that it *killed* me that you weren't at my bedside when I needed you, and you *burned* it. And you held it in your fist . . ." She raised her hand in the air, her hand in a fist, and her weeping consumed her. "You wanted me to see . . . at the train window . . ."

"No. No. Oh, no, no, no, no, no," I said, as I realized. I put my hands to her cheeks, to turn her face toward me, to get her to look into my eyes. "No, no, no," I said. I felt washed in relief. *A mistake*, I thought. She had made a mistake. We could correct the mistake. We just had to come to this. It was this easy. "I didn't burn the letter, Cecily. Mrs. Margaret burned it. I wanted you to see that . . . I just needed you to see that I couldn't read it. Cecily, I don't know what you wrote in that letter. Mrs. Margaret burned it." I felt such regret over my foolishness. *Of course* it had looked like *I* had burned the letter. *How could I be so stupid?*

She seemed to be weighing this new information, considering it. She had stopped crying. She pushed my hands from her shoulders, and she stepped away in a daze. She leaned against a column, putting her forehead to it. "It doesn't matter," I heard her say. But I knew that it did. I was certain that this all mattered to her deeply. I walked to her. I ran my fingers over her cheek, pushing away the strands of her hair caught in her tears. I put my lips to her cheek, and she allowed it. I then kissed her neck. And when she let me do that, I brought my lips to hers. I put my arms around her waist, and she put hers around my shoulders. We kissed not with intensity but with tenderness, sadly, as if we were saying good-bye.

She then said, "I need to go. I need to get back to the table. I've been gone too long."

I kissed her cheek, her neck. "Don't go," I said. "Won't you just get into trouble?"

"I can slip back in without him even noticing," she said. "The fashionable ladies don't rustle anymore, you know. We wrap ourselves in a cashmere shroud to keep ourselves silent." She reached down to lift her dress enough to show the thin lining beneath.

The garden door squeaked open and we both jumped at the noise of it. "There you are, Mrs. Wakefield," Wakefield's sister said. I felt Cecily's heart quicken. "Your husband is worried about you," Billie said.

Cecily hurried from my side without a word and walked past Billie, their skirts sweeping against each other with a whoosh of silk. Cecily left the garden, dry leaves dragged along behind her, caught up in the train of her dress.

"Thank you for finding her, Ferret," Billie said. She came to me holding out some folded dollar bills. Instead of taking the money, I grabbed her wrist. I pulled her closer, and I grabbed her elbow, and I pulled her closer still. I looked her in the eye.

"Oh, Ferret, don't be bitter," she said pleasantly as she squirmed. "This isn't a contest. And even if it was, how could you win?"

I held tight to her elbow. "I can't," I whispered in her ear. I could feel her breath on my neck. "But if I threw you off the roof, it might feel a little bit like winning something, at least. And why shouldn't I do something awful? To you. Then to your brother. What have I got to lose?"

Billie leaned away from me. She lifted her chin, squinting, examining. She brought her hand up to my face and I flinched at first. She then touched my cheek with her thumb as if brushing away a fallen eyelash. "I always liked you, Ferret," she said. "You've got a good soul. Don't let someone like her ruin you. She's not worth it."

When I yanked her closer again, she gasped with what I hoped to be true fear. I then took the money she still held in her hand, but only so that I could drop it at her feet. I said nothing else and walked to the door to the garden. It satisfied me to hear the sound of her silk as she lowered herself to collect the dollar bills.

THE DINNER GUESTS left the hall to be escorted into buggies and carriages festooned for a flower parade—President McKinley would ride at the end of the procession—down the Grand Court in the dazzle of the night's electric light. August would later educate me on all the flora, as he lay back in my arms on a patch of lawn to watch the parade pass. Forget-me-nots and myrtle wreathed and garlanded the manes of the horses, and clematis and daisies wove and wound through the spokes of the wheels. "Snowdrop, crocus, damask rose, hyacinth, hollyhocks," August would say, pointing, tapping his finger at the air.

But before I would take any moments of ease, I slipped myself in among the footmen and maids assisting the ladies and gentlemen into their carriages. According to a chart acquired covertly by the anarchists, Mr. and Mrs. Wakefield would be riding with McKinley, whose wife had stayed behind in the White House to crochet slippers and nurse her epilepsy with laudanum.

We were to hand every woman a parasol trimmed with fresh flowers. I hid beneath one to wait for Cecily, the parasol's silk rippling with fringed pink.

Though I'd only ever been afflicted with the slightest bit of hay fever, all my weeping and snuffling on the roof had seemed to aid with my suffocation—the fragrance was like a cloud of dust, working up my nose and down my throat, to tickle and scratch. I fell into a sneezing fit that shook the petals off my parasol, sending them raining down around me.

All the servants noticed my convulsing, but I didn't care. I didn't care if I got caught and exposed as a fraud. I'd had my moment on the rooftop. Cecily had left her husband's side to meet me, and I'd been able to tell her the truth. I'd kissed her and held her. And she'd believed me, a little, at least.

When Cecily and Wakefield stepped forth, I ducked low, hiding beneath the parasol, and I nudged aside a young maid who was prepared to hand Cecily a parasol weighty with the heavy heads of sunflowers. As Wakefield attended to the president, I held my parasol over Cecily's head, tilting it, blocking Wakefield out altogether. She put her hand on mine as she took the handle, but she dropped her eyes away. In all the confusion and fuss on the roof, I'd failed to give Cecily the scent bottle, so I now held it out in my open palm. Without any words between us, she took the bottle and tucked it into her handkerchief with a magician's sleight of hand. As she walked away from me, she carried my sneezing fit with her, such a lovely contagion. She sneezed and sneezed, knocking the flowers around as she stepped up into the president's carriage, which was covered in cowslip and primrose.

AUGUST HAD STAKED OUT a spot of grass on the promenade early, so we could watch the flower parade up close. The promenade was flooded with electrical light, the Grand Court as lit up as daytime but starker, brighter, the white light casting the thinnest and slightest of shadows.

Even outside of his fortune-teller's tent, August's attire had grown bizarre. He had on trousers and a suit coat like a gentleman, but beneath his coat, instead of a shirt, he wore a woman's corset he'd fashioned into a kind of breastplate, having stuck in some feathers and wired in pieces of bone.

"That reminds me," I said, touching a bone on his corset. I pulled from my pocket the gnawed-clean bone of a frog's leg I'd plucked from Cecily's plate as a waiter had carried it back to the kitchen. "Divine something from it," I said, handing it to him. And though I'd had no way of knowing it, he predicted the leg I would break when the balloon would fall.

He closed his eyes and tapped the frog's bone against his forehead. "A crutch," he said. "No spring in your step."

August had brought along a box of macaroons and a bottle of red wine, and we leaned back against the pedestal of a statue. Feeling sentimental, I put my arm around his shoulders, and he snuggled in close. I guzzled back some wine, and since I'd eaten nothing all day, it took quick effect, and any pangs of worry I had left were dulled away to nothing. Cecily was still married, and Doxie still in her crib in the house on the hill, but I would get them back soon. Soon. I was certain.

"Do you have any sense of time at all?" Cecily had asked, and her tone still stung. But I knew in my heart that I was the one she loved—we could throw all the clocks away and live only by the sun and the moon. I tapped my tongue against my teeth again, just as I had when waiting on the rooftop, ticking off the beat of her steps on the stairs.

As if sensing my inner rhythm, Rosie tapped the toe of his boot against the top of my head. He sat above us, atop the pedestal, at the feet of a naked-breasted angel, leaning back against her leg. He seemed mopey about the parade—President McKinley would be passing by in his flowered buggy unassassinated. McKinley was destined to survive our Fair, and all the anarchists were already feeling defanged by a sense of failure. It was a regret they'd feel even more severely a few years later, a deep envy, when McKinley would be gunned down at the world's fair in Buffalo, New York.

"Wallflower, foxglove, celandine, anemone," August said, poking the coal of his asthma cigarette at the air as the flower-bedecked carriages wheeled by. I took August's opera glasses and looked down the line, seeking Cecily at the parade's end.

The rapid pops and shots that suddenly filled the night air didn't worry me a bit, as I could see the source. The horseless carriage that the catalog company sold, that had been sputtering and popping up the midway all summer long, giving rides to and from, had joined the parade too, strewn with honeysuckle and buttercups.

But the sharp, loud firing of its pipes set the folks in the crowd to shrieking and shouting, suspecting they'd just heard the president done in. No one ran for cover. Instead, they stood on their toes and craned their necks. They stepped into the promenade, closer to the horses and carriages, hoping to get an eyeful of history.

The spectators then retreated, running away from the parade when they saw what they saw: a carriage pulled quick by spooked horses. The carriage tottered and bucked, knocking off its red and white carnations, flinging the flowers into the crowd. I was relieved to see it wasn't Cecily's carriage. The passengers in the runaway cart, we'd later learn, were two teachers from a one-room schoolhouse in the little town of Aurora, who'd been rewarded for their commitment to the children of Nebraska with a place in the president's parade. The teachers screamed and clutched at each other, their hats toppled and their hairdos wrecked, their skirts in a flurry.

While all the rest of us scrambled up the steps of the Electricity Building, away from the danger, Rosie got to his feet on the pedestal. He held on to the angel's wing to lean out and forward to see all he could. And he surprised us by leaping onto the promenade into the thick of it.

Rosie stumbled at first, falling to the bricks and nearly rolling into the rush of the hooves, but he righted himself in time to run alongside the runaway horses. He grabbed hold of the harness of the horse nearest him and seemed to be trying a cowboy trick, intending to kick himself up and over and onto the horse's back, to slow the horse and steer it to safety.

But Rosie kept tripping on his own legs, and he took a few kicks from the horse. He abandoned the Wild West move and collapsed instead, using his full weight to pull and yank on the harness. The horse, weary of dragging him, bared its teeth and slowed to a gallop, then to a stop. The schoolteachers were saved. The two women wept and laughed all at once. They wouldn't even step down when some gentlemen offered to help. It was as though they could only feel at ease by loitering in this moment of death averted.

August and I elbowed and shouldered our way through the crowd, but before we could even reach Rosie, he'd become the Fair's hero as he lay groggy and wrecked, flat on his back on the bricks. Snippets of rumors passed quickly from person to person, and his heroism became more and more embellished along the way. We could hear everyone muttering. By the time we'd reached his side, word had spread that he'd saved not only the schoolteachers but also, somehow, the president and the president's wife, who wasn't at the Fair at all. And Rosie, we heard, prevented the trampling of an orphan; we then heard it was an orphan on crutches, then a one-legged orphan with a little mangy dog, then a whole choir of legless orphans who'd been singing a hymn.

"Did I live through it?" Rosie asked us as we knelt next to him, the ambulance wagon within sight.

"It doesn't look like it," I said. I put my hand on his naked chest, plenty bloodied and bruised. His shirt had been torn, the rest of his suit ripped and dirty. He had a black eye and a purple nose and a mouthful of even more missing teeth. "Don't you know you're supposed to run away from a runaway horse, not into it?"

August smoothed back Rosie's hair from his forehead, and leaned down to kiss a cut above his eye. "You'll outlive us all, you mean cuss," August said.

A few doctors and nurses attended to Rosie with stethoscopes and cotton balls of ointment before struggling to lift the beast onto a stretcher and into the back of the wagon. August and I attached ourselves to the outside of the ambulance, clinging to the sides and standing on steps, and we traveled from the Grand Court and into the midway.

The ambulance took Rosie past the Fair's hospital to Roentgen's Wonderful Ray of Light, a carnival attraction—Cecily and I had paid a dime each to stand in its beam to see our skeletons. "Your skeleton is much skinnier than I thought it would be," Cecily had told me after.

The doctors and nurses pushed past the fairgoers in line for the X-ray. "Medical emergency," a doctor explained to the ticket taker. We would later learn that the doctor had been waiting all summer for a chance to sneak a patient into the X-ray. But the doctor was nonetheless disappointed by the picture—Rosie didn't have so much as a crack in his bones.

November 27, 1898

Dear Cecily,

   We've begun to build the Emerald Cathedral.

   *Emmaline woke in the night, only hours ago, so inspired she
couldn't speak. I leaned on my cane and followed her, as quickly as
I could limp, to the barn. She wore only a nightgown and no
slippers, and though the wind was still, it was cold. She didn't feel
it, though. She was feverish. Her chin dripped with the sweat that
rolled down her cheeks. She paced the barn, she ran, she danced and
spun, picking things up, putting things down, laughing, crying,
possessed. Hester threatened her with a trip to the doctor, and
Emmaline finally spoke. <u>Pick up everything you see</u>, she said.
<u>Move it over there</u>. She pointed to the west wall of the barn. And
we began to work. <u>Even this?</u> we often stopped to ask. <u>Even that.
Even everything</u>, she said.*

   *The tools and materials of the Emerald Cathedral had been in
the barn all along.*

   *In my weeks as an oracle, folks often brought sentimental
objects to my side. At first they only brought the little things they
kept near their hearts—old keys to old diaries, frayed ribbons,
dented thimbles, lockets with locks of hair. But the more often
they came, the more they brought. They hoped for me to divine
something from the everyday. In the twisted logic of the
inconsolable, they concluded that the answers they sought rested in
all the things that seemed to have no meaning. They wanted me to
tell them something. Anything at all. They thought I might be able
to intuit something from the dull scythe of a dead son, or a*

grandmother's cracked butter crock. They brought old sleds with rusted blades, moth-eaten quilts, broken carriage wheels, splintered school desks.

Hester had not allowed the debris to be dragged into her house. _Leave it all in the barn_, she'd said. _He'll get to it_. But I never did, and they kept bringing more.

Word of the cathedral had all day to spread, and when night came, the folks from town and from neighboring farms brought even more of their junk, and they brought wire and rope and pitch. Most of us have gone to bed, even Emmaline, but I can still hear the few that remain in the barn. The wind has dropped to nothing, and I can hear their every word, and every tooth of every saw cutting through something. I hear glass break, and pulleys screech. I hear boozy laughter. And I fall asleep to the noise, comforted, knowing that it's all begun.

Ferret

October 1898

26.

I N THE DAYS AFTER our reunion on the rooftop garden, my letters
to Cecily went unanswered, perhaps unread. I could easily lose an
hour of an afternoon, slouched over my typewriter, coaxing forth poetry for her, hoping to sound hopeful. And I could lose the hour after
that, collapsed on my bed, imagining her collapsed on her bed, my
letter opened, a letter opener in the shape of a sword gripped in her
hand, my words keeping her restless.

I hope to see you at Rosie's tea, I wrote to her a few days after the
president's dinner. Rosie was being honored as a hero by the Fair's board
of lady managers in the gallery of the U.S. Government Building. He
was to receive a patchwork quilt, stitched from burlap bags by a girl in
Iowa who was deaf and blind, and a framed certificate signed by President McKinley.

I wasn't all that surprised that Cecily never arrived, but I kept my
eye on the entryway, watching for her, fooling myself into seeing a
little bit of her in every woman that turned the corner. I even found
myself recognizing her in the shape and flow of a few ladies' shadows,
or a peal of polite laughter, or the click and skip of a heel on the floor.
The afternoon ended up being a nonstop stuttering of disappointment.

I sat with August at Rosie's table of honor near an exhibit of
things confiscated from federal prisons—dinner knives that had been

sharpened into saws, the pine of broken broom handles whittled into keys. The tea in our pot was a strong and awful Lapsang Souchong that tasted of wet smoke.

ROSIE HAD BEEN patched up well, his few grisly gashes covered with gauze, his sprained wrist wrapped tight. But his gums were so sore from the few teeth he broke, he couldn't keep from licking his chops and smacking his lips. "Give up on her," Rosie said, as I cast another glance across the gallery. "Stumble off and go trouble some other lass. And then some other lass after that. There are worse fates than a life of stringing dollies along." He whistled his *s*'s, still getting used to the extra holes in his grin.

"Besides," August said, "you'll become more desirable to her if you desire her no more." August had just come from his tent in the Indian camp, still in his petticoat and corset breastplate. Across his shoulders was a woman's fur stole, and he'd covered his face entirely in white paint but for a little blossom of red at the very kiss of his lips. He'd taken a new name: *Cinnamon Bear*.

August and Rosie, despite their motley appearances, were absolutely right. My cupids were putting away their quivers of arrows. No matter how carefully I scrutinized every minute that passed, Cecily would not suddenly be where she'd never been.

And Cecily certainly had no use for a man broken by love, even if it was her love that had broken him.

ROSIE AND AUGUST helped me even more in the days that followed, setting me up in an office across the hall from August's apartment, above his father's bookshop. Half the room served as August's laboratory, where he brewed his potions of frostwort and horse nettle and hemlock bark, and the other half, the half by the window, would be my office of literary assistance. Even injured, Rosie could lift and haul. He one-handedly took one end of a desk I'd bought secondhand from the stenographers' college and helped me carry it the few blocks to the office and up the narrow stairs. I installed my typewriter and a few chairs, a few lamps, and a hatstand. I propped a sign in the window: *Bartholomew "Ferret" Skerritt, Literary Assistance.* I placed an order for a telephone line, and August's father's shop printed me some sheets of letterhead and envelopes.

And all the while I was certain I'd see Cecily again. She was waiting for the right moment. The truth *did* matter to her. *It must.*

I placed expensive, illustrated advertisements in the *Omaha Bee* and the *Omaha World-Herald*, with money August loaned me. The ad featured a picture of a ventriloquist's dummy that the ad man had had in his files—it had looked a little like Oscar. *Put Words in Your Mouth*, the headline read, along with details of my grand opening: *All love letters half price.* Mr. and Mrs. Wakefield couldn't possibly miss the advertisement in their daily papers.

On my first day of work, I arrived at the office early. From my closet at the Empress, I'd selected the costume of the captain of a paddleboat casino, for luck—a red satin vest and a necktie patterned with horseshoes. The actor who had donated it to me explained that the vest's pink buttons had been made of mollusk shells fetched from the river and cut into shape by the orphan girls of Council Bluffs, Iowa.

I was too excited to sit at my desk, so I paced the room, situating everything just so. I rolled a sheet of paper into the typewriter. I adjusted and readjusted the window blinds. I sharpened pencils. I moved my desk around, pushing it against one wall, then another, studying the room for symmetry.

I had plenty of time that afternoon.

My one and only customer, on my first day of work, was the one-eyed automaton.

27.

Mrs. Margaret, out of costume, in a shirtwaist and small straw hat decorated with crocheted sunflowers, carried a cake box by the twine that tied it closed. "Pork fruitcake," she said, sitting across from me. She put the box on my desk and cut the twine with a pocketknife.

"Pork, you say?" I said, looking in at it. I sniffed for poison in among the scents of cinnamon and clove.

"Some salt with the sweet," she said. "You'll like it." She cut off a slice as I gathered a few sheets of letterhead to use as plates. We had no forks, so we tore at it with our fingers. But I paused to let her take the first bite. When she saw I was waiting for her, she stopped.

"I read in a penny dreadful once that you can smell almond when there's cyanide in something," I said.

"Yeah, cyanide smells like almonds," she said. "And so do *almonds*." She ate the cake, so I ate too. I didn't care for it much, so I only nibbled.

At first I thought Mrs. Margaret was laughing when she started wheezing. She buried her face in her handkerchief. She boohooed and blubbered, her wails broken by her shaky breath. She flipped up her eye patch to dab at the tears there.

Seeing her cry was somehow like seeing a snake swallowing a mouse, gulp by gulp. But it was jarring in other ways too. I counted on her cold indifference, I realized. Without her hardness to rage against, I felt a wall I'd built falling down.

She'd pinched and blown her nose until it was as purple red as a beetroot, like a drunkard's. Finally she cleared her throat and took some deep breaths. She snorted back the phlegm she'd worked up. She took the folded newspaper from the corner of my desk and fanned her hot, red cheeks with it. "I need a letter written," she said. She snapped the eye patch back into place, blessedly hiding the milky glass. Her unseeing eye seemed it could see right through a person.

"I thought you only *burned* letters," I said.

"I'll pay you whatever you need to get paid," she said. "I don't have much, but I'll get you whatever sum you ask for."

"Seeing you in such misery may be sum enough," I said.

As she spoke with her head lowered, she picked at a loose thread in the embroidered violets of her handkerchief. "Cecily can't look at me without getting sick with rage," she said. She sniffled. She whimpered and whined. "She won't let me see Doxie. She doesn't want my inky black soul infecting the child, she says."

"Maybe it's for the best," I said.

Mrs. Margaret slapped the flat of her hand on the top of my desk, rattling the pen in my ink pot. I jumped at the noise and she looked me in the eye. "Understand something, Ferret. I'd sooner swallow glass than live without those girls. Nothing in this world matters to me but Cecily and Dox. I couldn't love them more if they were part of my own blood and guts. Why do you think I've tried to kill you so many goddamn times? I can't have nobody taking them away." I still said nothing, and she sat back in the chair and returned to picking at her needlepoint violet. "You're kinder than I am, Ferret," she said. "I know you think you're tough because you're a boy who grew up in an alley, but can you imagine being a *girl* growing up in an alley? You learn your way around your reflexes awfully fast when the men come creeping, even in the daylight. And I know what you're thinking . . . you're thinking who'd be so hard up they'd go after an ugly toad like old Mrs.

Margaret in the light of day? But back when I was young, I was only half this ugly. And even if I'd been double as ugly as I am now, I still wouldn't have been safe, because they ain't looking to show you off to their mothers."

I folded my hands atop my desk. I sighed, exhausted. "What am I supposed to do for you, Mrs. Margaret? Cecily won't see me either."

"She trusted me to take that letter to you, and I didn't," she said. "It's unforgivable that I set fire to it, she says."

Cecily's lack of forgiveness consoled me. She had turned Mrs. Margaret from her home for being cruel to me. To *me*. "What do you wish me to do?" I said, mimicking Oscar's creaky voice box without quite meaning to. I turned in my swivel chair—its coils still squeaking though I'd oiled them three times in my boredom that day. I touched my fingertips to the typewriter keys, drumming my fingers gently, making the letters on the thin steel bars shiver. "What is it you want to say to her?" I said.

"I don't want to say anything to her," she said. "You won't pose as me, you'll pose as yourself. In your own voice. You'll tell her to forgive me. She will if you say so."

She will if you say so. I could've listened to Mrs. Margaret all day, the two of us analyzing Cecily's unforgiveness.

And then it occurred to me—my fee.

"If she forgives you," I said, turning away from the typewriter, "then you have to get her to meet me. Trick her if you have to. I need to be alone with her."

Her nod of agreement was so slight, it might have just been a little tremor of disgust.

I had installed a bottle of whiskey in a bottom drawer. "A gentleman's contract," I said, bringing out the bottle and two shot glasses. I'd barely finished filling her glass when she'd picked it up and tossed it back. I poured more in, and she drank that too, and held the glass out for another shot. I'd not had a chance to take a single sip of my own.

"She's not good," Mrs. Margaret said. At first I thought it some feeble attempt to convince me I shouldn't love Cecily. It had been Cecily's own strategy a time or two, in her attempts to send me off to Pearl: I'm no good for you, Ferret. I'm no good.

But then Mrs. Margaret said, "She's sick."

"No," I said. "No, she's getting better." I thought of all those postcards. *Took the waters, leaving today, took the waters, leaving today, took the waters, leaving today,* her recitation sounding like a train on its tracks. But I also thought of how pale she'd looked on the roof. "The travel did her good," I said.

"No," she said, "the travel made her worse. Or something's making her worse. I spent time up at the house when she first got back. She'd been to ten sanatoriums, had been prodded and fingered by perverted old doctors, and yet she couldn't even lift Doxie out of the crib. She's getting so big, she'd say, but Doxie isn't getting so big. She's not even as big as she should be. Do they even feed her? That little heiress is as thin as a waif."

I shot the whiskey back, then poured some more, shot it back, catching up with Mrs. Margaret as she spoke of her dread. "I had a little girl of my own once," she said. "I was just a little girl myself. What did I know about looking after a living thing? I didn't know nothing, and she didn't live long. And I knew she was dead a month before she died. Even when she was still alive, she was a ghost in her own skin. She was haunting her own bones. She was so afraid."

I stood up too fast and knocked over the bottle, but Mrs. Margaret grabbed it before it spilled a drop. I fell back into my chair, dizzy. I shook with rage, and I felt my throat constrict. I felt it burning with the liquor. Wakefield was killing Cecily as sure as if he had his hands at her neck, pressing his thumbs in, inching her windpipe closed.

I would not write a letter. I would not scheme for a secret meeting of begging. I would not hope for the best. I would kill him. I would go to wherever he was, press the point of a pistol to his temple, and pull the trigger. And they'd hang me for it. They'd lynch me, so they could all have a tug on the rope.

Even before it had all flickered through my head, I resolved myself to this fate. Nothing in my life had ever seemed more certain. I took another shot, straight from the bottle.

Mrs. Margaret seemed to be seeing into my head and all the pictures of my execution. She put her hand on my wrist and squeezed hard. "I need your help," she said. "If you go off half-cocked, you won't get anywhere. You won't get *near* Billy Wakefield. You think a man gets so rich from being a saint? You think you're the first one to wish him dead? Get Cecily to forgive me, and I can keep watch. And I can get things fixed."

It had a kind of hypnotism, her cranberry eye, the whites shot through with red. I believed her. We would save Cecily. We would get her and Doxie out of the house on the hill.

I turned back to the typewriter. I typed *Dear Cecily*, then stopped, defeated. "I don't think my letters even reach her," I said.

"I can get it to her," Mrs. Margaret said. "I know where she's going to be. I can even put it in her hand today if you finally get to writing the damn thing. It doesn't have to be much. She just needs to know I was here, making things right."

I concentrated. I considered. But everything I wrote was wrong. I would type a few lines, then rip it from the typewriter, to crumple the paper. Only when I imagined myself sitting with Cecily, speaking right to her, did the words come to me. *Only one person has ever loved you and ol' Dox more than I do, and that's that Mrs. Margaret of yours,* I wrote. *Forgive her. She was only thinking of you when she was so awful to me.*

I folded the note too slowly for Mrs. Margaret. She grabbed it from the desk, stood, and turned to leave the room. "Mrs. Margaret," I said, and she paused with her hand on the doorknob, wiggling it with impatience. I said, "What did Cecily's letter say? Did you read it before you burned it? I'd just like to know a little something about what it said." I somehow felt, as coconspirators, we could rely on each other. And I could finally ask her what I'd so longed to ask. I was desperate for even the least fragment of a sentence, even a word or two more. Cecily had confessed on the roof what she'd written—*I told you that I loved you.* How, exactly, had she said it to me?

"You idiot," she said, snorting. As she stepped out the door, she said, "Where would somebody like me have ever learned how to read?"

And it was as if she took a match to that letter once again.

Dear Cecily,

The Emerald Cathedral hasn't an emerald in it. There isn't much of anything green. In the sunlight that creeps in between the cracks of the barn's walls, the cathedral does glisten with a few green sparks here and there—shards of jelly jars catch the light, and green glass bottles and lightning rod insulators and a window excavated from a church, the whale that devoured Jonah swimming in a blue-green ocean.

And it's not much of a cathedral. There's a cross of crystal doorknobs, but no door. There are no rooms within with pulpits and pews. Its spires suggest steeples, but for the most part, it has yet to take shape despite its hulking mass. The Emerald Cathedral seems it might fall apart from the strain of reaching toward heaven—it looks like a collision caught in the middle of collapse.

We use anything useless: bent nails and rusted wheels and broken pitchers; warped window frames of abandoned sheds, the ball-and-claw foot of an old bathtub, the clapper of a church bell. We built a scaffolding around the growing altar. We use wire and plaster and nails, tar and rope. The beauty of it, I came to see after only a minute or two, was how it stood always on the verge of ruin.

We dismantled all the implements rusting in nearby ditches and lying broken in neighboring creeks. The plows, the harrows, the cultivators, the weeders, the potato diggers. These winter days are mild, and the cathedral creeps along the walls and rafters, and swirls and towers, like a stilled tornado in the middle of tearing apart a town.

We add dolls to the cathedral, sundials, croquet mallets, mole traps, cherry stoners.

We've forgotten about Christmas coming. Many from across the countryside come every night to the barn, bringing along the birds they shot and plucked and cooked for our supper. We hang lanterns from every hook and we have evenings of waltzes in the flickering amber glow. A farmer plays a dulcimer, his wife a ukulele, and we dance across the barn floor after dark, at the foot of the altar.

Somehow it seems the cathedral belongs to everyone around. It's a reason to gather and to work. The harvests used to be like this, I'm told. When the crops were healthy, they would tend each other's fields and gather for festivals. They would eat together, and drink, and they'd stay up past midnight.

We're anxious to be finished with the cathedral, but we never want these days and nights to end.

Ferret

28.

A ND CECILY RETURNED TO ME, like a blessing. Within only a
minute of being together again, it was as if we'd never spent a
minute apart. We didn't talk about the burned letter, or the summer
just past. We didn't talk at all. She wouldn't let me speak. "Sh-sh-sh-
sh-sh," she said, when she saw me.

Mrs. Margaret, not only forgiven by Cecily but given a job at the
house, had arranged for us to meet in the offices of the Chinese doctor
on Douglas Street.

Cecily had expected me, and took my hand the moment she walked
in the door. She led me down a hall, through a dimly lit rabbit warren
of little rooms and sleeping berths.

Sh-sh-sh-sh-sh. "I've grown to hate hellos even more than I hate
good-byes," she said, as we ducked through a curtain. She shook my
hand, gentlemanly. "It's a pleasure to meet you, mister, ma'am, miss, a
pleasure, a pleasure, a pleasure. The pleasure is all *mine*, to be sure." She
curtsied, she bowed, she tsk-tsked and tut-tutted, and she handed me
her fur stole and her scarf and her hat, flinging them all into my arms
with the lazy wrists of a wealthy matron.

She took off a winter glove lined with white rabbit, and she held
her bared hand to my lips when I went to speak again. "Sh-sh-sh-sh,"
she said. "The doctor needs absolute silence."

Dr. Gee Loy had come in, and he placed a sheet across a black table inlaid with pearl. "When you're allowed to speak again," Cecily told me, "remind me to buy a new chameleon from the doctor." Pinned to the breast of her dress was a little chain with a ring at the end of it. A leash. "The fashionable ladies wear the chameleons as jewelry," she said. "It's sweet to have a little heart thumping against mine, while I'm buried in cadavers." She sneered at the head of the muskrat propped up on the fur stole in my arms. "I'm cold all the time, so he keeps buying me furs." She unpinned the chain and stuck it into the lapel of my coat. She leaned in to whisper. "The chameleons keep getting away from me, but if I don't rescue them from the doctor," she said, "I don't know what's to become of them."

Any chameleon in Dr. Gee Loy's apothecary would likely end up dried or powdered. The doctor's methods of treatment crawled with dead bugs and reptiles. In the apothecary jars on the shelves of the office that fronted the street were the roasted larvae of grasshoppers for headaches, and the dusty husks of silkworm moths for fainting fits, and dead scorpions for rheumatism. There were little red-spotted lizards dried to a crisp, and rattles without their snakes. I suspected it was all for show, all the labels facing out, promising cures you wouldn't find anywhere else. It seemed nothing but hocus-pocus, just like everything else did those days.

But Cecily, to my great relief, seemed better somehow. Much, much better. She had color in her cheeks, life in her eyes. When she turned her back to me, lifting a few stray tendrils of hair up from her neck, asking me to undo the buttons of her collar, of the back of her dress, I was with her again on the night we first met, backstage at the Empress. I placed the fur stole and the hat in a chair, and I brought my fingers to the buttons, and I worked slowly, so slowly, and she let me. She stretched her neck forward. She touched her fingertips to mine. Once I'd opened her collar, I leaned forward to kiss her skin, and she reached back to run her fingers across my cheek.

I was willing to trust anything Dr. Gee Loy prescribed, even the vial of tiger's blood and the tincture of dragon's tooth.

Cecily stripped to a suit of underthings every bit as fancy as the dress itself, with all its ribbons and ruffles of lace. The doctor held a candle to Cecily's tongue to study the pink of it. He put his fingers to her wrist and whistled a tune to the rhythm of the beats of her pulse. I helped Cecily onto the table, and she lay back. I sat in a chair to watch.

A girl with a braid assisted the doctor. She held quills of bamboo. He heated the skin of Cecily's arms and shoulders, of her neck, by pressing against it an enamel pot of burning mugwort.

"Don't I make a pretty porcupine," Cecily told me as the doctor gently riddled her skin with the quills.

"Sh-sh-sh-sh-sh," I said.

She said, "Yes, yes, sh-sh-sh-sh-sh . . . This is the only place I can sleep anymore," and she closed her eyes and drifted off. I became mesmerized by the rise and fall of her chest as she breathed, and as her breathing slowed more and more. Her breaths shivered the little silk roses at the knot of a ribbon between her breasts.

In the twenty minutes that the doctor worked, I considered what I'd say to her when she woke. I knew I must be careful. If I said what I wanted to say—*Leave with me now*—she might never return. I would have to let *her* let *me* know what to say next, and when.

The doctor finished, removed the quills, and said, "Wake her," as he left the room. I stood next to the table. How could her breaths fall so far apart? She seemed to be barely breathing at all.

I leaned over to kiss her lips, and as I kissed her, she kissed me too, and she held her hand to the back of my head. I helped her from the table, and when I tried to speak again, she shushed me once more. "We'll talk tomorrow," she said. I helped her with her dress, and her fur, and her hat, and her gloves. When we weren't looking, the doctor had brought a little paper box containing a new chameleon. "Help me think of a name for him," she said, and she slipped past the curtain, and down the hall, and out the back way.

· · ·

CECILY VISITED DR. GEE LOY, and me, every day after that. As Wakefield spent his afternoons attending to the Fair in its final few weeks—in an endless parade of backslapping and celebratory lunches for a job well done—Cecily slipped from his side and into the coach, and she stole into town for our secret afternoons. She claimed to Wakefield, and to her driver, to be putting together her winter wardrobe, and needed to devote hours to the dress department of Brandeis. At the store, she had tea as the shopgirls modeled gowns, and she stood for fittings, allowing herself to be spotted by the gossips and scandalmongers. She then snuck away to weave through the store, around the shelves and manikins, and out the back. She moved then, in her furs of blue fox and chinchilla and electric seal, in her silks and diamonds, a veil across her face, from back alley to back alley, across the dirty, broken bricks, through inky puddles, past the skittering of rats and the grumbling of bums, until she came to the back door of Dr. Gee Loy's. We would spend an hour together, then she would leave alone to retrace her steps. As she hurried through Brandeis's again, Pearl would hand her paper bags full of boxes, of novelty shirtwaists, of boots, of a pigeon wing to clip to her hair with a diamond-studded clasp. For Wakefield, a silver match safe etched with a parrot. A doll for Doxie. Italian marshmallows for Mrs. Margaret.

Wakefield would tease her at breakfast about her shopping, amused by her girlish pleasure in fashion and jewelry. They would spend their mornings in the conservatory, the autumn sun hot through the glass overhead. Wakefield would eat a steak delivered directly from one of the slaughterhouses he owned in South Omaha, and he would feign shock and disgust over the Brandeis bill, open at his side. He read aloud the list of clothing and gifts, clucking his tongue. More often than not, Cecily would not have even opened the boxes yet, and she would only just learn of their contents from Wakefield's recitations. She was always caught up, she told me, in thoughts of our afternoons together. Cecily would butter her blueberry muffin with butterine, also from the slaughterhouse, made from cattle fat and oil, and she'd drink Hawaiian coffee, sitting in a kimono of blue satin, relaxed, happy, distracted.

I imagined that Wakefield loved playing the part of a husband who indulged his spoiled wife too much. I could picture him boasting to other men: *My darling canary, gilding her cage.*

Meanwhile, behind his back, Ferret the Weasel robbed the very rich groom of his very pretty bride. Cecily and I met every day of those few weeks in October. She wouldn't allow me to walk her through the alleys, afraid we'd get caught together lurking about. So every day I waited in a room lit only with the low flame of a linseed-oil lamp hanging from the ceiling by a chain. This was not the private room where Cecily took the acupuncture, but a room full of people sleeping. Each wall was lined with berths like in a train car, three beds high. Some patients snored behind curtains, others lay with the curtains open, the pipes falling from their hands as they dropped into sleep. The room had a haze of vapor that had no way out, as there were no windows, and only the one door, always kept shut.

"And if we get caught, it's over," she said. "He would never let me out again." From Cecily's little black hat hung a lace veil tatted to resemble a cobweb. Cecily pulled out the hatpin at the top of the veil, the pin's head spider-shaped, the spider's abdomen a teardrop pearl.

I took off my boots, my coat, my collar, my cuffs. Dr. Gee Loy stepped in with a tray, and on the tray, a long bamboo pipe and an opium lamp. We never smoked the stuff, but Cecily liked to inhale the medicinal haze puffed up by all the other smokers in the den. "Not opium," the doctor explained to a new patient on the other side of the room. He set down the tray and tapped his finger against the pipe's bowl. "Swallows' nests. Crushed lizard bones. Pipe tobacco. Maybe a little, little—just little—bit opium." The pipe's red enamel was patterned with bats. "Bats bring the happiness," the doctor said.

"What do the characters mean?" the patient asked, running his fingers along the calligraphy that lined the top of the bowl.

"Opium better than money," he said. He tapped again at the pipe's bowl. "But no opium here. None. Just a little. So little, it is almost none at all. A little opium to ease you away from it."

This room was where addicts gathered to kick the habit.

"When you start to see your dreams," Dr. Gee Loy told his patient, "lie back and look."

Cecily whispered to me. "This medicine ain't for the weak," she said. She winked at me and tugged on my chin. We both lay back on the bed together, our heads on the same pillow. I put my hand on her hand. Her skin was like ice.

"Leave him," I whispered. "Get Doxie, and run away with me."

After a moment, Cecily said, "I will," and I could have wept at the sound of it. *I will*, as precious as a wedding vow.

BUT SHE DIDN'T RUN AWAY with me that afternoon, or the afternoon after that. "I just need time," she said, when we met again. Back and forth, she went. One day she would try to convince me that Billy Wakefield was no villain, that he'd always been sweet to her, that he loved her and cared about her, and the next day she'd tell me how powerful he was, how careful we must be, how doomed might be our every plot.

But I don't think she feared him, truly. She wasn't frightened. She thought only of Doxie, and of how much her little girl would lose. To leave Wakefield would be to rob her daughter of the kind of future neither of us would have dared imagine.

"He rescued us," she said, in between kisses, as we lay in our sleeping berth.

"From me," I said.

"That's not what I mean," she said. She kissed my ear and whispered in it. "That's not what I mean." I closed my eyes, so pleased to believe her every word.

I begged her to promise me that she'd only ever been mine. I wanted to believe that Wakefield's gifts had never mattered, that she'd never paid him a minute's interest in those days before he stole her away.

"I never kept anything secret from you," she said.

AFTER TWO WEEKS of our lost afternoons, the autumn began to feel wintery. "Your body senses a shift in the weather coming," Dr. Gee Loy said, as he plucked away the bamboo needles of her acupuncture. "We will work with the storm." I helped Cecily down, and the doctor's little girl pulled the sheet away and set the very same table for tea. Cecily sat only in her underthings as the doctor poured the tea into cups carved from the horn of a narwhal.

He then led us down the hall to the sleeping berths. There wasn't a single lick of lamplight, and I felt I was back in the orphanage, in among its crooked corridors and damp little rooms, marching off to a whipping. The nuns who'd managed the children's home had been renegade, not Catholic at all, with a mission of poverty and nothingness. They'd been an order with no order at all; their habits and wimples hadn't even matched in color or cloth. Our house had been a house of sticks, ramshackle and cast-off, no sturdier than the cardboard in our shoes. Sister Patience had loved me, but she'd beat me too, and I would lie in my bed, my skin stinging from the switch, and I'd stare at the cracks in the ceiling, praying for the roof to fall in on us all.

As we sat on the thin mattress, Cecily said, of the doctor, "I'm not sure I believe he's even Chinese. I once met a Chinese magician who was just some hayseed from Kentucky. All he did was buy a costume and a trunk of tricks off a real Chinese magician."

I saw Cecily's earbob bobbing, a tiny silver swan on a little chain. I touched the swan. "Can I tell you something that you can't tell anyone else?" she said, taking the swans from her ears.

"Of course you can," I said.

"These swans," she said, "I saw them in a hotel shop in one of those towns with the mineral springs, and I thought of you, and of us," she said, "and I couldn't take my eyes off them. And that night, at dinner, Billy gave them to me, in a pretty velvet box, and I thought I'd got caught. I thought he knew, somehow, how much I missed you." She stopped speaking, and I was afraid there was nothing more to the story. She lay back in the bed.

I lay down next to her. "I slept in the same iron crib from the time I was a baby until I was ten," I said.

"No wonder you kick in your sleep," she said.

"No, I don't," I said.

"How would you know if you do or you don't?" she said. "You're asleep."

"You know me best, I guess," I said.

"I do."

"So how did Billy know?" I said. "About the swans?"

"He didn't," she said. "He thought I was thinking of the swans we watched together in the town before, in a park, where we had a picnic. Beautiful swans, some black, some white. We tossed some crumbs out on the water. He didn't know I was thinking of you then too."

I whispered in her ear. "Stay with me," I said. "Don't go back."

She tried to breathe in deep, but her breaths were shallow. "I can't live without Doxie," she said.

"You don't have to," I said. "I'll take care of both of you."

"Doxie lives in the house on the hill now," she said. She put her hand to my cheek, and met my eyes with hers. "Don't you want the very best of everything for Dox? Shouldn't she be far better off than we ever were? Just picture your miserable self in that old crib. If you hadn't run away from the orphanage, you'd probably still be sleeping in that crib today." When I said nothing, she put her forehead against mine, and she nodded, making my head nod too. "See, you agree with me," she said, smiling.

"How do you know I won't run away with you when you fall asleep?"

"Because I never sleep anymore," she said, and with that her eyes dropped closed, and her breathing slowed, growing easy, and quiet, and she slept and slept.

Somehow, I wasn't worried. Without a doubt, she was mine, not his. And soon enough, it'd be summer, then soon enough, summer again, and we'd be alone with our little girl. We would live in a state of contentment and melancholy, arm in arm, anxious for the next moment, and the moment after that, even as we watched our lives leave us, minute by minute.

29.

THE NEXT AFTERNOON I lay in the berth, in the back of Dr. Gee Loy's, waiting alone. I suspected Cecily had been slowed by the cold, icy drizzle that slicked the walks. I got up often to go to the back door, to lean out and look up and down the alley. I lingered there, as if I could see her figure in the mist and fog just by staring hard enough. Finally I walked to the front desk, to check if there'd been any word. Dr. Gee Loy had a telephone. She might have called.

But before I even asked, I saw, out the window, the Wakefield coach parked in front, the coach that delivered Cecily to the front door of Brandeis every afternoon. The black umbrella that the old driver had wired to his perch drooped with a few broken spines, hanging above his head like a listless bat. The old man's mouth was wrapped around tight with a woolen scarf.

I stepped outside, suddenly remembering a dream I'd had the night before. I was happy it came back to me. In the dream, Cecily circled the cart of a flower peddler in the street, plucking off a petal here, a petal there, stealing a whole flower's worth of petals that she kept clutched in her palm.

I opened the coach door, wanting to tell Cecily of the sweet, strange dream, but only Pearl sat inside, Cecily's handkerchief, with the initial stitched in, twisted in her grip. Her eyes and her nose were red.

"Get inside, Ferret," Pearl said, "so I can tell you."

Wakefield caught her, I thought, with a catch in my gut.

I sat next to Pearl and closed the coach door. I took Pearl's hands in mine. "Tell me," I said. She began to cry.

My worry, in the moment, was only for Pearl, this sad girl here at my side, Cecily's friend, so wrecked. *Cecily and I will find a way*, I would tell her, to comfort. *She loves me.*

Pearl tried to steady her voice to speak. In a moment, she said, "Cecily died this morning."

I took my hands from hers. *A lie*, I thought, but not with anger. Pearl was only confused. Or Wakefield had invented this, to take Cecily from me again. If it was true, how could Pearl possibly know? How was such a thing knowable? Who would have told her? Who was she talking about? I couldn't ask. I couldn't think. *Stay confused. No one knows. There's no truth.*

"Did you hear me, Ferret?" Pearl said.

"No," I said. "No."

"She became very ill, Ferret," she said. "Something overtook her. And she died."

"*Who?*" I said, though I don't know what answer I wanted. *Who died? Who did this?* I still expected Cecily to look in the window, to open the door.

"Cecily died. Ferret, Cecily is gone."

The coach sat in the street, its stillness filling me with fear. It stopped my breath. I opened the door to let in the wind and sleet. *I was with Cecily yesterday.* We would be late to our bed in Dr. Gee Loy's. We wouldn't have enough time. We would lie there, sleep a wink, then she'd have to leave.

Pearl leaned across me to pull the door closed. "So cold," she said.

And with the closing of the door, the snap of its latch, I believed it. I believed I was here, in this coach, hearing the truth. Pearl had no reason to lie. Cecily's death was cold and exact, and it shuddered through me, through all my bones, a slamming of doors. And yet Cecily wasn't gone yet. Her death was only in that handful of words, *Cecily died this morning.* Her death didn't exist anywhere else. It was confined to those words. We were still in that cloud, when what was said could still be unsaid. Or *more* could be said, and everything could change. *Do you have any sense of time at all?* Cecily had asked me on the rooftop at the Fair, after the president's dinner. And I didn't. That moment on the roof was so near, the memory so vivid, I felt I could step back into it and leave myself there. Each moment with Cecily was close enough to touch. I could have every moment back.

I opened my mouth to speak, and my words caught on my tongue, and they fell apart, into noise, and I sobbed. I tried to finish my sentence but only stammered. Pearl hushed me, whispering "sh" in my ear, her arms around my shoulders.

"I was waiting for her inside," I managed to say, through my weeping. "I was waiting and waiting. I thought she'd slipped in the rain."

Pearl put her arm in mine, and her hand to my wet cheek. "The rain," she said. "It's heaven fallen down on us."

"I can't stop crying," I said. "I can't speak."

"You don't have to stop," she said, even as she shushed me some more, rocking me in her arms. "Sh-sh-sh-sh."

I looked at Pearl, and I didn't have to ask her to tell me more. She took a breath and told me everything, in great detail. This was what we needed to do, it seemed. We needed to go over everything, minute by minute.

"Mr. Wakefield sent the coach around for me this morning, thinking I could help ease Cecily into some sleep," she said. "She hasn't slept for days and days. It was all too bright, she said. She wore a mask over her eyes. They put her in a room with the windows blacked out. And last night was the worst yet—she was disoriented and sick. There's been a doctor there, who Mr. Wakefield brought in from Europe, and he said she needed desperately to sleep."

"But she *did* sleep," I said, as if she could still be saved, if only everyone knew. "I know she did. I promise you. She slept."

Pearl nodded. "She was sleeping when I got there," she said. "They'd given her something to get her to sleep. Everyone was so relieved. You could feel the ease in the house. It was like the air was of silk. Not only was she sleeping, but she was restful. Her breathing was easy. We all felt the worst was past. The doctor was with her. He wasn't worried. We busied ourselves. Me and Mrs. Margaret and Mr. Wakefield and his sister. The staff. We played cards. And then the doctor came down from her room, only a few hours ago. He told us she'd passed."

"And you're certain?" I said.

She nodded. "We saw her," she said. "We went upstairs and saw her. She was sick all along, I guess. She was sick." And though Pearl described Cecily's death no further, I couldn't help but picture her myself, in her bed, her eyes closed, her life gone.

I pushed open the door and jumped from the coach. I went back into Dr. Gee Loy's, and down around the winding of its back halls, and out the door to the alleyway. I didn't run, but I walked quickly against the sleet, my coat's collar upturned, my hands buried in my pockets, my head low. I followed the path Cecily would have taken that very afternoon, if she'd ever arrived.

And when I reached the back door to Brandeis, I turned and walked back to Dr. Gee Loy's. I returned to my berth. I took off my coat. I took my feet from my shoes.

The doctor didn't ask about Cecily. He prepared a pipe and a lamp.

Everyone in the berths was awake, but they paid me no mind. They smoked. They breathed deeply. Their breathing was all I could hear, as if it were my own, as if I held my hands to my ears and listened only to the sound of the air filling and leaving my lungs. The doctor handed me the pipe. He ran the lamp beneath the bowl, raising the vapor.

The smoke choked me, catching in my throat like dust. I felt nothing else at first, nothing but a cottonlike covering of my tongue.

After only a minute with the pipe, I lay down to rest, and I slept. In the middle of a dream, Cecily shook me awake. *Don't wake up*, she said, crying and crying and crying. She pushed against my chest. She clawed at my cheeks. She pounded her fists on my shoulders. *Don't, don't, don't*, she said. *Don't wake up. Don't, Ferret, don't. Don't wake up.*

I won't, I said.

I can't hear you, she said, putting her ear to my lips.

"I won't," I said, and I said it aloud, waking myself with the effort to speak. Cecily was gone, though someone cried somewhere, there in the room. Someone a few berths away.

I held my hands to my face, covering my eyes, and I cried along with her. I cried myself back to sleep, to dream again of Cecily so frightened, shaking me awake. *Don't, Ferret. Don't, don't, don't wake up.*

30.

I QUICKLY GREW ADDICTED to the doctor's addiction cure. "It's all right, it's not opium," I whispered to August as he dragged me from my bed in the back of Dr. Gee Loy's. "Don't worry, I'm fine. I've only been here a minute." But I'd been there often, off and on, in the handful of days since Cecily's death. But I'd had no sense of time. For all I knew, I'd been there every hour, every second, for weeks and weeks.

I feel as light as air, I meant to say, but I wasn't sure any of my words left my mouth. As I was lifted from the bed, heavenward, I felt I should tell August I was levitating. *Hold me down.* But my tongue felt too heavy for my head. The weight of it sank my chin, and I felt my heart grow heavy too, and my stomach, and my spleen, wherever it might be. I felt tugged along by the wires of the Flying Waltz or by puppet strings.

August was to the right of me, Rosie to my left, and when I saw the black coach out the front window, I feared that Cecily had died again. Pearl would be inside, waiting. They were taking me to Pearl, the angel of death, the character she'd been born to play. *I know already*, I tried to tell them. I tried to stop them. *This happened already.*

We were cogs in the guts of a clock. We were on a stage, on wheels, on a track, appearing nightly. We stepped outside and snow fell from the rafters, little puffs of pillow feathers and shavings of bone, catching

318

in my eyelashes and melting on my red-hot cheeks. A pale gray scrim served as the winter sky, and actors and actresses in minor roles moved from one sidewalk to another, crisscrossing from corner to corner, pretending to talk to one another, moving their mouths for soundless words and empty phrases. The peddler pushed his flower cart along the streetcar tracks. Was this the same flower cart and flower peddler from my dream? The dream where Cecily picked the petals? *Had* that been a dream? Was I dreaming now?

But the cart wasn't the same cart, and the coach wasn't the same coach. This wasn't the same day. August and Rosie helped me inside, into the packed crowd of it. Still hallucinating, I saw anarchists and actors, a few of the Waltzing Dwarves, a nanny from the incubator exhibit, a magician's assistant, an elephant wrangler. There was Josephine the ragtime player, Mandelbaum the lion tamer, Zigzag the clown, and though he'd washed the makeup from his face, he had the same bulbous, gin-blossom nose and baggy eyes. *There's no room*, I tried to warn, *I won't fit*, but there was room, and I did fit. A few people spilled out the other side, and they crawled up to ride on the roof, despite the snow and the cold. And the coach pulled away.

I was the widowed husband. I wore an old undershirt, the neck of it sagging down my chest. I wore the trousers of my lilac suit and woolen socks. Rosie had grabbed my shoes from beside my berth, and he put my feet into them, and knotted the laces, as we rode along in the coach. August helped me into a long black topcoat, and a top hat, with a black lace rose pinned to the hat's black band.

"Mistletoe tea," August said, putting a cup to my lips. *Mizzle toad-ee*, I heard, and I saw mizzle toads, whatever they were, filling the coach like a plague.

"You should feel his heart," August told Rosie.

"You should feel my heart," I whispered.

Mistletoe tea. "Missed ol' Dox-ee," I said. I sang it, in a low howl, like the serenade of a sick dog under the porch. *Missed ol' Dox-ee* was how the song started, a song for the parlor, about the tragedy of the second Mrs. Wakefield. I couldn't remember how the rest of it went, but it didn't end well. That much I knew.

My hand was too heavy to lift, and when I looked at my open palm, I saw Cecily's heart, it having grown big enough to bust the rusted birdcage she'd kept tucked beneath her corset, and under her ribs. It weighed my hand down more with each tremor and beat.

"Here," August said, holding the teacup to my lips for more. "Here."

Here. Here. I'm here. Hear *me*.

"Drink."

"What is it?" I said.

Mistletoe tea.

Miss Cecily.

THE ROADS HAD TURNED to mud and slush, the snow and sleet having grown heavy. The coach slid and rocked, the tea sloshing in my cup. August had brought a whole pot full, and every time I spilled some tea, he poured in more.

The coach was not as crowded as first I thought—some among us had been only an illusion. We were all of us in black. The incubator nanny sat feathered, with a half-eaten apple in the hand in her lap, the red of it like a spot of blood. She was a shot crow. She stopped her chewing when I caught her eye. She smiled with closed lips, and furrowed her brow with sympathy. *I was the widowed husband.*

After the long drive in the rented coach, north, and up the hill to the Wakefield house and into a slow caravan of carriages and phaetons, I'd sobered up. They were taking me to see Cecily, for prayers in the parlor. Wakefield was having a service, of sorts.

"But he wanted no funeral, it seems," August said. "There'll be no sermons." He took from his pocket a mourning card he'd collected from the undertaker's parlor. The card was black with white illustrations. I ran my fingers over the embossed feathers of the angel wings and along the droop of the willow.

In eternal loving memory of Cecily Wakefield was etched into a gravestone that sat between two urns.

Wife & Mother

Who fell asleep in Jesus, on the month, the day, the year.

My sight fell past the white and into the black night of the background. How was any of this a comfort? The engraved cards, the mourning lace. Eternal memory? Eternal death. Every word of all this angelology was just another shovelful of dirt. There was no beauty in this. All the night and all the black there ever was, and could ever be, could never blind us. As long as we were alive, our dead would keep dying.

"I keep forgetting she died," I said. "I keep thinking of new ways to try to take her from Wakefield. Just this morning I thought of the balloon at the Fair. Maybe if we went up in the balloon again, I thought."

"They don't even gas the balloon up anymore," August said. "The Fair's winding down. Some of the midway attractions have already started heading to Philadelphia for next summer's fair."

"Take me home," I said, and by *home* I meant my sleeping berth, my healing pipe. It felt like I hadn't slept in days. "I need to get some rest," I said. "It's important that I rest."

But we were already there. *Now we are there*, I'd read to the orphans, from the story about the Paris exhibition. *That was a journey, a flight without magic.*

We stopped at the gate. We heard conversation, then dispute. We heard yelling and swearing, from the driver, from the men standing sentry, from the anarchists perched atop our roof. The anarchists' anger shook the coach as they stood up to hurl down insults. Rosie stepped outside, and his shouting and curses joined the noise.

Those of us in the coach sat silent, listening, trying to interpret the nature of the ruckus. The guards at the gate kept us out, it seemed. You could only pass through with a wreath on a hook. The day before, every florist in the city, and every florist in every city nearby, had wound and wired fresh lilies and fronds into funeral wreaths. They'd filled wagons with the wreaths, and horses had galloped along every street and lane, slowing only long enough for a boy to jump off and deliver a wreath to a door of someone who was allowed, by Wakefield, to mourn his wife.

Without a wreath on your coach or carriage, you were sent away. You were among the uninvited.

"We're her *family*," Rosie shouted at them, as he opened the door to step back into the coach. He was bright red with rage. Josephine took his arm, petted his sleeve, to settle him. And the driver pulled away from the parade of coaches, steered the horses around, and headed back the way we'd come, past wreath after wreath, the lilies' petals and leaves wilting, burning, in the cold. The anarchists on the roof kept shouting, kept cursing, back at the guards and ahead to the mourners in line.

Rosie saw me trembling and spilling more mistletoe tea. In the hour or so we'd been in the coach, all the mystifying smoke that had clouded my head had lifted. Rosie said bashfully, "I'm so sorry about all that."

But I was grateful. My old anger at Wakefield jolted through me, pushing the blood up my veins, shortening my breath, the rush of it all so familiar. My hatred of Wakefield made sense, the *only* thing to make sense in the days since Cecily's death. Now I wanted nothing more than to go into that house. I was the only one in all the world who deserved to mourn alongside little Doxie. I was afraid before that I would weep and wail, but now I needed it, I needed to fill that house with my pain. *I am the widowed.*

"I want to go back," I said, and no sooner did I say it than Rosie had the door open again. He jumped from the coach and pulled me out by my sleeve, both of us slipping in the snow and nearly falling beneath the coach's turning wheels. I'd only just righted myself before Rosie had opened the door of another coach, one moving slowly up the hill toward Wakefield's gate. He pushed me up and inside, in with an old couple sitting across from each other. The gent withered on his bench, cringing, wide-eyed, clutching his cane to his chest, while his wife leaned forward, ready for battle, brandishing her mourning umbrella of black lace and raven's feathers.

I sat next to the lady, and Rosie sat next to her gent. Somehow, through all that, I still had the empty teacup in my hand.

"You are so kind to offer passage," Rosie said.

"You absolutely *must* leave at once," the woman said.

When Rosie crossed his thick legs, his foot was suddenly in front of us all, and he leisurely tugged at the knee of his trousers to lift the hem above his sock. There, in a holster buckled to his calf, was a lady-like pistol with a mother-of-pearl handle. In all his weeks as a conspirator to assassinate, I'd not once seen a weapon.

The old man and the old woman leaned back, away from Rosie's armed leg. "So sad when there's a funeral," Rosie said, tapping his toe in the air. "But I guess we should be happy it's not our own, ay?"

Rosie tapped the toe of his shoe against my knee with affection, and he kept tapping, calming me with the rhythm as we rode up through the gate, and through the orchard, and up the winding lane to the house.

THE HOUSE SMELLED WARM, of cinnamon and ham hocks. The dining room thrashed with the well-meaning buzzards that hover at funerals, the undertakers with their folded hands and tics of sympathy, the church wives with their mince pies and mints handmade from cross-shaped molds. An aunt fussed with flowers, an uncle nipped at mulled wine.

They all looked my way, studying me in my topcoat and top hat, in my ratty undershirt and lilac pants. Rosie had plucked a lily from the coach's wreath and poked its stem through the buttonhole of my lapel.

You can't see me, I thought, even as they stared. None of these people were Cecily's. These people were only here for Wakefield, to shed polite tears, to compliment the undertaker's art, to chatter about all the life that burned in Cecily's dead, red cheeks. *So peaceful*, they said.

But the old anger I'd worked up in the coach had dulled back to a sadness that seemed to thicken my blood. My skin felt too heavy, and every hair on my head weighed me down.

Though feeling queasy, I decided to eat. I wasn't ready to go to the parlor, where Cecily rested in her casket. I sent Rosie in without me. "Go see her, and come back," I said. "Tell me if I can bear it."

I picked up a little china plate from a stack on the sideboard, and I nearly dropped it. My every finger was too weak.

An old woman, kindly recognizing my grief, came to take my arm, and my plate, and she led me to the table. The ladies' group of a Lutheran church had brought casseroles and stews, cakes and ices.

"Pickled figs in the bowl there," the woman explained to me, "calf's liver here, kidney stew in the pretty tureen, eggs fricasseed." I followed her around the table as she pointed at the dishes and platters. I would nod, and she would nod back, and she would ladle a spoonful onto my plate.

My eye traveled up from the table to the portrait on the wall—a life-size picture of the first dead Mrs. Wakefield seated, her little boy in a sailor suit leaning against her knees. Had Cecily eaten all her last meals under the eye of her mister's old missus? I feared the whole of her life there in that house had been haunted by the other Mrs. Wakefield. Cecily wore lace the first wife had tatted. She ate off the first wife's wedding china and spent her sleepless nights in the first wife's sheets. It wouldn't have surprised me to learn that the mortician had dug up the first Mrs. Wakefield to put Cecily in her burial gown, and on her pillow, and in her box.

After all the church wife's work of heaping my plate full, I said,

"I'm sorry, I'm not hungry. I should have told you. I can't eat." I put my hand on her thin, fragile wrist and I said again, "I can't eat," and she nodded, and she forgave me all the trouble I'd put her to. And that forgiveness lightened me somehow. I didn't want to step away from her act of kindness. I longed to pick up another empty plate, and to ask her to fill that one too.

Instead, I left the dining room to search for another room where Cecily wasn't, but Rosie found me, took my elbow, and led me back. I was relieved and leaned against him. I thought we might be leaving. He'd gone into the parlor, he'd looked, and he'd decided I shouldn't see her. *This was all a mistake*, he would promise me.

But Rosie eased me around a corner, and into the parlor, and I saw her before I could look away from the black coffin surrounded by wicker baskets of white roses. Before I could see too much, I turned my head toward the bay window, where the light glowed a powdery white, as if the sun were trapped in muslin.

In front of the window sat Mrs. Margaret, Pearl, and a nurse in an apron and cap. A quilt covered their skirts, and the women slowly stitched without speaking, cobbling the clumsy memorial blanket together, all its squares at crosspurposes.

When Pearl spotted me, she seemed agitated at first, but then stood and came to take my hands in hers. Her thimble-less thumb was bloody from the needle. She wore a black dress trimmed in crepe that crackled as she pressed against me to kiss my cheek.

For a second, my anger rose again. "We were turned away at the gate," I said.

"I'm so sorry," Pearl said, and the fact that she didn't seem at all surprised only wounded me more. "There's such confusion in a house when there's been a death."

"I wouldn't know, I guess," I said. *You wouldn't know either*, I wanted to tell her. *You don't belong here.*

"We have to help each other at times like this," Pearl said.

Nail the coffin shut. Throw ashes in the river and the wind. None

TIMOTHY SCHAFFERT

of it would work to spirit the lost life away or to shut it out. We were all fools, fattening up the undertaker, paying handsomely for the panto-mimes of grief. I wouldn't be a part of it.

"Let's go," I said to Rosie. Rosie tugged at my arm, to lead me to the coffin. "Why?" I said, through locked teeth.

Rosie leaned in to whisper. "Let it ruin you," he said. "Let *this* be the very worst thing you have to get through. Get through it, and move on along."

And when I saw her so still, I felt my own soul leave.

Tucked into her hands folded just beneath her breasts was a hand-kerchief, but not the one I'd given her. This handkerchief was a souve-nir of the Fair, the battleship *Maine* embroidered in the corner of it, in gray thread. It was all wrong. It was all so terribly wrong. I had to be-lieve Wakefield saw some sentiment in the gesture. Was it because he had been introduced to Cecily at his masquerade ball, with the sinking of the toy ship on the lagoon? Was that it?

I watched for the handkerchief to lift, the lace of it to rustle, her chest to rise and fall gently. Her breath before had always been so soft and slow, so barely there. If you didn't know her like I knew her, if you didn't know the rhythm of her sleeping breath, where to look, where to listen, you might not see the breath at all. But I knew. I'd watched her sleep so many times. I knew well the flutter of her lashes as dreams crossed her eyes. I knew how her tongue clicked as she ticked off each breath that left her lips.

I knew the best way to wake her, to ease her from sleep. I knew to stroke her neck.

I didn't give much thought to touching her neck just then, to slip-ping my fingers beneath the silk and lace of her collar. When I did, I wasn't astonished to feel the pulse of her heart. She was there with me, for only a beat. It was the pulse of my heart, in my fingers, beating against the skin of her neck. In a lost moment, quicker than a heart-beat, than a wink, I mistook my heart for hers, and she woke for me, just for me, for just that moment, one more time. And though it was only a heartbeat, only a wink, it was time enough. I had time to say good-bye to her.

THE MORTICIAN HAD signaled concern to the others in the room, as I'd stood there, touching Cecily, *his* corpse, *his* creation, and suddenly Mrs. Margaret was breathing her foul breath in my face, twisting my arm behind my back, leading me away from the coffin and toward the parlor door.

"I want to see Doxie," I told her, in between gasps of pain.

"Doxie's upstairs," she said, spitting, her wretched breath now a mist, "where she belongs. She's with her family. She's a Wakefield now."

"No," I said.

"Yes," she said. "I'm doing this for your own good, Ferret. Get out and stay out."

Rosie came up next to me and elbowed Mrs. Margaret away. "We're going," he said.

"We're not," I said. I stopped and turned to shout through the halls, up the stairs, "We're not going!" But Rosie pushed at me, taking my arm, leading me toward the door.

I turned my head to shout back, "You can't keep me from Doxie! You can't keep me away from my girl!" But even as I shouted it, hearing my voice bounce from the walls and echo, I knew I'd lost her forever too. "She's mine!" I shouted. But nothing had ever belonged to me.

December 15, 1898

Dear Cecily,

 *Yesterday I fell. I'd grown quite capable without my cane, able
to climb and burrow, and I got too confident, scaling the Emerald
Cathedral so that I could place a brass candlestick exactly where
Emmaline wanted to see it, up among some bird's nests the birds
had built themselves. I fell, and I grabbed at the balloon's rope.
We'd built the basket and the rope into the workings of the
cathedral. The basket was a sacred relic, of sorts. And that rope
saved me from crashing. It burned my hands as it slowed me,
and I hit the ground hard enough to crack my cast.*

 The Old Sisters Egan were at my side before anyone else.

 *Hester said nothing. She just lifted her hammer and tap-tap-
tapped the crack deeper and longer, until she could pry the cast off.
She and Emmaline then helped me to my feet and I walked. I
strutted across the room and everyone applauded. The pretty
daughter of the man who grew clover, a young woman named
Eleanor, slipped herself into my open arms, tipped her hip against
mine, and gently swept me into a waltz. We danced, circling close,
as the others gathered around and clapped out a rhythm for our
steps. We stopped to watch as Eleanor's father carried the pieces of
my cast up onto the shrine, binding the plaster to a statue of Mary,
Mother of God, salvaged from an abandoned prairie hospital. He
attached the cast to her plaster gown, winding a string of barbed
wire around and around.*

 *And last night I dreamed Emmaline's dream. She and I had
the exact same dream on the exact same night. In the dream, the*

Emerald Cathedral was finished, and it glowed as green as the grasses in the valley in springtime. Emmaline took my arm, and we walked to the front of a row of old, splintered church pews. We sat down. Behind us was a whole congregation, people humming and chanting the language Emmaline had created. We suddenly knew all the sounds for all the symbols. And the man who Emmaline had once loved was there. He was old now. He spoke to her in her strange language. "I had a long unhappy life," he told her. "I died a broken man." He took from his pocket the same emerald ring he'd given her years and years before. The emerald for Emmaline. She had dropped it into the sea on the day he left her for someone else. When she took the ring from him now, he faded away.

I then realized that the cathedral is a monument to our grief. It is a shrine for all our dead, constructed of the wreckage of the lives that have fallen down around us.

In my dream, I could picture you at rest within it, entombed but afloat, as if buried at sea. The emerald of the cathedral was the ocean, and you were caught falling in its waves. Your curls were tangled in the coils of a bedspring, your sleeves lifted and pricked by a thicket of nails. Your back arched over a wheel, your legs bent around the petrified branches of a tree.

In my dream, I cried myself to exhaustion. I curled up in the pew to sleep, and I dreamed within the dream that Doxie had grown up to look just like you.

Ferret

31.

THE SNOW BLEW ITSELF into a blizzard on the night of Cecily's funeral, then settled, then quit. The snow was light enough to blow away in the gusts of evening, sweeping itself from our paths and our walks, away from our steps and our skirts, to drift in corners and doorways. We huddled in furs and held scarves to our cheeks. We warmed ourselves with whiskey, bellying up to the stoves in saloons.

In the first of the morning light, a dusting of snow glittered on eaves and windowpanes, in the manes of horses, in the cracks of the bricks of the sidewalk and street. The horses' snuffling lifted in clouds of vapor as they lowered their heads against the last of the cold. By noon, it was warm, by afternoon warmer, and the snow went away. And as October ended, we were treated to a few days that seemed like spring. We opened our windows to let out the flat air and to let in the cool, to let in the smell of wet soil and leaves, the sealike breezes blown off the river and up and down the avenues.

I didn't return to Dr. Gee Loy's. I didn't go much of anywhere. I slept, and when I couldn't sleep, I sat at the window and let the hours pass. But I did return to the Fair on its very last day.

It was Halloween, and many went to the Grand Court in costume. It seemed I could see something of Cecily in every masked woman I passed.

I would feel a quick beat of recognition in my heart when a woman happened to be looking up and off the way Cecily always had, like she was studying a pattern in a cloud or following the flight of a bird. And I don't mean to say Cecily was ghostly even before she died. She was not some illusion. She was never dreamy, never doomed. Never. She was none of those things. That's why I still saw her, alive, living, everywhere I looked.

I made quite a fool of myself in front of a woman dressed as Marie Antoinette. She had a girlish habit of Cecily's, of twisting a loose strand of hair around and around her finger, but it was all part of the contraption of her disguise. With each tug of the curl, she fluttered the wings of the three toy butterflies in her wig. I wore a mask—a simple pink face with pinhole eyes—and I pushed it up to settle it atop my head. I watched the woman for minutes and minutes, convincing myself Cecily had returned, even as I failed to see much of anything of her in the stranger. I became certain, though, that I knew very well the beat of her tiny pulse in her throat, and a freckle at the inside of her wrist. I followed her as she wove through the street, the crowd parting for her and her grand skirts that bounced like on a spring. I finally said her name, touched her elbow, and she turned, a mask of peacock feathers held to her face by a stick in her hand. I touched her wrist, to lower her mask. Those weren't Cecily's eyes, not her lips, not her pale, tender throat. I didn't recognize this woman, but she recognized me. I mean to say, she recognized my sadness, and her happiness fell, and she stepped back, away, her mask returning to her eyes.

Everyone was thieving. They were like Hansel and Gretel, tearing away at the buildings of sugar. They broke windows, toppling cornices. They snatched spoons and saltshakers. They dug up the canna and lily bulbs. The Fair was to be torn down, beam by beam, the lagoon drained, the carpets rolled up. It would all be gone, whether we took it or not.

A little stationery shop in the Manufactures Building sold its goods for cheap. I bought an ink pot and a long fountain pen shaped like an alligator. I bought a bundle of postcards tied together with a white ribbon, and I walked down the Exposition Hall to the booth of a distillery, to sit at a stool at a cask and sample some scotch, my mask still pushed up into my hair. At first I attempted to describe the flavors, noting them on a postcard. *Tumbleweed, cowboy bonfire, salted apple peel, black mulberry.*

And then I wrote to Cecily.

The Fair ends today, my love, I wrote. *I'm so glad you won't see it.* I wrote her name on the card, and dropped it in the mailbox. I stuck the rest of the postcards, and the pen, in my back pocket.

I imagined what would happen if the Fair wasn't razed but left to decay, nature taking the land back, returning it to the miles of dying fields it was before. If they would let the place fall apart, I thought, I would visit the ruins as an old man, a better man than I ever could have imagined I'd someday be, in top hat and overcoat and monocle. The swan gondola, its long neck broken, would sit shipwrecked at the bottom of the dry lagoon, the fossils of leaves speckling the winged hull. The fairgrounds deserved to become a sad, battered monument to every lost thing of beauty.

"You really are afraid, aren't you?" Cecily had said the night we'd gone up in the basket of the balloon. She had asked me to steal her away. And it was true, I had been afraid, but why? What was there to be afraid of? Falling? Death? There'd not been a day that had passed, not an hour, that I hadn't wished I'd cut that rope and carried her off, at the risk of everything.

On this last day of the Fair, the Civil War balloon rose again. The men pulled it down and sent it up, down and up, all morning and afternoon, lifting people into the air to the very end of its rope, to wave at the city below.

I'm not sure at what point I decided to escape with it. I'd walked the entire length of the midway, as the showmen and managers tore down and packed up. The tracks were rolled, the tents collapsed, the carousel horses unharnessed. The Turkish Village, the Moorish Village, the Filipino Village—whole civilizations fell.

The Indians had abandoned their camp days before, with the first eddies of blizzard, and they'd torched their makeshift tepees and wigwams, setting their whole fake city ablaze. They'd put their belongings on their horses' backs, shrouded themselves in blankets and hides, and walked against the ice and wind, away from the burning camp and down the midway, their hundreds of footsteps fading behind them as more snow fell to cover their paths. They walked through the Grand Court and past the lagoon, where the fairgoers watched while wrapped in their own coats and furs in the wind-rocked gondolas, their umbrellas knocking into each other. They watched, and some applauded, assuming it was all spectacle, a parade of tribal nations.

August's tent—its brightly colored walls made of ball gowns and tablecloths—was nearly all that remained in the vast vacant lot scorched black and gray. He'd added to its drapery in recent weeks, stitching on ruffles and stretching a wall by adding bolts of kimono silk, crimson, yellow, violet, patterned with cranes, butterflies, cherry blossoms. He attached a weather vane to the tip of the tent pole—a wooden mermaid that spun around and around no matter the breeze, the points of her pink fin pointing north, south, east, west.

August wasn't inside, but I went in to sit anyway. He'd dragged in a wrecked velvet settee. But he'd taken most of his own things—his samovar, his framed painting of Sarah Bernhardt playing Hamlet, the skull of Yorick in her hand like a puppet.

I'd turned August away several times in the aftermath of Cecily's death. I hadn't meant to be cruel; I just refused to be comforted. I turned everyone away. And I went to my new office only once, to telephone the Wakefield house. To speak to Mrs. Margaret. "The nanny, please," I told the servant who answered. "I'm the infant's doctor."

"Don't call again," Mrs. Margaret told me, in her harsh growl. "You can expect nothing from me. This is what Cecily wanted for her little girl. And I'm here to look after her, so you don't have to worry.

You have no business worrying. Respect Cecily's memory, and allow the little motherless mite a good life."

I had not intended to give up so easily, but I didn't know what else to do. I couldn't think. *When the Fair ends*, I promised myself, *my life will start back up.* I would move forward, toward whatever might be next, once the Fair was over. When the Fair was over, I would be ready.

So when I reached the balloon, I'd not meant to commit a grand theft. Stealing it hadn't even occurred to me. I just wanted to go up in it again, to see all that Cecily and I saw that day. I wanted to go up, and be unafraid.

But the winch was loose, and nobody knew it but me. In my nervousness, I had stood aside, working up my courage, watching, inspecting every inch of the rope, seeking any slight fraying of the hemp. I lowered my mask back to my face.

The rope that kept the balloon captive was wound around a winch that was grounded in a block of cement. With every winding and unwinding, the crank turned and the winch rattled, loosening itself from its anchor.

The cement was cracked and crumbling, and when no one else stood in line for flight, and as the balloon's managers flirted with the trapeze artist, sharing a cigarette with her, I stepped forward, kicked my boot hard against the failing winch, and pushed myself up and into the balloon's basket. I gave the rope a yank, freeing it from the winch, and set sail.

I was tucked into the basket of the balloon like a rabbit in a hat. *Now you see him, now you don't.*

Under hypnosis, a man could shake his sense of fear. You watched a watch swing—ticktock, ticktock—or you followed the crushed eggshell that trickled through the neck of an hourglass, and your torment ticked away too, like magic. Or so they said. I'd once been on the same bill as a hypnotist who mesmerized for show, not medicine, and he'd put me in a trance without me even realizing. It had been easy to fall into it.

As I watched a rapid cloud, and as the balloon lifted, I felt myself slipping away.

I rose higher and higher, gripping the sides of the basket tight, the wicker sticking into my skin. I heard the shouting below, the beckoning, the begging, but it sounded no more boisterous than all the happy racket of the fairgoers. In my fear, I kept my eyes downturned, watching my feet on the floor. When I finally looked up, and over, and across, I saw the New White City no longer beneath me. I saw farms and pastures, the lines of furrows in the plowed ground.

I lowered myself to the bottom of the basket, unwilling to watch the world drift away.

BOOK THREE

Ghosts

December 1898

32.

E VERY CHRISTMAS EVE, late into the night, the Old Sisters Egan told the ghost stories they'd grown up with. They would go to church to hear the children sing the carols, and then return to the farm for oyster soup, cooked goose, and plum pudding with a puddle of rum burned away with a match. They would then have brandied figs by the hearth, their legs covered with quilts, and retell old tales of the unsettled dead.

But on this, my first Christmas Eve with the sisters, a snowstorm kept us in. This pleased me, of course. I'd left the house once that day, and did not feel inclined to leave it again. We'd gone to town, to the dry goods store, where I bought Cecily some jasmine-scented soap wrapped in pink tissue. I bought Doxie a toy elephant that fluttered its ears when you wound it up. Emmaline had loaned me a handful of coins for the gifts. "The poor darlings should have something under the tree, at least," she'd said.

I'd gone to the library alone afterward—a little room with too little light and too few books—and spent the rest of the morning reading while Emmaline and Hester had tea and doughnuts down the street with the listless Mrs. Peck, the ether addict.

At the library, I wrote Cecily a letter. *I'm looking for ways to turn the*

Emerald Cathedral green, I wrote. *I'd like that to be my Christmas present to Emmaline and Hester. A promise of some green, in the middle of winter. In a manual on painter's varnishes, I found a recipe. You treat some sheets of scrap copper with crushed grape skins. You soak the sheets in tubs, then wash them with turned wine. Eventually you build up a coat of verdigris. We'll scrape it off and sprinkle the cathedral with the crystallized emerald.*

I tore the wrapper from the soap and tucked it into the envelope. *I hope the scent lasts long enough to reach you*, I wrote. *Merry Christmas. I love you.* I had then posted the letter, and collected the mail.

And in the mail was a letter addressed to me, but I didn't have to open it to know who it was from. I'd written August Sweetbriar just once, to let him know I was alive, and he'd written back, in early November, a note so full of peevishness and disappointment, I'd had to read it several times, each time hoping to see something gentler in his screed. He'd not believed me when I'd said it was all an accident—it was as if he thought I'd gone up in the balloon and that I'd broken my leg, all as a plot to escape without saying good-bye. What I'd explained as a strange kind of fate, he'd dismissed as cruelty. *I don't believe in fate*, he'd written. And he'd written me a few other times since, each letter a little crankier than the one before it. I tucked this one in my jacket pocket. I knew I had done a heartless thing to him, even if by accident, and didn't need the reminder.

I would read it later, though, when I felt better fortified against his moods. Charitably, he had sometimes sent news. Rosie and Josephine had married on the first Saturday in December. Pearl had gone to Paris to study the window dressing of the dress shops there. Doxie's baptism, and her long, silk christening robe, and her new name—*Dorothy Wakefield*—had been featured in the Sunday pictorial section of the *Omaha Bee*, with the sainted Wakefield holding her over the baptismal font. August had enclosed the newspaper clipping.

I decided I would wait to read August's new letter until after Christmas. Or maybe after the first of the year. Or maybe never. I missed August, and I loved him, but if he could only scold, I couldn't listen.

Or could I? His letter, unread, occupied my thoughts all the ride home, as Hester drove the horses, me sitting between the two sisters. In that envelope might be the unforgiveness I needed. I needed him to be inconsolable, so that the old life of mine could finally fall behind and fall away.

But I kept the letter tucked in my jacket, and as we drew nearer to the farm, the air grew gray and sharply cold, and I had to bury my hands in the pockets of my trousers. The morning had been pleasant, with no chill or wind, and I'd worn no overcoat or hat or gloves. The Old Sisters Egan had dressed lightly too, and as the mercury dropped and dropped and dropped, and the first of the snow began falling, we didn't speak a word to one another. We worried we'd not outrun the blizzard, and we were all distracted by our misery, by the burn of the icy wind which seemed it'd never stop. We leaned forward on our bench, as if we could lean our way right into our house, right up to the hearth.

When we were finally inside, and we'd built the fire and lit the stove, as we'd stamped our feet and slapped at our own arms to get the blood to pump, we laughed. We started laughing and couldn't stop. We laughed at how miserable we'd been only minutes ago, back when we'd thought we might die.

"Can you believe how *awful* that was?" Emmaline said, wheezing with laughter.

"How did we survive it?" Hester said. Despite her laughter, she seemed truly curious.

"*Did* we survive it?" I said.

"We did!" Emmaline said, smiling, nodding, sipping from a glass of scotch whiskey. "But only just."

When we fell quiet again, I thought of Cecily, and the night she couldn't stop laughing at my jokes, at Oscar's jokes, as I'd stood on the stage on the rooftop, after Wakefield's masquerade ball. I had thought I'd never forget the sound of it, so sweet it was.

But now I couldn't quite hear it. I heard her speaking, when I listened back, and I could hear her singing the little lullabies to get Doxie to sleep. But the exact sound of her laughter escaped me. And I realized I couldn't remember the sound of anyone's laughter, no one's but Emmaline's and Hester's, which I'd only just heard. And now, in the silence, I had no memory of the sound of theirs either. I could see, in my mind, whole audiences, shaking with laughter, their mouths open, their eyes watering. What did it sound like? For the life of me, I didn't know.

With such deep regret I thought of all the times Cecily and I had strolled past the phonograph booth on the midway, where you could speak into a horn and record yourself. You'd take home your own voice, its rhythms etched into a wax cylinder. "I have nothing to say," she'd said the first time I'd suggested we step inside.

She wouldn't have had to say anything. I could've told jokes, and she could've laughed. And I'd have that laughter still.

As THE WIND BLEW HARD, then died down, then blew hard again, its every gust sounding like a great beast slithering against the house, rattling the panes, knocking away shingles with the brush of its tail, Emmaline stood at the front window, watching for the snow to stop. She had dressed for churchgoing in a cape of possum fur— "Siberian marten," she insisted—and a fur cap stuck through with quail feathers.

Hester called us to the table in the kitchen, the room still warm from all the roasting. Emmaline gave up on the storm ending, and she took off her cape and hat. We sat down to another of Hester's fine feasts.

"Did you visit the Filipino Village when you were at the Fair?" Emmaline asked me. "Do you believe them to be a tribe of cannibals?"

"I don't believe anything about the Fair," I said. "Why do you ask? Are you thinking if we get snowed in for too long we'll have to eat each other alive?"

"Perhaps," she said, "but we have a cellar full of canned birds and meats. And pickles and preserves. To turn cannibal would just be an extravagance."

After dinner, after dark, we exchanged gifts—the sisters gave me a monkey-leather wallet for all the money I didn't have, and a jade letter opener with a little circle of magnifying glass on one end of it.

I'd made each of us a pair of green goggles—pieces of a broken bottle wired together into spectacles. I'd tucked them into the stockings that hung from nails hammered into the mantel. As they reached into the socks, I warned, "Don't cut your fingers. Sharp edges. And don't cut yourself putting them on."

We hooked the wires behind our ears and looked up and around, at the fire, at the candle flames on the Christmas tree, at the lamplight, casting a green glow across the room with our every glance.

"In the morning," I said, "in the sunlight, the cathedral will be emerald, finally."

"Oh, I love them, Ferret," Emmaline said. "I never want to see again without them."

But no sooner had she said it than she took them off. We all did. And we settled in for ghost stories, and stayed up half the night. I found myself nodding off in the middle of my own telling of one, right at the minute of its grisliest twist. When I woke, I'd been covered with a quilt, and Hester and Emmaline had gone up to their beds.

The room wasn't bright, but it wasn't dark. It wasn't daylight. It was silvery in the room, like it was lit with moonlight, but the moon was clouded over, and it still stormed outside.

Every Christmas I always felt sunk in nostalgia, longing a little even for the orphanage and the tin bird with the windup wings Sister Patience had once snuck beneath my pillow. So I got up from the floor, took up August's letter and my new letter opener, and sat near the window. I needed the sound of his voice in his words, no matter what his words said.

There was enough of that pale, winter light to read by, though morning was hours away.

August had been using the typewriter I'd left in my office, and it appeared from my name on the front of the envelope that he'd got the thing repaired. Before, all the *r*'s had hovered above the other letters—the couple of *r*'s in *Ferret* and the couple of *r*'s in *Skerritt* looking like fangs lifted, about to strike—but the *r*'s had now been knocked back in line.

But only a moment after cutting through the envelope flap, before even lifting the letter out, I realized that August had not sent this. He would never have been so cruel, no matter how angry he was. He would never have scented his letter with Cecily's perfume.

><

My dearest Ferret,
  I'm here.
  Yours always,
  Cecily

><

33.

I READ THE LETTER, and I read it again and again and again. I picked up a pen and ran its dry nib over Cecily's words—*I'm here, I'm here, I'm here, I'm here*—over and over, following the slants and dips of her cursive.

Even if it was only a hoax, I would let myself be fooled. I would play along. I could imagine Mrs. Margaret, or Wakefield's sister, or Wakefield himself, weary of all the letters I sent to the house. I could imagine them wanting to taunt. Those three, they did love a dirty trick.

But I knew my way around the pitfalls of forgery. In my literary business, I'd been asked a time or two to mirror and mimic, to fake a wife's handwriting or a husband's signature, for seemingly deceitful purposes. If Cecily's letter had been written by someone else, there'd be stops and starts. There'd be tremors and tracing. Letters would fail to connect. You'd be able to see past the words to all the toil and industry in it.

And this, with little doubt, was truly Cecily's hand. I'd become an expert in her bad penmanship.

So, for a few hours in the night, my head not straight, I considered her *death* the hoax, not this letter in my hands. I closed my eyes and looked past logic. I returned to the funeral, lighting here and there like a fly in the room. *How did he do it?* I wondered as I studied the plot for its hinges.

Wakefield was a master of spectacle. Maybe Cecily's death had been nothing but a week of theater. Had he spoon-fed Cecily a poison that only slowed her heart, that hid its fragile beats away long enough to convince the undertaker? Had he buried a wax wife and locked Cecily in a cellar?

I began to see other things I hadn't seen at all. In my memory, Cecily appeared at an upstairs window of the Wakefield house as we left the memorial. She parted a drape, her breath frosting the glass.

In my response to Cecily's letter, I gave no greeting. I didn't sign my name. I wrote only, *You're cruel to deceive me.*

34.

A M I CRUEL? she wrote in response, in a letter that arrived only a few days later. *Am I deceiving? I don't mean to be. I've read your every letter, and your every letter lifts my heart. I make a ritual of it all. Before sitting down with your latest, I pour some quince brandy in my little ruby-red glass from the Fair. You seal your envelopes with golden wax, and you stamp the wax with a honeybee. I cut the wax with a kitchen knife. The knife has a handle of whalebone, and carved into the handle is the tail of a whale. Your letters smell of tobacco and smoke, and I picture you puffing on a pipe as you consider what to write to me. I hold the paper to my nose. I've lost my spectacles, so I run a magnifying glass over your words. I study every scratch of your pen, I follow every curve of your every letter of every word.*

I don't get your letters until they're gone. He gets them first, and he throws them in the fire. They burn away to nothing. And then they're mine.

To all you who hate me,

If Cecily's a ghost, why won't she haunt me in my own house?

Yours truly,

Ferret Skerritt

My dear Ferret,

Burn this letter before you even lay eyes on it. I don't deserve a single sympathy. I'm sorry to be such a puzzle. I won't write again.

With all my love,

Cecily

Whoever you are,
  Don't stop writing.
  F.

Dear Ferret,

I should never have written to you. Before you knew I was reading them, you wrote me such beautiful letters.

Yours,

Cecily

———————————————————— >–< ————————————————————

Dear Cecily,
  How are you writing me at all?
  Ferret

———————————————————— >–< ————————————————————

Dear Ferret,

How *am* *I writing you? I can't lift a feather. How am I reading your letters? I have lied, I confess. There's no ritual. I can't swallow a measly drop of quince brandy. I can't smell the tobacco on the page.*

I can't pluck a string of the mandolin in the corner. My breath won't fog the mirror. I can't write my name in the dust. The room could be locked. Or not. I can't turn a knob. I don't come and go as I please. I hear Doxie when she cries on the other side of the wall, but she can't hear me hushing her. How can I haunt the place? I can't rattle a chain or knock the pictures off the wall. I'm not a ghost, I fear. I'm less than a ghost. I'm less than the words written on the paper in your hand. I didn't write them. The ink in the pot is dry.

Cecily

>‹

Dear Cecily,
  Tell me something only <u>we</u> know.
  F.

>‹

Dear Ferret,

1. The day we danced a waltz hanging off wires.

2. The day you pressed into my palm a scent bottle made of shell, and when I twist its stopper, it smells of caraway seeds and flower petals.

3. On Sundays, those days the Fair was dry, our favorite waiter at the midway café served us our beer in teacups.

4. On the days Dox and me felt melancholy, you called us "colly-molly" and it cheered us up.

5. At the glassblower's booth, you bought me my little ruby-red glass, etched with my name, almost—the old man hadn't heard you right, so he left the y off. And you called me Cecil for days after. You pronounced it See-sill.

6. The shoes you gave me on the day it rained.

7. Mexican cigarettes.

8. Dandelion honey.

9. That place you kiss on my neck.

I am,

Cecily

January and February

1899

35.

EVERY DAY I DROVE Hester's haggard horse to town. Some days there were two letters from Cecily waiting for me. Some days, three. Some days, I posted two or three myself. I got in the habit of reading the letters there at the post office, and I would write in response right on the page, my words twisting around hers, my script weeding along the margins and around the roses and posies embossed in the corners. I believed in her. *If this is deception*, I once wrote, *deceive me*.

When the wind bit too harshly, the librarian let me stay among the books. I curled up in quilts under the table, breathing in the smell of worn leather and glue, and the vanilla scent of old paper, just as I had on the nights of my childhood, when studying under Mr. Crowe. When I couldn't sleep from the noise of the ice and snow, I read and reread Cecily's letters at the window. In the thick of winter it never got dark—there was always that haze of silver and gray that bounced the moonlight around.

The librarian was a young woman named Eulalie—when I first saw it spelled on the plaque on her desk, I thought it was pronounced *You-lay-lee*. After weeks of my saying it that way, she finally said, "You-LAH-lee."

Confused, I said, "I lolly?"

It was the very end of January, and a table was covered with lace and crepe paper, scissors and glue; she'd been instructing the town's lovelorn on the construction of valentines and the composing of poems. "My name," she said. "It's Eulalie, with a *la* in the middle." She raised her scissors and waved them like a wand, like conducting a choir, and she sang, *"La-la-la-la-la-la-la."*

She twisted an expert poppy from tissue paper as she sat on the edge of the table. She crossed her thin legs, and I saw the heavy winter boots she wore, a farmer's boots with buckles, lined in lamb's wool.

Eulalie knew I was all caught up in letters from a lady friend, and she naturally assumed my love was a woman who lived. "When will you go find your girl?" she asked. She wired a stem to the bloom. "There's nothing here to keep you, is there?"

"There's nowhere to go," I said.

"Hm," she said, holding the flower before her, as if confiding in it, "what could he possibly mean by that?"

"Do you believe in ghosts, You-la-la-la-lee?"

"I believe in the spirit," she said. "I believe in the soul."

"I'm talking about unholy ghosts," I said. "The ones that aren't in heaven."

She held the paper flower to her nose. "The ones that rattle the windowpanes?" she said, as the windowpanes rattled. She smiled and stood from the table. "No," she said. "I suppose I don't." She shrugged her shoulders. "No ghosts have crept up on me. But I trust others when they say that they've seen them. I believe in other people's ghosts, I guess." She took a book from the shelf, and thumbed through its pages. She finally found what she looked for, and she marked the page with the wire stem of the paper poppy. She handed me the book—*Around the World in Eighty Days*. "This made me think of you," she said. "Read this instead of those." She nodded toward the stack of letters I carried around with me everywhere. I helped Eulalie on with her coat, a threadbare thing that had already had a long life as a patchwork quilt. She lived only a few doors down, in a room above the drugstore.

Her flower marked a page with an illustration of a hot-air balloon. I read a little of the book's middle, before backing up to the start. I sat by the library window and stayed up all night, reading front to end. When I got to the part about Phileas Fogg riding a sledge with a top-mast and jib over the snowy fields and creeks of Nebraska, across the frozen Platte, catching a winter wind and sailing to Omaha, it seemed I could step out the door and into the story.

I finished the novel before morning, and I wrote Cecily a letter on one of the paper hearts, following the line and curve of the edges, turning the heart as I wrote, spiraling the sentences inward. *I'll rig a sail to a sled and get to you by nightfall,* I told her.

36.

IN THOSE FIRST DAYS of February, it had never been so cold in all the history of writing things down. The temperature fell past zero, past minus ten, past minus twenty, past thirty, past forty. The numbers on our thermometers didn't even go so low. And as the temperatures dropped, the drifts rose. Four inches, six inches, twelve. The snow closed the roads, slowed the trains. The coal ran out. A fire in town raged as the firemen watched, the water from their nozzles turning to ice and falling like hail.

I couldn't get to the post office to collect my letters, but even if I'd made the journey, and even if I'd survived it, there'd likely been no delivery at all. Later, when we were able to see a newspaper again, we would learn that the blizzard hadn't been only ours. The quilt of white spread out far past our fields. We'd shared the blizzard with much of the country, though we'd had no way of knowing so at the time. The storm had muffled our noise, trapping us in our rooms. No words reached us.

Hester, who wasn't typically biblical, nonetheless now suspected I was a messenger of the Revelation. "'And I saw another mighty angel come down from heaven, clothed with a cloud,'" she recited, as we high-stepped through the drifts, the two of us, on our way to a neighboring farm. "There are prophets who say the world will end when the century does," she added.

The temperatures had finally begun to rise, the mercury inching back to zero. We'd covered our faces with woolen masks and buried ourselves in coats and scarves. We were off to help a farmer feed his struggling cattle.

"I'm no angel," I said, my voice cracked from the cold.

"You are today," she said. "We're doing a good deed." Hester was the closest thing to a veterinarian anywhere nearby. She often helped her neighbors contend with livestock illnesses—hog cholera, tuberculosis, swine plague. She'd picked ticks off other farmers' pigs, led infected cattle through paraffin dips. She'd splinted the broken bones of horses. She'd committed herself to the animals' well-being, even here, during the coldest winter of the century, even at the age of seventy something. And she even moved quicker than I did, springing her legs up and over the tall drifts like a hound after fox.

She then told me a story I'd already heard from Emmaline, but Emmaline had insisted I never tell Hester I knew anything of it. "It was too painful a mistake," Emmaline had whispered.

"We only had cattle on our own farm once," Hester said, the vapors of her breath so cloudy in the cold, I couldn't see her eyes as she looked back at me. "Just a few summers ago," she said. "I don't know what possessed us. Has Emmaline told you about it?"

"No," I lied.

They'd shot the sickest of their cattle during an epidemic of blackleg. The killing, Hester said, not of all the cattle, but the youngest, strongest ones, the ones that this particular fever found most vulnerable, had changed both the Old Sisters Egan, unalterably so. Emmaline had not allowed Hester to take on the assassination alone. "In all our years together," Hester told me, "in a house of guns, Emmaline had never learned to fire one. So that one early Sunday morning of the slaughter, I taught Emmaline how the rifle worked."

"I'm not an excellent student even in the best of situations," Emmaline had told me. It took well over an hour for her to master the loading of the gun, the holding of it, the proper stance against recoil. Hester, slowly, in gentle voice, had exercised such a grave kindness, Emmaline had wanted forever to be under her instruction, in that awful, tragic dawn.

"But I'm the one who had nightmares after," Hester said. "Every night, every hour, I'd scream and yell. I didn't even wake myself up. But I sure as hell woke Emmaline. Every hour, every night, for two years, I woke that poor girl."

"I've never heard you scream," I said.

"The nightmares stopped when you got here," she said. "And Emmaline got to sleep through the night again. And when she got to sleep again, she started dreaming up that language and that Emerald Cathedral."

Emmaline hadn't told me any of that—she hadn't told me about the nightmares, and when they started, and when they ended. My legs grew even heavier, my steps slower in the snow. I belonged here. This farm had pulled me from the sky.

37.

THE MOMENT THE AIR was no longer so cold it'd kill you, the neighbors returned to our barn. They came to the farm in the heavy fur coats they'd stitched from the prairie wolves they'd shot. Sometimes the wolves' legs and tails, still attached to their pelts, dragged in the snow behind them. The farmers wore hats made from the rabbits from their gardens, the rabbits' ears sticking out from the men's heads, and they pulled along children's sleds, the junk piled on—rusted pump handles, chamber pots with cracks, tin buckets full of bedsprings, gas chandeliers with broken glass globes. They toiled for hours, reverent and purposeful, attaching these fragments to the Emerald Cathedral with great care.

The farmers had persevered through flood and drought and now the worst winter on record. Some came to the cathedral because they heard God's voice in their ears, like Old Testament Noah, and they longed to be touched by divinity, for their faith to be restored by this inexplicable mission. Others came in defiance of the God they'd lost, the cathedral their own Tower of Babel, their own godless, renegade church. Regardless of what brought them, they left invigorated by the wonder of it all.

I watched from the window. All I could think about were the letters from Cecily, so I lost the thread of the cathedral—I could no longer sense where it was going. Whereas I'd once seen in it something taking shape, now I saw only shapelessness. I worried we'd gone too far with it—I worried we'd reached its completion weeks before, but we hadn't known enough to stop. On the nights when the whole county converged on the barn, for a dance or a feast, I feared it would fall in on us all, wiping us off the map in one fell swoop, like the slap of a tsunami.

I would serve as oracle as I always did, a few hours a day, for those who came to the house, but the rest of the time I read and reread the notes from my ghost. I read them out of order. I read pieces from this one, pieces from that.

Did I already tell you that he buried me in an electromagnetic corset? she'd written once. Had she told me already? I didn't know, because I no longer read the letters in order.

In her death, Cecily wrote often of her health. Not only had she and Wakefield traveled to many hot springs in late summer, but they'd gone to hospitals and universities. They'd sat through seminars and experiments. She'd spent a week in hydrotherapy, swathed in wet shawls, stepping barefoot through wet grass and across wet stones. She'd had private sessions with a swami, who guided her on matters of truth and existence. Attached to her ankle she'd worn a cylinder meant to feed her extra oxygen.

Please understand, Ferret, she wrote. *Billy was no villain. He loved me somehow. I say "somehow" because how could he love someone he knew so little? Why would he want to save a stranger? But when he saw me, he saw his dead wife, I suppose. I looked nothing like her, but she and me must've shared the same rotten insides. Beneath our skin, she and me were the same. Our hearts were little clocks ticking the same last minutes away. If he saved me, he'd save her, in a sense. And in a sense, he'd save the boy by saving Doxie, which may be the saddest story of all. They'd gone to the Chicago World's Fair, him and his wife and the boy, and they'd gone home and they'd built their own little White City with matchsticks in the library. And after the train crash that killed the boy, Billy vowed to build a world's fair in his memory. So he devoted himself to the New White City. He formed boards and committees. He hired architects. He built our Fair up from nothing but a field. And the wife faded away. And she died while he designed his memorial to his son.*

That was the letter I read the most often. Because it pained me the most, I suppose. It seemed written by somebody else. I didn't want Cecily to be so forgiving. I didn't want to know how sympathetic she was to the man who stole her from me. I wanted her letters about Wakefield to be full of accusation. I wanted her to blame him. I wanted all his cures to have been her killer. *The electromagnetic corset sapped my strength*, I wanted her to confess.

I DROVE A SLEIGH TO TOWN, my legs under a lap robe of rabbit fur, a bed warmer once hot from its coals stuck in under the cushion of the bench. I looked like an old beggar woman with my head wrapped all round with a scarf, hunched against the wind, a quilt thrown over my shoulders. By the time I reached Bonnevilla, my beard was white with icicles, my cheeks a raw red.

The mail had resumed, and a postcard waited for me, its delicate paper lace only slightly tattered, its ribbons still in their proper knots. At the center of the heart-shaped card was a cupid stamped in gold foil, and on the back, Cecily had written in a tiny script:

I used to know a girl named Gertie who worked in a factory making valentines. She sat in a line, and every girl added a little something else to the same heart. Gertie would add a paper rose, or little satin lovebirds, or a little linen card with a poem printed on it. She said sometimes she'd add a strand of her own hair, maybe twisting it around a button, or tucking it into a stitch of thread. She had to quit the factory when she went blind from it. I guess this isn't a very romantic story, so I'll end here.

But she didn't end there. She ended with an invitation. *Meet me at the Fair*, she wrote. *At three o'clock. In the Agricultural Building on Valentine's Day, where we once watched the pigeons escape through the hole in the roof.*

My ghost wanted to be seen.

ON THE TRAIN TO OMAHA, on Valentine's Day, I was filled with dread. That very afternoon I would be faced with Cecily's imposter. I'd orchestrated my own undoing. I was a morbid, lovelorn fool who'd gone off to dig up another man's dead wife. The train hurried on its tracks, at an ungodly speed it seemed, the train perhaps trying to make up for all the hours lost in the storm. And I regretted leaving the farm at all. If I'd stayed behind, I considered, I'd still be miles from discovering anything at all.

I was playing right into Wakefield's hands. It was him, wasn't it, behind all this? All he'd ever wanted was everything I ever had. Why *wouldn't* he resurrect Cecily just to kill her in front of me? My torture was his hobby. I would suffer more than him.

On the farm, I'd come to believe in the logic of dreams. I believed in magic, perhaps even a heavenly order. I went up in the balloon so the balloon would come down, so Emmaline would dream, so the cathedral would rise, so Cecily would speak. Not only did I believe it, but it seemed insensible to believe anything else.

But as the train approached Omaha, black clouds rising from the stacks of the smelting works ahead, I felt I was the pawn of a darker magic altogether. There was only cruelty at work. Nothing else. I existed only to be Wakefield's victim.

I thought of the pretty little gun Rosie had strapped to his calf. I could tuck that gun up my sleeve, and as Wakefield stood before me, in the winter ruins of the New White City, I could promise a magic trick. *Nothing up my sleeves*, I would say, and as I lifted my cuffs to demonstrate that nothingness, I would drop the gun into my hand, and I'd send a bullet into his heart.

Could I murder a man? *Yes.* I could aim the gun, and if it was meant to go off, it would go off. And if the bullet was meant to stop his heart, it'd stop his heart. I was nothing but a victim of my own fate.

I felt a tug at my sleeve, and I realized I'd had my head in my hands. A little girl stood in the aisle wearing a white eiderdown coat, her blond hair as pale as a winter breath. "Are you all right, sir?" she said, with a pitying wrinkle of her brow.

I nodded. I smiled. "Yes," I said. I smiled again, and nodded again. "Yes, thank you." I felt ashamed, as if this angel had been dropped down to earth to look right into my head. I thought of my own little girl, my motherless Doxie.

She stepped back to her seat across the aisle, next to her mother, who glanced up at me with kind eyes before returning to her book in her hands.

There's nothing to be frightened of, I wanted to say.

As the train pulled up to the platform, I could only see the city through a fog of frost. Sunlight only barely burned through a spot in the haze, and the snow that fell lightly was ashen, as if from the clouds of smoke that collected up above.

The fog seemed to muffle not just the city's light but its noise too, stripping every sound down to its echo. Nearby voices sounded thinned by distance, and the horses' hooves on the cobblestones had a hollow clip-clop.

I headed straight to Thirteenth Street, to the Vendome Hotel where I knew I could get a squalid room for nothing much. It was the hotel where traveling salesmen perched as they passed through town to bilk old widows with real estate schemes and monogrammed Bibles. But on the sidewalk out front was a small shanty of boards and tin, and inside the shanty a cop kept cozy with a tiny stove as he watched the hotel's front door.

"Nobody goes in, and nobody gets out," the cop said as he pushed the door open a crack. "Hotel's under quarantine." Before I could ask for the specifics of the sickness, he'd shut his door to return to the apple he ate. I looked up at the hotel windows, to his prisoners, men and women who pressed close to the glass to see as far up the street as they could.

August's was only a few blocks away, so I headed off to his shop. I needed his forgiveness, I realized. I would fib, if I had to. I would tell him the balloon's rope had come undone on its own. Somehow, this had to be settled.

The door to the stairs in August's building, to his apartment, his lab, to my old office, was locked, so I stepped into his father's bookstore. The only customer was an old salt in a yachting cap studying a map with a magnifying glass. A long table stretched all down the middle of the shop, and the walls were lined with books packed tight in bookshelves. Atop the shelves were framed posters of all the somewhere elses to go—Paris, Berlin, Morocco.

I looked over the man's shoulder; the map depicted some island in some sea, and the mapmaker had playfully inserted a kitten-whiskered sea monster in the corner of the ocean, its serpentine tail crushing a ship.

At the other end of the shop stood a clerk with his back to me, but when I asked after August, and the man turned, I saw that this was August himself, in a kind of decline. *He* would consider it a decline, anyway—he looked every bit the dignified businessman. He'd cut his hair to the very nib and he wore a brown suit, a brown vest, a brown tie. The only sign of August anywhere in this serious gent was the cloud of perfume that hovered over him, some scent as precious as peonies, so strong it watered my eyes.

"Ferret," August said, and the relief in his voice made me relieved too. He rushed into me, pressing himself against my chest, wrapping his arms around. I brought him closer, put my head to his.

August stepped away and glanced at the carpetbag at my feet. Before leaving the farm, I'd shoved my few scraps of clothing into the bag. Emmaline had unpacked it, pressed the clothes, and packed the bag up again. "Are you back to stay?" August said.

"I was going to check into the Vendome," I said.

"Oh," he said. "The Vendome." He lifted his hand to his mouth and whispered, "*Smallpox*." He said, "We're all afraid of an epidemic. There are a handful of houses locked up by the police, the families stuck inside, waiting for the disease to come or go. They've been trying to build a smallpox hospital at the edge of town, but it's been too bitterly cold to get the walls up." He stopped, then took my hands in his, and squeezed them. "But don't worry, love. There are only a very few sick from the pox. And a few others sick from the pox vaccine. You'll stay here, up in my room."

I heard hardly anything he said. I was too caught up in his transformation. "What happened to you?" I asked, reaching up to give the prickle of his head a big-brotherly rub with my knuckles.

"My father fell on the ice," he said. "Hit his head. Had a hemorrhage. He can't speak." He rattled it all off, but I wasn't convinced it was an answer to my question. August had changed too much.

"I'm so sorry," I said.

"So I'm keeping respectable to save the family business," he said. He inspected his fingernails.

"You're a good son," I said. "Will your old man be okay?"

"It's too sad to talk about," he said. "Everything's too sad. Cecily died. The Fair ended." He paused to look me in the eye. "You left," he said. He kept my gaze for a bit, then looked toward the front window. "I don't think winter will ever leave. Summer will come and everything will still be frozen."

August rushed the old sailor out, and locked up the store to take me upstairs to Rosie's den. "I turned my laboratory over to Rosie, and he built a darkroom around the sink," August said. On our way past a hook near the door to the shop, August plucked up a silk scarf. He wrapped it around and around his neck as we climbed the stairs, the pattern bright with parrots with berries in their beaks. And with that scarf flittering from his throat, I began to recognize him again.

"He uses the apothecary for his chemicals," August continued. "He photographs his lovelies right there, then sells the pictures to men by appointment. He made a quaint little sitting room with wing chairs and a stove. And a humidor. And he peddles more than just his photographs; he deals in all sorts of respectable filth. They're things that can't be sent through the mail, so they're brought in by smugglers."

Rosie welcomed me with a back slap and a vigorous shaking of my hand that threatened to yank my arm from its socket. Then he pulled me in for a hug that crushed my lungs and stopped my breath. He grabbed my head to hold it still while he pushed his lips against my cheek in a kiss.

"Rosie missed you most of all, I guess," August said, taking a seat. He crossed his legs, flicked at some dust on his trousers, and spoke rapidly, as if bored. "Where have you been, what did you do, why are you here?"

I sat in a wing chair and ran my hands along the arms, along the freckled deer hide with the hair left on. Rosie's parlor was a dizzying display. There were apples and poppies in the wallpaper, and strawberries and lilacs in the carpet. The lamps had red glass globes painted with golden dragons. In a gold-painted cage, two lovebirds thrashed their wings in a lovers' quarrel. And covering one whole wall, ceiling to floor, were framed paintings of women wearing nothing or next to nothing, naked on a beach or in a field or in a bath. A woman's nightgown slipped off as she stood from her bed in the morning light. Another woman lifted her skirt to lower her stocking.

Rosie set a tray atop a low stool at our feet, with a cut glass decanter and tiny goblets, and a plate of little cakes decorated with candied violets.

"I have an engagement," I said. The men just looked at me, expecting more. "An appointment," I said. Silence, still. Then I said, "A business meeting."

"I'm so glad," August said, seeming genuinely pleased. "I'm glad you're getting back to things." He leaned forward and reached out to put his fingers in my curls and to pull at them, to examine their length. "You should let me hack at that hair with my scissors," he said.

I gently took August's hand from my head. We sat there, hand in hand, for a moment.

"Tell me what I've missed," I said.

Rosie told me about his Josephine, his missus now, and how she'd taken up giving piano lessons to the city's rich, and played ragtime at night in the orchestra pit of the Orpheum Theater for traveling vaudeville acts. And August told me about Pearl, and how she, like Rosie, was stripping ladies too, but for a more moral purpose. Upon returning from Paris, she'd stopped dressing the manikins of Brandeis to take to the road with Susan B. Anthony, the "suffering sisterhood" as they were known, preaching about the hazards of how women dress. Pearl was part of a campaign to get women to send their corsets to the navy, so the steel ribs could be used to build ships.

"I think you can see the ladies' hemlines inching up a little off the ground," August said, inching up the hem of his own trouser legs as he spoke, baring his ankles. "Back when Omaha was at its filthiest, a lady could drag her skirts through all kinds of muck. Vermin, dead or alive, could be swept right up." August tiptoed his fingertips, like mouse steps, across my hand and up my arm.

Rosie crossed his leg too, his trouser cuff lifting, but the holster wasn't there.

"And what about the Fair?" I said. "Is the White City still standing?" I hoped for disappointment. I hoped for them to tell me the whole thing had turned to rubble. Then I could get back on the train, that very afternoon, and on the ride home, I would write Cecily. *It breaks my heart to tell you this. There's nothing left of the Fair.*

"The buildings were supposed to be gone weeks ago," Rosie said. "But there's a dispute over wrecking contracts. So the flimsy things are just collapsing in on themselves, under the weight of all the snow."

"The Fair was supposed to save Omaha," August said, pouting, "but I believe it ruined it. It was the Fair that brought the smallpox. People carried in with them all sorts of plagues. And any money that came in just fattened the wallets of the corrupt. Even the girls at Anna Wilson's brothel are struggling—the Fair brought to town every prostitute within three hundred miles, and now that the fairgoers are gone, any poor whore could starve. And we'll all of us be lucky to survive this awful winter."

"I met a professor of the weather," I said. I picked one of the candied violets from one of the cakes, and let its sugar melt on my tongue. I poured myself some of the liquor from the decanter. "He keeps all kinds of whirligigs and rain gauges on his barn roof. Weather balloons tied to windmills. He could never get much to grow in his dirt, so now his eighty acres is covered with contraptions and motors. He says the farmers brought on their own droughts and their own floods. They break up the soil, and they release all the gases, and they stir up the clouds."

"Wakefield's lake froze over as always," August said, "but he didn't even have the ice cut away. He defaulted on his contracts. There's an ice shortage, and the other ice dealers can't keep up. We're freezing to death and dying for ice."

"If the smallpox doesn't kill us," Rosie said, "the fetid meat will."

Another silence fell, most likely from the mention of illness and death, and the suggestion of Wakefield too grief-struck to do business. Then Rosie said, "Do you want to know something about that Wakefield?" He leaned forward, one eye squinting, and the old Rosie I loved returned—Rosie the bitter, the broken-backed, the down-on-his-luck killer of presidents. His top lip lifted in a snarl. "I had a gentleman in here just the other day, a former business associate of Wakefield's. He was here to buy the diary of a whore, and he had a few glasses of hooch, and he said he hadn't worked a job for years. He was rich on account of a company he'd owned for a while with Wakefield. It was how Wakefield first got money—a syphilis cure."

I listened, the glass of liquor at my lips, the warm smell of it, its fumes, filling my head. Wakefield and this friend, it seemed, won the syphilis business in a poker game twenty years before. They started advertising in the newspapers, and before they knew it they had more orders than they had bottles. Wakefield grew richer and richer, and when a newspaperman, his syphilis uncured, threatened to kick up a scandal, he just bought the newspaper and fired him. He continued to sell the syphilis remedy, and then began to sell a remedy to the remedy, a cure for the cure for the addicts who took more than a spoonful a day. And with all the money from the city's syphilitics, he bought Omaha, block by block by block.

"He knew the poisons he was pouring down Cecily's throat," Rosie said. "He killed her as surely as if he'd stuck a knife in her gut."

I swallowed back the booze, to chase away that image of Cecily knifed, and when I returned the little goblet to the tray, its stem snapped off. I had only meant to set the glass down, to stand up, explain that I was late and must leave, but the little snapped stem startled me. I saw a few drops of blood on my trousers leg, then brought my cut finger to my tongue. All the damage was so minute, but it echoed. It magnified. The room shrunk around me, and I found myself crouching, sensing the ceiling pressing against my shoulders, pushing my chest toward my knees.

I shut my eyes tight, and when I opened them again, a watery vision, a trick of the winter light, danced near the ceiling, a spinning of color, a prism of pale blues and pinks, like Cecily's gown of chameleon silk in the mirrored dome of the Flying Waltz.

The New White City still stood, and Cecily would be there soon, to meet me. I was certain of it.

"What would you have me do?" I said, sounding more angry than I'd meant to. "Call the police? Have Wakefield arrested? For giving his wife something for her headache?" I stood. "Would you have me stick a knife in *his* gut?"

Rosie looked me steady in the cye. "Save the girl," he said. "Take Doxie away from him."

It wasn't that I had never considered it. But it had seemed to me impossible. I couldn't imagine ever being allowed to even sneak a glimpse of the child, let alone get near enough to lift her from her pram and spirit her away. It was cruel of Rosie to taunt me with it.

So I left. When I reached the bottom of the stairs, I heard August at the top of them. "Don't go, Ferret," he called down.

"I won't," I called up to him, stumbling off the bottom step as I turned back. "I'm not. I'll be away just a minute. I'm late." I faked a cheery voice so he wouldn't feel inclined to follow me. As I stepped out the door, I said, "I'll explain later," so that I wouldn't have to explain at all.

38.

I CAUGHT UP WITH a cabbie who drove me north, to the ruins of the White City. I unfolded the cab's hood when a drizzling of ice began to fall. I could hear the ice sprinkling the trees' skeletal branches, a soft tune without melody, like chimes or shards of shattered glass swept into a dustpan. The white sky went whiter, paler, the clouds of frost sinking in, and I didn't see the Fair coming until we wheeled right up to it. The New White City's tall walls and rooftops bled away into the mist.

I walked into the Grand Court past a gate leaning open on broken hinges. I wasn't alone. Off on the far end, near where the fountain's waters had played, were two boys in breeches with their bicycles leaning against the railing. The statue of Neptune had either lost his head or had had it stolen, and the boys sought to sever him of his other parts. They pitched snowballs likely packed with ice toward the statue. One fell just short of the god's gut, another nearly hit the trident. I could see the boys had piled up a pyramid of them.

The buildings turned to ruin in the winter, some of the walls fell in, a few rotundas collapsed. Windows were boarded, and some statues had been pulled from their pedestals and left in pieces on the bricks. Wings had been plucked from angels. A naked god was riddled with gunshot. Eve's arm with the apple had been broken off and taken away, and so had the serpent from the tree. Wild turkeys ran by, pursued by two men with rifles, running past the *No Hunting or Shooting* sign tacked to a toppled column.

And on the lagoon was a trio of young women skating across the ice, wearing black fur caps and long black coats of fur. One of the girls had her hands in a muff. One had a long scarf that trailed behind her and wrapped around as she spun. With everything so decayed, I worried about them on the ice, though I knew the water had been frozen solid for weeks. I thought I could hear the brittle sound of cracking.

"Is the ice cold enough?" I shouted down to them, but they couldn't hear me above their own chatter and the slice of their blades, which was just as well. They probably would have laughed at such a question.

Inside the Agricultural Building was vast emptiness, all the exhibits having been packed up and carted away months before. A few of the ornate birdcages of brass and bamboo that had housed the German songbirds had been left behind, feathers clotted in the cages' bars. There were carts and baskets of fruits and vegetables gone bad, then frozen in their state of rot. Pumpkins had burst and peaches had wrinkled and browned. I walked through the barren hall, my heart beating hard. The echo of my heels made it sound like someone was behind me, but I was alone. All alone.

Last summer, locked in their dovecotes to be judged and exhibited, had been more varieties of pigeon than I'd ever known existed. I stopped now to read the labels on the wire gates of the empty cages. Short-faced bald heads and long-faced tumblers. Barbs, dragoons, fantails, and trumpeters. Chinese owls, English owls, African owls. Magpies, jacobins, priests, and nuns. The chanting of it brought me comfort, and I remembered the afternoon Cecily and I strolled through the hall and lucked upon the sight of a few of the birds escaping their prisons. Their wings had sounded too heavy to lift them, but they rose to the rafters. They'd swooped and glided overhead, suddenly seagulls in the open air.

I checked the hour on my pocket watch. It was several minutes past three. But then the lonely echo of my boots went on and on, too long, and I felt dizzy, like from some sudden suck into my lungs of poison air. The sound of my steps kept going, but I wasn't walking, I wasn't moving. I sniffed the air, to try to place the scent. *Extract of sweet pea.*

"Cecily," I said, turning. I could feel her close to me, as if she stood at my back, her fingers light at my neck, but not touching, just stirring up static.

A figure in black approached. She was dressed in widow's weeds, a heavy black veil hanging from her hat and hiding her face. She carried at her side a mourning parasol trimmed in black feathers, the tip of it scratching across the wood planks of the floor as she dragged it along.

All air seemed to have left the room even as the wind picked up and spun little whirlwinds here and there, catching the skeletons of leaves and slips of paper. The husk of a dead cricket flew up to buzz past my ear. I could only take shallow breaths that felt too short to reach my lungs, and I tried to say her name again but couldn't.

The woman in black slipped her hand up under her veil, and she seemed to be scratching her head. Her hat shook. She then began to part the veil. "Cecily," I said, though I had yet to see her face.

The woman looked up, and her mouth dropped open, her eyes rolling back, her eyelashes fluttering. A bright, burning redness rose to her cheeks. *Pearl.*

"I'm here," Pearl said. She leaned her head back more and her hat tumbled off. She swayed on her heels. Her knees gave out, and she collapsed, falling forward, into my arms.

39.

I N T H E C O A C H, Pearl tried to explain. She leaned against the door as the old driver, out on his perch, drove us away from the fairgrounds. Even in her lack of posture she posed as Cecily. She sat collapsed in the corner, her forehead against the window.

"I don't remember putting on these weeds," Pearl said. "I don't remember leaving the house. But I've learned this is not unusual."

"*Not* unusual?" I said. I'd raised my voice more than I'd meant. I'd not wanted to be snappish, or I feared I'd frighten her and she'd reveal nothing at all.

"Not unusual for a spiritual possession," she said, slowly, cautious. She watched for my response. I looked out the window and shook my head. I couldn't bear to be part of this. Grief had stunted us. We'd all become disoriented. If we didn't set our minds to righting ourselves, we would become corrupt. As tempting as it was to trust her madness, to follow this all to some awful conclusion, I needed disbelief.

"August told me you'd left," I said. "He said you were touring with Susan B. Anthony." Even that detail had been surprising, I realized. Pearl was soft-spoken and skittish. I could barely even picture her pushing leaflets on people, let alone speaking to a group. She was far too shy.

When Pearl looked down to her hands, I saw she held the handkerchief I'd given Cecily. She ran her fingers along the embroidery of the letter *C*. "I've had to tell some lies," she said.

"You don't say," I said, and again I wished I'd said nothing at all.

"I helped Billy Wakefield with the funeral, and with Doxie, and he needed me to stay," she said. "He bought Mrs. Margaret a train ticket and sent her away, off to the Pennsylvania World's Fair, to catch up with her theater troupe. There's a world's fair somewhere every summer now. He didn't like the way she looked at him. And he sent his sister off to Egypt, to dig for antiquities with a professor from the university. He's hoping she'll marry him, though he's practically a mummy himself, he's so old."

"So you've been with Doxie?" I said. "How is she?"

"She has everything she could want."

"But in a letter from . . . in one of the letters you . . ." I stopped for a moment. I took a breath. "One of the letters says Doxie cries, alone in her room."

"She's never alone," Pearl said. "She cries some, yes. She misses her mother. But she gets all my attention, and all the attention of the servants. With that sweet little face of hers, she needn't ever worry about being alone."

"Let's go there now," I said. "Let's go spend a little time with Doxie, and forget all this. This didn't happen at all, none of it. We didn't meet at the fairgrounds. You didn't write the letters. I never got the letters. None of it. None of it happened."

"You think I'm insane," she said. She watched my eyes, waiting for me to console. When I said nothing, she looked back down to the handkerchief. "And I probably am, aren't I?"

I took Pearl's hand. "You've been hiding in the Wakefield house?" I said. "You quit window dressing? That's a shame. You used to travel."

"I'll travel again," she said. "But I'll take Doxie. Billy wants me to take her to see the world. I'm her nanny, in a sense. I'll be her tutor. He's paying me much more than I would have ever made at Brandeis. And I have the run of the whole house; Billy spends all his hours in a shed in the back. I eat dinner with the servants every night in the kitchen. I love listening to their gossip, though half the time I don't know who they're talking about. They talk about a maid who was worthless, and who was fired long ago. But they still find remains of her ineptitude in the house—a spice in the wrong jar. A broken china saucer hidden far in the back of a drawer. A coat in the wrong closet. They blame her for everything."

"You deserve better," I said.

"Oh, Ferret, you don't know anything," she said. She pulled her hand away from mine. It was the first I'd ever heard her speak with such a lashing tongue. "*Don't* you know anything? A woman living alone? Working as a shopgirl? Do you think I've ever been given a nod of respect? People are *suspicious* of a woman who works so hard at a job that pays so little. Even just my bedroom at Wakefield's is bigger than the room I had at the women's hotel." She looked out the window. "*You deserve better,*" she said, with a shrug, with a snort of derision. "Yes, I do. I do deserve better. But who are you to say what's better and what's worse? What would you know about it?"

We rode in silence for a while, my hands folded in my lap. Then I said, "Just please don't write to me anymore. I beg you not to write me more of those letters. My soul can't take it."

This just seemed to nettle Pearl all the more. She laughed and rolled her eyes. "Why would I write you letters?" she said. "Why would I put *myself* through all this? I open my eyes, and a whole afternoon is gone. And I'm not in the room I was in. There's ink spilled on my sleeve. I've gnawed my fingernails to the quick." She calmed down and put her hand on mine. "I loved the letters you wrote from the farm. They tore my heart in two. I kept every one, tied with a ribbon. My bedroom used to be the boy's room. On the mantel of the hearth is a beautiful box, with bluebirds painted on it, and the letters fit perfectly inside. One day Billy collected the mail, as he never ever did, and there was a letter from you. He read it and was furious. He demanded I bring him the others. He tossed the letters in the fire."

"When?" I said.

"In December, I think," she said. "Before Christmas. And for the next several days, he insisted on collecting the mail himself. And he would throw your letters in the fire without even reading them. And then he just slipped away again. He forgot about them. He didn't have the energy to walk to the gate to collect the mail. He stayed in his shed. When your letters seemed to suggest that someone was writing you in response, I suspected Wakefield himself. But he couldn't have been seeing your letters. I would collect the mail, and I would read your letters while standing in front of the fire. And I dropped them into the flame as soon as I finished. I pushed at the paper with the fire iron, stabbed at it, until it was ash. And it was a short time after that when I realized it was me, not Wakefield, who wrote you. Cecily was communicating through me. She was using my hands to write you. At first I would blame those missing hours to the headaches I had. I thought I was fainting from them."

It was then I realized that the coach had not just stopped, but that it had parked. We'd reached some kind of destination. I leaned over Pearl to look out her window. "I don't know this street," I said.

"Ferret, please come inside with me," she said. "Ella Winnows is a clairvoyant. She has a room on the top floor."

"No," I said, "no, no, no, no, no."

"Ferret," she said, clutching my arm, "just come with me this once. Allow me this one chance to prove the truth of it."

"No," I said.

"Ferret, the letters won't stop," she said. "They won't just stop coming because we want them to. Bind my wrists. Bury me in a box. She'll find some other way to write to you. Or not. And that would be the worst yet. You mustn't silence her until she's said all she's needed to say. Ella says this isn't at all unusual. She says spirits often ramble until they find the ease they seek. None of this is in the slightest bit unusual, Ferret."

I held my hand to Pearl's cheek, and I felt her skin grow hot. As disappointed as I was, as frustrated and as foolish as I felt, I did pity her. In her despair she'd fallen some charlatan's victim, willingly or otherwise. And I wasn't so wise myself; I'd fallen too, after all.

The town was plagued with clairvoyants—like beetles and silverfish, these men and women infested attics and undergrounds. They kept dim, moonlit parlors on every city block. They were just as plentiful and just as cheap as the churchless preachers who bellyached on street corners, predicting damnation with gin on their breath. And along with the mystics with business sense, the ones with telephones and advertisements in the *Evening Bee*, were those only passing through, renting theaters and halls to bilk the believing for a nickel a head before packing their trunks and moving on to the next congregation of ninnies. Add to them the hobbyists, the amateur psychics and spiritualists, who followed instructions in a book to save them the cost of a proper séance. It was a sport and a religion, and in our grief, we begged to be deceived.

I'd heard tell that Omaha was particularly rife with mysticism due, in no small part, to Wakefield. For a time, after the death of his son, then the death of his first wife, he spent outrageous sums in hopes of hearing their voices again. He had sought spiritual guidance nightly.

"No clairvoyant," I said. Pearl needed me to turn cold and skeptical to the whole to-do, even if she didn't yet realize it. If I didn't disapprove, if I played along a second more, she'd be making sense of her every dream and headache. "No, Pearl, I'm sorry." But then I felt, in the small of my back, some pressure and pain, like the sole of someone's boot. I arched my back and groaned. I turned around and, of course, no one was there. But in my ear, as clear as if she rested her chin on my shoulder to whisper, I heard Cecily's voice. *Stubborn*, she said.

40.

Ella Winnows, a psychic with a lisp, had been a shopgirl at Brandeis before opening her attic parlor. She answered the door to us, hugging an open book to her chest, her wispy red hair wired with static. You could practically hear it sizzle and snap. "You're early," she mumbled, a cigarette burning in the corner of her mouth. "I have to find my glasses before I can get anything going."

"You're wearing them," I said.

She brought her fingers to the lenses in front of her eyes. "Dear God," she said. She took the glasses off and held them up toward the skylight, checking for smudges. "Why can't I see through them? I'm blinder with them than without them. Sit."

The tabletop was covered with open books about the spirit world and the astral plane. She dropped her cigarette into her cup of coffee and slapped all the books closed, gathered them in her arms, and tossed them into the corner, into a wing chair so battered the springs stuck through. There was nothing about the room that would give a disbeliever faith. The wallpaper was torn and streaked with grime. Cobwebs gathered in the corners of picture frames. No one, alive or otherwise, had sat at this table in a while. I wrote Cecily's name in the dust on the wooden arm of my chair.

"I wish you had come when it was pitch-dark," she said, sitting down and placing her hands on ours atop the table. "You should have come when it was summer. It's better to summon spirits in the summertime by the light from my insects and fungus." She nodded toward a cabinet; on a shelf was a jar of dead fireflies, marked *fireflies* on a piece of tape, and a jar of dead glowworms, marked *glowworms*. There was a pot of withered mushrooms. "The mushrooms glow blue around the gills when they're healthy," she said. "I don't know if any of this will work at all. Don't blame me if nothing happens. You should come back in the summer." Her hands fidgeted. "I really just read tea leaves, as a rule."

We sat there, around the table, holding hands for several minutes. The room was cold, but our hands grew sweaty.

"My hands are hot," Pearl whispered.

Ella shook her head. "Doesn't mean anything," she said. "Not necessarily."

The wind picked up outside the window, so I tried to help things along. "There was no wind before," I said.

"The wind comes, it goes," she said. "I wouldn't read anything into it."

I heard a buzzing, like a short in a light, and I thought I saw, from the corner of my eye, the flicker of a firefly in the jar. When I turned to look, the jar was dark. And when I returned my eyes to the table, I thought I caught sight of the blue glow of the mushrooms. The table trembled. Ella didn't seem to feel it.

"Sometimes nothing happens," she said. "It's not unusual for nothing to happen."

My nostrils stung with the smell of a struck match. It gave me a headache between my eyes. Pearl's grip tightened on my hand. Her grip grew so tight, I worried for my fingers and I wriggled my hand from hers.

"Pearl," I said, as she straightened her spine, segment by segment, as if some heavy sob was working up from deep in her body. She leaned her head back and opened her mouth.

Pearl made no sound. She stood abruptly, and turned, the rustling of her skirt causing her chair to tip back and to spin on one leg before it tumbled to the floor. Blind as a sleepwalker, Pearl tripped forward into the wall. She ran her hands along it, as if feeling for a doorway. She followed the wall, whimpering and moonstruck.

I stood to take Pearl's shoulders in my hands, to turn her to me. I was spooked but not by spirits. There was the threat of death in the room. There was damage. Pearl had fallen ill, and it was illness that terrified me.

She looked past me, her eyes wide. Her mouth gaped open, her chin shook. It was as if her jaw had locked. She clawed at the skin of my neck until I pulled away and she broke from my hold. She stumbled toward a barrister bookcase and she struggled with a glass door.

Ella came forward, her shoe lifted. "Hold her back," she told me. "It's a tricky latch." She banged the heel against the latch until it came unstuck. Pearl again pulled away from me. She lifted the door and grabbed from the shelf a blue box, all the while whining and sniffling.

When she returned to the table, she opened the lid—it was a stationery kit. She took sheets of pale-blue paper from the box and an ink pot and a pen. She rocked back and forth as she wrote on the page.

The longer she took to finish the letter, the more the spell of the dingy room lifted and the more impatient I got. She wasn't caught in the fits of a seizure, to my great relief. This was some dark theater, her every move deliberate, even when her shaking hands knocked the ink pot over. She was left to dip the nib into the stream of ink that flowed across the tabletop and drip-drip-dripped off the edge.

I held my hand gently at Pearl's back. "Please stop," I said. "Let's quit this," I said. She kept writing, so Ella and I waited.

When Pearl finished her letter, she shoved the paper across the table, and she would have pushed it right into the spilled ink had I not leaned forward to snatch the pages up. Pearl's teeth chattered, as if she were out in the cold.

"Oh, Pearl, oh, Pearl, oh, Pearl," Ella said, clutching Pearl's shoulders, "you're all right, dear, you're all right. There's nothing to worry about, nothing at all."

Pearl held her hands to her face and fled the room. I headed off after her, but Ella grabbed my sleeve. "You haven't paid," she whispered. I took a coin from my pocket and flicked it with the top of my thumb to bounce across the tabletop. Ella grabbed my sleeve again. "And I gotta replace the ink pot in my stationery kit now." I took all the change from my pocket and slapped it into her open palm, and I ran from the room and down the stairs. I reached the street just as the coach pulled away, Pearl's dress caught in the door, a bit of fabric flapping at me like a taunt. I watched as the coach neared the end of the block. The door popped open enough for Pearl to pull her dress in, and then the coach turned a corner and was gone from sight.

As I walked to August's, I read the letter. I read it more than once, circling the block, passing August's door again and again. Though Pearl had written without posture, without her eyes on the page, she'd again captured Cecily's handwriting, down to the slant of her *b*'s, and the short, squat loop of her *l*'s.

When I first read the first line, I laughed. I rolled my eyes. *Dear Ferret*, she'd written, *Please don't be too hard on poor Pearl.* But by the next sentence, I was already hearing Cecily's voice again. *I guess we should have suspected her.*

41.

S HE WAS VERY GOOD *at forging my signature*, the letter continued. *On the days I went to Dr. Gee Loy's, Pearl signed my receipts at Brandeis, so Billy would think I'd gone shopping. He never suspected, and yet he studied those receipts like an accountant. I suppose if I'd developed a gift as worthless as signing a dead girl's name, I'd be happy for the chance to put it to proper use too.*

And so the mystery is solved. I don't exist. I'm a parlor trick. I always was, I suppose. They'd chop off my head, then, lo and behold, it was back, right where it always was.

But I don't possess people, Ferret. I didn't slip my hand in the hand of someone else to write you this letter. I'm not a morbid entertainment. It seems to me if there's a spirit world beyond the understanding of the material world, then in the material world the spirit world would be beyond our understanding. So how would you know how I do what I do?

Are there stains from tears on the letter you hold? And if so, could they be mine? Or were they sprinkled there, with a sleight of hand, for theatrical effect?

How is it that I felt your hand in mine at the psychic's table?

Maybe I am only a gimmick, after all. A wire and a wheel under a sheet. I hang in a clairvoyant's cabinet, whistling through a harmonica on cue. But there are worse eternities, I'm guessing.

And now your letters will end. And I'll haunt strangers for a nickel.

Please write me one more time and tell me how you might be convinced. What would it take to fool you completely? How can I make you give in to my illusion?

Go to the house. Look in the room. See if I'm there.

Always,

Cecily

42.

I SLEPT ON AUGUST'S FLOOR every night that week, and spent my every day in mystics' parlors. I saw palmists and astrologers. The Widow Gustafson ran her fingers over my skull, to read bumps and dents, and it comforted me so, I just wanted to sleep with my head in her lap as she predicted all my misery to come. Mrs. Fritz served me a flower tea that tasted of Cecily's perfume, and when she read the leaves left in the dregs, she said she could see me tortured by lies my whole life long.

In the lounge of a defrocked Chinese nun who called herself Miss Mulberry, I wrote a letter to Cecily on paper of silver foil. The nun stirred coals in a porcelain bowl on her windowsill and we dropped the letter in the flame. We watched it burn, our eyes following the wisps of smoke as they twisted toward heaven.

I don't believe you wrote that letter in the clairvoyant's parlor. I don't believe you're reading this. I don't know what to say. I don't want to write you ever again. I'm only writing you now because I can't keep myself from it. I can't bear to be the one to stop. I write to respect your memory, not to stir up mischief. I write, under the spell of sadness.

And it was through this coven of witches I learned of Madame LeFleur and her midnight séances. She didn't advertise in the newspapers, and she had no parlor in town. She snuck nightly onto the condemned stage still set for *Heart of the White City*, in the theater of the Grand Court, and she did all her seeing in the near dark.

The theater looked as if it had been abandoned in a mad rush, as if the audience had run away from the Ferris wheel as it had slipped off its axis and rolled into the aisle. The wheel now lay wrecked in the seats, leaning against a wall, creaking as it rocked. The paper flames of the fire that rose above the buildings still crinkled with the drafts that flowed through the theater. A train had jumped its tracks and into the orchestra pit. A gondola sat shipwrecked in the curve of the crescent moon that had fallen off its chains and down from the riggings to crash on the floorboards. But the buildings of the backdrop—all made of white stone—still stood as the theater fell down around them.

Madame LeFleur served as what they called an in-between—she would quiz the dead and perk her ears for their answers from the afterworld. People would bring to her the things their loved ones left behind, the ribbons and rings, the Bibles and poems, the windup toys, the tatted lace, the spectacles, the neckties, the snuff bottles, the tintypes.

These men and women, and children, would beg for any word, no matter how harsh or unwelcome, just as the men and the women of the farms had begged me. But Madame LeFleur was notorious for giving the living the dead's worst regards. Through Madame LeFleur, the dead rekindled old feuds once settled, confessed to love affairs, aired grievances, and revealed the secrets they'd taken to the grave.

I arrived at the theater only a minute before midnight, and I took a seat in the back as an organist pumped out funeral hymns. The organ's elaborate system of pipes reached to the domed roof, stopping just short of the hole the winter had made. Birds fluttered in and out, and wind blew in to lick the flames in the oil lamps that lined the foot of the stage. The lamps reminded me of the old theaters of Omaha, without electricity or gas, the ones I snuck into as a boy, where the saloon girls kicked their legs out from under their petticoats in the dim glow.

The audience was sparse. People alone, or in pairs, sat here and there in the dark. When the organist finished, Madame LeFleur took the stage without introduction, entering in a hooded cloak. She undid the clasp at her neck, took off the cloak, and draped it over the organist's outstretched arms. From where I sat, she was only a shadow, despite the lamplight.

From her very first words—"Let's burden the dead with our questions"—I recognized the gravel and bark of her voice. I even imagined I smelled her rotten-onion breath. I leaned forward.

I'd brought along August's opera glasses, and I now held them to my eyes. The woman stepped up to the edge of the stage and bent down to take a book a man handed up to her. The light played across her face, a mask of shadow and flicker. "I'll be damned," I mumbled. This Madame LeFleur was Mrs. Margaret, eye patch and all.

As the automaton on the midway, she'd barely moved, but as a medium she never stopped. She spent about an hour letting the phantoms go in and out of her. She paced and wrung her hands when possessed by a woman who fretted. She whistled and skipped when a little girl slipped in. She cursed and swore as she swaggered, finding the sea legs of a soldier shot in Cuba. She wept. She pointed fingers of accusation. She was even a dog once, dropping into a squat to howl at the moon.

When the séance was over, Mrs. Margaret lowered her shoulders into a slouch. "I can't do no more," she said. "Get your ghosts away from me." She left the stage, stepping into the wings, as the organist returned to blow out the flames of the lamps. Everyone left, but I lingered out front in the frozen night, the air like glass. Mrs. Margaret stepped past me, huddled in her cloak, and she paid me no notice until I said her name.

She stopped, paused. She turned to me, shaking her head.

She said, "You're the bad penny that keeps turning up."

"I could say the same of you," I said.

She was like a chimney spouting smoke, vapor puffing up out of her with her heavy, labored breaths. I could hear a few squeaks of a wheeze, like from a slow accordion.

"I already grieved over you," she said, smiling. "I figured you for dead. I heard you were in the balloon that got away."

I slapped my left leg. "Escaped with nary a limp," I said. "I can't be killed, even when they drop me out of the clouds. I heard *you* went to Pennsylvania."

"You heard I was *sent* to Pennsylvania, maybe," she said. "When you don't get on the train, the ticket takes you nowhere."

"Why didn't you go?"

She shrugged. "I can't leave Doxie here," she said, "even if she ain't mine. Even if I ain't welcome in the house. I promised Cecily as she breathed her last that I'd look after Doxie, and I'll do it until I'm dead. I'll always look after her even if I can't never see her."

"Wish I could work up an ounce of sympathy for you," I said.

She hawked up some phlegm and spat on the bricks. "You pity me for even a second and I'll take a pig snouter to your jiggling bone," she said, nodding at my crotch.

"It's probably talk like that that got you tossed out on your ear," I said.

"When I'm in among a *decent* lot, I'm sweet as sugar back to belly," she said. She gathered her hood tighter at her throat. She sighed, looked up at the moon. Her voice was wet. "Does anybody up at that house even know when the baby's birthday is? She hasn't had one yet." She sniffled. "She's not some mutt they saved from an alley, you know." She looked back to me. "How'd you know it was me doing these séances?"

"I didn't," I said. "Why would I go *looking* for you? I came looking for help."

"You're one of *them*?" she said, nodding her head toward the theater, toward the audience that wasn't there anymore.

My throat had gone sore, and I could only barely croak my words. "I have the same ghost you do."

She turned and walked away. "There's a saloon nearby that's open to all hours," she said without looking back. "It has a stove in the corner."

I TOLD MRS. MARGARET everything. I told her about the letters, and about Pearl. I told her I didn't know what to believe anymore.

We weren't the only lost souls in the joint. Others had braved the killer chill of the night to warm their bones with liquor. "Is there any truth to what you do on the stage?" I said.

"No," Mrs. Margaret said. "Before we started up on the fair circuit, the Silk & Sawdust Players was legitimate theater. I'm a classically trained actress. I've been in *Romeo and Juliet*. I played the nurse."

I told her about the farm, and the Emerald Cathedral, and my own performance as an oracle. "I only communed with their dead because they begged for it," I said.

"The century's about to turn," she said. "There's a lot of call for soothsaying. If we didn't do it, somebody else would, and they'd be the ones to get the coin." The boiled whiskey in her copper cup burned her mouth, so she blew on it. The sourness had somehow left her breath and I could have sworn it'd gone pleasant. Her breath smelled of spice cake hot from the baker. "And what do *we* know?" she said. "Maybe the spirits guide our tongues when we lie."

I leaned forward to whisper, though no one in the saloon was listening to us. "Do you think he killed her?" I said.

Mrs. Margaret took another drink. She put the cup down and folded her hands, prayerlike. She watched the skin of her hands as she rubbed at the wrinkles with her thumbs. She nodded. "Yes," she said. "But I don't think he wanted her to die."

"He thought he was healing her with all that poison?" I said, incredulous. "It was an accident?"

She shook her head. "It wasn't an accident," she said.

I had finished my drink, so I reached across for hers. I took a swallow, but the cheap burn of it made me even more peevish. "Why do I bother asking you anything?" I said. "What would you know about it?"

But Mrs. Margaret remained patient with me. I think she was pleased to have an audience for her tale of intrigue. "He wanted her *weak*, but he didn't want her *dead*," she said, speaking slow. "He wanted to keep her just a little bit sick so he could keep saving her. He wanted to keep her at the brink, keep her needing him, so that he could rescue her with some new doctor or drug. He was addicted to her salvation."

"No," I said, but I didn't doubt Mrs. Margaret's theories. But the closer I got to the truth of it all, the more the thought of Cecily's murder terrified me. I couldn't stomach it. I could have saved her. We could have been together always.

"When you're rich, everything's a trifle," she said. "So what if he gives her a little extra pinch of headache? He takes it away eventually. So she's up all night because the moon's in her window; she'll sleep tomorrow, or the night after that. The rich invent their own morality. Especially a man like Wakefield. He thought he paid for his sins already. So he just sinned some more."

"I thought he just wanted to save her because he couldn't save the wife who died," I said. "Or did he kill that wife too?"

"He took his first wife to surgeons, Cecily told me," she said. "She had nerves in her eyes snipped. She had something cut out of her womb. It's all too grisly to speak of."

But we did speak of it, for much of the night. Speculation, mystery. It kept the dead from dying entirely. When you're angry, you grieve a little less.

"Would he ever hurt Doxie?" I said.

"When I lived up in the house," she said, "he didn't even know she was there. His neglect might be a blessing."

"In the letters," I said, "there's been mention of a room."

Mrs. Margaret looked at me, an eyebrow raised. "Yeah?" she said.

I shrugged. "She says she can hear Doxie crying on the other side of the wall. Or, that's what Pearl says, in the letters she writes as Cecily."

"When Cecily was at her sickest," Mrs. Margaret said, "she spent time in a room in the upstairs. It was next to Doxie's."

"She had her own bedroom?" I said, somewhat hoping.

"No," she said. "It was where she looked after her hobbies. She said she kept her scrapbooks in there. She pasted her cigarette cards in the pages of one. In another one she pasted newspaper clippings about the Fair. But she kept the room locked. There was only one key. A skeleton key wouldn't even work in it. She insisted, when she married Wakefield, that he give her one room all to herself."

"In Pearl's mind, Cecily's in a room she can't get out of," I said. We sat without talking. I listened close to the wind just to be grateful I wasn't out in it. "How do we get Doxie away?" I said.

"There's no way," she said. "He might not care about her, but he needs her. He covets the attention of a man suffering. He's already been in the newspapers three times with our little girl, showing her off, so they can all talk about how lucky the little urchin is. She's already a legend—she's just like the Little Match Girl, but with a happy ending." She paused. "But if I can get back in there, I can look after things. You need to get Pearl to have a séance up at the house."

"Nobody up there's going to fall for your Madame LeFleur act," I said.

"Not Madame LeFleur," she said. "You get an actress who could use some work. We pay her to say what we want her to say."

"What do we want her to say?"

"That Cecily wants her friends around her," she said. "That she wants Doxie to get to know us. She wants us around Doxie all the time. If the clairvoyant is convincing, Wakefield will fall for it. He believes in ghosts because that's all he's got. And he needs forgiveness, I'm guessing, no matter what kinds of laws he lives by."

"Every time I conspire with you," I said, "it ends with me getting strangled. I'm not interested."

Mrs. Margaret pushed up her sleeve and wiggled her fat wrist around, showing off the bracelet with the scent bottle I'd given Cecily the day of the president's parade. When I reached out for it, she snatched her hand back and pulled her sleeve down. "You be a good little kitty," she said, "and I'll give it to you. And I'll give you other things too. Wakefield fired me because he caught me taking things of Cecily's after she died. But I wasn't stealing. She would've wanted me to have them. And on the day he fired me, I snuck away with her jewelry box. And this pretty thing was in it." She let the abalone shell of the scent bottle shimmer in the fire from the stove. "And a few other odds and ends of interest."

"Like what else?" I said.

"Like a key," she said. "That might open a door."

IN THE MIDDLE of the night, a few whiskeys in, the plot had seemed foolproof. In the light of day I was certain of doom. I wanted nothing more than to wrestle myself from another of Mrs. Margaret's death grips. But it was actually Doxie's grip that held me, and I'd been in it ever since she'd first wrapped her fingers around my thumb.

All the gears of the scheme were clicking along by afternoon. The only actress in the city of Omaha who I knew I could trust was Phoebe St. James, from the burlesque at the Empress Opera House. It'd been nearly a year since I'd seen her. I thought she'd left town, just before the Fair, to act in an open-air theater that had been hacked into a patch of forest. She went there, somewhere east, every summer to play actresses in Russian plays. "All the best plays are about actresses," she would say. The theater consisted only of a stage built from the trees they'd felled. The audience sat on rows of stumps.

"I didn't go this summer," Phoebe said, when I tracked her down. It had been easy—she had a telephone, and her name was in the directory. "You didn't notice I wasn't gone, I guess."

She had a little cottage of her own, and it looked like you could lick it. Some of its bricks were pink, others were white. The shingles were yellow and rippled like waves of ribbon candy. The wallpaper was striped like peppermint. I sat in her parlor with my hat on my knee.

"I'm sorry I fell out of touch, Phoebe," I said. "I had a very . . . a very *complicated* summer. How'd you get such a fine house?"

"I met a soldier off to war," she said. She picked up sugar cubes with tiny ivory tongs, and she seemed to drop about ten of them into a teacup. "He fell in love with me after only one day. We woke a judge in the middle of the night to marry us. And my soldier left in the morning. His family was wealthy. They were furious. I can't say I blame them. I wouldn't want *my* son to marry an actress." She poured tea into the cup of sugar, and brought the sickening brew to me. I set the saucer on the knee that didn't have a hat on it.

"So I made do," she continued, "taking whatever work there was. I was paid by a horse thief to play the part of a reverend's wife one afternoon. He had me take a Bible, with saws hidden in the pages, to his partner in crime who was cooling his heels in jail. I was so convincing, no one even suspected me when he cut his way out. Oh, and maybe you heard of Dizzy Daisy, who thieved on the midway? *Watch out for Dizzy Daisy?* No? I would pretend to faint from the heat, and the gentlemen who caught me would be relieved of their wallets and watches."

"You must've done a swift business," I said, studying the pretty swoop of the gold handle of the teacup.

"Not really," she said. She cut through a coconut cake with a silver-handled knife. "I got my money from yellow fever. My soldier died from it."

"Oh, Phoebe," I said.

"And the family paid me well to go away," she said. She picked up a flake of coconut and put it on her tongue. "They paid me to not have his name anymore. They paid me not to wear black and not to grieve. They paid me not to be a widow. And so I don't grieve, and I'm not a widow." She held out to me my slice of cake, and when I went to take the plate, my hat tumbled from my knee. I sat there, holding the saucer on my one knee with my one hand, and the cake plate on my other knee with my other hand. But I wasn't hungry for cake or thirsty for tea, so it didn't much matter that I couldn't lift a finger.

As a cuckoo clock clucked the hour, its little doors snapping open and shut, Phoebe said, "So I guess my summer was *complicated* too."

I told Phoebe of my own loss, and I think she took some comfort in it, in knowing that love and death had touched us both. The polite state of shock she'd seemed to be in as she'd served the cake and tea began to lift, and it was just us again, like always before, Ferret and Feeb, backstage at the Empress. We moved to the music room and sat slouched on the sofa, her arms wrapped around mine, her cheek on my shoulder.

"I'll be Madam Seymour," she said, thrilling to my scheme. "Madam Seymour sees more."

THE WAKEFIELD HOUSE, even though so far up the hill, had a telephone now. I called the house from Rosie's den. I spoke to Pearl about Madam Seymour.

"I've been to every parlor in the city," I said. "Madam Seymour's the finest."

"I'll see what Billy says," Pearl said. "I'll ask him this evening over brandy."

"No," I said. "*Tonight* must be the séance. Madam Seymour is impatient. She says Cecily needs us there. All of us. She needs all her friends with her." Pearl said nothing. I listened for her voice in the crackling of noise on the line. *I knew this wouldn't work*, I thought. My heart sped, my stomach turned. We'd failed. *Just help us*, I wanted to plead. Instead, I said, "Pearl? Don't you believe in Cecily's ghost? Has this all been a fraud? Pearl? Tell me. Has this all been a fraud?"

Pearl said, "I'll ring back in an hour."

And in an hour she called with an invitation to summon ghosts in the parlor. But Wakefield was not happy, she said, and he'd have no part in it. "I had to beg him, Ferret," she said. "I broke down in tears."

By evening, we had rented a coach and driver, and had gathered our friends. August ran a stick of charcoal around Phoebe's eyes, painting exotic sweeps. He plummed her lips purple with some kind of rouge and he got her lashes to sparkle with silvery dust. She wore a lace shawl over her head. The six of us crammed ourselves into the coach, with August, Phoebe, and me sharing one bench. Across from us, Rosie and Mrs. Margaret took up all of a seat, so Josephine sat on Rosie's lap.

The weather worsened, growing as wet and cold as it had on the day of Cecily's funeral. The sky was just as stark-white. Maybe *we* were the ones who weren't real, caught up in a dead woman's dream.

Mrs. Margaret had given me the key to the secret room, and I held it tight in my fist. I was going to the house to open a door. It kept me anchored, this piece of iron.

WHEN WE ARRIVED, Pearl ushered us into the parlor, the same parlor where Cecily had laid in her open-lidded coffin on the day of her memorial. Servants rushed in and out, not only with extra chairs to bring to the table but with decanters of wine and cut glass bowls of candied fruit. They brought in cakes and pies and plates of marrow on toast. They brought us mutton puffs, boiled sweetbreads, and oysters wrapped in bacon. "This was the best we could do on short notice," said the head cook, a stout woman they called Lady, as she stood in the parlor and worried.

"You shouldn't have brought out anything at all," Pearl said, scratching at the back of her head. "This isn't a party."

Rosie popped the cork on a bottle of champagne and insisted the servants sit with us. "Cecily needs her people," he said. The evening was like Christmas, with its snow at the window and the servants carrying in suet pudding and macaroon custard. With some coaxing the maids and the butlers, and even old Morearty, consented to a splash of the wine. Pearl stood at the doorway, gnawing a thumbnail, refusing all drink.

Phoebe, as Madam Seymour, moved around the room with her eyes shut, wiggling her fingers in the air in front of her face like she was feeling for cobwebs in her path. "There is a room that is locked," she said, in an accent thick with fraud. *"Zere eees a vroom zat eees lok-ka-da."*

Pearl stepped forward. "Yes," she said, tilting her head. "At the top of the stairs. There's a room." I felt a pang of guilt seeing Pearl so curious. I nearly stepped forward to confess, to hold the key out to her. Pearl's deception—her possession, her letters—seemed somehow less dishonest than mine. This burlesque of ours, this séance, seemed a crooked act. Poor, gentle Pearl had only wanted connection. In my foolishness, I started to speak, to apologize for all of us, for drinking and dancing on Cecily's grave. But Mrs. Margaret elbowed me in the ribs and nodded her head, happy to see Pearl so easily fooled.

"Doxie's birthday's in April," Mrs. Margaret whispered in my ear. "I didn't think I'd get to spend it with her." She began to weep a little and held her handkerchief to her eye.

"Don't eat the calf in the cow's belly," I said. "You're getting ahead of yourself."

Madam Seymour opened and closed her hands. "Someone has the key in their fist," she said. *Some-vun az ze key in zere vist.*

Everyone held their hands out, palms up, even all the servants. They all looked around, looking for the hand with the key. "Ferret," Pearl said.

Pearl snatched the key from my hand and walked quickly to the stairs. We all followed, and we surrounded her in the narrow hall. The key fit through the keyhole, but it would only jiggle around in the lock, and the knob wouldn't turn. She tried and tried, until finally Morearty stepped forward to take the key from her. "The locks in the house can be fussy," he said. He put the key in and looked up and off, as if divining his way through the lock's twists and turns. We stilled our breaths and waited.

When it became clear that the old man could not unlock the door either, Rosie took him gently by the shoulders and led him out of the way. We all suspected what Rosie was up to as he pressed his palms against the door, testing for give. We stepped back, to allow him room. He rammed into the door, leading with his shoulder, shaking the whole house, it seemed. A picture fell off the wall. A hall lamp flickered and went out. But the door didn't open. Rosie struck again, this time harder, knocking all breath from his lungs with a loud oomph. He slammed into the door a few more times, until he was clearly in great pain, and Josephine came forward to beg him to stop.

"Is the door bricked up, for God's sake?" Rosie said.

I slipped away from the others and into Doxie's room. The room was dark, and her crib was empty. I walked to the window and looked out into the backyard, and the gardens, where the cyclone had spun Cecily up from the ground and into the rosebushes. At the edge of the yard was a child's house I hadn't noticed before, a playhouse painted bright blue, like a box of sky against the bone-gray of winter. A light was on inside.

WHEN WE'D GIVEN UP on the door, we all returned to the parlor where Madam Seymour suddenly doubled over, clutching at her womb. "The child," she said. "Where's the child?"

"She's playing with the maid's little girl downstairs," Pearl said.

"Fetch her," the psychic said. "Cecily wants her among us."

Pearl began gnawing at her thumbnail again. "I don't think that . . ."

Madam Seymour bellowed as if gutshot, bending over even more. "*Pleeeeeease*," she said, with a low growl. Pearl rushed to the back stairs that led to the servants' quarters.

While she was gone, I walked down the hall to the conservatory that led out into the garden. I stepped through the French doors and followed a snow-dusted lane of stone. When I reached the playhouse, I ducked my head around the gingerbread woodwork of the doorway's eaves to let myself in. Wakefield, in a fur coat, sat hunched over a carpentry bench, the top of it scattered with the wheels and mechanisms of windup toys and trains. The room had a small hearth, and the little bit of heat from its fire struggled against the bitter cold. I closed the door behind me, and Wakefield looked up slowly, unsurprised by the noise.

"Ferret," he said in dull voice.

The carpentry bench took up much of the room, having been shoved in among the furnishings of a child's pretend life. I kept bumping my head against the low ceiling, so I took a seat on a wooden chair painted blue. Wakefield returned his attention to his bench, and a penny cart with a wooden horse. He picked up the horse of willow to whittle at its flank with a knife. "How goes the ghosting?" he said.

I shrugged. "Have you ever been to a séance?" I said.

He nodded. "Many séances," he said. "Many, many, many. But all my ghosts are punishing. They won't speak to me."

"Cecily seems to have some things to say," I said.

"I'm skeptical," he said.

"There's a locked room," I said.

"Yes," he said.

"I'd like to unlock it."

"No."

"I just think that Cecily—"

"*No!*" Wakefield said. He stabbed the point of the knife into the wood of the bench, and left the knife to stand there. He covered his face with his hand, then pushed his hand back through his hair. He took a deep breath and said, "That room is something between Cecily and me only."

A gust of wind knocked against the house and blew so harshly, so firmly, it seemed it'd blow the walls over. A draft worked in from somewhere, playing with the fire and rattling the paintbrushes in the jar on the bench. And just at my back, I heard the familiar tapping of shoes against the wall. I turned to see a puppet much like Oscar hanging from his collar by a hook. But I knew it wasn't him. This dummy's face was unmarred by dents or chips. His suit looked new and he wasn't missing a single finger.

I reached up to touch the dummy's hand. "Could this be Oscar?" I said.

Wakefield turned. "No," he said. He then reached for a box on his bench—a splintered crate with oranges painted on. He pulled it down on its side, and my dummy spilled out, grotesque, stripped naked, plucked apart, dead. The door to his chest had been ripped off its hinges, and he'd been hollowed out, robbed of all his tricks and gimmicks.

I fantasized picking up that knife from the bench and stabbing it into Wakefield's throat. But I had no one to blame but myself for the damage done to my favorite toy. I'd taken Wakefield's money.

"Did you know he could do this?" Wakefield said, taking his dummy from the wall and propping it on his knee. He tugged a string, lifted the dummy's hand, and a fountain of silver sparks flew up like from the wick of a Roman candle. Its whistle was shrill, and I plugged my ears with my fingers. The show finished with a pop, and feathers flew like from a shot bird.

"Yeah," I said. "I knew he could do that."

"Well, this one couldn't," he said, bouncing the doll on his knee. "Not until I fixed him with the pieces of Oscar. This one belonged to my boy. My boy, Sylvester. He and I found the dummy at the world's fair in Chicago. The dummy was full of tricks then. Then it started to fall apart. Trick by trick by trick. The manufacturer fled his debtors, and was nowhere to be found. The factory closed. There was no way to repair it, except to gather up the parts of the dummies that somehow hadn't collapsed. After Sylvester died, I did everything I could to put old Humpty back together again. I contacted ventriloquists around the world, and magicians' clubs. I contacted antique shops, and doll hospitals. It was a needle in a haystack, it seemed. So when I saw you on the midway, it was a miracle. Here the doll was, right in my own town. It was as if Sylvester was trying to speak to me after all."

"So what now?" I said. "What good is it, anyway?" I tried to sound cynical, but my teeth rattled from the cold.

He looked at me. He squinted. "That's right," he said. "You don't know about the voice box."

"I know about it," I said. "It's nothing special. He doesn't say anything interesting."

He worked his fingers back behind the dummy's head, flipped the switch, and the dummy spoke in a voice I hadn't heard before. The voice box crackled with noise, and turned the voice to mush. But it was clearly the sound of a child reading aloud.

I couldn't make out all the boy's mumbled words, but I knew the rhyme from my own youth—a tale about a little lad who got a little wife, a wife who wouldn't stay within. He wheeled her in a wheelbarrow until the wheelbarrow broke. The wife took a fall. "That put an end to the wheelbarrow, little wife, and all."

The boy had had to read in a rush, to fit all the rhyme in. Even so, his recording stopped halfway through the last word, *all* left to echo with only its *ah*, the *l*'s lost to time.

"I'm not cut out for murder," he said, "but I might have gunned you down in the street to steal your doll." He placed the dummy on the bench, on its back. "My boy read the poem into a horn at the world's fair," Wakefield said. "Into a machine that made a tiny wax cylinder." He sighed, touching tenderly at the dummy's throat. "Smaller than a chicken-wing bone. When the dummy's phonograph quit, it took his voice with it. The cylinder wouldn't work in anything else. I hired engineers. I called Edison himself. No one could fix it. No one knew how it could ever have worked to begin with."

"What happens when this voice box quits too?" I said. I meant to be cruel. It seemed it'd be a blessing and a curse to have his dead son's voice always at the tip of that dummy's tongue.

He looked at me with shock, as if such a thing hadn't occurred to him, as if I'd stabbed him after all. He started to speak, but stayed silent, and he turned to again hunch over the bench. He picked up a wood locomotive and scratched a square of sandpaper at its edges.

"I suppose you think you're the only one she visits," he said.

"What? Who?"

"Her ghost," he said. "You think the ghost is all yours, I suppose." He put the sandpaper aside and put a jeweler's loupe to his eye. He cowered lower over the locomotive to tinker more, taking a screwdriver to it. "I loved her, and she loved me," he said. "Invent all the fictions you want. Make me as evil as you can. But it was me she needed as she fell ill. And it's my house she haunts."

My teeth were rattling more, and my voice shook. "But you didn't save her," I said.

"I saved her from *you*," he said. "It was your poverty that killed her. The way you lived. The dirty water you drank. The food you ate." He looked up from the train but stared at the wall ahead of him as his voice rose. "And are you so stupid as to think I don't know about the Chinese doctor? How would I not know something like that? Do I seem a man who is easily fooled?" He slammed the toy train against the bench, sending a few of its gears spinning away. *"Do you think I'm a fool?"* he shouted.

And he would kill me next, I thought. In all my daydreams of vengeance, he fell at my hands. But I hadn't expected this. He hated me as much as I hated him.

I stepped forward and Wakefield put his hand on the handle of the knife he'd jammed into the wood of the bench. It seemed he might mean to stick me with it, but, no, his hand was on the knife to keep me from taking it and cutting his throat. But I had no interest in the knife. I'd stepped to the bench to take Oscar back. I grabbed my doll by the neck and walked back into the cold.

I STEPPED FROM the little play cottage, ducking my head around the gingerbread again, and stood in the wind, my collar snapped up, my hands in fists, my fists deep in my coat pockets. Oscar was missing a few more of his fingers, but the metal hooks were still screwed into his wrists, so I was able to carry him on my back as I always had. The familiar weight of him, my spine of bone against his wooden one, consoled me.

In the house, I heard laughter. Down the hall, in the parlor, they'd quit with their séance, it seemed. They'd given up their ghost, which was just as well. I was desperate to leave.

I then heard the sound of what they found so funny. A child's squeals and hiccups. *Doxie.* My darling Doxie.

I hid at the doorway, around the corner, in the curtain, and watched. Mrs. Margaret kissed Doxie's neck and tickled her ribs, and Doxie threw her head back to giggle. Everyone swooned at the ring of it. They all sat around the table, the servants too, and they passed Doxie around, lifting her up, sweeping her away, swinging her. They cradled and rocked her. She loved it all and couldn't stop laughing.

Her fine, fair hair, which had grown so, and had curled into ringlets, had a little red to it now. It'd been so many months since I'd seen her last, her eyes were different, and her cheeks, and her chin. I could barely see the baby she'd been. And in her every gesture was the person she'd someday be—she had the charms of an actress. She had curiosity and amazement. She was filled with delight over every new discovery, and she discovered something new every second.

I was about to join them all, and to beg Doxie to let me hold her, when a hollow voice echoed down from up the stairs. It was a song being sung through a horn, it seemed. The voice, a woman's, shook and wavered, the music popped and skipped, and it sounded as if carried in through a distant window. I couldn't recognize a single word, but it was something from an opera, I was certain.

I followed the music upstairs, but once I reached the crooked hall of the second floor, the music seemed from somewhere else. It grew even fainter, and it seemed to be coming from the rooms I'd just passed. And the more I listened, the more it left me. I lifted my ear, cupped it with my hand. The opera I thought I was hearing fell apart, and the noise collected again into the rumble of a furnace and the whistle of wind.

I was about to return to the stairs, when I tapped a finger against the doorknob to Cecily's room. And something in just that little tip-tap made me think I should try the door one more time. I turned the knob, and felt the give. The door, somehow, had come unlocked.

43.

I PUSHED THE DOOR OPEN, into the room, and the rush of air stirred a small, white feather that had dropped on the floor. I closed the door behind me.

The room was nearly pitch-dark, with only a thin stick of moonlight coming in from between the closed drapes. I stepped slowly toward the window, my hands at my knees to save my kneecaps from bumping the corners of tables and chairs.

At the window, I parted the drapes. The moon was only a sliver away from full, and its light shone in, washing everything in a faint silver glow. I noticed swans in the pattern of the drapes—tiny swans lost among a design busy with plums and honeybees. I ran my finger along the curve of a swan's neck, touched by the sight of it and by the thought of Cecily standing at this window, seeing these swans every day. *Did you think of me then?* I wondered. I looked more closely at the swan, the bluish-white thread of the embroidery unraveling a little. Had Cecily stood here, right here, running her thumb along the swan too?

I could barely turn myself away from the swans, and from the notion to find each one, to count them all. Then I noticed a lamp on the table next to the window, so I reached to twist its switch. The brass base of the lamp was a swan too, the lamp's workings wired through the swan's bent neck.

And when I turned on the light, and I looked upon the room, I saw swans everywhere.

In a painting on the wall was a winter scene, a man and a woman bundled in fur, riding across the snow in a swan-shaped sleigh. And the wallpaper behind the painting was covered in swans swimming, every swan doubled, their reflections stretched along behind them. There were swans woven into the design of the rug on the floor, and swans in the plaster molding at the base of the chandelier overhead.

Though the sofa along the wall had no swans in its silk—it was pin-striped pink and blue—the pillows had swans on them and a peasant girl feeding them. I sat down and clutched a pillow to my chest.

This was the place she sat when she couldn't sleep.

The fact of her death stunned me just then, making my heart stumble, as if I'd only just been told of it. I felt so afraid for her. I trembled from the cold in the room. My teeth chattered again. I brought my hands to my face and tried to steady my breath. I tried to muffle the clack of my rattling teeth. I didn't want anyone to hear me. I didn't want anyone to come in and ask me to leave.

I thought of Wakefield down in his cottage. I thought of him telling me that this room was only his and hers. *It's not yours*, I wanted to tell him. *It's not yours. It's mine. And it's Cecily's. The swans belong to us.*

And I wept with such relief. No matter where she'd been, no matter where she'd gone, Cecily had been always with me.

OPEN ON THE TABLE in front of me was a scrapbook, its pages plastered with newspaper clippings about the Fair. It looked as if Cecily had only just stepped away. A clipping had been cemented, but not pressed against the page. There was a pair of scissors open, as if in midsnip, and an open jar of rubber cement, and a roller next to it.

Under the table was a stack of newspapers saved from over the summer and fall.

And tucked beneath a doily of lace, as if hidden there, was a thin tin box, about the size of my thumb, in the shape of a book. *Omaha World's Fair, 1898* was engraved on its cover, and when you pushed at a hinge, a drawer swung out from the inside of it. The hidden drawer of this hidden book held slips of paper, and on the paper, on every tiny page, was Cecily's handwriting again, but with the words so minuscule they were nearly impossible to read. I licked my fingertip so I could flip through, and I squinted.

A picture of an actress on his cigarette card, she'd written on one page. And beneath that: *He throws his voice.*

She'd written *the swan gondola* on the next page, and *They call him Ferret.* She wrote, *Shoes with a nail that clicks in the heel so I don't walk home in my stockings.* She wrote, *He carried Doxie.* She wrote about waltzing with me on wires, about the rose I turned from white to red, and the henna in her hair. Cecily had devoted the whole book to our summer, telling our story in snippets, in glimpses. *I keep this diary secret*, she wrote.

I thrust the box into my pocket, not wanting to risk having it out a second more, of getting caught with it, of having it taken from me. I'd never stolen anything more valuable in all my life. And the theft would inspire me. Before the night was over, I would take something even more precious.

LATER, whenever I thought of that room, I would remember even more swans, many that hadn't even been there at all. Had the ink pot been swan shaped, a pen tucked into its green-glass wings? I seemed to remember a teapot with a swan-neck spout and a teacup with a swan-neck handle. I would go through the next several years noticing every swan object I passed—and I passed many. The world was ridiculous with swans—a hat, a soup tureen, a pincushion, a flowerpot, a perfume bottle, a flask. A lap harp, a saltcellar, a candy dish. A porcelain figurine for your vanity, where you kept your rings slipped over a swan's fingerlike neck. I'd find myself collecting everything in my mind, in my memory, and it would all end up in that room.

I HEARD FOOTSTEPS on the stairs and I rushed to the lamp, treading lightly on the balls of my feet so as not to creak the floorboards. I turned off the light and closed the drapes and held my breath. It was Pearl, in the hall now, cooing at Doxie as she carried her to her bed.

Had anyone even noticed I'd wandered off? Standing in the dark, listening for Pearl to return to the stairs, I wondered how long I could live there, hidden in that room. Maybe there was a swan-shaped chamber pot. I could just empty it out the window. I could sneak from the room at midnight to eat from the icebox, my noises scaring them all, keeping them hidden under their bedsheets. Eventually they'd be so afraid, they would deny my existence, and I'd sit right down with them at their supper table and eat the food off their plates.

I wanted to turn on the light even at risk of getting caught. I wanted my brain swimming with swans. And what did it matter if Pearl knew I was there? She'd probably unlocked the room herself. I was her puppet, after all. From the moment she became Cecily's ghost, writing a dead woman's words, I'd fallen into step.

I listened to Pearl's silence, to her waiting in the hall, to her stillness. Soon enough, she would step in. And then what? What awful wails of grief came next?

I heard Pearl leave. I heard her steps on the stairs. And I heard Doxie on the other side of the wall, kicking her feet against the end of the crib.

AFTER SNEAKING FROM the room and into the hall, I stopped at Doxie's open door. She stood in her crib now, her wet eyes sparkling from the bit of moon that got in past her closed curtains. "Hey, love," I whispered. She bounced in her crib, and she held her arms up.

I walked over to her and I made a face to make her laugh, scrunching up my mug like a cranky old codger's. I tickled her under her arms, and she squealed.

"Muffle it, sis," I said, giving her a peck on the cheek. "Sh-sh-sh-sh-sh-sh." I put my thumb in her hand to let her squeeze it, for old time's sake. She brought her other hand to my mouth, to pull my lip. She dug her sharp little fingernails in, tearing at the dry skin. She then put her fingers all the way inside my mouth, and hooked them around my teeth. I pretended to eat them, smacking my chops with my tongue. She laughed some more.

Doxie then brought both her hands to my neck, leaning forward to wrap her arms around me, trying to climb me, to get up and out of the crib.

"Whatever you say, darling," I said, and I lifted her and tucked her into the crook of my arm. We waltzed around the room, but the dancing didn't please her. She began to whine, leaning toward the doorway, reaching out. "Doxie, Doxie, Dox, Dox, Dox," I sang, rocking her in rhythm, yet still she fussed.

I looked around the room for something to distract her. I picked up her little plush tam-o'-shanter of pale blue. When I put it on her head, I thought she might toss it right off. But she pulled it on tighter. She then reached toward the wardrobe, to where her coat hung from the knob. She wiggled her fingers at it.

I felt my pulse speed up. I felt the sweat bead up on my brow and trickle its salt in my eye. Once the thought had entered my head—the thought of putting her in her coat and taking her away—I felt sick with it. I felt feverish.

I moved forward without thought. I didn't think how I'd get out of the house with her, or down the hill, or out of town. I didn't think at all.

I was Doxie's father. The only father who'd ever loved her.

I'd never been so afraid in my life. But I wasn't afraid of getting killed. I'd heard tell of men shot for taking babies from cribs, and though that worried me more than a little, it wasn't what frightened me most. I was afraid I didn't know right from wrong anymore. I heard Wakefield's voice in my head. As much as I hated him, his words rang true. What could I give a rich little girl but my poverty?

That was the good angel on my right shoulder talking. When the bad angel over on the left spoke up, he got all my attention. Doxie belonged with me, not in this necropolis. I'd give Doxie *such* a life. The rich girl she might be would envy the poor girl I'd make her into. We'd have an act, for one thing. I'd finally become a master ventriloquist, my lips as still as a corpse as my dummy did all the talking. I'd follow Mrs. Margaret's recipe for woodenness, draping Doxie's face with cheese-cloth and patting it with powder. I'd draw lines around her eyes to make her lids look hinged. I'd plop a ratty wig on her head. And she'd sit on my knee and pretend to be speaking with my voice, a lively contraption of strings and joints.

I set Doxie on a stool and put on her coat. I then wrapped her in a quilt and held her close. I put my lips to her ears as I walked down the stairs. "Sh-sh-sh-sh," I said, over and over, to keep her hushed. She played with Oscar's fingers at my throat. I even took off my shoes and stuck one in each of my back pockets, so I could slip across the floor in stocking feet.

Doxie conspired with me nicely. "Sh-sh-sh-sh," she said to me too, into my ear.

They'd drawn closed the curtain at the doorway to the parlor and I could hear the faint ruckus of the séance resuming—it seemed the table might be trembling. I heard Phoebe, with her awful accent, calling for Cecily. *Seeeee-seeeee-leeeee.*

And I stepped out the door and right to the coach that had brought us up the hill. The driver sat inside drinking something brown from a bottle. "Get me out of here!" I barked, and he jumped up and corked his bottle. "To the city!" He took his place at the reins, and we jolted and stuttered forward.

I sat perched on the edge of the bench, careful not to bust up Oscar any more than he'd already been. The ride seemed endless, even just to get to the end of the winding road of the orchard. The gate to the estate had fallen off its hinges in the terrible winter, and it now lay in the bushes next to the wall, warping from its own weight. We rode on through, and picked up speed on the road down the hill. Doxie fell fascinated with the tassels of the curtain at the coach window, and she watched them swing, and she played with the fringe.

"Where can we hide until we can sneak out of town?" I asked her. They would notice her gone soon enough, if they hadn't already— Pearl and the servants could have easily heard the horse's hooves and the creak of the coach as we'd pulled away. For all I knew, the police were not far off. Maybe there was even a new ballad being sung in some saloon—"Wakefield's Latest Heartbreak." Already I could be the worst there ever was, as far as the rest of the world was concerned.

I would direct the driver to take me to August's. There I could take a loan from the cash register and pay the driver to keep mum about where he dropped me off. And Doxie and I would hide in the basement.

But then I began to worry, and when I began to worry, I became all the more befuddled. August's might be the first place they looked, and I hated the idea of dragging him down with me. *The Fair*, I thought. We'd find a place at the Fair. We could build ourselves a yurt in a corner of an exhibit hall, and burn the broken columns of plaster and wood for heat. We'd have a crèche, with Doxie nestled in the straw of a fruit crate. It would do, until things quieted, and we'd make our way out to the Egan farm, to the places the maps didn't chart.

No. It was too cold to sleep outside. My mind stumbled over all kinds of rotten ideas. Seek the mercy of the evil nuns of St. Joseph's? Check into the smallpox hotel, where no one would come near?

The coach slowed before we even passed Wakefield's shuttered resort by the lake. It stopped. I was about to lean out and yell, when the door was pulled open, Doxie was snatched from my lap, and I was dragged to the ground and punched at the back of the neck. I couldn't tell if I was falling, or if I'd already hit the dirt. Everything up was down, and down was up, and all went black to the sound of Doxie crying.

44.

I WOKE IN A JAIL CELL ALONE, flat on my back on a moth-bitten blanket on the floor. Whoever had knocked me down had worked me over. There was pain in my ribs and in my neck, and both my eyes were swollen half-shut. I could feel the promise of a limp, like an itch, working up the leg I'd broken before.

"Stand up," a deputy yelped. "There's a lady present."

My skeleton felt to be without gristle, all bone against bone as I tried to move my joints.

"I said, *stand up*," he said, and he banged on the bars with a club. "You're not allowed any visitors, but I never could listen to a lady weep without getting my heart in a knot. So you show the poor thing some kindness. You tell her you're no good and that she needs to find a man on the *right* side of the law."

I put a finger and a thumb to my one eye to peel it open. On the other side of the bars, standing in the corridor was the deputy, a homely young wretch with arms as thin as a broomstick, and next to him was a woman in an old-fashioned dress of wine-colored velvet. The dress was fat and frilly, the skirt of it looped and draped. There was fringe and tassel and buttons of gold. The deputy flirted, a sneer on his face, as he pushed a lock of the lady's hair back behind her ear.

But this was no lady. I would know August Sweetbriar anywhere, even with my blinkers knocked and bruised.

"Is it today?" I said, my voice hoarse and sore in my throat. "Or tomorrow?" The cell was all brick, with no window.

"Is *what* today or tomorrow?" August said.

"Now," I said. "Is *now* today or tomorrow?" I sat up on the blanket and pressed my fingers at the pain in my temples.

"It's the morning after yesterday," August said. He didn't disguise his voice much—he gave his words a little more breath and music than he might have otherwise, and a proper-sounding lilt and lift. *Moooorning . . . yistir-dee . . .* He clutched his handkerchief at his chest and feigned a tearful sigh that shook his breath. "Pearl was nervous all evening long, wondering where you'd gone off to," he said. "She figured you were snooping through all the rooms. We heard the coach's wheels during the séance, and she flapped around like a hen. She ran upstairs, saw Doxie was gone. She went out for Wakefield, and he came into the house in a rage. He tossed the table over. He threw us all out. We had to walk down to the streetcar, in the wretched chill, to take it back to town."

"How's Doxie?" I said. I brought myself to my feet, pressing my hands against the wall, climbing my way up, and feeling every bone snap into place with a stab.

"We didn't see her again," August said.

I took a few steps toward the bars of my cage, but the deputy banged the metal again. "You stay where you are," he said. "And keep your hands back. They make guns so tiny they can fit in a lady's ring. A blade can be passed in a handshake. And then you use that blade to cut the vein in my wrist when I'm doing something kind for you, like passing you a cup of water. No, sir," he said, "I know all your cowardly ways."

At that, August burst into phony sobs he buried in his hankie, and the deputy tut-tutted, patting his shoulder. Though the deputy was at least a head shorter than August, August fell into the deputy's arms. The deputy's sneer returned, and I could tell he was pleased to fondle my lady friend in front of my eyes. But for all the deputy's molestation—petting August's side, close to his padded breast, and stroking his back down low and lower and lower still, until he was rubbing August's ass beneath the bustle—he didn't catch on to August's disguise. The deputy even nuzzled August's wig and didn't smell the dead yak in it.

The deputy also didn't notice August fiddling with the keys in the iron ring hooked to his belt loop. As August sobbed into the deputy's collar, he worked his arm around the deputy's back, and spidered his fingers over all six keys, testing their lengths and points, determining the one most likely to open the cell door. When his fingers landed on the one he wanted, he sobbed louder, right into the deputy's ear so he wouldn't hear the jinglejangle as he slipped the key off the ring and into his palm.

I was curious as to what would happen next—the whole exploit seemed like something right out of the dime novels August sold in the shop—some prairie tale of Deadwood Dick. *Omaha Sweetbriar; or, The Damsel's Got a Trick Up Her Skirts.*

August wrapped the key in his hankie as he pulled himself from the deputy's arms.

"Can't I at least kiss Ferret good-bye?" he said. The deputy worked his jaw around, thinking. "You can hold my hands behind my back," August said. "I'll just lean in. We'll only touch lips."

"Only if you give *me* a little kiss too," the deputy said, with a pout. "I've been awfully sweet to you, you know."

"And you have," August said, and he puckered up. The deputy leaped for it, grabbing the back of August's head with one hand and pressing his lips hard against his. I heard their teeth knock together. It looked as if the deputy had never kissed a woman properly in all his life.

When the deputy finished with a *smack*, August leaned back and held his hand to his own jaw, wiggling it around on its hinges, working the feeling back in. And while the deputy seemed to be waiting for some kind of compliment, August returned to his sobbing, lowering his face into his hankie. It was then that August fed himself the key.

"I'll show you how it's done, pip-squeak," I told the deputy, and I leaned forward for my kiss. August leaned in too. He gave me a wink, and I winked back. We touched lips. I opened my mouth, and he opened his, and I waited for the key. But the key didn't come. He kissed tenderly, and I felt a whimper tremble his lips, and felt the breath of a sigh. I would let my friend have his kiss. And I kissed back. He just kept kissing me, his keyless tongue sliding around with mine. Finally, I tapped my tongue against his teeth to let him know I was impatient. Still no key. I went in for it myself, my tongue darting around his, working the key away from where it was tucked into the inside of his cheek. I'd only just licked it into my own mouth when the deputy pulled August away with a jerk.

"Enough violation," the deputy said. He took August by the arm and escorted him down the short hall and around the corner, to where the office was. I sat on the floor, the key in my hand, wondering what good it was. I contemplated the particulars of my escape as the deputy continued to flirt at his desk. I heard some clucking and cooing, and the clinking of glasses. I heard him do a ventriloquism act for August, telling jokes with Oscar on his knee. I heard August leave. Ten minutes later came a crashing of glass and the bang of a chair falling over.

I didn't know the deputy's name. "Kid," I called out. No answer. "Hey, kid."

I reached my hand around to the lock and stuck the key in the keyhole, half expecting August to have lifted the wrong one from the ring. At first I could feel it not fitting, tumbling inside like the key in the lock to the room with the swans. But fit it did, and out I was. One of the benefits of being an outlaw is you have outlaws for friends— friends who know their way around a jailer's collection of bones.

I crept around the corner into the office. The deputy was passed out on the floor, a glass and a bottle of whiskey broken at his side. August had put all his talents to work for me—he'd flashed the drag, fingered the key, and played chemist, dropping some sleeping potion in the boy's liquor. Poor Oscar hung from a hook by the door. I took him into my arms and stepped right out of my prison, into the street. I walked deeper into the city, and I moved among the men and women going about their guiltless lives.

45.

Ａ UGUST SAT AT HIS VANITY, his wig on the floor. He still wore
his dress, but he'd unbuttoned the back and the dress hung on
him limply.

"Oh, Ferret," he said when I walked in. "Wasn't I wonderful?"

"Why didn't you give him the knockout drug *first*?" I said. I paced
as I undressed, dropping my ripped jacket and shirt to the floor, and
kicking off my shoes. On the walk back, I'd worked myself into a
panic, worrying over all the ways everything could've gone wrong. "It
would've been easier. You could've knocked him out, and there'd have
been no risk of getting the wrong key."

August sighed. "You're such a stickler for plot," he said. "He
wouldn't trust me at first. I'd brought along a little breakfast of doughnuts and tea, but he refused to let me see you. So I offered *him* the
doughnuts and tea, and then some whiskey, but he wouldn't touch any
of it. So I cried and cried, and I wouldn't stop until he let me see you.
And when I let him kiss me in front of you, he sensed I was a bit of a
cotton top. So he agreed to some whiskey before I left." He uncorked a
bottle and dampened his hankie with some sharp-smelling unguent.
He came to me to dab the medicine at the undersides of my eyes.

"Cotton top?" I said.

"Respectable in appearance but cheap beneath it all," he said. "Like stockings of cotton with silk at the feet."

"He don't know the half of it," I said. August helped me pack my carpetbag, folding some clothes, knotting up some socks, tucking in a bottle of booze and a slim tin of Turkish cigarettes. I stuck in the morning's newspaper—the front page ran an artist's sketch of me sneaking from the Wakefield house with Doxie in my arms. We'd made the paper, me and my girl, and it wasn't a bad likeness of either one of us. With a gasp, I remembered the little tin book I'd taken from Cecily's room, and I stuck my hand in my pocket. I felt such relief when I felt the book still there.

I suspected I'd make the evening paper too, and probably the next day's edition, and the day's after that, for a week or so, until somebody cut somebody's throat or something equally awful happened. The *Omaha Bee* loved to pile on the agony, to turn a common man's mistakes into vaudeville. The tattered little newsboys would get a nice boost in street sales when word of my escape hit the papers.

Rosie brought over his beaver fur coat, and it was so big that Oscar and I could easily disappear into it. The front-page illustration had made much of the wild curls of my hair, so I concealed them by shoving them up into Rosie's giant derby hat. I pulled the brim down past the tops of my ears.

I headed off to the Old Sisters Egan again, this time on foot, and this time with purpose.

I FOLLOWED THE PAVED STREET until it became a dirt road, and then followed the dirt road until it stopped in an empty lot. I crossed the lot into the next lot over, and into the next, until I was crossing the fields of the countryside, the city falling small behind me, the filthy clouds above the smelting works growing fainter with my every glance back. The frozen snow cracked like burnt sugar under my shoes. After dark, I lucked on an abandoned farmhouse with a stone hearth, but I didn't sleep a wink—every snap of the fire sounded like twigs and ice under the sneaky steps of wolves prowling.

I left the house before morning, and once the sun came up we finally got an inch of spring. I took off Rosie's fur coat and carried it over my arm until it got too heavy, and then I dragged it by its collar. I left the derby hat in a ditch.

When I reached the Platte River, I discovered I'd walked too far and was nowhere near the bridge. I did what I could to lessen my load, to make myself featherlight to cross the ice. I left the fur coat on the riverbank, and my carpetbag. I kept only the clothes on my back, and my shoes. And Oscar.

I closed my eyes as I crossed, to better sense the threat beneath my steps. It seemed I could feel the thump of fish bumping their heads as they swam. I could feel water rushing, the unlikely warmth of it coming up through the soles of my shoes. I thought of all the hot springs that couldn't save Cecily. I tried to give myself faith in magic. I tried to make myself vanish. I pictured myself up off the ground, in the hot-air balloon, no heavier than a cloud of ether. I kept my eyes closed, and every time I opened them, I seemed even farther from the shore.

Finally, I survived. I reached the other side, blew the ground a kiss, and soldiered on. I stayed terrified of the river and its thin ice, as I walked and walked, as if it might curl around and strike again, like a serpent. Or maybe it was more like a hunter in the woods, dodged once but still on your trail. I had no compass, no pioneer's instinct. To be only streetwise was to be unwise in everything that mattered.

The hunger in my gut reminded me I hadn't eaten anything since that coconut cake at Phoebe's, and that had been a few days before. August had packed me a little tin of eats when I'd left, but I hadn't looked inside. He'd said something about a pickled egg and some hog jerky. I entertained myself by inventing the feast I'd left behind. In my daydreaming, I sat down to a turkey leg and a mutton chop. Gingerbread. Johnnycake. Boiled fish. Lima beans. I sang it all in a hearty song and marched to the beat of it.

It was still daylight when I saw the little red spot of Hester and Emmaline's barn. But the sun went down and I still wasn't there. The terrible cold returned, needling up my pant legs and down my sleeves.

When I finally arrived, the Sisters Egan were eating a late supper. Hester threw a quilt over me fast, like dousing a fire, and Emmaline held a jelly jar of whiskey to my lips.

"You're blue," Emmaline said.

"I am," I said. She could see my sadness. It felt so good to be known so well. I began to cry.

Emmaline dabbed the tears on my cheeks with the cuff of her sleeve. She wiped my nose with her hankie. And Hester said, "She means your *color*. Your *skin* is blue." She covered me with another quilt, and led me to the stove.

They stayed up with me as I slept. They kept touching my head, hoping for warmth. I would wake every time to their whispers. "Feels a smidge warmer to me," I heard Emmaline say. Then Hester would test my temperature with the back of her hand at my cheek. "Wouldn't you say so?" Emmaline said. But Hester wouldn't. She'd offer no hope.

"We'll know he's better when we stop worrying," Hester said.

Hester fixed a pot of a chilblain's cure, to rub on my red, frozen feet. She recited the recipe, like reading a poem or singing a lyric, and I fell back to sleep to the sound of it—"oil of sweet almonds, lanoline, beeswax, Venice turpentine."

But in the morning I had to leave my place by the fire. Detectives had been by the day before—in my letters to Cecily's ghost, I'd spoken of the Sisters Egan. The detectives had been rude. They'd made Emmaline so sick, she'd spent the day in bed. We feared the detectives would be back, again and again, and they did return a few more times. But I was hiding within the Emerald Cathedral. I was able to burrow in like a pack rat, to build a nest of my own, at the risk of sending the whole shrine crumbling by shifting, unknotting, shoving. I hammered and dismantled. I lived in the narrow quarters of a monk. I mined my chamber with booby traps. If someone were to try to get in uninvited, they might be crucified, a nail in a foot, a hook in a hand. They might be knocked in the head with a hot-water bottle filled with cement. They might be kicked in the groin with a steel-tipped boot on a spring.

I learned how to worm in and out without tripping any of my wires. It became instinct, my wriggling around the triggers.

Mr. Crowe once gave me a book about wolf boys; and when I'd been eight or nine, whenever I'd had a wish coming (from blowing a fallen eyelash off my fingertip or from seeing a newborn calf), I'd begged fate that I'd be snatched from the orphanage by wild dogs and kept in a cave in the country. Some nights in my bed, when I'd closed my eyes tight, I'd felt myself go lupine, my skin tingling with hairs sprouting on my cheeks. I had run my tongue over my teeth, certain the edges were sharper than before.

I lived now like the wolf boy I'd longed to be, leaving the barn only to squat in the dry creek and to piss in the patch of Russian thistle. The neighbors cooked, and they left their pots and casseroles at the foot of the shrine, like offerings to the beast. I gorged myself. I licked the pots clean and sucked the marrow from the bones. I worried my pants had shrunk, but they hadn't been washed for days. They didn't fit, because I was growing fat. I imagined myself getting too fat to fit through my tunnel.

Instead of leaving food at the door, Eulalie, the librarian, brought books. She brought novels at first, but I sent them back out with a note stuck in, requesting texts on spiritualism. She brought me back a stack of ghost stories, and I returned those unread too. *The* facts and fallacies *of spiritualism, please*, I wrote in my next note to her.

She brought me *The Spirit World Unmasked* and *Spiritualism and Nervous Derangement*. I read each one three times, by the light of a lantern, writing page numbers on my hand and observations on my cuffs and sleeves. I wrote names on my trousers. *Madame Blavatsky, Eusapia Palladino, Annie Eva Fay.*

I didn't quite know at first what I was looking for. But I came to realize I wanted to learn all the tricks, so I could convince myself I'd not been tricked at all. I'd not been fooled by fishing line, by a hankie made to float and wave farewell, by a self-squeezing accordion playing a sad polka behind a closet door. I read the books so I could dismiss their explanations.

And now that the letters from Cecily had stopped, I considered her presence in everything else around me. In my hovel, I had much time to watch the things that didn't move. I lay back on my mattress situated in the shell of a broken grand piano, and studied the rusty spigot, waiting for a tear to drop. I caught sight of her step in a peg leg, the rise and fall of her breath in the breasts of a corset form.

I LIVED IN the Emerald Cathedral for two weeks, until the manhunt was called off with little fanfare. I was no threat, it seemed. There was no longer any warrant for my arrest. Wakefield, always the gentleman, would not have me hanged after all.

I liked to think he was afraid of me, that he was scared of ghosts and of retribution. He could've killed me a thousand times over, but he feared what I'd do when I was dead. Once I was a phantom, there'd be no end to the grief I could give him.

Though I moved back into the house, I rarely left the farm. I became a deadbeat nephew, not even lifting my head from my book to eat. I'd sit at the kitchen table, a book in one hand, a fork in the other, to the gentle annoyance of the sisters.

Hester said, "Who knew this rabid tomcat would cook up so good?"

Emmaline said, "Ferret, don't you love it with the mouse droppings baked right in with the rat gizzards?"

"Mm-hm," I said.

Eulalie tracked down books for me, and pamphlets and articles, borrowing them from other libraries and ordering them from publishers. And August sent some from his bookshop, along with long florid letters, mostly in defense of his own psychic, Mrs. Bertha Long, who helped him dig up memories of the lives he led before he was born. His favorite self was a spirit guide, a girl-boy who grew up to be a woman-man, whose kiss could promise a warrior victory.

August also sent a clipping—*Wakefield to Marry*, the headline read. It was to be a long engagement of nearly two years, the article said; the wedding was scheduled for December 31, 1900. On the night the century turned, Pearl would become the third Mrs. Wakefield. And I prayed she became the first Mrs. Wakefield to live.

Somehow, I wasn't shocked by the news. I did worry about Pearl, but I was pleased for Doxie. Pearl would be a good mother.

What somehow struck my heart harder was news of August's affection for a wounded soldier of the First Nebraska Regiment. Despite peace treaties and cease-fires, our wars still raged. A man named Maddox had been shot in the lungs by insurgents in Manila, and he returned to Omaha, and lived in a boardinghouse around the corner from August's shop. He visited the shop every day to read about the war he'd just fought. And he studied maps of the places he'd been, and books about the Philippines.

Stuck into the pages of a book August sent—*The Witchcraft of the Planchette*—was a letter he'd written me about his new friend, and how the friend had no family, and how this friend's best girl from before the war had married another. So August gave him a job in the shop. And the soldier lived there now, in a room in the basement. *He looks like how an artist might illustrate a soldier in a children's book*, August wrote, *innocent and plucky, with apple'd cheeks and little dimples when he smiles, and hair that won't stay combed. A forelock, a rooster's tail, a cowlick.* But the lad had seen some horrors, it seemed, and on the nights he couldn't sleep, he wandered up the stairs to August's apartment. August owned a penny-in-the-slot phonograph machine he'd bought from the back room of a saloon; its cylinders didn't play music, they played actors performing lewd limericks and dirty prayers, and the soldier never tired of its jokes about bedsprings in whorehouses and old ministers defiled. *And then he does sleep, the darling boy, but I don't. I sit up the whole* night watching him. *I've never seen anyone so at ease as this soldier when he sleeps in my bed.*

And from then on, August stopped begging me to return. *I'm happy about your new friend,* I wrote, *but if your new friend ever gets unfriendly, and breaks your heart, I'll become unfriendly too, and he'll wish he'd never left Manila.*

And August wrote, *Don't worry your pretty head. You were, and will always be, the only one who can break my heart.*

Spring and Summer

1899

46.

E ULALIE BROUGHT ME *Phantasms of the Living* and *The Death-Blow to Spiritualism* and *The Weakness of Muscle-Reading*, but only after she'd read them herself. When the library closed for the day, she would bring me the books and we'd have our discussion. Together, we became scholars of flimflam.

As winter thawed away in April, Eulalie and I sat on the back porch drinking the dandelion wine she'd jugged the summer before. After analyzing whether *The Report of the Akrakoff Commission on the Occult* proved skeptical enough, I went into the house for the letters I'd received from Cecily's ghost. I hadn't looked at them for weeks. As I explained to Eulalie how I'd fallen victim, how convincing the fraud had been, as I ran my fingertip along the slopes and slashes of Cecily's handwriting, I felt myself falling once again. I believed. Here were her words before me, familiar and bewildering. And beautiful, despite her poor penmanship. The crosses of Cecily's *t*'s had never, ever pierced the *t*'s at all. They had scattered around the words, like arrows on the lawn of an archery range.

Eulalie ran the tip of her pinky along the words too, commenting on the sharp points of the *m*'s and *n*'s, the curls of the *p*'s and *q*'s.

I took Eulalie's hand in mine, twining my fingers with hers.

I asked her to marry me. I was surprised by the question myself.

When she didn't answer, I asked again.

"I heard you the first time," she said.

"Then why won't you answer me?" I said.

"Because for all your fussing," she said, taking her hand away, "you still believe in ghosts." She took a sip of wine.

It was true. For all I knew, it was Cecily's ghost who'd put the idea of marriage into my head. "I don't," I lied. "I have no ghosts." I shrugged. "I don't."

"Has this been a courtship?" she said.

"Has *what* been?"

"Exactly," she said.

"Say again?" I said.

"*This*," she said. She lifted her glass of wine, then gestured widely— at the porch, at the books on the table, at the landscape in front of us—*this*, has *this* been a courtship, as if to imply deception rested everywhere around us.

"Yes," I said. "Hasn't it?"

"I certainly hope not," she said. "You haven't asked me anything at all about myself. For all you know, I may be betrothed already."

"Are you?"

"No," she said.

"This is a very frustrating conversation," I said.

"It's not a conversation," she said.

We drank our drinks, and rocked in our rocking chairs.

After a silence heavy with the sense that someone should be speaking, Eulalie said, "Ask me again."

"Will you marry me?" I said.

"I don't mean ask me *now*," she said, with a gust of exasperation. "Because *now* my answer is no. But when you ask me again, some other time, I'll say yes."

"When will that be?" I said.

"I don't know," she said. "Maybe never. How will I know until you ask me at the right time?"

"Maybe I'll never ask again," I said.

"Oh, I'll be *devastated* with *regret*," she said, grabbing at her heart sarcastically. We then rocked and stewed in silence.

And this was how things would be between us. I'm not sure I ever did propose to Eulalie again, but somehow we married only a month or so later.

Eulalie quit her job at the library and moved to the farm in spring, and like a goddess she brought the land to life. She was a professor of everything. She knew, from books, the technology of seeds and the secrets of cultivation. She studied soils and root systems. She consulted almanacs and meteorologists, but learned the most from farmers' wives who, unlike their husbands, weren't afraid of confessing their mistakes. She kept good accounts, managed our money.

Myself, I couldn't even keep a vegetable garden. The watermelons burst before I picked them from the vine. The sweet corn grew tart and tasteless. The radishes were woody to the tooth and the green beans freckled with rust.

So I tended to the Emerald Cathedral instead. It did a swift business itself that summer, drawing pilgrims and the downtrodden from miles and miles around. People hung framed photographs from all the cathedral's stray hooks and points, from the legs of chairs and the handles of skillets. These were pictures of the pilgrims' dead, old and young, and strung among them were wreaths of twisted vine and dried roses tied round with ribbon. These people left donations in a coffee can in exchange for votives to burn.

I became the shrine's sole custodian and priest, but I no longer prophesied or spoke on behalf of the dead. If people came seeking comfort or healing, I only listened. August sent me tins of tea made from the petals and thorns he grew in a greenhouse on the roof of his father's building. I dragged an old tufted sofa of matted-down velvet into the barn, and a table, and I would sit with visitors, in the shadow of the leaning shrine, and we would drink the tea. I would tell them about the history of the Emerald Cathedral, and how it had saved many lives already, not the least of which was my own. The mystery and magic of it had given people faith, and the faith had healed wounds and stitched broken hearts. For many of us, the cathedral salvaged a childhood sense of wonder.

I would tell them they should trust in their belief in ghosts.

With the farm under Eulalie's management and Hester's oversight, Emmaline and I had the leisure time to become professional saints. We would take the donations we collected in the coffee can and dole them out as we saw fit. We weren't inclined to be anonymous. We announced our intentions to newspaper editors, dressed in our best, and posed for pictures as we distributed our wealth. With our money, we afforded legitimate cures for the sickly, we shoed the shoeless, we shingled the poorhouse, we filled the library with storybooks. And we were patrons of the arts. At the Bonnevilla Opera House, our money electrified the old gas chandelier. Emmaline and me, we got called angels daily.

Emmaline sewed a new suit for Oscar, from the scarecrow's pajamas, and we found him a new golf cap in a shop that sold clothes for dapper babies. We tore the pages from a book on papier-mâché and used the paper to paste and patch his broken head. We oiled his hinges and spit-polished his eyes. I then performed in hospitals and orphanages, with a repertoire of mild and inoffensive comedy. These were the most grateful audiences I'd ever encountered. I memorized their laughter.

47.

IN A FIELD IN LATE AUGUST, a carnival parked. They strung up a tightrope for the high-wire artists, and flew flags, and raced horses with pink plumes in their manes. Girls in short ballet skirts of tulle did handstands on the saddles, and clowns conducted and wrangled trained birds that circled and dove in the sky. The birds seemed tethered to the clowns' wrists with strings. But most of the amusement was confined to the shadows. A circus barker in a candy-cane vest would lift a flap, and if you did so much as peek into the dark of the tent, you then likely stepped in to see more.

The folks that lurked there on those slapdash stages—a woman scantily clad and wrapped in a python, a skeletal man napping on a bed of nails, a contortionist, a fire-eater, a cancan dancer, and others— spent a great deal of time at the Emerald Cathedral during their week in Bonnevilla. They came seeking wisdom and courage. They had questions about love. They came late in the night after the carnival closed, and early in the morning before it opened again, still in costume and in makeup streaked from the sawdust that stirred in their tents.

They instantly felt like old friends, and it was good to be among them. From the books about spiritualists, I'd learned about tea leaves and cranioscopy. Though I didn't claim to be an interpreter of anything cryptic, I did tell these visitors what a seer might see. They seemed, by nature of their perversity, more likely to have a healthier skepticism than my usual pilgrims. So I would shuffle the dregs of their tea, seeking symbols in how the wet leaves clotted. *If I was a reader of leaves I might see a bat there*, I might say, pointing my pinky at the line of the wings. *And maybe here I'd see a teacup.*

When a tattooed lady sat with me one afternoon, in the last days of the carnival's stay, I thought of Doxie's real father. Or, at least, I thought of the man that Cecily had described to me. His name had been Mercury, and he'd been a showman too, and had tried to convince Cecily to do as this woman had—to get covered in ink from forehead to foot. Inclined toward coincidence, I asked the woman her tattooist's name.

"Luther," she said. Most of her skin was hidden by her high-collared shirtwaist and her long skirt. The pink tentacle of an octopus twisted up from the lace of her collar and snaked around her jawline. On the back of one hand was an anatomist's sketch of the bone and sinew that would be under the skin. On her palm was a patch of lucky clover, in reference to her name.

Clover tugged at her skirt and stuck out her leg, but revealed none of the tattoos beneath her white stocking. "Luther was an old sailor," she said. "When Luther had a leg, he had a tattoo of a pirate ship on it." She tapped at her calf. "So when he lost the leg, and got the wooden one, he had somebody carve the same ship in."

I looked at the leaves in the cup, studying how they'd snaked into a perfect serpent. Or a river. Or the letter *S*.

I showed it to Clover. "The letter *S* mean anything to you?" I asked.

She shrugged one shoulder and squinted one eye to think. "I have an uncle named Stanley," she said, with little faith.

I told her about the science of graphology—the analysis of handwriting—and the book I had read in which I'd learned the letter *S* was difficult to interpret. "There's too little expression in it, I guess," I said. "But how could that be? Doesn't it seem the most expressive of all?" It was a viper coiled to strike. It was sex. It was lazy wisps of smoke that you let lift from your lips.

Sessily. Sessalee. Sissly.

I THOUGHT OF CLOVER often in the few days after her visit, and after the carnival tore down and packed back up. I guess I worried about her. The way those tea leaves followed that dark curvy line seemed ominous somehow.

"Ice skates," Emmaline suggested, as we sat at the table having tea of our own, discussing the performers who'd passed through. She ran her finger in the air, twisting her wrists around the curves of the letter. "You skate an *S* when you're skating your figure eights." She dropped her hand to the table with a thump. She gasped. "Clover will fall through the ice, to drown."

Eulalie said, "I think all the trouble's with that uncle Stanley of hers. Sssssstanley's going to ssssstab her with his ssssstiletto." She winked and smiled, and she studied her own tea leaves, which were too scattered to read.

As it turned out, it *was* a premonition I was having those days, but one that had nothing to do with Clover herself. I was rapt with her tattoos—she'd been a flesh-and-blood glimpse of Cecily's fate had she stayed with Doxie's dad.

And when the carnival left, Doxie arrived.

AT FIRST I DIDN'T recognize the child. Why would I? Not only had she grown since winter, not only did she now walk on her own two legs, but she was far from home, on forbidden land. I had resigned myself, absolutely and completely, to never being allowed to see her again. So when I did see her, there before me on my very own farm, she wasn't there. This was someone else's child, most certainly.

A woman all in black, and shrouded like a beekeeper, a dark, heavy veil hanging low from the brim of her hat, helped the girl down from the phaeton. They were alone but for the driver, a lanky lad from Bonnevilla who could be relied upon to slither out of his basement room whenever there was need for a cabbie or pallbearer or drinking chum.

In the back of the phaeton were steamer trunks, portmanteaus, hatboxes. This woman and her girl were refugees of the carnival, I figured. I wondered what sort of horrors might be hidden beneath the veil.

I'd been in the garden in my pajamas and robe, my pockets full of the stunted carrots I'd pulled, their leaves gnawed to twigs by rabbits. The two came toward me, the woman slightly bent so she could hang on to Doxie's hand, to help keep the little girl upright as she stumbled around the clods of dirt.

When the girl finally looked up at me with Cecily's eyes, I knew she was mine. The shock of seeing Doxie passed in an instant, and it was as if I'd been expecting her all summer long. I ran to her, and I swept her up and into my arms. She giggled and shrieked as I lifted her above my head. I tossed her in the air, up at the spot of sun. "More," she said, slapping at my wrists. *More.*

The woman in black lifted the veil up and aside with the whole of her arm, like parting a drape from in front of her. This was Pearl, of course, caught in those cobwebs, and I worried about her. I worried about myself. If she'd gone possessed again, I couldn't bear it. Though I no longer received letters from Cecily, or any word of any kind, Cecily was there with me always, whether she spoke or not. And I'd grown comfortable with the quiet.

"Pearl?" I said, hesitant.

She struggled with her hatpin as she resituated her veil. At the pin's head was a hornet of topaz. "I fear that I've . . . well, I think . . . I think I've left Billy," she said.

At the kitchen table, we all scrambled to entertain Doxie, look-ing for everything and anything that might pass for a toy. We let her upend the saltshaker and hammer the sugar cubes with the back of a spoon. We allowed her to tear a plum apart.

She sat on my lap and I ran my fingers through the tiny, fine curls of her hair. I didn't fret or dread. I didn't plot. I wanted only to be there with Doxie, letting every minute linger. I touched my fingertip to her ear, learning the slope of it. I put my fingers to her neck, gauging where best to tickle. She flinched, then laughed, then tried to tickle me back in revenge, her fingers sticky with plum, her face comically intent on my torture.

Pearl had changed from her black traveling dress in a back room and now stepped into the kitchen in a long bright yellow robe aswirl with pink paisley. She was dressed much like the actor from India who'd ridden down the midway atop an elephant. She even wore beaded carpet slippers that curled up at the toes.

While we entertained Doxie, Pearl opened and closed cupboard doors and put on a kettle for tea. Emmaline and Hester, who would normally object to anyone rummaging through their kitchen, paid no notice. The Old Sisters Egan became more animated than I'd ever seen them, as they clowned and mugged for Doxie and spoke in squeaky voices. Hester knotted and twisted a hankie into the shape of a baby in a cradle. She held each end of the little hammock and rocked it.

"How long will you be staying?" I asked, though I dreaded the answer.

"Only a day or two, if you don't mind having us underfoot a little," Pearl said. She examined the patched-up china teapot that had fallen from the cabinet the day my balloon hit the house. Hester had pieced the delicate thing back together sloppily, for Emmaline, with cement and plaster, and it looked to be forever bursting at the seams. "I've booked passage for Paris."

They'd only just arrived and already they were leaving. I held Doxie closer. "Then you need to go back the way you came," I said, with an edge of irritation. "Unless you're taking the long way around the world." But then I smiled, hoping she wouldn't sense my impatience. I would have to eke out to her every ounce of pity she sought, so she'd become addicted to my sympathy, so she'd escape Wakefield again and again, and bring Doxie to me, over and over. Pearl, so susceptible to spirits, would easily fall under the Emerald Cathedral's spell.

Pearl returned to the cupboards until Eulalie, unsettled by all the squeaking of hinges, stood to get the tin of tea from the spice cabinet. "Let me," she said, taking the teapot and nodding toward the table.

But Pearl wouldn't sit. She walked from the kitchen to the front of the house, to look out the window and up the road. Hester was begging to hold Doxie, so I handed her over, and I went to Pearl's side. "Are you worried Wakefield will find you?" I said.

"No," she said, but she continued to look out, as if expecting a late guest. "He's the one sending me off." Wakefield, Pearl explained, had arranged for her to see a doctor in Paris.

THAT EVENING I salvaged a broken-down bassinet from the Emerald Cathedral, prying it loose from where it'd been roped and nailed on. We put Doxie to bed on the screened-in porch, where there were some cool late-summer breezes that smelled of autumn must. We sat in the wicker swing and rocking chairs and watched the angel sleep.

Eulalie brought out our evening's cups of brandied plums, and we ate them with teaspoons as Pearl told the story of her escape.

"He wants me to conceive a child on the night of our wedding," Pearl said. She spooned a sodden plum into her glass of red wine. "On the first night of the new century. And he wants a son. Only a son."

"There are methods," he'd told Pearl. He'd consulted with scientists and witches alike. He'd studied folklore and medicine. "We're on the precipice of discovering all there is to know about everything," he'd said.

He'd already begun her on a diet of potato peels and red clover blossoms and alfalfa grass, horseradish, and dandelion leaves. *Alkaline*, he'd explained. She lay awake in her bed every night, worrying, some tonic undrunk on the nightstand beside her. She cried for her little girl that could never be. She began to feel herself going mad from it. Wakefield had spoken of having her womb *curetted*, a word she hadn't known. One of the maids, who'd worked for a time in an asylum, told Pearl it meant a scraping of her insides.

Then one afternoon Wakefield's twin sister, Billie, took Pearl to Brandeis for a private showing of the milliner's new wares. Billie and Pearl drank champagne on a sofa of white, and they would nod, gasp, cluck their tongues at the dramatic hats and compliment the shopgirls who modeled them. The girls would lean in to show off every hat's every frill—the glass grapes with leaves of calfskin, the stuffed doves with sapphire eyes, the blue beetles with stone backs pinned to silk ribbons, the feathers, the flowers, the gems.

And in between all the polite fuss, Billie offered rescue. "I'll help you get away," she said in a whisper, leaning her own head forward, the brim of her hat hiding her face.

Not yet trusting Billie, Pearl said, "I have nowhere to be."

"You're up all night crying," she said.

Pearl felt her skin grow hot, felt the sweat bead on her forehead, and she cursed her constant blushing and how her red cheeks always told all her secrets.

Billie would arrange for Pearl to go to Paris with Doxie to a special clinic. "What clinic?" Pearl said.

Billie said, "It doesn't matter. It doesn't exist." Billie would have materials printed, papers and advertisements that promoted the fictional clinic's expertise at selecting a baby's sex. Wakefield would find it irresistible and arrange the travel himself. And Wakefield's sister would send Pearl money, for as long as she needed it.

Billie spoke with her glass at her lips, her breath popping the bubbles of her champagne. "We'll tell my brother it requires months of treatment. And you'll tell him you're taking Doxie so she can learn French as she learns English. And you'll disappear into the city."

Pearl asked, "Won't he come looking for us?"

"Eventually," she said. "But he won't find you. And he'll forget about you. He's a broken man. He has no true capacity for love."

"Why are you doing this?"

Billie leaned over, ducking the brim of her hat in and under the brim of Pearl's, and she said simply, as the answer was obvious, "I want you both out of my house." She then smiled, fluttered her eyelashes prettily, and turned her attention to the shopgirl bent before them to show off the silk lilies twisted into the hatband.

So before Pearl left the country for good, with my girl, she found her way to the farm.

"We couldn't leave without saying good-bye," she said.

"I'm grateful," I said, but I was heartbroken. Only months before I might have felt inclined to follow her to Paris, to be near Doxie always. But now I was home, and I was home to stay. I'd come to rely so much on Eulalie. And as the Old Sisters Egan got older, they needed the son they never had.

After Eulalie and the sisters went up to bed, leaving me alone with Pearl on the porch, I said, "Don't go."

"Oh, I won't," Pearl said. "I'm not tired. I can stay up all night talking to you. It's so good to see you again. Can you believe how much we've been through?"

"I mean, don't go to Paris," I said.

"Oh," Pearl said, worried, looking down to the floor. She reached to the curled toes of her slippers, to touch at their tips.

"You can hide here as easily as in Paris . . . even easier," I said. "You can't trust the Wakefields. She'll tell Billy where you are, I know she will."

Pearl met my eyes. "But you see, it's all already settled, Ferret," she said. "She bought me my own shop. I plan to pay her back, but . . . *my own shop. In Paris.*" It pleased her so much just to say it. "I can sell whatever I want."

"Do you even know what it is you want to sell?" I said.

"It'll be a shop for the new woman," she said. "Dresses that fit. Cigarettes. Political magazines."

"Sounds just awful," I said, but I smiled, and I winked, as I said it.

"You'll come visit us," she said, which sounded even more awful somehow, and the words caught me by surprise. I felt my eyes tear up. In those words were all the miles of road and ocean between us. In that invitation to visit were all the visits we'd never have.

When I went to bed, I stared at the ceiling, two crickets in duet somewhere in the room. Every time I stood, my ear peeled toward the crickets' chirp, hoping to cup the bugs in my palms to toss them from the window, they got quiet, dropping mum at the creak of the floor. Only when I was back under the sheet would they sing again.

Eulalie was awake too, but distracted by other insects. "June bugs in August," she said. We could hear the soft thump of their hard shells on the window and the screen.

"What do we have to look forward to?" I said. It was a practical question—Eulalie was the expert on our crops and all the ways they might fail. June bugs in August sounded prophetic somehow. She knew the true villainy behind every summer song and flash of color. For her, the night quiet was always noisy with threat. As was a ladybug on a daisy petal. A robin perched on a fence post. The sight of any pretty thing could put a hitch in her step.

"'What do we have to look forward to?'" she said. "What a cruel thing to say."

"No, no, sweetie, no," I said. "What does it mean, June bugs in August? What kind of damage will they do? That's what I meant. What *damage* do we have to look forward to? To the crops."

But she'd already begun to cry. We lay flat on our backs. She put her hand to her face, and the bed shook with her sobbing. I got up on one elbow and held my fingers to her cheek. "Eulalie," I said.

She sat up to swing her legs over the side of the bed and rummaged through the nightstand drawer for a handkerchief. "They lay eggs in the meadow," she said. "When they hatch, they're worms that live in the sod. Then we cut the sod to put in the cornfield. And the grubs get in the roots."

"Is that anything to cry over?" I said, hoping to make light. I walked my fingers up the back of her nightgown, ladder-stepping the knots of her spine. "Worms in the roots?"

I sat on the edge of the bed next to her and took her hand in mine. She put her head on my shoulder. She said, "She's quite a little girl, isn't she?"

I nodded my head against hers. We could see the black shadows of the June bugs creeping along the screen. "What do we do about them?" I said. "The worms?"

"We turn the neighbor's hogs loose in the field to eat them up," she said.

I said, "I have so much to learn," and Eulalie laughed.

We lay back down, Eulalie in my arms. She put her hand at my cheek. "We've got skipjacks in the strawberry patch," she said.

"I like the sound of that," I said.

"Well, you shouldn't," she said. "Their eggs hatch worms too." I'd seen the beetles bouncing around the strawberry leaves. Eulalie explained to me the notches in their skeletons and spines. The bugs, when on their backs, could right themselves with a click.

"They're cute," I said. "I like how they pop up and around like acrobats."

She moved her hand to cover my mouth. "Sh," she said. "You make me tired."

I WOKE TO the noise of Pearl's shoes on the living room floor downstairs, as she paced back and forth before sunrise.

She'd already dressed for the day in her traveling suit of mohair, and she wore her veil again.

"What's wrong, Pearl?" I said, sashing my robe closed around my pajamas.

It seemed my every word anymore brought a girl to tears. With the question, Pearl began to whimper, and her shoulders to bob. I went to her and pushed her veil away from her face. I put my arm around her as she cried, and I led her to the kitchen table. I put on some water to boil. "You're leaving already," I said, standing at the stove, staring down at the kettle.

"Yes," she said.

"I thought I might have the day with Doxie," I said.

"Ferret," she said. "There's something I haven't told you."

"What more could there be?" I said, weary.

"I can't take Doxie with me," she said. I held my breath. Her words had been broken by her weeping. Had I heard her right? I was afraid if I asked her to say it again, she'd take it all back. "I love her with all my heart, but I'm no one's mother. I'm no one's wife. I never wanted to marry. I got lost in all of this. And now I can start over. I can be who I wanted to be. I can be who I am."

I sat at the table and took Pearl's hands in mine. I knew I must move slowly, but it was all I could do to keep from running to the porch, to where Doxie slept, and snatch her up before Pearl changed her mind. But when I felt Pearl squeeze my hands, when I looked at her wet cheeks, at her chin quivering, I knew she'd already let Doxie out of her life. Doxie was mine. I sat up straighter in my chair. I gripped Pearl's hand tight, and nodded, with my chin lifted. I took on all the stern and certain gestures I imagined a good father would have.

When the water in the kettle began to bubble, Pearl stood from the table to attend to it. She wiped her face with her sleeve, and she went about brewing our tea. "I'm not sure if I should tell you what I want to tell you," she said.

"You should," I said. "You should tell me."

She stood still, her back to me, steam leaving the room through the window open an inch. "Cecily sent me here," she said.

I welcomed it now, this ghost story. Pearl was on her way to Paris. It wouldn't hurt to indulge ourselves for a minute or two, for old time's sake. "You can tell me," I said.

Pearl told me that she and Mrs. Margaret had continued to secretly visit clairvoyants. Pearl would go down the hill and into town, hidden in veils and massive hats. Most often all the psychics' hullaballoo amounted to nothing—even the charlatans saw their tricks fizzle, with cogs skipping gears, lightbulbs flickering to black in their presence. Now that the room with the swans was unlocked, Cecily's ghost refused to haunt.

"Absolutely nothing, until we returned to Ella Winnows," Pearl said. It had been in Ella Winnows's parlor that I'd watched Pearl, possessed, compose a letter from Cecily on that gray day in February. And it was in that parlor again that Cecily wrote, only a few weeks before Pearl left Wakefield. "I'm *sure* it was Cecily," Pearl said. "Ella Winnows had a slate. We stared at the slate for the longest while. It was only when Ella picked the slate up and went to put it away that I saw the words. They appeared there suddenly. 'Let Dorothy go to the City of Emeralds,' it said. It couldn't have been a trick, Ferret. Ella Winnows didn't know that Doxie's real name was Dorothy. I don't think so, anyway. I don't think I would've ever told her such a thing. And she certainly couldn't have known about the Emerald Cathedral. It was our

Cecily, Ferret. It was our Cecily, and she was setting me straight, bless her heart."

"Bless her heart," I mumbled, like a muttered prayer. I wondered what Mrs. Margaret would have to say about that slate. I would've been just as happy to never see the old automaton again, but I wanted Doxie to someday learn all she could about her mother. Mrs. Margaret would have many stories that I didn't know. And I wanted to hear them too.

AT THE STATION, Pearl stood on the platform with her bags and trunks, and we all looked up along the tracks, hoping to see the train's lamp cut through the fog. The train was late, and it grew later and later, with no whistle in earshot.

We'd arrived at the station late ourselves, and we'd been so relieved to find we hadn't missed the train, we'd become giddy. We'd had a teary but cheerful farewell, with kisses and promises to write and visit, certain the train would be along in only a minute, to steal Pearl away to her new life and to leave us to ours.

It was only Eulalie and me with Pearl, Doxie in my arms, and the train's absence dragged on. We could think of no conversation. Every tick of the watch in my pocket made us tired and reminded us of the silence we shared. And we couldn't distract ourselves by playing with Doxie, as she'd fallen asleep, her head on my shoulder. I wanted to concentrate only on the weight of her against me, and her hot puffs of breath against the skin of my neck.

"She gets kind of heavy, doesn't she?" I whispered.

"She'll get lighter," Pearl said. "You'll get used to carrying her."

Finally Pearl sat down on one of her trunks, slapping her bouquet across her knees. Eulalie had tied together the last of the flowers for Pearl—some stems of echinacea and black-eyed Susans, and some sprigs of dill. "You should go," she told us. "Really, there's no need for us all to wait. I'm perfectly fine. You should go home."

"Oh," I said.

I was about to say, *Are you sure?* when Eulalie said, "Absolutely not. We'll wait as long as it takes."

"Oh, please don't," Pearl said. She began to cry again, and she took her handkerchief from the pocket of her jacket to dab at her nose. "Please go. I insist. It'll be easier for me. I can't go through another good-bye. I'm terrible with good-byes to begin with."

Eulalie sat next to Pearl on the trunk. "You'll have to suffer us, my dear," she said. "We're not leaving you alone at the station, for God's sake. We're family, and family waits. Right, Ferret?" She looked at me askance, as if she sensed I was eager to go. And I was. I couldn't feel certain that Pearl had left us all behind until she was no longer in my sight.

"We wouldn't even think of leaving you here alone, Pearl," I said.

And so we waited the two hours it took. Doxie grew fussy, and an old woman alone on a bench nearby brought us a naked china doll so small it fit in Doxie's hand. Much of it fit in her mouth too. I stuck my finger in to scoop the doll out, and she only fussed more when I refused to return it to her. She hadn't been at all close to choking—the gangly doll wouldn't have fit down her gullet—but I nonetheless pictured it clearly. I suspected I'd spend the rest of my life seeing the threat in seemingly harmless things.

When we finally heard the train's clattering wheels, we practically danced, bouncing on our heels, clapping our hands. Eulalie plucked away stray petals from Pearl's jacket and skirt, and Pearl raised the bouquet and waved it in the air toward the train, as if she wasn't about to leave but rather welcoming a lover arriving.

Our last minutes together were a flurry of kisses and sweet nothings. We made yet more promises we wouldn't likely keep, but in the moment they seemed the deepest of oaths. We were so happy and sad, so swept up, it seemed everything could change in a blink. Pearl might not leave, Doxie might not stay, every thread of our lives only ether.

When Pearl leaned in toward Doxie for one last kiss, Doxie reached for Pearl, and cried and begged, clutching at her collar. Doxie tried to climb from my arms and into Pearl's, and I wasn't sure what to do. To Doxie's frustration, I only held her tighter.

Pearl pressed her cheek to Doxie's forehead. "You'll always be mine," she whispered. "You belong to all of us." She then stepped away, blew us a kiss, and got on the train as a porter gathered her trunks. Once she was inside, we didn't see her again. She didn't sit at a window to watch us, but we stayed on the platform nonetheless, looking after the train until we couldn't see it at all. Its racket and whistle faded away, Doxie cried herself to sleep in my arms, and we were left with the quiet of the prairie. We could hear the wings of the wood thrush beating in the dry wheat in the field near the station.

The day felt mercifully wasted away, and we resolved to go home and do nothing. We deserved it, we decided.

I drove the horses, Doxie awake again in Eulalie's lap. We learned our way around her language, interpreting, figuring out what noises meant what words. I made up a fable on the spot, and it seemed to soothe her. It was the first chapter of many tales I would tell her, about a farm girl named Doxie Skerritt, and her mother who waltzed in the air, and a balloon that fell with a wizard in it, and a one-eyed witch that saw everything. In these early years, the story of her mother would be a wonder tale, solely for her pleasure, all the heartaches and nightmares left out.

Acknowledgments

My many, many thanks to the people of Riverhead, especially Sarah Stein, my editor, who contributed heroically to the care and feeding of these characters. Alice Tasman, my agent, is another of my heroes, always expertly guiding the way. Rodney Rahl, meanwhile, is my angel, offering support, inspiration, patience, and humor throughout every step of the process.

Thanks to:

—all the museums, libraries, scholars, and historians (amateur and otherwise) who have worked to preserve and archive Expo materials, including the Omaha Public Library; the Durham Museum; Douglas County Historical Society; Nebraska State Historical Society; University of Nebraska-Lincoln (notably Wendy Katz, Kay Walter, Jaclyn Cruikshank-Vogt, Laura Weakly, and Karin Dalziel, who have developed the new Trans-Mississippi Expo digital archive); and private collectors such as historian Jeffrey Spencer.

—Susan Belasco and the English Department of the University of Nebraska-Lincoln, including research assistants Sarah Chavez, Anastasia Bierman, Ryan Oberhelman, Danielle Metcalf, and Laura Dimmit.

—Matthew Clouse, for his research on turn-of-the-century health resorts and regimens, and Roxanne Wach, for her research on the mediums and clairvoyants of the period.

Thanks also to the many others who have offered support, insight, and inspiration along the way: Janet Lura, Judy Slater, Kurt Andersen, Lauren Ceran, Kate Bernheimer, John Keenan, Leo Adam Biga, Kathy Patrick, LeAnn Messing, Jessica Regel, emily danforth, Wanda Ewing, Loretta Krause, and Greg Michalson and the exceptional Unbridled Books. And, as always, much love and admiration to my parents, Larry and Donita.

And a special thanks to the booksellers (especially the Bookworm of Omaha) who serve novels and novelists so tirelessly.

Author's Note

The Omaha World's Fair, as depicted in *The Swan Gondola*, is a fictional approximation of the Trans-Mississippi and International Exposition of 1898. For my interpretation of the event, and of turn-of-the-century Omaha, I relied primarily on the collections of the Omaha Public Library (for which I thank Gary Wasdin, OPL executive director; thanks also to Kyle Porter, Amy Mather, Patrick Esser, Martha Grenzeback, and all the fine librarians and staff members of OPL). I also appreciated the extensive index of newspaper articles compiled by historian David Wells, and I benefitted greatly from reading the 1898 editions of the *Omaha Bee* via the website of the Library of Congress. Some excellent portraits of nineteenth-century Omaha can be found in *A Dirty, Wicked Town* by David L. Bristow and *Impertinences*, a collection of articles by *Omaha World-Herald* columnist Elia Peattie, edited by Susanne George Bloomfield.

From that foundation of fact, I developed the fiction, shaping the novel and its details around the demands of character and plot. And the narrator brings along his own biases, filtering his portrait of Omaha and its people, rich and poor, through the perspective of a young man who grew up in the alleys. To learn more about the Expo as it actually was, visit http://trans-mississippi.unl.edu for photographs, documents, and Expo publications.

Though some real-life personalities of the time (such as President McKinley and some of the lunch guests at the Pink Heron Hotel) do make appearances in the novel, all the novel's main characters are imagined. There was a John A. Wakefield who served as the exposition's secretary, but I know little about him, and the character of William Wakefield is in no way based on him. I simply liked the name; John A. Wakefield's wife, whom I know even less about—I've yet to even stumble across her first name—was one of the Expo's first archivists, putting together scrapbooks that are still housed in the special collections of the Omaha Public Library.

But long before I became interested in the Expo, I was interested in *The Wizard of Oz*, and the wizard's balloon emblazoned with the name of his hometown: Omaha. I grew up in Nebraska and was always curious about the wizard's humble origins as a ventriloquist's apprentice (as briefly described in L. Frank Baum's original novel of 1900). Though *The Swan Gondola* is not a retelling of the Oz myth, I did consult Baum's novel frequently, particularly the centennial edition with annotations by Michael Patrick Hearn. Throughout *The Swan Gondola* are many allusions to Baum's novel and to the novel's illustrations by W. W. Denslow.

I'd also like to note: the paragraph from *The Female Offender* in chapter 21 is a direct quote from the 1897 criminal study by Professor Caesar Lombroso and William Ferrero; a line about census figures in chapter 5 is paraphrased from *Official Guide Book to Omaha and the Trans-Mississippi and International Exposition*; and chapter 9 features lines from a speech given by John L. Webster during the opening-day ceremonies.